the mystery of kama
&
brahma's courtesans

JANE DE LA VAUDÈRE was baptized Jeanne Scrive and was married to Camille Gaston Crapez, who began styling himself Crapez de La Vaudère after inheriting the Château de La Vaudère from his mother. Her prolific literary work is very various but she was assimilated to the Decadent Movement firstly because of two scandalously scabrous Parisian novels, *Les Demi-Sexes* (1897) and *Les Andrognyes* (1903), and, more pertinently, because of a series of accounts of *moeurs antiques*, some of which—notably *Le Mystère de Kama* (1901)—set new standards of excess in their exotic eroticism and fascination with torture.

BRIAN STABLEFORD has been publishing fiction and non-fiction for fifty years. His fiction includes an eighteen-volume series of "tales of the biotech revolution" and a series of half a dozen metaphysical fantasies set in Paris in the 1840s, featuring Edgar Poe's Auguste Dupin. His most recent non-fiction projects are *New Atlantis: A Narrative History of British Scientific Romance* (Wildside Press, 2016) and *The Plurality of Imaginary Worlds: The Evolution of French* roman scientifique (Black Coat Press, 2016); in association with the latter he has translated approximately a hundred and fifty volumes of texts not previously available in English, similarly issued by Black Coat Press.

jane de la vaudère

the mystery of kama
&
brahma's courtesans

translated and with an introduction by
brian stableford

CONTENTS

INTRODUCTION

This is the third of six projected volumes translating fiction by Jane de La Vaudère (15 April 1857-26 July 1908). Five of those volumes each contain two of her short novels, while the second in the series, *The Double Star and Other Occult Fantasies*, contains a selection of her short fiction. The first volume, *The Demi-Sexes and The Androgynes*, contains translations of *Les Demi-Sexes*, originally published by Paul Ollendorff in 1897, and *Les Androgynes, roman passionel*, originally published by Albert Méricant in 1903. The present volume contains translations of *Le Mystère de Kama, roman magique indou* (Ernest Flammarion, 1901) and *Les Courtisanes de Brahma* (Flammarion, 1903). The fourth, *Three Flowers and The King of Siam's Amazon*, contains translations of *Trois fleurs de volupté, roman javanais* (Flammarion, 1900) and *L'Amazone du roi de Siam* (Flammarion, 1902). The fifth volume, *Syta's Harem and Pharaoh's Lover*, contains translations of *Le Harem de Syta, roman passionel* (Méricant, 1904) and *L'Amante du Pharaon, moeurs antiques* (Jules Tallandier, 1905). The sixth volume, *The Witch of Ecbatana and The Virgin of Israel*, contains translations *of La Sorcière d'Ecbatane, roman fantastique* (Flammarion, 1906) and *La Vierge d'Israel, roman de moeurs antiques* (Méricant 1906).

Jane de La Vaudère was baptized Jeanne Scrive; both her parents died when she was still a child, and in the social class to which her family belonged, which might be described as the "upper bourgeoisie," the standard practice when a young girl was orphaned at an early age was to put her in a convent, where she would be educated until her teens, and then marry her off as soon as possible. That appears to be what happened to Jeanne Scrive and her elder sister Marie. It is necessary to say "appears" because almost nothing is known for sure about Jane de La Vaudère's personal life and death, all of it covered by an obscurity that remains virtually impenetrable, save for the statements she made in a few newspaper interviews and a few objectively determinable facts.

In one such interview La Vaudère said that while in the convent of Notre-Dame de Sion she seriously considered remaining there permanently, the idea of living as a nun having a certain romantic attraction, but soon abandoned the idea. In fact, shortly after leaving the institution, when she apparently went to stay for a while with Marie, by then married to a military surgeon, she was married herself to Camille Gaston Crapez (1848-1912), who inherited the Château de La Vaudère in Parigné-l'Éveque (Sarthe) from his mother and styled himself thereafter Crapez de La Vaudère. The name with which she signed her books was not, as many sources report, a pseudonym, although she deleted the Crapez and anglicized her forename.

The Crapez de La Vaudères had one child, a son named Fernand, who apparently stayed with his father when his mother went to live in Paris, where she seems to have lived alone. Although she was never divorced, and her body was taken back to Parigné-l'Éveque for burial after her death in Paris, the separation appears to have been complete, no newspaper reports of her appearances at social events or interviews conducted at her home mention the presence of her husband. Nothing was reported about the circumstances of her death, and neither her husband nor her son appear to have been with her at the time; the unusual brevity of the death notices and the conspicuous absence of the customary post-mortem eulogies suggest a diplomatic silence, but we can only speculate as to what it was that was deliberately not being said about her sudden death at a relatively young age.

The circumstances of Jane de La Vaudère's early life evidently had a profound impact on her literary work, to which she turned a trifle late in her career. Before she began writing she had attempted to make a career as an artist and exhibited at the

Paris Salon; when she decided that her real vocation was literary, she first began writing poetry, and then wrote for the stage. Her first collection of poetry, *Les Heures perdues* [The Lost Hours] (1889) appeared in the same year as the production of her one-act comedy *Le Modèle* [The Model]. Her verse is Romantic and might have seemed a trifle old-fashioned at the time of its publication; she was certainly not unaware of contemporary trends in Symbolist poetry, for she was a very voracious reader and her influences were eclectic. *Le Modèle* was the first of many frothy one-act comedies, often in verse and often performed with musical accompaniment—fifteen of them were collected in *Pour le Flirt! Saynètes modernes* [approximately, Just For Fun, modern satirettes] (1905)—but she also wrote longer comedies and dramas.

She continued to write poetry and plays alongside her prose fiction, but there are very striking differences between her works in the three genres, and her prose work also shows sharp generic divisions. It is not unusual for writers to manifest seemingly different personalities in their prose fiction and their work for the stage, especially if the latter mostly consists of vaudevilles written as pure entertainment while the former is more earnest and intense, but in La Vaudère's case the difference is extreme. Even her contemporary Paris-set novels, which often feature female characters not unlike those routinely featured in her stage comedies—young socialites, actresses and artists' models—are far more mordant in their attitude and development, but the distinction is far more marked in the remarkable series of exotic novels set in far-flung places and times that make up the last four volumes of the present series of translations.

La Vaudère's first novel, *Mortelle étreinte* [Mortal Embrace] (1891) is the story of a young orphan brought up in a convent, who then goes to live with a relative, where she continues to live in virtual seclusion, in the psychological environment of her vivid imagination and the books she reads in abundance. She knows nothing about the real world and is utterly unready to cope with her own hectic emotions when she is first attracted to a man—a man who is also greatly attracted to her, but is, from every other viewpoint, quite unsuitable and incapable of providing her with the existential anchorage and security that she needs and desires.

The basic features of that story-line were to recur again and again in the author's work, even in the most bizarre settings. Its melodramatic intensity is inevitably restrained in *Mortelle étreinte* by the conventions of the society in which it is set, but when it is removed to ancient India or ancient Babylon, in the author's accounts of *moeurs antiques*, such shackles no longer apply and the pitch of that intensity is turned up to a level unequaled in the work of any other writer of the era. The sensation of having been brought up in an artificial environment, with little or no parental guidance, and then thrust into a world equipped with hopes and expectations that are certain to be betrayed, is developed in story after story, in variants that are extraordinarily wide-ranging, often wildly exaggerated, and almost always brutally tragic.

Several of La Vaudère's early short stories, including "Amour Astral" (*L'Univers illustré* 1890-91; tr. as "Astral Amour"), "Réincarnation" (in the collection *L'Anarchiste* 1893; tr. as "Reincarnation") and the novella "Yvaine," (*Gil Blas* 1896; tr. as "Yvaine") are tales of the occult, and the references contained therein reveal that she had become intensely interested in contemporary research in physiological psychology, especially hypnotism, and the possible connections between hypnotism and the magic and mysticism of the occult revival. She frequently cited the seeming supernatural accomplishments of Indian fakirs, as reported by contemporary travelers' tales, as good evidence of the reality of magic, and she obviously read a great deal of the proto-anthropological spinoff of those travelers' tales. Although the intensity of her interest in physiological psychology waned over time, her interest in proto-anthropological accounts of Indian culture did not, and the combination of the two interests was at its peak when she wrote *Le Mystère de Kama* and *Les Courtesans de Brahma*.

La Vaudère probably attended spiritualist séances in the 1890s, led by curiosity rather than belief, but we can only speculate as to how closely she was acquainted with Camille Flammarion, the brother of her principal publisher, whose weekly salon played host to many of the most celebrated mediums of the day, as well as writers and scientists, and often included experiments in automatic writing and drawing. One of the stories in *L'Anarchiste*, "L'étoile double" (also reprinted as "Dans une étoile"; tr. as "The Double Star") is clearly based on Camille Flammarion's ideas, but La Vaudère had surely read his bestselling *Uranie* (1891) and might well have picked them up from there. The question is of some interest because La Vaudère's fiction, which rarely stands up to rational analysis, often gives the impression of having been written in a self-induced alternative state of consciousness. That is arguably true of all fiction, but there are different degrees of writerly self-hypnosis and La Vaudère's more exotic work, including her visions of India, seems to have been exceptionally disconnected from careful pre-planning and rational afterthought. All of her novels seem to have been made up as she went along, with relatively little advance preparation, and they often meander or change direction in response to her reading or her mood, routinely lacking continuity, consistency and coherency. *Le Mystère de Kama* is a cardinal example of that apparent procedure, and the fact that *Les Courtesans de Brahma* had its ending partially preprogrammed by history did not serve to make it an exception.

Once begun, La Vaudère's literary production rapidly became prolific; she published more than twenty novels between 1894 and her death in 1908, and seven more appeared posthumously under her name. It is unclear why she wrote in such profusion, and the likeliest explanation—that she needed the money—cannot have been the only one. If her motives had been purely commercial she would surely have pandered to popular tastes and expectations far more than she did. The direction that La Vaudère's later work took, however, seems to have been largely determined by the sales of her first best-seller, *Les Demi-Sexes*, whose *succès de scandale* she tried hard to repeat in one of the strands of her subsequent work, to considerable effect. Equally important, however, was the evident inspiration she took from the great best-seller of the era, Pierre Louÿs; *Aphrodite, moeurs antiques* (1896), which sold three hundred thousand copies and, inevitably, launched a bandwagon chased by many Parisian publishers, including Ernest Flammarion, and especially Albert Méricant, who became La Vaudère's second major publisher in the last few years of her life, and the publisher of most of the posthumous works signed with her name.

Aphrodite carried forward a rich tradition of feverish antiquarian erotic fantasies begun with Théophile Gautier's "Une nuit de Cléopâtre" (1838; tr. as "One of Cleopatra's Nights") and continued by Gustave Flaubert's *Salammbô* (1862; tr. as *Salammbo*) and Anatole France's *Thaïs* (1890; tr. as *Thaïs*), and demonstrated in no uncertain terms that erotic extremism seemed more acceptable and more plausible to the contemporary French literary audience if its exemplars were set long ago and far away, in the context of a culture where moral standards and expectations could be presumed to be very different.

La Vaudère's first venture into exotic erotica, the Java-set *Trois fleurs de volupté* (1900; tr. as "Three Flowers of Sensuality") is not set in the distant past, and owes something to the French genre of "travelogue fiction," but its successor, *Le Mystère de Kama*, pulled out all the stops. In the works recorded in *Trois Fleurs de volupté* as "en preparation," *Les Amours d'un fakir*, which was presumably the working title of *Le Mystère de Kama*, is listed second, after *L'Amazone du roi de Siam* (1902), which might, therefore, have been written earlier, or perhaps simultaneously. If it was the publisher who chose to issue the India-set novel first, it was a wise move; even more controversial than *Les Demi-Sexes*, *Le Mystère de Kama* was the first of La Vaudère's novels to sell thirty thousand copies, and it set a pattern that was continued by a series of novels, initially issued at the rate of one a year, all featuring the same garish eroticism and many of them displaying the same fascination with gruesome physical torture—a fascination carried forward with extraordinary extravagance in *L'Amazone du roi de Siam* and *Les Courtesans de Brahma*.

At first glance, the perverse fascinations displayed in La Vaudère's erotic fantasies might seem odd, on the part of a small, seemingly frail, upper-class woman in her forties. To some of her contemporaries, at least, they seemed shockingly indecent, strangely perverse and frankly sadistic, although the politeness with which they were reviewed by the daily newspapers of the day, almost always in gushingly complimentary terms, also seems a trifle odd in retrospect. One reviewer described *Les Courtisanes de Brahma* as a "charming idyll," somehow neglecting to notice, let alone to report, that the later phases of the story are a virtual bloodbath, replete with murders, massacres and violent rapes.

It seems probable, in retrospect, that *L'Amazone du roi de Siam*—which was surely planned, if not actually written, before *Le Mystère de Kama*—was partly a reaction to another notorious Decadent novel of the era, which, although it did not sell as well as *Aphrodite*, certainly attracted a lot of attention: Octave Mirbeau's *Le Jardin des supplices* (1899; tr as *Torture Garden*). There is a fleeting reference to a "jardin des supplices" in *Trois fleurs de volupté*, but no actual torture; in *L'Amazone du roi de Siam*, however, the author seems to have deliberately set out to describe a torture garden that would make Mirbeau's look tame, producing a series of atrociously horrific images that were to recur frequently in many of the subsequent works in the series, concluding with *Le Vierge d'Israel* and *Les Prêtresses de Mylitta*.

That recurrence is more suggestive of psychological obsession than a straightforward repetition of a narrative move that had proved capable of generating sales, and the same is true of certain other recurrent features of La Vaudère's account of exotic mores, most obviously her accounts of childhood sexuality, very obvious in *Le Mystère de Kama*, which includes two striking portraits of pre-pubescent nymphomaniacs. All the works in the exotic series are obsessed with dancing girls—as, in fact, are many of La Vaudère's Parisian stories—and in particular with dancing girls kept and raised in closed religious communities dedicated to the worship of female deities. Although the images in question are frankly bizarre, it seems probable that their imaginative bedrock is the author's own experience of having spent her childhood and early adolescence in a convent. It is possible, of course, that her frequent depiction of very young girls obsessed with sex is completely imaginary, as is her frequent allegation—but not explicit depiction—of the brutal sexual exploitation of those same young girls by priests, Brahmins in the works contained in the present volume; nothing like those depictions features in her novels of contemporary French life, in spite of her occasional ventures in pushing the envelope of the conventionally-unmentionable. On the other hand, it would perhaps be surprising if such imaginations did not have firm psychological roots of some kind.

There is an inevitable temptation to charge writers describing scenes of gruesome torture as "sadistic," and it is necessarily the case that sadistic motives are credited to the characters responsible for the described torture, but that skips over the crucial question of whether the narrative is inviting the reader to identify with the torturer or the victim. Invariably, in La Vaudère's case, her narrative voice shares the distress of the victims and witnesses of torture, especially when they are her heroines, as in the cases of Viamalah and Assilinia, and offers the same facility to her readers. Significantly, the few central characters in her fiction who avoid mental torment—most conspicuously, the juvenile heroines of *Trois fleurs de volupté*—usually end up dead, although the pain of dying is often anesthestized by their boundless amour, and the fact of dying saves them from inevitable agonies to come.

Almost all of La Vaudère's literary work focuses intensely on "the mystery of Kama": the puzzling features of amour, at least in its classic literary representations, which tend to proffer the ideal of an exclusive, omnipotent, all-consuming and indefatigable passion, which surely has no existence in reality. Her work represents that ideal with an intensity and extremism that might well be impossible for someone not brought up in such remote isolation from the real word in an ambience of assertive religious pretense, but it is always replete with complications, although *Le Mystère de Kama* is exceptional in imagining a complication that is very odd indeed. For La Vaudère, perhaps to a greater extent than any other writer, the idea of extreme amour embodies both the idea of Paradise and the idea of the Inferno; it is simultaneously the most sublime exaltation and the ultimate torment, the only really worthwhile desire there is, but an essentially self-destructive desire, inevitably opening a gateway to damnation and eternal, inextinguishable fire. The symbolic dramatization of that ambiguity reaches an exceedingly strange extreme in *Le Mystère de Kama*, and although *Les Courtisanes de Brahma* is necessarily more restrained in its plotting, being a historical novel rather than a supernatural one, it does feature the most striking of the many female black panthers that play a sexually symbolic role in La Vaudère's fiction.

The exoticism of *Le Mystère de Kama* is, of course, greatly heightened by the supernatural element, which draws extravagantly on the author's interest in the Occult Revival—and it is perhaps surprising that she did not carry that supernatural element forward into *Les Courtesans de Brahma*, given that *Les Mystère de Kama* sold so well. Perhaps she was advised to leave it out by her publisher; it might be significant that the next novel into which she imported a strong supernatural element, and which refers back explicitly to the character of Nassudamy, *Le Harem de Syta* was issued by a different publisher. On the other hand, the most extravagant of all La Vaudère's supernatural fantasies, *La Sorcière d'Ecbatane*, was published by Flammarion, so he must have repented of his prejudice, if he ever had one.

Even in *Le Mystère de Kama*, however, the horrific aspects of the supernatural interventions are matched, and perhaps outdone, by the purely physical horror of the scenes of violence, which stand out all the more sharply in *Les Courtisanes de Brahma* because of the absence of any counterbalancing supernatural horror, and Flammarion certainly did not put a brake on that aspect of her work. There are not many authors of whom a reader can think that it would be pleasant to live inside their fictional worlds, even with a virtual guarantee of an eventual happy ending, but the prospect of being the heroine of one of Jane de La Vaudère's stories, or the confidante of such a heroine, would be a horrific one indeed. Although she seems to have been overlooked by historians of horror fiction, her contribution to that genre is by no means trivial; perhaps she was simply too far ahead of her time in breaking such new ground in the subgenre of erotic horror fiction.

Exactly what the psychological and experiential reasons were for that fascination with physical horror we cannot know, and it is perfectly plausible that she did not know herself. Whatever the underlying motivations were, however, their results were certainly fascinating. La Vaudère's novels have manifest flaws of construction, seen from a logical viewpoint, but they are sometimes all the more intriguing by virtue of the resultant dream-like quality. Few rudderless writers improvised twists and turns in their plots as boldly, as adventurously and as eccentrically as she did, and although she occasionally struck false notes, she also achieved highly original effects, which helped push back the boundaries of what it was possible to imagine and write during her brief heyday. *Le Mystère de Kama* was ground-breaking in several ways, and remains startling even after a century in which the literary ground in question has been thoroughly and repeatedly plowed. Although *Les Courtisanes de Brahma* is in many ways a repetitive exercise, it too remains very striking, still capable of evoking a visceral reaction

*

The translations of *Le Mystère de Kama* and *Les Courtisanes de Brahma* were made from the copies of the Flammarion editions reproduced in the International Archive Digital Library at *achive.org*.

—Brian Stableford

the mystery of kama

PART ONE

I
Viamalah

Benares, the holy city. At the temple of Durga, large gray monkeys with white beards are leaping from column to column, throwing flowers and peelings, and then going to look at themselves in the sacred pool that protects the image of the goddess. In the lateral galleries, supported by red or blue monolithic pillars, the cows consecrated to worship are wandering indolently. Glass ornaments surround their powerful necks, and their horns are silvered beneath strings of roses.

Inside, before the golden idols, sparkling in the convergent light of lamps, Hindu women, silent specters, are depositing perfumes, fruits, honey and mahua flowers; the most fervent prostrate themselves and lose themselves in mystic adorations.

"Let's go, Matou-Mahli," says one of them, getting to her feet. "I'm devoid of courage, the gods have abandoned me!"

"Why, Comet Flower, dear, Smile? The influence of Bisheshwar cannot be manifest yet."

"Shiva is against me."

"O Viamalah! Let's keep praying."

Viamalah shakes her head, and her black hair comes undone, falling over her slim hips and kissing the amber conch of her heels. Seen face on, she is a child with delicate limbs and slightly indecisive but infinitely harmonious forms. Her elongated face has a singular gravity; her profound, passionate, sad, soft and tender eyes are veiled by long eyelids fringed with silk; her mouth is ardent and as thin as a perfumed pepper; her nostrils quiver like jasmine flowers in a squall.

"Let's pray!" repeats the servant, tightening a blue gauze langouti embroidered with golden grapes, whose flaps fall forward between her legs, around Viamalah's supple waist. The fabric is light, but the jewels are heavy, and the young woman is covered with them from head to toe, like a frail and magnificent idol. Sapphire studs fasten on her shoulders and her thighs; her breasts show their delicate cups, the tips of which support a star of carbuncles. A triple row of pearls descends all the way to her belt, which is made of thick gold lamé and folded beneath a diamond clasp.

The priests are asleep on the steps of the temple; the shadows of the gods extend over the ground, emphasizing the menace of their attitudes; burning aromatic plants emit suffocating vapors that rise under the sacred vault, and chained birds are flapping their wings feverishly.

Again, Viamalah has prostrated herself, her arms extended and her heels together; then she has kissed the bronze table in front of the idol, placed three almonds in a triangle and scrupulously counted the beads of pink coral whose placement and number are determined by the ritual.

After her, women have offered coffee, saffron, alum and rice, and crimson berries that they have disposed so as to form mysterious figures, intoning a chant in unison, which fades away and dies on a shrill note: words of adoration or a curse. The richest have noses and ears laden with pendants, bracelets of glass and silver on their arms, and red toes ornamented like fingers by rings with glaucous bezels.

Viamalah's confidante remains next to her and sustains her. She is a tall brown young woman with sharp features, large metallic eyes like a cat's; brightly colored fabric striped with yellow descends to her ankles; a headband ornamented with shiny plaques grips her forehead and peridot buttons traverse her nostrils.

"Comet Flower, it's necessary to go back."

"Yes, the fiancé is coming. It's time."

Leaning on Matou's shoulder, Viamalah has left the temple of Shiva—or Bisheshwar, the god of poison. Matou-Mahli guides her ill-assured steps into a maze of dark and strangled back streets. They are so preoccupied that they do not even stop in front of the bazaars, which present, some in projection and others in retreat, displays of precious fabrics and jewels. The former have massive doors that hide the treasures of the interior from gazes; the latter have windows perforated like paper lace, which enclose bouquets of precious stones coquettishly in trays.

In the boutiques, open to all winds, crouching men turn between their fingers light muslins filigreed with gold, silk fabrics laméd with bright colors, and gauzes of an infinite delicacy; the fabrics of Dacca, in particular, are so tenuous that an entire sheet can be passed through a ring. The cobweb cloth is only visible when folded several times, and the Bengalis, in their picturesque language, call it "nocturnal dew." A piece of a hundred aunes is worth approximately a demi-lac of rupees, which is about twenty-five thousand francs. There are also kincobs, or constellated brocades, indurated with precious stones of an inestimable value.

The turbans of Benares have a great reputation for elegance; they are made of scarves woven with silver, wound around several times; others are in velvet in pastel shades embroidered with little pearls, sapphires and moonstones. Cashmere shawls are displayed everywhere, mingling their harmoniously melted mosaics, and the warm light of the sky gives them a range of tones that no exotic cloth could attain in our misty land. A pale ocher dust floats everywhere, the impalpable residue of alluvial Ganges mud, pulverized by the centuries and the billions of men who have trodden it.

Viamalah hangs on to the servant's arm more forcefully.

"It's tomorrow . . ."

"You love him, however, your handsome fiancé?" asks Matou-Mahli, with a little malice and a great deal of compassion.

"I love him . . ."

"In that case, dear Smile, it's necessary to flee with him and hide so well that no one can divine the place of your retreat."

"Nassudamy doesn't want that."

"What does it matter?" said Matou-Mahli, disdainfully. "Nassudamy is only a yogi of the temple of Durga."

Without responding, Viamahah starts to weep.

"Do you not, little flower, have the free disposition of your sentiments and your actions?"

"No. I am under the dependence of that man, and I must do, in spite of myself, what he orders me to do. He is the master. He pronounces mantras and the pitris hasten to do his bidding. He is omnipotent and terrible."[1]

"Follies!"

"This evening, again this evening . . ."

"Don't go to the rendezvous."

"Alas, I no longer have a will, since the day when I encountered him near the temple of the goddess. He is the servant of Shiva, and the Brahmins have put all their confidence in him. It was when offering a dove to Parvati that I saw him for the first time. He has drunk my breath!"[2]

"It wasn't necessary to talk to him—a yogi, a beggar!"

"Undoubtedly, and I resisted for a long time, but his voice is as soft as that of a cocila,[3] his eyes shine more strangely than those of a tiger and his face is as resplendent as the moon."

"Achilgar is better still and ought to seduce a woman; he's elegantly rich and of high birth. It's necessary not to hesitate between the two."

"I'm not hesitating, since my heart belongs to the former."

"So?"

____

1 The author inserts a parenthetical note in the text to define *pitris* as spirits. I have usually left such notes in parentheses, but it seems inappropriate to do so in dialogue, so I have moved those that require retention into footnotes.
2 The author inserts a note translating the last sentence as "He has taken my soul."
3 The cocila is also known as the Indian cuckoo.

"How can I express what I feel? It seems to me that an occult force is oppressing me, communicating thoughts and making me take resolutions that my reason would reject at any other time. Invisible hands are pushing me forward. I want to resist but my legs are as soft as after a long struggle, my failing energy is yielding to a mysterious power."

"Has Nassudamy given you a philter or a fetish? You haven't shared rice and saffron?"

"No . . . but I've swallowed golden pills!"[1]

"Don't accept anything from him. You'll belong to him forever."

"This evening I'll see him one last time and I'll beg him to go away, to let me follow the road of amour."

"Are the bayaderes of the temple of Shiva no longer sufficient for him then?"

"He doesn't look at them, Matou. It's not a body that he desires but a soul. He claims that, among all the virgins of Benares, I have the favor of the gods and that they have put into me the mystical ardors that make priestesses and sacred pythonesses."

"Nassudamy doubtless only wants your wealth."

Viamalah shrugs her shoulders scornfully. "He's of a noble family and he begs on the roads; he does that in accordance with his wishes, since he could have palaces and servants, like Achilgar."

While conversing, the two women have taken an infinity of streets bordered with houses of two or three stories and little temples sculpted like chess-pieces, and have crossed the paths of Brahmins and fakirs painted in various colors, with emaciated faces and shining, strangely mobile eyes. Semi-naked young women laden with rings bow as the holy men go past, offering them flowers and fruits, lowering their eyelids under the lascivious gazes that envelop them. Sometimes, the yogis, in exchange for their presents, give them cylindrical stones rounded at the

---

1 The author notes that these are the formulae of mantras rolled into balls.

end, which they press to their lips ardently. Matrons with jewels in their ears and noses only allow their withered beauty to show in strange eyes circles with kohl and antimony; they wear tight trousers like men and drape themselves in veils fringed with silver and hemmed with glass beads.

Pilgrims are stripping off their garments on the bank of the Ganges and descending into the current pell-mell in order to make their ablutions, while pretty children, with ingenuous and pensive gazes put on the costumes of Hindu divinities in order to solicit the pity of passers-by. Floating everywhere on the river are light pyres of reeds, cotton and dry leaves, the modest sacrifices of those who cannot immolate lambs or goats.

In front of the temples there are also little pale pink bulls with wet muzzles, with gilded horns terminating in little metal balls, and strange cavaliers mounted on horses tinted with henna and indigo, with manes braided with pearls.

II
The Fiancé

Viamalah is now in her garden with her father, who is exhorting her mildly. Doves in the surrounding palm trees are cooing plaintively; peacocks and parrots seem, in their capricious flight, to be juggling with the gems of their wings, while very tiny birds, like golden scarabs, are asleep in the calices of flowers. Fig trees and pomegranates pierce the white crowns of cotton-bushes; mimosa, mango trees and bamboos launch toward the sky, sheltering baskets with warm and honeyed odors.

"Your fiancé will come, Viamalah."

"Yes, father."

"And you will be tender for him; it's necessary not to cause him any more chagrin."

The girl shivers at the memory of the anger of her fiancé, Achilgar, whom she has wounded profoundly. However, he pleases her, the handsome young man with the dark velvet eyes, and it is in vain that she tries to explain her eccentric humor.

"You will be good and submissive," commands the old man.

"Yes, father."

The day is declining slowly; black bees, heavy with pollen, are returning to the hive. Questing moths with heavy wings blotched with mauve and pale blue replace them, fluttering silently from one perfume to another in the midst of horned bats and luminous flies, which extend a gold-studded mesh over the abysm of the sky.

Matou-Mahli brought a kind of triangular harp encrusted with agates and opals, and offered it to the young woman, who began to sing in a voice that was sometimes grave and profound, sometimes light and crystalline, to the accompaniment of the humming strings.

> *Taï tou moucouty conda*
> *Rouné canny pomlé!*[1]

The popular song, full of idyllic rumors, became animated, burst forth in a joyful fanfare, and then died into an amorous lament.

Silence fell, and Achilgar appeared under the roses.

He was tall and slim with a pale and passionate face, eyes as profound as the night, and lips of shining bounty. When he was close to Viamalah he raised his hands to his forehead in a sign of adoration, and waited for her to be kind enough to speak to him.

"Achilgar," she said, "I will do as my father wishes. However, the mysterious signs that have never deceived me have warned me to be careful. May the wrath of the gods be turned away from us!"

The young man looked at her sadly. "For what would the gods punish us? What have we done against them?"

---

1 Author: "Bring jewels, young virgin of Aruna."

"Doubtless without wishing to, we have displeased them."

"Viamalah, you don't love me!"

She stood up, put her arms on her fiancé's shoulders, and brushed his cheek with her burning cheek. "Yes, I love you with all my strength."

"Then let us be married."

Discouraged, she let her arms fall again, and turned away. "Don't you want to wait a while, Achilgar? What are weeks and months when one is sure of loving forever?"

But he held her against him again, impetuously.

"No, no, tomorrow you will belong to me . . . tomorrow . . ."

"I'm afraid, my friend. I don't believe that I'm free . . ."

He laughed arrogantly. "You are mine, Viamalah!"

With tender words and seductive gestures, he told her the reasons he had for believing in their happiness, the certainty that he had of the indulgence of the gods, and how, that very morning, he had made a sacrifice to the goddess Kali, the most terrible of the Hindu divinities.

The goddess Kali bears all crimes and curses within her; she only takes pleasure in images of death, and scenes of murder and carnage. She is represented with four arms; one of her hands holds a sword, another the grimacing head of an executed man, and the other two hands are open. A large necklace of human skulls surrounds her neck, and her tongue hangs down to her breasts. Her ankle is ornamented by a bracelet of fleshless fingers, which rattle when fanatics drunk on arak and opium massacre one another before her pedestal.

At the name of the goddess, the young woman had shivered. Achilgar hugged her more forcefully and fastened her lips with an irresistible kiss.

"Do you not love my embrace and the softness of my mouth, Viamalah? Be mine. I will have the sacred fire carried to the Brahmin's house, I will spread kusha grass over the ground, and we will be married without witnesses, in accordance with religious prescriptions. The ceremonies will come afterwards, with all the magnificence due to our rank. If you prefer, I shall lift you on to my Sikh horse and offer you betel in the shade of the banyan of Shiva."

"Shiva does not want it! Just now, I consulted him again . . ."

Achilgar leaned toward her ear and whispered the charm of amorous words, which makes young women shudder from the nape to the heels, and delivers them defenseless to a man's desire.

"I will caress your breasts with my lips and I shall penetrate the flowery secrets of your body; your flesh will be burning with kisses, and you will no longer want to detach yourself from me."

She closed her eyes, swooning. He went on: "There will not be a tiny corner of your body that I do not know; every charming covert will be the nest of a kiss, and those kisses will fall gently upon you like the fluttering wings of little birds, making you laugh and cry with joy. Then there will be yet more kisses, rare and precious kisses, kisses as light and silky as lily petals; there will be so many that if the gods had the power to make precious stones of them, they would cover you with a fulgurant mesh."

"Stop," she said. "Your words are like flames in my heart."

"You will know the supreme joy, you will die and be reborn voluptuously; you will only want to exist for that, and I will teach you, with science and slowly, the sixty-four fashions of Kama . . ."[1]

"Ah," she said, dolorous and feverish.

He slid into her hand a curiously-mounted and sculpted jewel representing a lingam, made from a single ruby of great purity.

---

1 Kama features in the present text primarily as the name of a god—the Hindu equivalent of the Greek Eros—but it is also one of a set of four supposedly fundamental objectives of life (desire), along with dharma (virtue), artha (material prosperity) and moksha (liberation). *Kama Sutra*, an ancient Sanskrit text analyzing and commenting on the role of sexual desire in life, is best-known in the West because of its exhaustive list of positions for the accomplishment of sexual intercourse (to which Achilgar is presumably referring here), although it offers a far more elaborate account of "the mystery of Kama."

"Wear it," he said, "for love of me." And, delicately, he fixed the little chain to Viamalah's slender wrist. She was to longer defending herself. When he wanted to remove the light gauze retained in front by the diamond clasp, she pushed him away fearfully.

"No, not that . . . Tomorrow perhaps . . . yes, tomorrow."

He had knelt down, like a Brahmin, before the triangular stone that penitents bear to their lips. With a sigh, he got up again.

"Tomorrow," he said. "I have your promise."

And he drew away between the double hedges of flowering shrubs, with the scents of pepper and honey.

III
Haunting

Tomorrow! She had said tomorrow. A veil of mist descended over her thoughts; she closed her eyes in order to isolate herself from the real world, to forget, to the extent that it was possible. But that moment of mental anesthesia was only of short duration, and the fear of the future that awaited her returned more sharply.

She went on to the terrace of pink sandstone and Rajputana marble, the foot of which was bathed by the Ganges. At Benares, the Ganges is astonishingly wide; the holy city, on the left bank, is arranged in stages. To the right are the Maharajah's palaces and gardens, magically grouped in a glory of towers and silver- and gold-plated cupolas. Every Hindu prince has a duty to possess a palace on the bank of the river, and several of those splendid domains contain a following of several thousand individuals.

Viamalah, of illustrious origin, lived in one of those vast dwellings, with porphyry columns encrusted with jade and ivory, with galleries of white marble full of the twittering of fountains in profound basins.

Her childhood had been pleasant, in the midst of attentive servants who anticipated the least of her desires and solemn Brahmins who initiated her young soul into the mysteries of their religion. Sitting on silk cushions filigreed with gold, her slender hands crossed over her knees, she listened to the grave words of the ministers of Mahadeo and did not tremble at the account of his barbaric exploits.

Already she had shiny little bells on her ankles and precious rings in her ears. Her hair, mingled with jasmine, spread around her, and she was prouder of it than the rarest jewels. She was accompanied by three favorites with complicated and sonorous names: Honeycomb, Glory of the Moon, and Celestial Perfume. All four ran away at night to go and dream in the starlight in the solitude of the gardens or dip their feet into the sacred waters of the river. They thought about amour, as all Hindu girls do, who are only brought up to worship the gods and give pleasure to men.

Brahmanism is a mixture of pantheism and polytheism. All murders, all excesses, all the delirious inventions of the mind and the criminal temptations of the senses are divinized therein, along with the elements and matter. By means of a series of transformations, the Brahmins have made the deification of life and generation the very essence of the religion.

The worshipers of Shiva wear a ring on the left arm that sustains the lingam-yoni, the venerated jewel of amour and joy, the obscene and troubling symbol that young women adore ingenuously. The fervent followers of Vishnu have a tilaka on the forehead, a kind of trident traced from the origin of the nose, whose central vertical line is red and the straight lateral lines white; that too is a symbol of youth, strength and fecundity.

The Brahmins have introduced dolor and pleasure into everything connected with their worship. They encourage and advise human sacrifices, the periodic assassination of children and virgins.[1]

____

1 Knowledge of Brahmanism and other Eastern religions in nineteenth-

Viamalah remembered having presided over a bloody sacrifice at a time of epidemic disease, mortality and famine. She had followed the victim to the edge of the river, where she had been bathed in order to dress her in silk clothes florid with precious embroideries. Then, to the sound of a tambourine made with two skulls stuck together and a flute pierced in a human femur, she had been accompanied, preceded by a troop of dancers, to the place of sacrifice. The child had smiled, thinking that it was a game. She trembled, however, when the man was bound in order to break the bones of his arms and legs. He did not cry out, intoxicated by opium and datura, presenting his breast to the priest in order that the heart could be cut out and collected in a silver vase.

And Viamalah could still see that heart, fuming and quivering, the blood of which was escaping in impetuous bubbles, reddening the flowers that she was holding in her hand. That vision of horror still pursued her, and she had talked about it to her little friends Honeycomb and Glory of the Moon, stammering fearfully.

Apart from that terrifying day, her life had gone by without significant events. She had sung, danced and prayed to charm the gods, had impregnated herself with the essences of roses of Gazipur, had combed her long hair, smiling at her image, between the red lotuses of the pool of Durga.

Then the fiancé came to intoxicate her with burning words, but she has not dared to allow herself to yield to the sweetness of amour, because a fanatic, at the exit from the temple of the god-

---

century France was largely based on the reports of missionaries, which were heavily laden with slanderous propaganda, routinely including lurid accounts of rituals of human sacrifice. A significant role in popularizing the myths adopted and greatly elaborated by La Vaudère was played by the French missionary Jean-Antoine Dubois (1765-1848), whose account of *Moeurs, institutions et cérémonies des peuples d'Inde* (1825; tr. as *Hindu Manners and Customs*) remained a standard text for many years.

dess, a yogi charmer,[1] had placed himself in her path and forbidden her to lend her flesh to a mortal being.

Achilgar, however, is of noble origin like her; he is young, eloquent, and he has everything required to charm the imagination of an ardent virgin full of desire too long contained. What, then, is the power of that stranger whom she encountered by chance and who has the pretention to govern her desires?

"You should not belong to a man," he had said. "Your body belongs to the mysteries divinities that govern us. They have chosen you as a sacrifice, because you are the most beautiful . . ."

Viamalah rebelled, and tears flowed from her eyes like a broken necklace of pearls.

"Who has given you the right to speak to me thus?"

"The Pitris, whose advice I follow and whose servant I am. By means of the possession of Maya,[2] I govern the earth."

Nassudamy had placed himself before the young woman, half-naked, displaying a torso that was harmonious in spite of fasting, an energetic head with features hollowed out in sharp ridges, and long hair retained by a white ribbon. In his passionate and tenebrous face, his immense eyes were reminiscent of two flowers of precious stone, and the virgin had been unable to support the extraordinary glare of his gaze. He had extended his dominating hand toward her and she had bent her knees in dolorous humility.

---

1 La Vaudère sometimes uses the word *charmeur* [charmer] to mean "snake-charmer," although she also uses the more restrictive word *psylle* for that purpose, but she usually uses it in a more general sense, to mean something more akin to "magician." I have only translated *psylle* as snake-charmer, even where *charmeur* seems to have the same reference.
2 The author inserts notes here and elsewhere defining Maya as "the Illusion," but the meaning of the term is more complex; in early Vedic texts it seems to imply supernatural power and wisdom, and it is only in later ones that the implication is added that such power is based on illusion—an implication sometimes generalized philosophically to suggest that what we assume to be reality is actually a kind of illusion. The name is also used in Hindu mythology to mean "goddess," and, more specifically, the goddess Lakshmi—a meaning obliquely cited by the present text at one point.

"Other women are better and more fervent. Why prevent me from following the law of amour?"

"You shall know amour, Viamalah: the amour that is not submissive to the caprice of men."

"I love my fiancé."

"You believe that you love him. Demons are inspiring you. Is not this Kiss softer than that of Achilgar?"

And without Nassudamy having moved, Viamalah felt on her lips the caress of an avid mouth, an invisible mouth of which she had nevertheless felt all the voluptuous sinuosity.

She had wanted to flee, but, even though there was no witness to the scene, two arms had gripped her forcefully and the kiss, the intoxication of which she savored unconsciously, penetrated more profoundly, taking away all sentiment of reality.

When she recovered consciousness, Nassudamy was no longer with her, but between her joined hands, a bunch of violently-perfumed tuberoses sprang forth.

IV
Nassudamy the Charmer

By day, Viamalah thought about her fiancé, and by night about the unknown charmer. As soon as the shadows descended over the holy city, she summoned Matou-Mahli in order to have herself conducted to a mysterious place where she knew that she would encounter the fakir.

The servant threw a thick veil over the young woman's radiant beauty, a sort of dupatta, which hid the gems of her adornment and the gems of her body; then the two women climbed into a dingui—a long boat fitted with a cabin—and followed the shore of the Ganges. The boat was governed by a tendal, or chief boatman, and six macouas, oarsmen of the caste of fishermen, accustomed to taking the worshipers of Durga to the florid temple of the goddess.

They saw the frail minarets reaching into the sky, like golden pistils emerging from the massive corolla of domes and towers. Then there were long arcades sustained by marble columns, elevated quays, terraces garnished with balustrades perforated like lace, designed in guipure relief against the foliage of tamarinds and banana trees. There was no coherent plan in the architecture: a forest of walls, cupolas, turrets, porticos and pillars, admirable and crazy ornaments, solemn and light, denoting a highly developed sense of everything that stirs the nerves and the imagination.

The Ghats—monuments of a sort composed of four pilasters linked together by a unique cornice and placed at the summits of giant staircases that dipped their final steps in the sacred waters of the river—are the only quays that ancient city possesses, the former Kasy of the rajahs of the primal race. All day long they are covered by coolies loading and unloading ships, hastening around merchandise from India, Europe and Asia, which aliments the markets of upper Bengal.

Of all the temples of Benares, the most venerated bears the name of Bishishar-Kumardil, or the Holy of Holies.[1] It is a construction of a particular genre, very rare in India. It is made of granite, rather low, painted bright red and filled with stone sculptures representing Brahmanic bulls and the symbols of various Asiatic cults. During fêtes, the bells ring at full tilt, punctuating their joyous cascades with the shrill clamors of pilgrims.

But Viamalah gave no thought to the Holy of Holies. The temple of the god Hanuman, who is a great green monkey, ardent and bellicose, did not arrest her attention either. Snake-charmers, however, descended the steps of the Ghats, with snakes wrapped around their wrists. They whistled in a plaintive fashion and the cobras swollen with venom raised their little flat heads toward them, sticking out their triangular tongues in a caressant fashion.

---

1 This name and definition, as well as the subsequent description, originate from *Himalayan Journals; or, Notes of a Naturalist in Bengal* (1854) by Joseph Dalton Hooker, and are only to be found in copies of his account.

Viamalah recognized one of the charmers as Nassumady and made a sign to the oarsmen to put into the bank. The man carrying the reptile drew away, without turning his head, and she followed him meekly.

They marched in silence for a long time to find a cooler place. Now the foliage joined overhead; they were in a deserted spot, a kind of mysterious zenana where the paths, scarcely traced, were invaded by a thick tangle of grass and lianas. Nassudamy guided the young woman to the usual place of their rendezvous, a ruined temple of which the anterior and lateral facades were covered by reliefs representing sacred animals and human couples engaged in sexual intercourse. A rectangular gallery, to which the disjointed steps of a granite stairway gave access, was still dressed in places by a kind of stucco prepared with pulverized shells, which the sun and rain had colored with opaline tints. A sarcophagus stood in the middle, under the high arched arcades that the climbing plants had decked in light and sumptuous drapery, as florid as a betrothal feast. Petals, incessantly falling and swirling, put the softness of a smile over the black sepulcher.

The charmer stopped and turned to the young woman.

"You have seen your fiancé and you have given him your word?" he said, in a hoarse voice.

She tried to deny it but he interrupted her. "Why lie? The Pitris have informed me. Nothing that you do remains hidden from me."

"Well," she confessed, "I have obeyed my father, who desires this marriage. What do you want of me, since you cannot love a woman? Fakirs cannot marry, Shiva forbids it. The god of somber justice forbids those he has endowed with the power of evocation, illusion and metamorphosis to occupy themselves with other concerns, which would deflect them from the mission that they have received."

"Certainly Shiva loves those who devote themselves to his laws. He loves them with a capricious and jealous amour . . ."

"You see! Your mission is all sacrifice. To misunderstand the law of Shiva would be the cause of the greatest punishments for you. You must charm all those who hesitate or revel, all those who reject your beliefs and deny the manifestations of the spirit emanating from the superior power. Your family is the Universe. You ought not to love a woman."

"I love you in spirit, Viamalah, and, without touching you, I can savor the same delights as the most impetuous of lovers. Is not the will to govern one's heart and senses sufficient to attain omnipotence? Carnal joys are trivial if one experiences them passively, or solely by virtue of the need of an imperfect nature. Has not my amour troubled you more delightfully than that of Achilgar?"

The young woman lowered her eyes. "I don't know . . ."

Nassudamy went on vehemently: "You have tasted his impure kisses early, and he has given you that jewel, with which you do not fear to adorn yourself before me!"

Unconsciously, Viamalah had folded her arm over her breast in order to protect the sacred jewel; but without the charmer making a gesture, the golden chain that retained it suddenly broke, and the lingam fell on to the funerary stone like a ruby tear.

The virgin bowed her head sadly and the charmer went on: "I have no need of jewelers or sculptors to ornament your beauty. Look!"

A large crimson corolla was swaying over the forehead of the amorous adolescent. Nassudamy plucked it, and, holding it delicately before his lips, pronounced fateful mantras over it. Immediately, the pistil overflowed the petals, grew, and rounded out graciously, presenting the perfect image of the lingam emerging from the calyx of a flower: the lingam-yoni.

"Thus," he said, "you will have the complete symbol."

And he bent the stem, which changed into a chain of aqua-marines.

"Oh!" she said, marveling, as she took the bracelet. "Can you realize all my desires, then?"

"All your desires, if you feel strong enough to belong only to me, spirit and will."

"No," she groaned. "What you're asking of me is impossible. I have promised!"

He smiled disdainfully. "I can disengage you from your promise."

"How?"

"I know the herbs that give sleep and sensuality, life and death. I can also render you invisible."

"Render me invisible?"

"Yes, by rubbing your eyes with a lotion that I will teach you; thus you could act without dread. A few drops of the juice of this plant . . ."

"No, no!" she said, with horror. "I hate you!"

And she tried to flee. But her feet remained riveted to the ground, and a kind of torpor invaded her. With a sigh, she closed her eyes and abandoned herself.

V

A Strange Dream

Nassudamy laid the young woman down on the moss and, kneeling beside her, contemplated her ardently.

Wandering holy men have a mysterious and terrible power that troubles the mind and confounds reason. No one has yet been able to discover the means employed by the Brahmins to fanaticize their adepts. The latter, on quitting the pagoda in which they have lived in prayer, fasting and perfumes, must not reveal to men the secrets they have been taught. If they make use of magical formulae and incantations for their astonishing experiments, it is in a low voice, always unintelligible for the witnesses. To any questions that a traveler might pose, they reply that they are nothing, and that the Pitris alone give them the power to go for months without eating or sleeping, or to be buried underground in a strange and terrifying catalepsy. Maya assists and charms them; she is the magician who reigns over hearts and governs consciences.

Leaning over Viamalah, Nassudamy suggested his desire to her.

Gradually, the spirit of the fakir entered into union with the spirit of the sleeper. Solely by means of the evocation of pleasure, he possessed all the voluptuous flowers of her young flesh: the jasmine of her mouth, the tuberose of her armpits, the pale carnation of her breasts, the golden rose of her lap,[1] soft and ambered like a tuft of carunas, and, lower down, the sacred lotus of secret intoxications. No veil was disturbed, however, over the slender body of the virgin, who, lips parted, was also intoxicated by the fictitious kisses. Her heels touching under the gauze of the dupatta, her arms folded over her pearl necklaces, were not brushed by the hands of the charmer, who penetrated her with all joys by the force of his will alone.

"Oh," she said, without waking up, "the wind that plays in the clove-trees is blowing from the Himalayas now! I can hear the buzzing of bees in the barbed darts of the patali, like the quivers of Smara, the god of amour, and the petals of the palasa are like the fingernails of Kama, which bruise and caress by turns . . . come to me, come inside me, it is the hour for embraces and harmonies . . ."

"I am yours, I am inside you," sighed the charmer, who had not budged, but whose face was contracted by the intense and prolonged sensation of the dream.

Broad rays of moonlight pierced the foliage.

In front of them, a lawn extended seething with bubbles of pink florets, so crowded that the grass could hardly be seen.

---

1 Here and elsewhere, I have translated Le Vaudère's euphemistic *giron* as "lap," that being the most familiar English equivalent, but the great majority of her readers would have been sufficiently familiar with female anatomy to know what she really meant [the pubic region], even though she distinguishes it here from the "sacred lotus" [the vagina].

Leaves, dentellate or bristling like sword-blades extended above, and the branches, frosted with pale clarities, disappeared in their turn beneath the network of lianas and the velvet tunic of mosses.

Over the mirror of a pond, large birds with metallic reflections circulated, with breasts of quicksilver with green and azure sheens, and throats of lilac silk with crimson and gold scales . . .

"I am yours, I am inside you. Your tresses are somber veils that palpitate in the night like the plush wings of bats, and your ardent lips have the taste of the bloody flower of Bandhujiva. Your eyes are stones of mysterious and changing adora, which speak of sidereal splendors and let nothing penetrate. Your ear is the nacreous shell in which the amour of the waves sings. I would like to put my tongue therein, like a coral pistil. Your breasts are twin cups, in which rubies set in gold tremble. Your belly is a jade buckler, which no weapon has violated, and the secret of your divine body is like a hive of honey lost in flowers . . .

"You are a virgin, Viamalah, but you have known supreme ecstasies! You are no longer ignorant of anything of the complete embrace, but no caress has ever attempted to break into the closed calyx of your loins. In thought, I have drunk from the cups of your breasts, I have tasted the honey of your lips, and, without having put my tongue into the supreme source, I have intoxicated myself recklessly!

"Viamalah . . . !"

The young woman uttered a faint cry and opened her eyes, her body burning, her limbs exhausted, as if after a long struggle. Her dupatta still enveloped her, and not a single pearl of her necklaces had budged.

The charmer allowed her to stand up.

For a moment she remained silent, anxious and surprised, her eyebrows furrowed; then she became indignant.

"Adieu! You will never see me again. I don't know to what bewitchment you have subjected me, but I blush at what I've experienced! If the gods are against me, let my destiny be accomplished!"

"You will have wanted it."

"Yes," she said, resolutely. "Your practices are culpable and you violate the laws of nature. Desire has been unleashed within me, and my senses aroused, in a futile fashion, and I want to experience the satisfaction of amour."

He shrugged his shoulders. "Go, you are free—but you belong to me, and no man, while I am alive, will know the sweetness of your flesh."

VI
The Ruby Lingam

Matou-Mahli was waiting for her mistress on the path.

"Quickly," she said, "day is about to break. How late you are, Comet Flower!"

Viamalah suddenly felt the weakness of the entire being that is the aftermath of the vertigo of amour. Her nostrils quivering, she inhaled the perfumed air of the woods impetuously. She took a few steps at a run and then stopped, indecisive and torpid, feeling a kind of anguish in her side that flowed into her legs, now limp and uncertain.

Painfully, she went back to the dingui that had brought her, and, while the six oarsmen rowed ardently, she placed her head on the servant's shoulder and wept quietly, like a child caught at fault.

"What's the matter?" asked Matou, anxiously.

"I've . . . oh, what's the point? You wouldn't be able to understand . . . what happened to me is so strange."

"The holy man predicted an unhappy future for you?"

"Yes, the fakir is cruel . . ."

"Bah!" said Matou-Mahli, who was a Buddhist, "the fakirs are as mistaken as the Brahmins. The best thing is not to attach any importance to their pretended science."

"Nassudamy is no ordinary charmer; what he can do surpasses everything you could suppose . . ."

"Really? What can he do, then?"

Confused, Viamalah did not reply. Matou went on, disdain-fully: "He's made seeds germinate and flowers bloom . . ."

"Yes," said the young woman, "he's a skillful man. He knows what pleases women."

"Women with feeble minds . . ."

". . . But a vivid imagination."

"Really? He's a great sorcerer!"

"Look," said the young woman—and placed her burning hand in Matou's. "Do you see this jewel?"

"You have a fever, Comet Flower!"

"It doesn't matter. Look at that lingam."

"It's a ruby from the Oxus."

"He made it spring from a crimson flower that was dangling over my head, and the flower itself became . . ."

"That jewel is inestimable for the purity of its gems and the perfection of its details. Doubtless the fakir had hidden it in a bush. It's a marvelous gift."

"What is it necessary to do with it, Matou?"

"It's necessary to throw it in the Ganges, Comet Flower."

"You think so?"

"You only ought to accept presents from your fiancé, Achilgar."

"That's true . . ."

Having kissed the fetish, she attempted to remove it from her arm, but the chain resisted, tightening around her frail wrist, and in spite of all Matou's efforts, it could not be detached.

The servant was trembling slightly. "By Buddha! The devils are mixed up in this. May the evil spirits withdraw from you!"

"No, leave it, since it's the will of Shiva."

"What will Achilgar say?"

"He'll think that it's the lingam he gave me, and I'll be careful to hide it under other jewels . . ."

"That's all right," said Matou. "His wasn't nearly as beautiful."

VII

The Affectionate Friends

Before going to sleep, Vialmah wanted to purify her body of all pollution, and, having summoned her favorites Honeycomb, Glory of the Moon and Celestial Perfume, she plunged into a porphyry basin above which eight elephant heads poured embalmed water at different temperatures out of their jewel-encircled trunks. Imperceptible showers filled the air like diamond dust, and thousands of little bottles of various tints, illuminated internally by fireflies, spread a mysterious light.

Glory of the Moon, who was pale, with long, burnt topaz eyes and hair that caressed her heels, picked up her rebab—a sort of viol in the form of a calabash with a long handle of green ivory—and caused its two copper strings to vibrate.

Celestial Perfume, who was small and plump, with a minuscule red mouth as moist as a fruit, started to sing: "*Taïtou, mon couty conda . . .*"

And Honeycomb, gliding lightly on her bare feet, ringed with turquoises and sapphires, lifted up her gold-laméd dupatta, for the "amour that collects pollen," which she executed with voluptuously enticing undulations.

But Viamalah, agitating her hands in the warm water in order to mix in the vehement perfume of tuberose that she had chosen, sighed dolorously.

"No, not that."

The adolescents stopped, and contemplated her in silence.

"Your games fatigue me," said the bather, languidly. "I don't want songs or dances . . . but I want you to cosset me like a wounded turtle-dove whose wings one kisses . . . Get into the pool with me, quickly."

Without taking off their jewels, which sparkled under the water like the reflection of minuscule stars in a pond, they slid in next to Viamalah and took her in their arms.

"Cuddle me," she said, closing her eyes. "I'm sad . . ."

And the little girls ran their quivering and caressant lips over her shoulders, like agile bees violating a basket of roses.

VIII
Around Shiva

Day dawned, and the virgin, weary but unsatisfied, her mind and nerves still subject to the strange suggestion of the charmer, tried to sleep.

Around the palace, the mirror of pools reflected the long galleries with colonnades of pink and green marble, shaded by clove-trees and bamboos. In the distance, the brick chimneys of the manufacturers of aromatics were fuming, and merchants of every sort were selling subtle spices, delicate glassware as slender as flowers, prayer wheels, objects of carved odorous wood, unpolished gemstones framed in copper and silver, plant essences for embellishing the face and crushed stone pastes for polishing the skin. Snake-charmers were whistling softly in the countryside, summoning serpents, and pilgrims on the bank of the Ganges were commencing their customary ablutions.

Nassudamy, with a few other fanatical yogis, was evoking the Pitris in the temple of Durga, while the bayaderes consecrated to the divinities were circling around them slowly or fixing themselves in lascivious poses, which the sacred monkeys with white beards did their best to imitate.

All religions, including Christianity, have admitted the existence of astral forms possessed of intelligence, under the name of devas, angels, saints or spirits, playing the role of intermediaries between humans and the superior worlds. Hindus believe firmly in apparitions, hands of fire, miracles, good and evil presages, deadly influences and bewitchments. Yogis or fakirs, in particular, exercise a great influence over crowds. By means of an incredible energy of will or fanaticism, sometimes pushed as far as dementia, they condemn themselves to tortures that our reason can scarcely conceive.

Some of them remain motionless for years, crouching, kneeling or even buried to the waist. Their legs and arms atrophy, stiffening in the pose they have given them, and no effort is able to flex them. They remain thus until death, often a long time coming. Others exhaust themselves in repeated fasting, place themselves between two braziers in order to stimulate the decomposition of their organs, arriving at a state of spectral thinness, almost diaphanous.

A large number of travelers have assimilated the fakirs to assassins and highway robbers; the truth is that although these fanatics are dangerous, because of the influence they exercise over crowds, the philters they distribute and the black magic that they practice, one cannot impute other crimes to them. They must have been confused with the affiliates of the terrible sect of Thugs, or death-worshipers, who kill out of devotion—even in the interest of their victims—and form beyond the Indus a secret society of the most redoubtable character, which has resisted all efforts attempted against it for three thousand years.

There are, moreover, fakirs of all conditions. In the same way that Catholicism, in the times of political domination, created religious orders, the mission of each being to act in its own sphere upon the social class that it was charged with directing, in India, where the regime of castes still subsists, there are yogis in each one, of a similar condition, who associate themselves with its destiny and share the esteem or scorn that it inspires.

Some of those holy men, by means of mysterious practices or the omnipotence of their will, succeed in modifying the mental character of humans, and even their form. They can unleash or prolong the existence of epidemics that decimate regions or cities in a matter of days. They can embellish themselves or disfigure themselves, changing the color of their eyes or hair, the dimension of their body and the natural sound of their voice. They can efface their wrinkles, render themselves invisible or seem suddenly to arrive at the final extreme of decrepitude. Finally, they are masters of Maya, like Krishna, who showed himself at the same time in his sixteen thousand eight hundred palaces, occupied in rendering his duty to his sixteen thousand eight hundred wives.

IX
Petty Digressions on Black Magic

India, which, so the kabbalistic tradition informs us,[1] was populated by the descendants of Cain, and to which the children of
Abraham and Keturah subsequently withdrew, is, *par excellence*,
the land of goetia, incantations, bewitchments and illusions. The
accursed science of black magic is perpetuated there, with the
original traditions of fratricide, rejected by the oppressive castes
and expiated by pariahs.

India, the ancestor with the dark secrets, with a past of murders, spoliations and rapes, has seen all idolatries flourish. The
dogmas of its gymnosophists could teach us wisdom if they did
not begin by familiarizing us with the most diabolical practices and the most monstrous vices. The terrible trimurti of the
Brahmins is composed of a creator, a destroyer and a repairer.
Their Addha-Nari, who depicts the divine mother or celestial
nature, is also named Bohawnie, and the Thugs or Stranglers offer human sacrifices to her. Vishnu, the repairer, only incarnates
himself in order to kill a demon who is invincible because he is
incessantly reborn by virtue of the will of Rutrem or Shiva, the
god of death.[2]

It is from the Kabbalah of India that the Gnostics borrowed
their voluptuous and perverse dreams.[3] It is Indian magic that,

---

1 This allegation, contained in a manuscript held in the Bibliothèque de
l'Arsenal in Paris and known in English as *The Book of the Penitence of Adam*,
was cited in *Histoire de la magie* (1860; tr. as The History of Magic) by
"Éliphas Lévi," which became a central text of the French Occult Revival.

2 The details of this paragraph, and much else in the chapter, appear to be
derived from *Addha-Nari, ou L'Occultisme dans l'Inde antique* (1893) by
Ernest Bosc.

3 This remark might be particularly relevant to the present text, the fundamental plot of which seems to be based on the legend of the relationship between
the alleged Gnostic known as Simon Magus and a woman named Helen, an
incarnation of Ennoia [Sacred Wisdom], with whom he is said to have travelled

presenting itself from the outset with its passions and its vices, attracts and frightens imaginations smitten with the marvelous. The great ritual magic, the book of Indian occultism, the *Oupnek'hat*,[1] informs the fakirs of the physical and mental means to consummate their mysterious power and arrive by degrees at the divine state, which, it is necessary to admit, also has its cruel dementia.

The *Oupnek'hat*, the most ancient of grimoires, is divided into five sections. It is a sky of darkness streaked with lightning. One finds marvelous sentences of virtue and abnegation there, alongside the most culpable oracles, abominations worthy of stryges, empusas and lamias. In order to procure visions, to produce the phenomena of second sight, the Brahmins put themselves into a state related to sleep, death and madness. Their science is also that of poisons, and their pupils, the yogis, are not ignorant of any of their secrets. They even claim to be able to kill by congestion or by the sudden subtraction of astral light, when, by means of a series of strange and dolorous exercises, they have made their nervous apparatus, flexible to all tensions and all fatigues, a kind of living galvanic pile capable of condensing and projecting forcefully the light that intoxicates or devours.

The great arcanum of the *Oupnek'hat* is the absolute in immortality, fatality and mortal quietism. This is what the book says on pages 35 and 92 of the first volume of the Anquetil translation:

"It is permitted to lie to facilitate marriages and exalt the virtues of a Brahmin or the qualities of a cow.

"God is called truth, and in him shadow and light are only one. The man who knows that never lies, for if he wants to lie, he

---

while preaching and working miracles—a story reprocessed by several writers of the Symbolist school, including André Lebey in "Ennoia" (1896).

1 The text known to occultists as the *Oupnek'hat* is a selective translation of the Hindu Upanishads—ancient Sanskrit texts summarizing and elaborating the philosophy of the Vedas—made circa 1801 by the Indologist Abraham Hyacinthe Anquetil-Duperron, but it was better known in the form of a somewhat distorted summary published in 1805 by the journalist Jean Denis, Comte Languinais. It is not a book of black magic, and is said have been a key inspiration of Arthur Schopenhauer's philosophy.

makes a verity of his lie. Whatever sin he commits, whatever evil work he does, he is never guilty. Even if he were a parricide twice over, even if he were to kill a Brahmin initiated to the mysteries of the Vedas—in sum, whatever he does—his light is not diminished, 'for,' says God, 'I am the universal soul, in me are good and evil, which are corrected by one another. The man who knows that is never a sinner; he is as universal as I am.'"

Sure of impunity, the fakirs, profaners of temples, purveyors of pyres, have mixed the bitter narcotic juices of henbanes and hemlocks and the caustic milk of tithymalus, have poured philters of aconite and mandrake with innumerable venoms and strange semens. Forgetting their vow of chastity, they have made themselves loved to the point of murder by young virgins submissive to their influence, and, in spite of the disgrace of their bodies, have been desired madly.

X
The Enamored Bayaderes

Nassudamy, who was handsome and well-built, remained prostrate before the image of Shiva. His muscular body, only gripped by a narrow strip of cloth, stood out against the whiteness of the marble, and he extended his arms in a tragic gesture.

"O terrible god," he said, "god of somber justice and punishment, god of amour and death, listen to the prayer of the most ardent of your servants. O formidable god, Ugra, Sthanu, Rudra, Sana, you repose on Mount Kailasa and you grant your incomparable favors to the beggars of the roads . . . Master with the black throat, the long hair and the deformed eyes, are you not the visitor of palaces and tombs, you who carry the club ornamented with a skull and the skin of an elephant? I have come with a humble and fervent spirit, to make the sacrifice of my flesh to the destroyer of Tripura, and only to love a woman in thought.

"Give me, Ugra, the strength never to place my lips on her body in flower, and let dream alone enable me to know the supreme delights . . . but let the one that I have chosen belong to me in imagination and intelligence, as I belong to her, if such is your will! May she understand and obey me, in spite of distance and time! May she be my faithful slave and the source of all joy. O lord of riches, Kirtimukha, friend of the heart of the goddess Gauri, womb of the universe, father of Kumara, god of sacred cows and powerful bulls, you who serve as a way to the sense organs, grant my wish of purity and amour!"

The bayaderes around him accelerated their dances, brushing him with their supple bodies rubbed with aromatics, imbibed with essences, aureoled with effluvia, and sometimes risking a more direct caress, for he was one of those men that young women notice.

Habituated to satisfying the complicated caprices of Brahmins, they smiled ingenuously at the young fakir, coveting the new feast that seemed to be offered.

"Nassudamy, I have skin fresher than the pulp of the modhavi."

"Nassudamy, I burn the like flame of pyres, and the wax of the amra tree melts on my flesh."

"My tongue has the musky taste of tamala!"

"I arrived here yesterday, my body is like a bunch of flowers. Look, I am only six years old!"

"Myself, I am ten, but I know pleasant games."

"Would you like me to recite the sixty-four manners of Kama? You'll recognize that I'm an assiduous pupil . . ."

"We'll read the Kama Sutra together, in order better to penetrate ourselves with it."

"I have the tender mildness of a dove."

"I circle like an eaglet above a sparrow."

"I die twenty times in one night and resuscitate like a butterfly in the light . . ."

"I have the convulsive spasms of a wounded panther."

"I have a surprise in reserve for you . . ."

"So do I!"

"You'll see! You'll see . . ."

They made their necklaces tinkle over their naked breasts, with tips heightened with rouge, gliding softly, their toes parted by the bezels of rings, their ankles heavy with rings and gems. An indefinable odor, warm and tenacious, with hints of vanilla and spices, emanated from them, and their skin shone like gold under the nacreous transparency of scarves.

Three children of six or seven, who did not quit him, harassed him more than the others, trying to put chains of roses around his arms and legs.

"Take all three of us, Nassudamy, we're sisters and still virgins. You'll make us suffer a little, and that will be more amusing . . ."

Laughing, they threw red petals at him, tearing their veils in order to show their frails nudity, the smooth chests of prepubescent girls and their narrow hips.

Gently, the charmer pushed them away.

"Save yourselves for the Brahmins who like leaves in bud and unopened flowers."

But they pulled faces. "What's the point, since they no longer have the strength to violate the mystery of calices? The Brahmins have passed the age of the larcenies of amour. You're young and handsome; your body is supple and strong, made for the embrace and the caress; your eyes are like two stars in a stormy sky. We love you . . ."

"Why don't you want us, Nassudamy? You don't know what you're refusing!"

"We've brought you lotus wine and honey cakes . . ."

Disdainfully, the fakir drew away without replying. Then the children, chagrined, offered their honey to the monkeys.

XI

Demi-Confession

"Am I pretty thus?"

"You're like a ray of moonlight on the mirror of the sacred waters."

Kneeling in front of Viamalah, after having given her the customary ablutions, Matou-Mahli polishes the pink agate of her toenails lightly, and wraps her slender legs in garlands of jasmine mingled with pearls, which spread out in three glorious tufts over the emerald clasp of her belt, positioned very low down. Her dainty breasts, the tips of which support two scintillating diamond stars, stand up proudly above the narrow corselet of precious stones, and her loose black hair, shiny and heavy, makes her a royal mantle that throws her head back arrogantly.

"Have Achilgar come in."

Trembling with happiness, Achilgar is already before her.

"Achilgar, I want to talk to you."

Her solemn tone makes him anxious, and he notices with surprise the strange circles around her long eyelids.

"What is it, Viamalah, dear Smile, little Comet Flower?"

"I have . . . I have . . ."

She stammers, confusedly, at the memory of the voluptuous dream that she had had, the dream that penetrated her, although a virgin, with the most profound of caresses.

Achilgar senses the claw of jealousy in his heart. Vaguely, but dolorously, he senses a possible treason.

"Explain yourself," he says. "What have you done since our last conversation?"

"I've prayed to the gods to come to my aid."

"Only that?"

"Yes, I swear it, but the gods have disheartened me, for they oppose our union. They're unjust and cruel."

Achilgar respires, preferring the hatred of the gods to the amour of a man.

"You must have misunderstood. In what fashion did they manifest their resentment?"

"By giving me extraordinary dreams."

"Frightening dreams?"

Viamalah sighs, and bows her head, nervously biting the stem of a lily.

Fully reassured, the young man adds, in order to say something: "Dreams have no importance."

"You think so? Even those that initiate us into . . . the joys of amour?"

"Certainly. I authorize the dreams, my beloved; I summon them, if they are agreeable to the gods . . ."

"Then you have no fear?"

"I fear nothing."

"You want to marry me even so?"

"More than ever. The virgin who knows everything and extends herself to the kiss, like the flower to the bee, is the most adorable of mistresses . . ."

XII
The Possessed

"Achilgar, have you not proposed to marry me secretly before the consecrated feasts, always so long for people of our caste?"

"Oh! You consent . . . ?"

The young man, bewildered, contemplates her rapturously, not daring to believe in so much joy.

Viamalah, her lips dry, her eyes brilliant with fever and desire, continues in a hoarse voice: "I had to tell you about my dream. It was pursuing me, haunting me. I want to escape it, you understand? So, since you know everything and you consent . . . let us both be happy. Go, my love, go seek the consecrated fire in the Brahmin's house. During your absence I will spread the kusha grass over the ground, after the fashion of the Gandharvas, or the

Vampires of Manu; in that fashion our marriage will be indissoluble. Go, my beloved, hurry . . .”

Alone, Viamalah shook her heavy hair and looked at her wrist, for she had seemed to feel a slight pressure of the accursed bracelet. Again she attempted to detach it, but the chain resisted all her efforts, as it had the first time. Terrified by her solitude, she summoned Matou-Mahli, who came running, meekly.

“Matou, I’m giving myself to the lover I’ve chosen.”

“You’re giving yourself? When?”

“In a moment.”

“You hope to escape the charmer thus?”

“I hope so. Cover me with red roses, light the pale algae in the silver tripod and strew the sacred herbs on the ground.”

The young woman lay down on cushions and the servant, having undressed her entirely, simply knotted a cordon of crimson roses around her loins, and poured perfumes mixed with powdered gold over her head.

Viamalah closed her eyes, abandoning herself. But she went on: “Rub me again with those balms with the subtle and fresh essences. Tint the insides of my hands with vermilion, pass antimony over the edges of my eyelids and elongate my eyebrows with that mixture of gum, musk and ebony, which goes so well with my amber skin. It is necessary that Achilgar’s amour doesn’t weaken and the reality is inferior to the dream . . . the beautiful dream I had!”

“What dream?” asked Matou, disquieted by the adolescent’s gleaming eyes. “I know that dreams are of great importance. If you desire, I’ll explain yours.”

“No need, Matou, it carried its explanation within itself.”

And Viamalah, once again, lowered her somber eyelids over the ecstasy evoked.

She was naked, supple, thin and plump, her cleavage straight and pure, starry at the tips of the breasts, with corollas of diamonds maintained by slender chains. Her hips rounded softly above tapering legs like colonnettes of pale gold. Essences floated around her, evaporating from her flesh in gusts that were some-times agile and sometimes heavy.

Achilgar came back in with a small stove containing the sacred fire of the gods. He threw a handful of Chaba pepper into it, and a little uchala root and hedysarum; then he offered the young woman a cup of milk mixed with fennel juice and whipped with three sparrow's eggs. When she had drunk it he put a bamboula—a betel nut and leaf—on his tongue and pre-sented it to her thus, kneeling before her. Their lips met and they whispered words of love. Then he held her against him, kissed her hair, her forehead, her mysterious eyes and her delicate ears, slowly, as one savors a delicacy long coveted. His ardor was in-creased by those slight caresses, causing his temples to throb, and if he refrained from possessing her brutally, it was to prolong and refine his pleasure.

She looked at him, charmed to sense herself loved so com-pletely and in accordance with the wishes of nature. What she had sensed, under the influence of the yogi, could only be the ef-fect of dangerous evocations, of spells. A frisson ran through her at the memory of those singular sensualities, almost dolorous in their acuity. Achilgar was the grave and passionate lover that all women desire, the lover tender enough and skillful enough never to make the disdainful pride of his triumph felt.

He held her against his breast, felt her flanks quiver; the warmth of her body, rubbed with unguents with vehement scents, exasperated his desire to take her, to make him his irresistibly. He lifted up the stars of her breasts in order to place his lips thereon, tore away the chain of roses that hid the softness of her sex, his fingers crazed and tremulous, irritated by obstacles.

Viamalah seemed dead, motionless in the red petals, which were like drops of blood.

Marveling, dazed by rare sensations, he admired the erect and turgid breasts, amber cups inverted on the altar of sensuality that her charming body presented. The adolescent's firm flesh rebounded under his mouth, he traveled over it all, surprised by that perfection of forms, impatient with ardent joy, hungry for pure kisses.

When he had touched her here and there, like a great maculate flower, he tried to open the calyx of her loins, but the young woman had the rigidity of marble. It was in vain that he called her by the most tender names, sighed, moaned and became desolate. It was in vain that he covered her with kisses and bruised himself in trying to conquer her; the slender legs, stretched out on the roses, remained riveted together; not a muscle of that virginal body twitched.

He realized then that she was in a state of catalepsy.

XIII
To Ward Off Maleficent Powers

Viamalah woke up in the midst of the lamentations of her favorites Glory of the Moon, Honeycomb and Celestial Perfume, who were rolling at her feet like affectionate kittens.

"The Dream!" she said. "The Dream again!"

"O Viamalah! Comet Flower! Divine Dew! Lily Petal! Stainless beauty, what has happened, then?" the little darlings asked, taking her hand. "Your fiancé Achilgar has run over the terraces and told your father that you are possessed by evil spirits."

"Me, possessed? Why?"

"Because he could not accomplish the sacrifice of amour that you desired, as he did, and you were insensible to the most ardent caresses. The stove is there, however, red with the sacred fire, for the Brahmin had blessed your union."

Silently, Viamalah contemplates the end of her naked foot, tinted with carmine.

"It's necessary to care for you," Glory of the Mon resumes.

"To fetch a doctor," Honeycomb supplies.

"Or an exorcist," risks Celestial Perfume.

"An exorcist?"

"Of course! When we came in, a blue flame was fluttering over your head, which indicates the presence of Rakshasas—ironic demons."

"Personally, I saw green jackals hiding behind the wall-hangings; they were certainly Pishasas and Asuras, sly and maleficent spirits."

"Myself, I think that the gallant, overexcited, wasn't up to the height of his mission."

"What are you saying, Glory of the Moon?"

"I'm saying that the handsome Achilgar hasn't done honor to his engagements . . . you understand?"

"Can that be possible? A fellow of such proud manner and such high reputation!"

"He might have encountered a piebald horse on his route—everyone knows that brings bad luck."

And the adolescents laugh madly, forgetting their recent tears.

"You don't know, Viamalah? It'll be necessary to make him take Chaba pepper."

"Or pods of premna spinosa."

"You could also fustigate him with chains of roses . . ."

"Or tickle his feet with a hummingbird feather."

Viamalah sighs, her lips swollen.

"I don't know, I was doubtless asleep, and my dream was strangely voluptuous."

"Perhaps you dreamed that your fiancé Achilgar was caressing you?" asks Glory oft he Moon, interestedly.

"That would only be a demi-misfortune," remarks Honeycomb, "for, after all, from the moment that you belonged to him, whether it be in a dream or reality, it would have been a pleasure for you anyway."

"It wasn't a question of my fiancé," the young woman admits, wearily. "But let me be—I want to reflect, to weigh things up . . . try to make a resolution. You, Celestial Perfume, lull my thoughts with the song of the Cocila . . ."

The young woman with the minuscule coral pink mouth picked up her rebab, and began with a cascade of light and vibrant notes, something like the rustle of the wind in branches or the irritated murmur of wavelets against a reef. Then she sang in a faint and monotonous voice.

> *The Cocila has shown me the road to amour . . .*
> *I await the beloved, impatient and fearful,*
> *All my flesh extends toward him,*
> *As if he were the day star.*
> *O my lover, penetrate me!*

Meanwhile, Achilgar had come back to lie down at Viamalah's feet, for a truly smitten man cannot be put off by obstacles. Obstacles stimulate impetuous chargers, which only recoil in order to take a better run-up.

"I know what it is," he said. "The gods desire that we marry in great pomp, and they were irritated by the scant splendor of the ceremony. Let us marry in a fashion worthy of our birth and our tenderness. Do you want that, Smile of Smara, Petal of Tuberose, Dew of Nenuphar?"

"Alas!" she sighed.

"Yes, let us marry, my lovely lover, escorted by three hundred elephants, five hundred camels and all the bayaderes of the temple of Shiva!"

"The bayaderes!"

"If, after that, the divinities hold us in rigor, it's because they're exceedingly difficult!"

XIV
Voluptuous Nostalgia

For two days, Viamalah did not leave her apartment. She sat motionless, eyes wide-open, obstinately staring into the void, frozen by the horror of an obsession; then she sensed even that idea blurring and fading into a nightmare. Then, in spite of the light songs of Celestial Perfume and the feline stroking of Honeycomb, she fell into a nervous slumber full of terrifying visions.

The adolescents interrogated one another anxiously with their gaze, not daring to deliver themselves to their customary games, or to ornament themselves with flowers and burn incense in honor of voluptuous idols.

Sometimes, Viamalah woke up abruptly, as if someone had cried out beside her. She lent an ear: nothing, no friction to cause the silky cloth of the draperies to rustle; the dainty servants were asleep in one another's arms, displaying their slender nudity, lowered here and there by the cold gleam of a stray gem. Regular breath emerged from parted lips; eyelids partly lowered in the ecstasy of a youthful dream veiled the double star of the gaze imperfectly.

Then Viamalah wept silently, bruised her bosom with the bezels of her rings, and implored the gods to inspire her, to come to her aid. No glimmer of light was manifest, however, in her troubled mind. She belonged in spirit to Nassudamy, and by heart to Achilgar. The former dominated her, the second charmed her . . . and she dreaded, by disobeying the former, causing harm to the latter.

Solely preoccupied by the thought of her lost love, she nevertheless welcomed the unformulated hopes that were gleaming within her. In her memories, in her dead life, in the shadow of her youth she marched and rolled, listening and looking at everything as a presage, sometimes good and sometimes bad. Her desires, whatever they were, collided with one another around one permanently fixed desire, and she trembled at being unable to vanquish it. She fretted like a lioness in a cage, stirring a thousand extravagant projects that she subsequently abandoned, wearily.

Achilgar hastened the preparations for the marriage, throwing gold around with full hands in order that the fête would be truly regal. Never had so many invitations been sent, even for the daughter of a rajah, and it was expected that the procession would last several hours.

In the presence of his fiancée, however, the young man was able to extinguish the fire of his gaze and not to attempt a caress, for fear of displeasing Shiva.

"But when we're united before men and the gods," he said, "oh, then, my Brown Lotus, we'll make up for lost time superbly!"

And she, with her eyes lowered and her hands feverish, repeated in a faint voice: "When we're united . . ."

XV
The Wedding

The inhabitants of distant quarters are running, agitating palms, the children are laughing and jostling one another, climbing trees in order to get a better view of the princely wedding procession, while the young women address whispered prayers to the goddess Durga, who will not be able to refuse them anything on such a day of rejoicing.

The sounds of a barbaric orchestra, punctuated by cymbals and tambourines draw closer, the rumor of the crowd undulating and increasing like a rumble of thunder. Here come the musicians dressed in indigo and yellow, leading the cortege, then a large number of horses, harnessed with large plates of sculpted silver, with crimson covers heightened with gold and necklaces of pearls. Each stallion, with a proud neck and a long floating tail, is led by the hand of an indigenous servant wearing his master's colors.

After the whinnying troop, in a quiver of silk, amulets, spangles, gauzes and feathers, come frail maidens with long velvet eyes, carrying on their shoulders beribboned hurdles filigreed with gold covered with beatific or hideous idols, monsters with glaucous eyes. Some are raising overhead honey-cakes in the form of miters, crystal ewers containing jujube and lotus wines, or hardened golden banners like stained-glass windows. In flowery baskets there are also vases of every form filled with perfumes, caskets encrusted with chrysoberyls and cat's-eyes, cassolettes of agate, sardonyx and tourmaline, swung on long chains by the nonchalant fingers of little girls.

There is an archipelago of muslins, in which incense swirls in little blue clouds, and the song of half-closed mouths resembles the distant murmur of waves. The bride's favorites, Glory of the Moon, Honeycomb and Celestial Perfume, are carrying Achilgar's presents to his beloved on cushions of jasmines and roses. There are inestimable necklaces, hairpins, shoulder-fastenings and waist-clasps as large as turtle-shells, bracelets for the wrists and ankles, diadems and girdles.

Between the gilded carts and the tall idols that preside over all the magnificence, beautiful children, completely naked, but painted in pastel colors and tattooed with spangles stuck to the skin, are incessantly drawing handfuls of lily- and rose-petals from baskets, which they throw at the spectators. They are chained to one another by bonds of foliage that surround their thighs and they jump all along the route.

Here come the Sikh cavaliers, clad in hyacinth and crimson cloth, prancing on their black horses with long manes braided with coral, ears ornamented with pompoms and foreheads surmounted by sprays of precious stones. Others, very bellicose, have coats of mail and armbands; a few, more ornamented, wear long plumes on their helmets, like owls with outspread wings. A few dark-skinned warriors are bare-chested, tattooed with bizarre designs in ceruse white and cobalt blue, with leopard-skins around their loins. Important guests are riding elephants whose saddle-cloths and howdahs, encrusted with topazes and carbuncles, are suggestive of fragments of sunlight.

"Aya! Aya!" cry the people, agitating green palms as a sign of delight.

Now it is the turn of the elegant men of Benares and the banks of the Ganges. They wear silky veils like women, enveloped in gauzes with delicate hues, retained by cameos of great price, but they are holding gourgouris in their fingers—little pipes that they raise nonchalantly to their lips. The Akalis, dressed in somber colors, have high turbans ornamented with daggers; they are followed by the savage Afghan chiefs, swaying on their immense camels with tufts of red wool fringed with little bells.

It is an extraordinary crowd, a fantastic pell-mell of men, horses and flamboyant divinities, terrifying monsters of gold and precious stones that no description can render . . .

And in that dream of hashish or morphine, Viamalah, on a colossal white Sikh horse, with legs painted pink below the knee and harness of silver and turquoise, attracts all gazes. Her veils are so transparent that they do not appear to be covering her, but sliding over her like crystalline water. Two sapphire stars retain the cobweb fabric to either side of her forehead; a loose girdle of diamonds and sapphires, beneath the floating veil, fastens a narrow skirt in a network of fine blue stones, ocellated with diamonds and opals, like frost on a moonbeam. The amber skin of her bosom and arms is visible between the rings, plates, cabochons and pendants of her jewels, primarily composed of blue and white gems.

She seems unreal, like a dream princess; she is astonishing, and somewhat disquieting, by virtue of her mysterious and suffering beauty, with the feverish gleam of her crespuscular eyes consuming the face.

But she has shuddered from head to toe, and her staring eyes have capsized in anguish, for she has recognized Nassudamy in the first rank of the crowd, who seems to be challenging her and ordering her to follow him. The young woman's hand has made an abrupt movement, clenching on the mane of the huge horse, which makes a sidestep and rears up, whinnying with anger. Servants launch forward to the animal's bridle, master it and drag it away.

Momentarily stationary, the cortege resumes its pompous march. It is now the turn of the bayaderes in tight trousers and narrow corselets, who are agitating pink, white and mauve streamers and twirling graciously. The undersides of their eyes are gilded, their noses, foreheads and temples so laden with gems that it is difficult to make out their features. Their legs and their hands carry tortoiseshells of tiny juxtaposed mirrors; they are as delicate and shiny as scarabs. Some have vinas, tals and macabou flutes; others are singing a hymn to the god of amour in high-pitched voices.

Achilgar is following close behind his beloved, similarly mounted on a white horse of noble race and proud gait, covered in a mosaic of gems. His azure mantle, retained over his forehead by a gold headband constellated with diamonds, which hangs down behind all the way to his horse's hooves, is confounded from a distance with the color of the sky. Above his head extends an awning ornamented with heavy fringes, borne triumphantly by captains in cothurnes and steel leg-guards. Behind him, to either side, march two long lines of soldiers, and the procession is eventually terminated by the crowd of relatives and guests, mounted on more than eight hundred elephants.

In India, the splendor of a marriage is the great pride, the foolish vanity of the rich classes. The ceremony occupies a pre-ponderant role in the annals of a family. In order to appease the evil spirits and attract the benevolence of the gods to him, Achilgar had wanted to do everything royally. In any case, his fortune permitted it.

XVI
The Lingam Again

On the pink sandstone and marble terraces of Rajputana, the tables are now ready, and the guests have an evident desire to do honor to the dishes. The gardens are furrowed with bushy pathways where maidens are wandering two by two. At inter-vals, baskets display crowded, ardent, feverish flowers still warm from the kisses of the sun, which alternate with idols of wood or bronze, fantastic beasts, tongues darted and claws extended, and monstrous stone lingams. An odorous rain, like diamond dust, falls from jets of water into porphyry basins or disperses in the air, carried by the breeze of huge flabella incessantly agitated by young women. The latter wear scarves with a golden backcloth, from which human figures stand out embroidered in brightly colored silks; crowns of jasmine surround their foreheads.

The guests have made libations with milk and honeyed wine, they have perfumed their hair and they have kissed the great idol of Durga that presides over the feast. In the treetops, the monkeys seem to comprehend the general delight and utter bizarre cries, while imitating the gestures and expressions of the guests; she-monkeys fan themselves with banana leaves, dancing to the sound of the tals and malatans that children are beating frantically.

Brought on huge jade platters are insects, fruits, saffroned and curried eggs, vehement pâtés with spices and flowers. For the foreigners who like flavorsome meats there are goat-kids cooked in the juice of aromatic plants, buttered hazel-grouse, cutlets of camel in cumin, and warblers with gilded breasts on slices of pineapple. Between each course, the guests wash their fingertips in medlar-, rose- and clover-water. There are roasted herons, cranes and swans, venisons in verjuice and coriander, vehement dishes with rosemary, basil and ginger, elephants' trunks coated in honey, guinea-fowl and peacocks with all their feathers, and for those—very numerous—who do not eat meat, there are jujube and lotus cakes, rice in all its forms, salads with eggs and caraway, flower jams, roots candied with sugar or vinegar, sprinkled with cinnamon and pepper. Pyramids of fruits collapse into tuberoses, for the tables are literally covered with embalmed petals, disposed in such a fashion as to form arabesques and words.

A few delicately sculpted golden ewers contain a viscous liquor charged with cinnamon bark and musk, speckled with precious stones and crushed pearls. That is the wine of rajahs, which is only offered on special occasions.

Night fell, and the lines of white flowers along the pink terraces described great parabolas like spindles of the Milky Way. The waters of the Ganges splashed gently, and the flames of torches carried by servants trembled as they were reflected therein, in the ripples of the bank. The conical roofs of heptagonal temples, minarets, domes and turrets were silhouetted against the profound violet of the sky, and the golden roof of the temple of Durga resembled a formidable shield extended toward the arrows of the heavens.

"Viamalah!" sighed Achilgar, entering his beloved's bedroom.

She was waiting for him, anxious and impatient. "How late you are," she said. "Time has never seemed so long to me."

The young man opened the window.

"The fête has scarcely begun. Can you hear the joyful voices?"

"Yes, they're celebrating our happiness. I would like to believe that the anger of the gods has turned away from us, but I'm besieged by somber presentiments."

"Let's not think about anything any longer but our amour. Although the Brahmin's blessing of the consecrated fire was insufficient, it appears to me to be inadmissible that the magnificence of our wedding has not appeased Shiva's resentment. Have we not had an entire flock of sheep sacrificed, not to mention the princely gifts that we have made to the temple of Durga?"

With an abrupt movement, Viamalah sprang from her cobweb veils like a golden lotus from the mystery of the waves, which was not calculated to calm Achilgar's amorous fervor. She paid no heed, however, to the bestial gleam that shone in his eyes, and continued her own train of thought in a grave voice:

"Human destiny is unknown. No one, in spite of his cleverness, is able to direct existence to his whim. It is an error to think that will-power alone can succeed in overcoming obstacles. In the final analysis, it is fatality that decides. In the hands of jealous powers, we are like grains of rice in the hands of children."

Achilgar was troubled by his beloved's sadness.

"In sum," he said, kneeling before her, "have you some reason for further anxiety? Speak without fear."

"Well, I would prefer to spend this first night in prayer."

"We'll pray together."

"Is that possible?"

"You'll see!"

"Oh, I believe that, in spite of your good resolutions, you'll attempt to approach me, and that the mystical charm will be broken."

"Why? Amour is not disagreeable to the gods, who have taken the yoni-lingam for their emblem."

As he spoke, Achilgar had put his hand on the jewel that Viamalah was wearing on her arm, and which he believed to be the one that he had given her. But he uttered a cry of pain, showing a little round wound from which blood was falling in hasty droplets."

"What's the matter?"

"It's your bracelet . . . you turned the fetish against me like a dagger!"

"I haven't moved."

Desolate, she staunched the crimson dew with her lips, and the young man, mad with desire, contemplated the harmonious line of her back, the dimples of her shoulders and the exquisite curve of her inclined nape.

"Come," he said.

XVII
The Corolla That Does Not Want to Open

As he took Viamalah toward the florid couch, the favorites climbed the marble steps that led to the nuptial apartment on tiptoe, and while Honeycomb and Glory of the Moon attempted to surprise the mystery of felicity from behind a curtain, Celestial Perfume, sitting on her heels, sang the couplets of the Cocila to herself.

"The Cocila has shown me the road to Amour. I await love, impatient and fearful. All my flesh extends toward him, as if he were the day star. O my lover, penetrate me!

"Approach, approach, O beloved! The flower stands upon the bank; the zephyrs are already caressing her; but on her lascivious corolla, she wants to feel your kiss. O dear lover, penetrate her!

"And the butterfly flies, flies toward the calyx still closed. With his golden wing he brushes it, and with his sting erect, he has caressed it!

"For her life, the flower has opened, and will collect the dew; dew of night, dew of day! The blue butterfly of amour has alighted on the corolla, and has penetrated to her depths!"

The child interrupted herself. "What can you see, Honeycomb? What can you hear, Glory of the Moon?"

The curious duo did not reply, and Celestial Perfume, having approached in her turn, moved them aside in order to look in her turn.

"Oh," she said, "the room is full of thick smoke."

"Wouldn't one think that plush wings were stroking the walls?"

"Phosphorescent eyes looking at us . . ."

"And there, there on the couch, a white form . . ."

As they leaned forward, panting, the curtain was violently pulled and Achilgar, emerging impetuously, nearly knocked them over.

They uttered a cry; then, turning round, he showed them, on the bed covered with mutilated tuberoses and roses, Viamalah, asleep; Viamalah, as inert and pale as a virgin on her tomb.

"She's icy," he moaned, "and my most ardent kisses have done nothing for me or for her. The corolla is closed and the flower is intact. May the fire of Shiva violate her and annihilate her, since the desire of a man has not been able to open her!"

And, his head bare and his garments in disorder, Achilgar fled, as if he had heard behind him the infernal gallop of Rakshasas, Pishasas and Asuras!

PART TWO

I
The Husband is Everything, the Wife is Nothing

The most important affair for a Hindu is marriage. A man who is not married is regarded as devoid of status and useless to society; he is not consulted on serious questions of religion or the arts, no honorific or remunerative employment is confided to him. A man who becomes a widower finds himself in the same condition as a bachelor, and he hastens to remarry very quickly, while the inconsolable wife, on the death of her husband, is required to sacrifice herself on his pyre or to wear mourning forever. That mourning consists of a single strip of cloth that winds around her midriff, passes from right to left, coverts one breast and falls without any ornament along the body deprived of amulets, claps, necklaces and a belt.

The immolation of Hindu widows goes back so far in the past that it is scarcely possible to fix its origin by means of precise dates. The first fire of conjugal joy lit up in the night of time. One can be sure, however, that the custom was established by the Brahmins in order to prevent excessively numerous poisonings of Hindu husbands. Suttee, rather than being a mark of reckless tenderness that might flatter masculine vanity, is, on the contrary, only a preservative measure against the vindictive or eccentric humor of women. For a long time, that obligatory incineration was general in India; it was with a firm step that the fragile victims were seen marching to the torture, ornamented as if for a feast of amour, their eyes bright with pride.

If, before the marriage, the fiancé testifies his desire to the young woman by means of a thousand caresses, a thousand ur-

"

gent and prestigious offerings, afterwards the male reclaims his rights and affirms his power. And the girl inclines submissively, glad to give her unique thought and her silken body, the frail calyx of her enticing beauty, to a master who is often senile and debauched. Not yet nubile, they share the pyre of an unworthy spouse and, flesh against flesh, lips against lips, demand that the criminal work be concluded.

A Brahmin brandishes a torch, while the relatives throw kindling, aromatic oils, incense and dried flowers at the feet of the victim, which stimulate the fire and are agreeable to the iniquitous gods . . .

Viamalah had lost one of her dearest friends in that fashion, a child seven years old who had been sold to a septuagenarian Brahmin exhausted by late nights and perverse pleasures. The union had not even been accomplished, and the child had sacrificed her virginity to the stone god of the temple of Kama, in great pomp, before a curious crowd. Then the devadasi had collected in a lotus flower the blood that ran all the way to the golden rings on her ankles, and had offered it to the indecent idol. The child had only known of amour that frightful rape, and died a year later in the flames, to obey the last will of her husband.

Viamalah could still see her, quivering beneath the transparent undulation of her veils, her temples and cheeks so covered in jewels that even her tears could not fray a path there. She saw her, very thin, almost immaterial, with the ingenuous smile of her immense eyes and her long hair lifted by the wind. It was that hair that went up in flames first, suddenly, rising toward the blue sky like a dazzling rocket.

Viamalah had thrown her bracelets and rings into the furnace in order that her little friend might not suffer too much, and she had only heard one scream, a lacerating scream that drilled into her heart until she fainted.

When the last sparks had fallen back, crackling, on to the cooling fire, the ashes of the spouses were collected in little urns, and the people around the fire danced all night.

Sometimes, the sacred fire did not burn for one alone, and that is comprehensible in a land where polygamy is always in honor. The death of a man often entails the immolation of five or six women, who are assumed, in accordance with a masculine vanity that is always surprising, to accord all their adoration exclusively to a husband who only deigns to render them meager suffrages.

A very old Brahmin, not so long ago, had left forty-two widows, varying between five and twelve years of age, and for four days the voluptuous flames, avid for so much pure flesh, danced a mad round in a festival of amour, displayed in long ardent tongues along slender bodies imbued with essences, gemmed from the heels to the eyebrows, like marvelous corollas of precious stones on the branches of the pyre.

Aji, Prince of Marwar, left fifty-eight queens, and all of them resolved to perish in the arms of Agni, the god of fire. Tightly enlaced, semi-naked, each with a diadem of diamonds in her night-dark hair, they threw themselves into the flames, which sprang up toward the clouds with such brightness that the watchers thought they might be blinded.

That famous hecatomb was presided over by the victims' children, who never ceased to jump and sing, setting an example of lively delight.

Viamalah, a wife without a husband, a mistress without a lover, surrendered to bleak reflections after Achilgar's flight, Many women, she told herself, had suffered because of their husbands, but a case as singular as hers had certainly never been known before. Every hour brought her a new anguish, and tomorrow appeared to her to be full of menaces.

II
Conversation with a Dying Man

Achilgar, however, was even more unhappy than Viamalah. On finding himself on the bank of the Ganges, alone, his soul full of terror, he had told himself that Viamalah did not love him, and that all his tortures stemmed from that. To love is insufficient; it is necessary to know how to communicate amour and to make oneself loved as one loves. All terrestrial creatures have senses, and seek sensuality, but a man is only truly worthy of that name if he associates sentiment with that sensation, mingling with the carnal act a little of the divine essence that is within him. Passionate lovers only experience a real joy in the consciousness of a reciprocal tenderness, and the kiss of the heart is worth more than that of the lips.

Achilgar marched dolorously in his memories, in his dead life, in the shadow of his youth, disdainful now of good or evil presages. He had gone to the bank of the Ganges and abandoned himself to a despair in which all his sorrow and dejection were united. He thought that Viamalah was under the influence of spirits, or that she loved someone else to whom she had given herself, and that idea caused him a pain so intense that it paralyzed him there, before the mysterious waters in which so many crimes had been mirrored. The mortal frisson of jealousy and revulsion for the treason gave him, at times, ideas of murder. Then a sudden resolution caused him to raise his head, and he resumed his course in the direction of the temple of Durga.

The night was cool, one of those Indian nights sometimes so different from the days, when the caress of the sun is almost dolorous in its intensity. The wind was blowing, bitterly, from the Himalayas; the stars were shining in a profound ultramarine sky, like flowers of frost.

Achilgar hastened along the white terraces. The palaces appeared, capricious, with their turrets, their gilded domes, and their facades painted in pastel colors. Sometimes, there were bushes of flowering mimosas, shaking their odorous clusters, and the steps of buildings stood out in spite of the gloom against their curtain of palms, bamboo and eucalyptus. Jets of water hissed under the foliage, dispatching aromas of earth and flowers on the breeze.

The young man's dolor was no longer that of people who are acting and struggling. He was weary of struggling, tired of hoping for unrealizable things. In front of a pagoda particularly venerated by those despairing of life, those who seek the cessation of their cares and the sanctification of suicide in the Ganges, he lay down on the ground and contemplated the glaucous waves with the firm resolution of engulfing himself therein. He lay with his chin supported by his hands; large tears fell between his fingers, sliding into the sand, making little dark patches there, which the wind immediately effaced.

As he became torpid in his chagrin, a troop of pilgrims passed close by, following a Brahmin who was reciting the hymns of the Veda. Before a gigantic idol with three faces representing Brahma, Vishnu and Shiva, the sacred trimurti, which garlands of jasmine were already ornamenting, the priest lit the fire in the Vedic manner, by means of the friction of Arani sticks. He stimulated it with his breath with all the strength of his lungs, sprinkled it with oils with keen effluences and threw into it herbs, grains of rice and dried fruits, which the pilgrims offered to him in blue and red jars. The flame crackled, inclining eccentrically, disengaging a perfumed mauve mist that veiled the faces. Two she-goats and a he-goat received precise instructions from the sacrificer, who spoke into their ears for a long time, and then offered their blood to the black idol, in the midst of songs and cries.

Achilgar gazed at those men, who had decided, like him, to die. They were thin and stooped, with very pure aquiline noses. A few had pale skin, others retained something akin to the ardor of the desert upon them. All were expert in religious stratagems, disciplines and fasts. They appeared calm, and yet a somber fire was shining in their bewitched eyes, and their faces were frozen in a morbid desire that made him shiver.

When they had concluded their singular practices they prostrated themselves one last time, and went into the water.

However, although they wanted to die, it was not in a simple and rapid fashion, for their sacrifice would not have been agreeable to the gods. It was necessary, in order to be worthy of the maleficent powers they served, to make the anguish of suicide last, and, by means of ingenious imaginations, to show oneself superior to others.

Some of them gouged out their eyes and floated at random, their heads maintained above the water by a collar of cork. Others opened their veins, leaving behind them thin threads of crimson. Others attached enormous pitchers under their arms and, by means of little abrupt movements, filled them slowly, sustained to begin with and then dragged down beneath the surface.

Achilgar approached one of the fanatics, who was reddening a needle in the fire on the altar, in order to pierce his breast with it.

"Before you die, I would like to ask your advice," he said.

"Speak, but hurry, for I'm in haste to know the exquisite tortures that will permit me to approach the divinities of the trimurti."

"I'll be brief. Like you, I want to put an end to my days."

"For a god?"

"No, for a woman."

The pilgrim smiled scornfully. "A woman! You're weak enough to suffer for a woman, and you're mingling with our glorious troop!"

The young man hung his head in confusion.

"A woman! An eccentric, unconscious being! A little bird that smoothes its plumage from evening till morning! A goat-kid that leaps from bush to bush, avid for perfumes and delicacies!"

"But . . ."

"Woman has been given to man for his pleasure; he owes her nothing and can dispose of her, like plants and beasts."

"However . . ."

"A woman! What religion do you have, then, to take seriously that being, as fragile and perverse as everything that is only made for the joy of the eyes? You have no religion, my son, for all of them inform us that man alone is the master, for he is the stronger!"

"That's true. I'm very young, still, and very ignorant. However, I recognize that religions are in accord on that point. Woman is the servant of man."

"So?"

"I can't possess the one I love!"

"Take her by force."

"It's impossible."

"Marry her."

"I have."

"I no longer understand. You're young, handsome, supple and vigorous."

"A power superior to mine protects her."

"What power?"

"I don't know."

Serenely, the yogi made his flesh sizzle, twisting the sharp weapon in the wound, and as Achilgar recoiled, offended by the odor of burned skin, he said: "You are not worthy to die, since you're troubled by such a little thing. See, the blood is flowing; I have labored my body profoundly, and yet, I feel nothing but an inexpressible wellbeing. Would you, too, like to try your courage? Here, seek my heart, and go gently; it's necessary to delay the supreme spasm for as long as possible."

Achilgar presented the long golden pin to the flame and, seeking on the fanatic's breast for the place where the heart was throbbing, already exhausted, tried to impale it like a great red butterfly in its narrow prison; but his hand trembled, he closed his eyes, and he lost consciousness.

III

Ourvasi the Seller of Forgetfulness

When he recovered consciousness, at the foot of the gigantic idol of the sacred trimurti, the fire was going out over the aromatic plants, next to the bloody corpses of the three goats. As for the pilgrims, a few were still adrift on the water, their eyes ecstatic, allowing a last hymn to Shiva to escape from their blue lips with a last gasp.

Daylight was beginning to appear, and the young man, tottering as if emerging from an opium dream, resumed the route to his dwelling. Fleeing the river, however, he penetrated into the narrow streets full of women going to the temple of Bishishar-Kumardil. They were half-naked, with eyebrows elongated as far as the middle of the forehead, lips reddened by betel and nostrils charged with rings with brilliant stones. One of them approached Achilgar and whispered a few words to him.

"Yes," he said, wearily, thinking that he might find in the simulacrum of amour a remedy for his suffering.

"Where?" she asked. "Your home?"

"No, walk ahead, I'll follow you."

Meekly, she took the lead, making her hips sway under a scarf of light gauze and the bracelets of her ankles ringing. Her long hair, mingled with coral, hung down to her knees, and she had eyes of somber velvet, widely separated beneath thin eyebrows. She was not from Benares, and was reputed to be very learned in the voluptuous science. Doubtless she was returning from some fête, and desired to make an offering to Bishishar-Kumardil of imminent intoxication.

Ourvasi—the nymph—was proud of her body and had the right to be. Her breasts were firm and harmoniously rounded around the amber pink nipple, her waist was slender and her loins powerful, in order better to give and receive. Her slim legs were wrapped with strings of pearls mingled with red flowers, and beneath the transparency of her girdle other ardent corollas blossomed in bushier bouquets.

Achilgar did not speak, but he walked behind Ourvasi, who often turned round to smile at him, proud of the morning of amour that flattering conquest promised her. Through the somber and bizarre alleyways, in the compact and confused mass of brick houses, huts made of mud and reeds, and little conical temples populated by Brahmins, monkeys and sacred bulls, she led him to her dwelling.

At the extremity of the city, it was a low building daubed with ultramarine, surrounded by aromatic bushes of roses, saffron, mulberries, rhododendrons and magnolias, where thin jets of water hissed in basins.

A terrace with a perforated wooden balcony gave shelter to a multitude of parrots, iridescent peacocks and other birds with gemstone plumage, which the courtesan amused herself by nourishing. When Achilgar arrived, they flew away with a great clatter of wings, and Ourvasi, having lifted a curtain fringed with wool, invited the visitor into her abode.

As soon as he had entered the cool and perfumed room, the young man let himself fall among the cushions, and, his head buried in the silky fabrics, he began to weep. A relaxation took place within him, and his tears sprang forth almost without bitterness.

Ourvasi undressed in the next room, sparkling with glass mirrors from Ceylon and Ormus. On sideboards enameled with lapis lazuli, bottles and boxes were lined up, large and small, containing ointments and essences: snake- and crocodile-oil for tightening the epidermis; musk, antimony and crushed fly-legs for elongating the eyes; crimson foam and ceruse white to brighten the complexion; unguents of black elderberry seeds and beans to firm up the breasts; myrrh berries, mint and ginger to awaken the senses; cantharid powder and the bones of camels, owls, vultures and peacocks to augment the seductive power of woman over man; mandrake herb, star-stones and hippomane to get rid of a rival.

Completely naked, Ourvasi summoned her maidservant and had her rub her body with a paste of narcissi, gum, honey and incense with subtle effluences; perfumes mixed with gold powder were poured over her hair, and, without any other adornment than a girdle of red flowers, she threw herself on to the bed where Achilgar was still sobbing.

"I can see that you have a chagrin, but I respect your secret. I will offer, for you, to the goddess Kali, whose festival is about to be celebrated, doves and grains of rice. When one does not offend her, the goddess of death is not malevolent, and she listens willingly to the daughters of amour."

"You're compassionate," Achilgar said between two sobs.

"Yes, and yet, I ought to be annoyed, for your pain comes from a lover that you prefer to me. I am only the consoler. Is that true?"

"It's true."

Ourvasi bit her crimson lips, and, as if involuntarily, asked: "Is she pretty?"

"As lovely as a flower of election in a field of wild flowers! As a crystal stream under the grass! As a glorious star in the mantle of the night!"

"You're exaggerating."

"No, words cannot comprehend her exquisite smile."

"I too am pretty."

Achilgar raised his head and looked at her indifferently. "Certainly . . ."

"Oh," she said sadly, "you can't admire me because your eyes are full of another beauty. And that beauty, you admire all the more madly because she refuses you, while my possession is too facile. How can you submit to the caprice of a slave of sensuality? Are you not the master?"

Thus, the courtesan on her bed of pleasure spoke like the pilgrim on the bank of the Ganges. The woman who gave herself to amour and the man who gave himself death thought the same!

Achilgar told himself that a kiss was, in fact, very little, and he took Ourvasi's lips between his own.

She showed herself expert and supple, with the delicate caresses and passionate surges that make every lover believe that he is the most cherished, and double the pride of triumph.

On her knees before him she murmured: "What more do you want me to do to prove my ardor and my submission? Do you want the game of the bee or that of the imprisoned corolla? Would you like me to be the rapid hawk or an indolent panther? There is not one of the mysteries of Kama that I do not know."

But he was a little weary, he desired nothing more than an immense repose. He closed his eyes and put his head on Ourvasi's shoulder, requesting the helpful gods to annihilate him in eternal slumber.

In fact, the courtesan found him to her liking, admiring his noble face and the magnificence of his garments. She remained still, with a soft indulgent gaze beneath her long, painted eyelids.

"Sleep," she said, with melancholy. "Women always cure the suffering of men, while men only know how to inflict new wounds on women. Sleep, little prince with the tender heart; I've consoled many more unhappy than you. You're weeping? Bah! The breeze will carry the tears away. I know so many kisses . . ."

IV
Feline Sensualities

Achilgar had the age for caresses; Ourvasi had the science. Together, they found new embraces and intoxicated their bodies, unable to intoxicate their hearts. There was a fury of possession in the warm clarity, a frenzy of frictions and bites. Under the trees in ardent flower, he came with her, avid for perfumes and birdsong. His gaze lost in the distance, he burned with the spectacle of the silvery sheet of the river, annealed by stripes of golden red or green, like an immense necklace stretching all the way to the horizon. The quays of Benares were animated by the disquieting life of a formicary, and the boats with white sails seemed to be spreading the wings of nostalgic gulls.

The sun's rays illuminated myriads of spangles in the quiet wavelets of the Ganges, the indigo and cinnabar facades of the palaces were aureole with light, the minarets of the mosque of Aurang-Zeb put steeples into the current, and the bizarre chanting of Bengali sailors resonated in the distance, celebrating the puja—the festivals—of the benevolent gods. A sort of yellow powder, the impalpable residue of the alluvial mud of the

Ganges, seemed a rain of fire drowning the roofs of innumerable petty temples or sanctuaries, which rose up everywhere.

At the foot of the slope, at the level of the giant stairways, the faithful were saying their prayers, and women were plunging huge jars of shiny bronze into the water in order to accomplish the sacred rites. Young women were entering the river holding hands, and their pure voices could be heard singing the glory of the gods of sensuality, while priests, perched on light towers, were haranguing the crowd.

It was not only the practices of religion that struck the eyes, but scenes of amour and death, and he saw, without astonishment, couples embracing one another and kissing one another on the lips in front of the fire of aromatic wood that was completing the consumption of the body of a relative.

Achilgar tried no longer to exist as anything other than a plant gorged with sunlight and dew. At the crepuscular hour, however, when he leaned over the terrace in the mauve of dying days, suddenly anguished by the imminence of darkness, he languished in the sadness of the troubled hour, thinking, even so, of the one he had desired among all, and who, alone, had refused him.

Then Ourvasi approached on tiptoe, her bare feet circled with gold, and put her hands over his eyes abruptly.

"I don't want you to think about Her! Here, my mouth is better. It's a magic fruit that calms the thirst and the hunger of amour."

Feverishly, he pushed her away. "No, leave me alone; the fruit of your mouth no longer has any savor."

"Oh, you say that, but in a moment you'll allow yourself to be convinced even so by my caresses . . . and I know others, many others . . ."

"Later, when night has come."

"So be it. Listen to this song, then; it's as soft as the dying light."

"Yes, sing; your voice is more soothing than your words."

Ourvai had a deep and captivating voice, which charmed her lover. The bass notes, a trifle hoarse, descended, tearing apart on a final chord of her rebab; then, after a moment of immobility, she threw the futile instrument away and, with her hands raised above her head, spun slowly, making her torso undulate and displaying the somber veil of her hair. Then her knees parted, her thighs flexed, she lowered herself and raised herself up again, uttering a plaintive cry, like the appeal of a wounded bird.

He became interested, in spite of himself, in her game, and that was what she wanted. As he drew nearer to take hold of her she said: "Wait a little; I've danced for pleasure, I'll dance for desire and then for delirium . . ."

After supple and feline poses, torsions of her upper body, she made her breasts and belly move in voluptuous frissons, dared all attitudes, and only consented to abandon herself when the young man begged her, his gaze shining with desire, not to let him languish any longer. Thus, to please the man she wanted to keep, a little for his sad male beauty but mostly for his situation and magnificence, she made herself seductive, tender, lascivious and demonic—a courtesan, in sum, all the way to the little fingers of her bewitching hands.

V

Viamalah Obeys the Occult Power

On waking up, Viamalah had found her three confidantes weeping at the foot of her bed. Her head aching, and her lips dry, she tried to get up, but her head fell back on the roses and the vervain with which the cushions were strewn.

"Achilgar!" she moaned.

"He's gone!" sobbed Honeycomb.

"Gone!"

"As if the Rakshasas had carried him away in a tempest. Your bedroom smelled of mandrake and sulfur; over the walls, there is the plush frisson of the wings of vampires and owls . . ."

"Glaucous pupils shone in the shadows, and thunder was rumbling in the distance!"

With fearful gestures, the adolescents huddled against the bed.

Viamalah tried to laugh. "Imagination!"

"No, no! We saw and heard!"

"Yes," said Glory of the Moon. "Being curious, we parted the curtains, because, you know, a wedding night is always full of useful education, and if you look hard, you can also experience its pleasure . . ."

"It's almost as if one were cuddled in a lover's arms," confessed Celestial Perfume, lowering her eyes.

"You counted our embraces?" asked Viamalah.

"Your embraces? You were as cold as Soma, the goddess of night, and your spouse called you all the names of the Mahabharata, but you didn't budge any more than a stone idol."

"Oh," said Honeycomb, "Achilgar was so desperate that he might well throw himself under the wheels of Kali's chariot at the imminent festival!"

Viamalah hid her face in her hands.

"I'm so unhappy!"

"Yes, it's singular that so many kisses weren't able to move you."

"What do you know about it?" said the virgin, vehemently. "I thought I gave myself as many times as you have rings on your fingers."

"Oh!" said Glory of the Moon, marveling.

"Only, it appeared that I couldn't share my joy. It was a dream, and in the dream, Achilgar wasn't with me."

"What are you saying?"

"I'm saying . . . I'm saying that I'm devoid of strength and will. Everything is overwhelming me, and the gods have abandoned me. Come closer, closer still, to cuddle me and console me, as Matou-Mahli did when I was little."

Honeycomb and Glory of the Moon took Viamalah in their arms and rocked her like a sick child, while Celestial Perfume threw the withered flowers of the bed into a fold of her belt, in order to decorate a statuette of Kama, the god of amour, which she had in her room.

Viamalah did not go out during the day, and did not want to see anyone. The doors were barricaded, and the sealed room was only illuminated by the pale light of jade and ivory lamps. The noises from outside scarcely arrived there, muffled and disfigured. At times, the cry of a merchant of balms or glass beads pierced the walls, and the quarrels of the sacred monkeys and the shrill cries of cockatoos could also be heard over the rooftops.

Viamalah was pensive, her forehead leaning on Honeycomb's shoulder. The latter sometimes kissed her hair very softly, or cooled her temples with a few drops of perfume.

What should I do? the virgin asked herself, and it seemed that her self was metamorphosed, and that new desires were manifest within her. Elite natures, being more impressionable, are consequently more liable to vary in the wake of a great chagrin, a keen emotion or a physical or mental shock. Neat and violent changes are rare, however, and the transformations of health, behavior and character generally proceed by alternations, by slow infiltrations, from which a sort of malaise results, an astonishment for the cessation of habitual functions.

So many unexpected causes trouble the course of an existence in changing its goal! Life is a stream, which a stone or a tree branch can cause to deviate, and although all those poor little streams return to nothing, they are no less involved for that in the great law of eternal attraction. Nothing is indifferent in the ensemble of terrestrial movements; the unity of the universe is constituted by the immaterial, imponderable force that moves the atoms.

Next to her little friends with feline gestures and lips ripe for kissing, Viamalah sensed things, her intelligence having developed under the magnetic influence of the yogi.

And suddenly, the voice of Nassudamy rose up distinctly beside her. It was in vain, however, that she scrutinized the depths of the room with her gaze; no visible presence was manifest. The little servants were asleep on the cushions, and the fakir's words, although very vibrant, did not seem to reach their ears.

"Viamalah!" sighed the mysterious voice. "What are you doing in this palace? Achilgar has abandoned you!"

"He'll come back," she replied, mentally rather than with her lips, knowing that the Pitris could read her like an open book. "Yes, yes, he'll come back. A tenderness like ours can't be forgotten."

"Your lover is in the arms of a courtesan, and their lips are sharing the betel of amour."

"Oh!"

"He's neglecting you before the possession. He's unworthy and unfaithful."

"Unworthy and unfaithful!"

Viamalah stood up so abruptly that Glory of the Moon, who was still hugging her, fell to the floor.

"You hurt me," said the adolescent, rubbing her eyes.

"It's nothing. I'll give you my beryl clasp to soothe your contusions."

Honeycomb and Celestial Perfume opened wide astonished eyes.

"You didn't hear anything?" asked Viamalah.

"No," they said, in unison. "No one came in, unless a big monkey permitted himself to lift the curtains."

"For myself," said Celestial Perfume, "I was actually dreaming that a green she-monkey from the temple of Durga was chasing me over the rooftops, and I was trembling so much that I nearly fell at every step. Feel, my heart's still hammering."

"It really is a matter of the green she-monkey from the temple of Durga. There was a phantom here that ordered me to follow him. My mission is sacred; the gods have designated me to accomplish prodigies."

"Prodigies!"

"Yes, and since my beloved has abandoned me, I'm leaving too."

"You want to leave us, Comet Flower? Who will kiss us when you're no longer here?"

"You, Celestial Perfume, will kiss your little god Kama; you, Honeycomb, will dance the steps of 'sensuality' with a pearl-encrusted dupatta of pink gauze and an emerald clasp at the place of your desire; you, Glory of the Moon, will mark the measure on the tal and the maladan. Then, when you're weary of dancing and music, you'll roll one another in the tuberoses."

"And you're not coming back?"

"I'll come back if that's the will of Shiva."

VI
The Seven Naga Heads

Once her resolution was made, the young woman tried to forget Achilgar, who had fled so cruelly. She assembled her precious veils, as well as a few jewels that she wanted to offer to the most redoubtable divinities, and then she purified her body in the porpyhry basin watered by the trunks of the eight ruby-studded elephants, and had herself rubbed with unguents and powders in order to stimulate her energy and her beauty.

Delicately, following Matou-Mahli's lessons, Honeycomb stuck three golden stars over her breasts and her lap, shook diamond powder over her shoulders, which made her resemble of huge flower under the morning dew, and enveloped her in a thick yellow cloth whose pleats fell back over the forehead, passed beneath the armpit, wrapped around the waist like a capricious flame and caressed her heels. They mixed cardamom, nutmeg and cloves with pure betel, for an offering to Durga, and then all four of them climbed into a dingui and sailed silently to the place on the Ganges where Viamalah knew that she would find Nassudamy, the fakir snake-charmer.

The minarets were reflected in the water, with the moon, which the ripples speckled with silver at the feet of the monumental stairways of the ghats.

In a fantastic light, the bank displayed its temples, its palaces and its ruins; garlands of roses, the offerings of devotees, were soaking into the water; the smoke of odorous resins rose up in light swirls. Semi-naked men were throwing wood for fires on to the immense series of steps and steep slopes; crows and vultures were flying heavily, awaiting the human remains spared by the flames.

Then, there were beggars, old men, children, who, crouched on the steps of the ghats, their hands extended, were asking for alms in lamentable voices; further away, the clamors of mourners resounded in long ululations. Those women, enveloped in veils, resembled huge snowflakes fallen at random, and in that foam of gauze, muslin and silk, children were agitating, clad in red and green, running after the snake-charmers. The latter were playing with spectacled cobras, which they wound around their arms, caressing them with their lips softly, and whistling melancholy tunes.

The serpent in question is sacred; it represents the god of destruction, and as such, has a right to the homage of men. When a pious Brahmin discovers one between two stones, he kneels down before it, consults it, venerates it, and offers it the milk and insects that it loves. The cult of the nagas preceded the Brahmanic religions in India, and it is found in various forms in many of the countries of the Old and New Worlds. It is the dragon of legend that vomits fire and smoke, a monster with rutilant rings and a forked tongue, with fiery eyes that frighten humans. It rears up on the mysterious thresholds of lairs of spirits and sorcerers, guards riches, and presides over enchantments. The diadem of Shiva is formed from seven naga heads tumultuously raised. Vishnu is protected by the reptile with a thousand stings.

The viper and the king cobra are less venerated than the spectacled cobra, but they are prettier, extending and elongating in the sand ribbons of azure ringed with ocher and cinnabar, resembling streams of fire spat out by some volcanic mouth, and the devadasi have no fear of picking them up in religious ceremonies.

Among the snake-charmers who were whistling softly to wake the nagas swollen with venom, whose coils surrounded their ankles and wrists, the young woman recognized the yogi.

"Come," he said, and plunged into the night.

The little confidantes prostrated themselves in the bottom of the boat, invoking the holy trimurti, while Viamalah, wrapped in her golden fabric, disappeared like a shooting star.

The temple of Durga is the most venerated after that of Shiva, the supreme being. The cult of the lingam-yoni is celebrated there, represented there in onyx and kaolin, which virgins come to adore, bringing the goddess rice, betel leaves or valuable jewels, in accordance with their condition.

Nassudamy, who was specially attached to the temple, professed Shivaism ardently; it, was, in any case, the natural religion of all literate Brahmins. Agastya was the first sage who taught Shivaist monotheism, basing it simultaneously on the Vedas and the Agamas—writings that have never been translated into any European language.

Shiva is the god of India who has the most sanctuaries. Every year, in certain countries, an immense lingam surrounded by foliage in which there is an infant who only shows his jasmine-crowned head, is paraded in great pomp. The people prostrate themselves as the procession passes and young women address fervent vows to the incomparable divinity.

The cult of Priapus in Greece appears to have had the same character, which only became erotic subsequently, and it is probable that it is necessary to seek in India for the origins of the phallic cult.

The ancients, who did not attach any equivocal idea to those images, but, on the contrary, venerated them as symbols of divine amour and fecundity, reproduced them in marble, metal and the rarest gems. They are found in necklaces, rings, ornaments and antique cameos. Candles and lamps, weapons and cups are made of them.

It is the predominance of male energy that continued in Greece, whereas in India, the female and creative energy gradually triumphed. Columns of a particular and precise forms stand at the entrances to all the naturalist temples of Cyprus and Phoenicia. Erudite men claim that the towers or steeples of our Gothic cathedrals have the same origin, not to mention the menhirs of Low Brittany. It is thus that everything in life is connected; only opinion changes, since the things once most venerated have become the most reprehensible, without anyone knowing why.

Nassudamy had stopped and was contemplating Viamalah, who remained immobile before him, her eyes lowered.

"You see," he said, "that you were unable to resist the Pitris. Their will is omnipotent."

After a moment of silence, the young woman asked: "What do you want of me?"

"First of all I want you, body and soul. Your vital breath has entered into my mouth. You belong to me."

She shivered. "Oh yes, I know . . ."

"Are those delights not incomparable?"

"Perhaps, but I'm afraid. It's not what nature desires."

"It's necessary to rise above her, since the gods have chosen you for the glorification of their cult."

"What will you do with me?"

"I shall take you to the priestesses of the goddess Parvati. Like them, you will put on a golden miter and you will dance before the idols during the sacrifices. But that will only be a stage. Later, you will follow me in my voyages through the world . . ."

"I'll follow you!"

"Yes, and we will accomplish miracles that will overturn the deceptive religions."

"Oh! My thought is hesitating on the edge of the gulf! I won't have the strength to resist the proofs and temptations."

"Whatever you do, Viamalah, your destiny will be accomplished."

"And Achilgar?"

"What does it matter to you?"

"Yes, I want to know . . ."

"You'll know later."

"No, right away."

Nassudamy hesitated for a moment, his eyes suddenly scintillating, his hands clenched; then he said, with a malevolent joy: "You're asking me what will become of Achilgar?"

"I'm asking you on my knees, and I beg you to reply."

"Well, he will die."

"He'll die!" Viamalah extended her arms, uttered a cry and bumped the ground with her forehead.

"Yes," said Nassudamy, bitterly, "you still love him; you're too close to nature to comprehend. I will struggle for the truth and you will end up submitting. Come now."

Groaning, she came to her feet. "Are we going into the temple?"

"Yes."

"Oh! Look!"

Large black-winged birds with bald heads and violet goiters were circling overhead.

"They're vultures searching for a prey."

"They're forming circles that are shrinking . . ."

"A presage of death for someone you know."

She shivered, and pressed herself against the charmer.

"Have no fear," he said. "My power is above life and death. In any case, life and death signify nothing, since we have never ceased to exist, and are only transformed until we reach perfection. Achilgar will not disappear, he will simply be elsewhere."

"Shut up—I don't want him to quit the earth. Now that I belong to you, spare him."

He shrugged his shoulders. "Come; you'll sleep tonight under the protection of the goddess, you're not worthy of my kisses."

VII

Flesh of Amour and Prayer

Nassudamy and Viamalah have entered the temple of Durga. It is formed of lateral galleries sustained by columns, in the center of which is the sanctuary, on monolithic pillars. There are bas-reliefs everywhere, carved in red marble, and golden idols that are resplendent in the convergent light of lamps, arms raised menacingly or placidly folded over the abdomen. Monkeys run along the branches curiously in order to see the visitors and demand fruits and honey from them, but the fakir drives them away. He claps his hands and pronouncing mysterious words.

Immediately, the sacred dancers, or devadasi, consecrated to the worship of the gods and the pleasure of the Brahmins, emerge from the temple tumultuously and prostrate themselves before him.

"O Nassudamy," says the most ornamented, extending her painted lips, "I can refuse you nothing."

"I know."

"Oh, gentlest and most handsome of yogis, is it the desire for amour that has finally led you to us?"

"It is not the desire for amour, it is amour itself that I am bringing you." Pushing Viamalah, who was hiding behind him, he went on: "This is my spouse before the gods. She is pure in body and unformed in spirit. Respect her flesh and maintain her soul!"

"But that young woman was married yesterday," said one of the bayaderes, whose name was Arna, meaning Nevermore. "We danced at her wedding before the idols."

"She is pure, I tell you, since she has only been possessed in a dream. Is that true, Viamalah?"

"It is true," she murmured.

"I have suggested to her resistance to the transports of a man. She has only known the bewitchment of my spiritual caresses."

"In fact," said Raksa (Evil), "you have made a vow of celibacy."

70

"Everyone knows what that means," murmured a beautiful young woman in full bloom.

The fakir smiled disdainfully. "Lotus Heart, I know better kisses than those of mortals."

"Kisses of the soul?"

"Kisses that burn like fire, envelop like the sea and bite like poison. Extraordinary kisses that recommence incessantly or last one night, according to my caprice; kisses that . . ."

"Stop," said the breathless dancer. "You're intoxicating us with your inflamed words, and we have no one to calm us down this evening."

"Yes," said a thin girl with long smoky eyes. "The stone idol."

"Good for you, Schahabalu," riposted Lotus Heart, hotly. "We prefer living caresses."

"The Brahmins are so old!" said the child, shrugging her narrow shoulders, solely ornamented by blue ribbons and flowers. "At least the god of sacrifice never steals away."

"Oh, if Nassudamy wished! He's young and strong! For once, where would be the harm!"

"Nassudamy loves Viamalah; if he forgot his oath of purity, it would only be for her."

"Well, let it be for her."

"They are both accomplished, and the spectacle of their embraces would be a marvelous thing," said Arna. "Around their ecstasy we could burn perfumes in agate cassolettes, we could agitate peacock-feather flabella above their heads and, to reanimate their ardor, we could pour them lotus wine spangled with gold."

"I assure you, Nassudamy," said a bayadere with breasts coved in opals, "that you won't find a better occasion to forget your promises. Then again, Durga protects you because you're handsome, she'll intercede for you with Shiva."

"In fact," the child with confused and heavy eyelids went on, "I've prepared a bed of roses in front of the idol I serve. I have bananas and figs, cakes and cinnamon bark and jujube, yams and rice, not to mention a piece of the sacred horse killed last tanguam. You'll never have such a feast!"

They surrounded the yogi, extending the tips of their breasts toward him in amorous battle, sticking out sharp tongues at him, avid for kisses, and shaking their somber hair over their impatient rumps.

They were almost all beautiful under the metallic headbands that barred their forehead from one temple to the other. Their wide eyes with fixed gazes, seemingly insensible, almost unfathomable, were separated by a thin nose of a very pure design that descended over a fragile mouth, open at the heart, in a puerile manner. They had faces of an unusual, disquieting regularity, primitive and superb, made of simple and impeccable lines. The Brahmins chose them carefully, and the noblest families abandoned their daughters to them without argument, proud of that rare favor. But the Brahmins wearied of them rapidly, and they languished in the temple, their souls unquiet, their senses perverted, always on the alert.

Often they were heard singing in a dolorous and nostalgic voice, hoarse and torn, like the call of a lioness in the desert. The youngest, who were five or six years old, and had not yet felt the spur of desire, took up the bizarre chant, which then became lively and light. One dainty child of eight, in particular, sang delightfully, and the others stopped to listen to her. The sounds fluttered and faded, floating like a breath of the soul of the Ganges, the soul of the wind blowing from the Himalayas, the soul of warblers and cicadas.

Nassudamy took a few steps to withdraw. "Look after Viamalah well; I'm going to evoke the Pitris."

"Stay with us!"

"No."

"We'll do for you what we've never done for the most demanding Brahmins! Here's a cup full of saffron and powdered sandalwood . . ."

"No."

"Why don't you want us, Nassudamy? Do you fear the vengeance of men? In that case, since you're a sorcerer, you only have to rub a lotion on your eyes that will render you invisible. We still have some; it contains, as you know, the ash of a mongoose, the eyes of serpents and the fruit of the long tumbi gourd."

The smallest clung to his legs, kissing his knees.

Viamalah, mute, watched those transports with surprise, which she would not have dared to imagine, and a little jealousy gripped her heart.

"No, leave me alone; you know full well that it's futile."

"Do you prefer the eunuchs to us?"

Nassudamy made a gesture of disgust.

"Oh, it was for a joke that I said that," said Lotus Heart. "We know that you only love what's pretty: the harmony of forms and souls."

"I love the creature in its divine essence, and I venerate the gods that have permitted me to scorn matter. Go back to the temple and try to sleep; tomorrow you must prepare to celebrate the goddess Kali worthily, who is presiding over human sacrifices. I want Viamalah, in order to be sanctified, to witness the ceremony, seated at the feet of the statue, and ornamented with all the diamonds of Golconda!"

Having spoken, he drew away.

VIII
The Advice of Lotus Heart

Viamalah followed her new companions into the part of the temple that was reserved for them. It was a high hall surrounded by porphyry columns, which only received daylight through the door. Six jade lamps hung down from the vaults, spreading a glaucous light over things. The entire room was full of bizarre gifts to Kama: banners indurated with precious stones, ornaments of copper and crystal, dolls with enamel eyes swinging on the end of strings, frightful masks, necklaces and weapons of every sort. It was no longer the severe temple but a retreat of sensuality, ornamented by the childish and passionate taste of female savages.

A violent perfume of essence of roses gripped Viamalah, who inhaled that breath of flowers avidly, imprisoned there, captive among the rich cushions and embroidered golden fabrics.

In the center, a stone idol erected his desire toward the insatiable priestesses, but many virgins also came to offer themselves to the divinity before belonging to a husband. The ceremony then took place in great pomp in the public square to which the sacred image was transported, in front of relatives, friends and foreigners ever avid for edifying spectacles. The bride, her hair mingled with jasmine and vervain, arrived supported by young women, covered, like her, in long floating veils and flowers; but sometimes, the shock was so violent that the lover, after having given herself to the stone god, lost consciousness, and was only reanimated inside the pagoda under the caresses of the Brahmins. They too, before the husband, had full authority over the woman, and if she was exceptionally beautiful, they kept her for several days, to the great joy of her relatives, very proud of that particular favor.

Without looking at the image, Viamalah went to let herself fall on to one of the little beds of precious wood, the parrot-feather cushions of which were strewn with freshly-plucked petals. Two cassolettes rose up at her feet, filled with aromatic herbs that were consumed slowly. On the ground, a metallic powder glittered, sown with bizarre signs agreeable to the gods.

The bayaderes, having burned perfumes extracted from hemp, the gigantic asclepiad and black datura, swayed their entire bodies two or three times, and then prostrated themselves and extended their arms. After the obligatory prayer to Shiva, Lotus Heart fetched carpets, which she laid out on the ground, and on great trays of enameled copper, in red clay vases, brought fruits, broths of wheat, beans and barley, yellowed by saffron, salads of mangoes and bananas, pâtés of ginger, mahua and angelica, fritters of acacia and rose, and creams of pistachio milk sprinkled with musk. Although it was forbidden to them, she also fetched liqueurs of cinnamon and jujube, and pink lotus wine speckled with gold, which foams and sparkles, and intoxicates adorably.

The little dancers lay down on cushions, nonchalantly parading their fingers, ringed all the way to the smallest phalanges, above the dishes.

"Come on, then, Viamalah," said Schahabalu, the girl with the bruised eyelids. "There's a place next to me."

"No, I'm tired."

"All the more reason. You haven't felt the profound sensualities that two enlaced lovers experience, though. A mouthful of this cinnamon wine will renew your . . . imaginary emotions."

"No, I'm sad."

"Sad? Why? Do you not have the mystic amour of Nassudamy, the most handsome of the servants of the temple?"

"I don't love him."

"You're very difficult. Here, we're all mad for him. Who do you love, then?"

"Achilgar, who has abandoned me."

They started to laugh, already slightly intoxicated.

"He's only a husband," said Raksa.

"He's not even a husband, alas."

"That's truly a cruel torment! The stone god will replace him," whispered Arna, the forsaken, laughing.

"He's never fatigued," said the girl with somber eyes. "You'll see; I'll initiate you into the games of the most famous priestesses. When you leave here you'll be instructed as a sacred courtesan. The Brahmins, you understand, aren't obliged to exercise their ministry with all the devadasi; they choose the youngest, almost always children, and neglect the others; but we console one another for that."

"Listen," said Lotus Heart, "to the advice of wisdom, and know how to conduct yourself in life. A husband is nothing; it's necessary to have generous lovers."

"If Nassudamy heard you!"

"Nassudamy is a fanatic who doesn't reprove amour in others. He only wants to conserve you for himself alone, egotistically."

"He knows all my actions."

"That's true," said Schahabalu. "He's in commerce with the pitris, and nothing can be hidden from him."

"Well," said Lotus Heart, "listen to my advice anyway, and make use of it when the fakir quits you in his turn—for all men are alike, you see; it's necessary not to count on them."

"Speak," said Viamalah, with lassitude. "What is it necessary to do, then, to attach them?"

"Not take them seriously."

"That's easy to say."

"Not to love, or, if you have too tender a heart, to act in such a way as never to allow your weakness to be divined, and above all, to mock oaths of amour."

"It's necessary to be a perjurer?" the young woman queried, beginning to be amused by that strange morality, coming from a priestess of Durga.

"That's of no importance. In any case, the gods scorn fidelity, since they give themselves to everyone . . ."

"That argument is incontrovertible. However, pyres are built for inconsolable widows, and they follow their husbands' remains there, voluntarily or by force."

"It's a prudent measure; husbands are too afraid of being sent to the other world; they've taken their precautions."

"You have an answer for everything, Lotus Heart. It's necessary to have lovers, then?"

"As many as possible—only it's important to choose rich ones, and only to give oneself to them in exchange for valuable presents. Look, these necklaces, breast- and waist-clasps, leg-bracelets and rings of incomparable workmanship have been offered to me thus . . ."

"I thought that the devadasi could only belong to the Brahmins?"

"Certainly, but the Brahmins are no less generous than other men, when one knows how to handle them. There's only that little fool Schahabalu here who is only ever decked with flowers, because she lets anyone see her temperament."

The child with the vague eyelids jibbed. "I have time before me, whereas you're old."

"Old!"

"You're twenty-two—everyone knows that. When I'm that age, my shoulders will be under pearls and brilliant plaques."

"You're more faded than me, and that's not astonishing, with the life you lead, Chi-chi!"

"Well, I enjoy myself! Ghirna!"[1]

"You'd do so anyway, and with a little cleverness you'd render it profitable."

Viamalah smiled at the women's words, languidly. It seemed to her that she was reading a bad book, but her heart was not soiled by it.

"So the gods pardon these mercenary thoughts?" she said. "They never become irritated?"

"They'd have too much to do. We're all like that. Anyway, the gods prefer quantity to quality. Like nature, they're good and evil at the same time, they only want amour and death."

"You're right."

"Fecundity and destruction—they don't care about anything else. Look at the beasts, which, like us, have souls . . ."

"Beasts don't care about presents."

"Because they don't have any need of them. But among them, too, it's strength and cunning that triumph. So the great sacred monkeys . . ."

"Enough," cried the children, drunk on kisses and lotus wine. "Enough! You're more tedious than the doyen of our Brahmins, who's ninety years old and doesn't even know how to tell a girl from a boy. You drone on like a chapter of the Dharma Shastra,

---

1 The author inserts notes to explain that "Chi-chi!" is a nasty insult and that Ghirna signifies "the scorned."

which claims that the Brahmins were born from the mouth of Brahma . . ."

". . . The Kshatryas from his arms . . ."

". . . The Sudras from his feet . . ."

"My beauties," said Schahabalu, yawning, "I'm going to find the monkeys—they'll distract us."

"Yes, yes, they'll eat our leftovers."

"Above all, bring Maddy and Baoudou, they're the nicest."

IX

The Game of the Bayaderes and the Sacred Monkeys

Maddy and Baoudou, two bastard chimpanzees[1] with pink muzzles between blue side-whiskers, with yellow bands around their eyes, making them enormous golden spectacles, came in walking on their hands like clowns. Then, that position putting them at the level of the dishes, they began to clean them very neatly, uttering slight joyful clucks, like those of chickens that have found a worm.

Raksa poured them fermented juice of cinnamon-bark, which has the privilege of making them merry. All the liquors of cinnamon and jujube went the same way, only the wine of the spotted lotus being set apart to sustain the strength of the devadasi and prolong their drunkenness. The intoxicating beverages stimulated the lust of the great sacred monkeys, flowing in their stomachs in fiery waves.

Lying on her stomach, Schahabalu excited them with her voice and her gestures, laughing like a lunatic on seeing them so greedy. When there was nothing left in the clay bowls and the bottles of sweet wine, the two quadrumanes raised their round and sharp eyes, with irises of burned topaz, to the women.

----

1 The temple monkeys would most probably have been gray langurs of the genus *Semnopithecus*, but the description given does not fit that species very well, and is more suggestive of some kind of macaque.

"We're listening to you," said Lotus Heart. "Quickly, thank us and be eloquent. Celebrate the praises of the god Hanuman, who has permitted you to resemble humans."

Maddy and Baoudou then intoned a bizarre duet, full of caressant notes and hoarse cries, phrases that were sometimes languorous and sometimes curt, in which there was gratitude, prayer, joy, impatience and irritation.

"There, there—calm down! You're good and pretty."

The devadasi had put bizarre dupattas on the monkeys and loincloths of foliage, sliding parrot feathers behind their ears. The she-monkeys walked with precaution, pinching their lips and simpering, rolling their eyes languorously, but they shuddered with jealous anger because the males were neglecting them in order to obey the young woman.

A skinny russet female, more irritated than the others, approached Schahabalu, who had taken Baoudou by the waist and was spinning frenetically around the idol.

"Look out! Be careful!" cried the dancers.

"Bah! Let her try to do me harm!"

And, laughing, the little girl spat in the face of the beast; but the latter gathered herself, bounded, and scratched her cheek profoundly with a thrust of the paw.

"Oh, the vermin!"

They both fell to the ground, wailing and howling. They were soon no more than a ball of flesh and fur, bristling with claws from which blood was trickling.

"Go on! Go on!"

"Here, Schahabalu, my stiletto!"

"No, no, that's not the game . . . let them be."

But the she-monkey, more muscular, had the upper hand. She bit her rival in the breast and, seizing her by the hair, thrust her head back so brutally that the skull hit the ground with a dull thud.

"Separate them!" cried Viamalah. "Can't you see that she's lost consciousness?"

"Oh," said Lotus Heart, bearing a grudge against the girl for her sarcasms, "it isn't the first time the she-monkey has knocked her out. Why did she steal her property? Everyone knows that Baoudou is married, and that it's necessary not to touch him."

The monkeys, however, fearing reprisals, had fled, still covered in their finery, and their precipitate gallop was audible outside, accompanied by shrill cries.

Schahabalu got up, went to look at herself anxiously in a copper mirror, and applied jujube balm mixed with honey to her wounds. A bloody gash striped her face from the eyelid to the chin.

"Will that be visible?" she asked, anxiously.

"A monkey's claw is poisonous. Little Kshirikita, who had also offended a she-monkey, lost her left eye after a quarrel, although only the lid was touched."

"What became of her?"

"Disfigured, she quit the temple, because the gods only want to be served by perfectly gracious and beautiful women."

"She quit the temple?"

"And no one looked at her any more. She took refuge in the mountains with the herdswomen, who beat her and treat her with scorn."

Schahabalu began to weep convulsively. Her frail shoulders rose and fell, and the garlands of flowers hung down her back, all withered.

X

A Secret Offering to the Stone God

The devadasi are now collecting themselves. Although still drunk on lotus wine, they are taking on grave expressions that belie the sly creasing of their lips. Their warm complexion, as if illuminated interiorly, is bronzed around ecstatic pupils, beneath smooth foreheads covered with the thick, black, heavy masses of their ruffled hair, mingled with shiny powder. In the smoke of aromatic herbs, the carpet and the scarves are taking on colorations so pale, so pastel and so faded that they are caresses for the gaze.

Veils are undulating like waves of light, belts of gemstones are dotted with sparks over the sea-green, glacier gray and crepuscular mauve draperies. It is a magical vision, to which the soothing magic of music has just been added.

The glaucous reflection of lamps, turned toward the idol, makes it seem almost alive. The god is seated; a skillful sculptor has carved him in pink stone, and has given him virile forms in excitement, harmonious and full. He is smiling, and holding out his arms as if to embrace the amorous women who come to visit him every day. The most fervent have attached valuable jewels to his wrists and legs; a necklace of Karmoul roses and moonstones hangs around his neck; elephant pearls fall from his ears and he has a diadem made of hummingbird feathers on his head.

Women sacrifice doves with coral feet to him, bring him rice, saffron, betel, dishes possessing the six delicious tastes, and give themselves to him. Thick smoke, which comes from cassolettes that are always lit, blurs his features and renders them mobile; his arms seem to be agitating and imploring amour.

Lotus Heart has hoisted herself up on to the pedestal religiously, and, with a camel-hair brush that she dips into a jar full of essence of vervain and tuberose, attends to the god's toilette, voluptuously caressing his shoulders, his breast and his belly, descending along the muscular legs all the way to the gold-ringed toes. Then, with a feather with fine barbs dipped in carmine, she reddens his mouth, and touches his nipples and ten toenails.

The others, swinging their heads slowly from one shoulder to the other, intone chants to the divinity, punctuating the strophes with stokes of the tal—cymbals of steel and copper that are struck sharply.

Lying on her couch strewn with jasmine petals, Viamalah does not move, her thought lost in an obscure dream. She is troubled by a confused emotion, full of pity, and perhaps of envy, for those hallucinates of pleasure who exhaust their ardent desire in that prison of flowers and perfumes, by means of images and dangerous simulacra. The poor things only emerge for nuptial ceremonies, processions and sacred festivals, when they have the mission to dance behind the chariots of the idols.

Some have escaped and have wandered in the arid country, fissured by ravines, where, at intervals, the white carcass with raised ribs appears of some beast that has died of hunger or has been sacrificed to the gods. The vultures and crows have butchered the body, and the bones will whiten on the dusty road for a long time.

But the daughters of amour have marched on, and have ended up finding bushy trees, boscages full of freshness and watercourses, over which nacreous dragonflies flutter, and butterflies with orange velvet horns and large quivering wings. And they have installed themselves in shady retreats, only going out in the evening in order to wait on the road for travelers and merchants, who sometimes go home with them, or quite simply take them in the grass and the flowers. Thus they live, with the constant fear of being recognized by a Brahmin—for that would mean death for them.

Those rebels and vagabonds are rare, however, the simulacrum of amour sufficing for their fever and their nature, more avid for sensations than sentiments. Under the temples there is a long subterranean corridor that descends to the bank of the Ganges, and it is said that at its extremity, culpable women or those deemed to be too old were killed, and their bones thrown into the water, weighted down with heavy stones to prevent them from resurfacing. Thus concluded the torture of their futile and morose lives, for a woman who is only an instrument of pleasure has no more reason to exist when the flame of her eyes and the honey of her youth no longer retain men.

Nowadays, dancers who fall ill or are enfeebled by age are simply reformed, after branding them on the thigh with a red-hot iron with the mark of the pagoda where they have served.

Viamalah was pensive, and Schahabalu was still weeping.

"Tell us," said Lotus Heart, laughing, "what you know about kisses."

"No," said the child, shaking her head.

"To amuse Viamalah, who is thinking about her fickle spouse."

"There are seven orders of kisses," murmured Schahabalu, as if she were reciting a lesson.

"List them, to prove to us that you're a good pupil."

"There is the nominal kiss, the moving, the touching, the direct, the tilted, the turned and the urgent."

"Good. Which one do you prefer?"

"I like them all."

"You see! However, you won't know any of them tonight, Chi-chi!"

"I don't want any; I'm tired."

"Ha! You're even disdaining the stone idol!"

"I'm too ugly; it wouldn't want me to kiss its stone foot."

"Oh, it wants all those who offer themselves."

"Go on then."

"We prefer one another."

The children removed the largest of the flowers that they all wore beneath their loose belts, and swooned under the kisses in which they went avidly in quest thereafter. One by one the scarves fell, and when they were no longer wearing anything but their necklaces and bracelets, they took one another by the hand and spun madly around the idol. Some were almost pale-skinned and had the feverish gestures of dislocated puppets; others, newly arrived, retained in their flesh the colors of the earth and the sun. A few were frank in those passionate amities and declared themselves happy; their relations became almost conjugal; they no longer had any desires except for one another, and only accepted the visits of the Brahmins with repugnance.

Those visiting days were desired and feared by the devadasis, for frightful unknown debauches were committed in the temple then, in the name of the goddess Durga. But aphrodisiac substances, mingled with jujube and lotus wine, were poured over the weariest; their breasts and certain parts of their body were rubbed with a mixture of peppermint, nutmeg, cantharide and phosphorus, which galvanized them to the point of rendering them docile to the worst experiences. They attempted with joy the most dangerous sensualities, and sometimes expired before the end of the night without crying for mercy.

Schahabalu claps her hands and excites them with her voice. They have picked up the golden lingams of their adornments and are clicking them like castanets. Their feet agitate frenetically, their torsos undulate, curve and sway in an increasingly rapid movement. Their tresses expand, displayed like fans and parasols, shaking a brilliant powder around them, which mingles with the smoke of the cassolettes. After the farandole comes the lascivious dance; the knees part, the thighs flex, the hands seem to be seeking the passionate lover who is waiting for them and imploring them; then they straighten up with a bound, clicking their sacred jewels more forcefully.

Now, having collected kisses from burning lips open like flowers, they draw away, laughing, pivot on the tip of a foot, beat the air with a muscular leg, and leap in order to pose further away in feline and cunning attitudes. With shrill cries they throw themselves upon one another, knocking one another down and fighting for a bite or a caress.

The most expert make their breasts and bellies move, roll their hips, rear up, lean back in a semi-circle, sweeping the ground with their hair; others lean over to seize a dream butterfly, which their slender fingers retain by its transparent wings, and with an effort, arms raised and rumps projecting, launch their winged desire toward the vaults . . .

Then, irises drowned in the nacre of the eye, eyelids half-closed, they remain motionless, showing the brown moss of their young bodies. In the end, they dare all attitudes, those that the devadasi mistresses have taught them and others that they have imagined.

They pursue one another and enlace one another, touching and swooning, fleeing and coming back, lips to lips, breasts thrusting and mingled. A fine sweat causes their amber bodies to shine, which become weary, enervated by the embraces.

Finally, they lie down, their limbs opening, the secret corolla of their flesh offered to the mystery of amour. They call out, they laugh, they weep, their voices become wheedling, cajoling, sobbing, moist with desire . . . and Lotus Heart, the first, approaches the stone god . . .

XI
The Brahmins and the Yogis

In the courtyard of the temple, Nassudamy has remained in prayer; then other yogis have come to join him, and, crouching on the ground for an hour, they have maintained the most absolute immobility.

They are naked, with white and blue tattoos on the body; some are mutilated, or retain the traces of profound burns.

Brahmanism, with its strange, cruel, murderous practices, albeit imprinted with a savage poetry, gradually pushes the soul into the gulfs of madness. The imaginations of the trimurti are horrible and obscene. In the theories of the Veda, the god of all science and all beauty is only manifest in rape and murder. All supraterrestrial revelations and all human progress are determined solely by a sanguinary and always triumphant conflict. The gymnosophists and the initiates of Zoroaster have drawn from the same sources, but it is the false Zoroaster, the black Zoroaster, who remains the master of Indian theology. By virtue of the pantheism that reigns in the ultimate degrees of that degenerate doctrine, one arrives at absolute materialism, while obstinately denying matter. The consequence of that pantheism is the destruction of all morality, liberty in vice and in death; the equal power of darkness and light.

In accordance with those dogmas, it is easy to understand the progressive exaltation of the Brahmins and their great ritual magic, the basis of the Indian occultism, the *Oupnek'hat*, teaches them the physical and mental means of consummating the perverse endeavor and arriving, by degrees, at the dementia that they consider to be the divine state.

That evening, the yogis, or pupils of the Brahmins, were awaiting their professors, who would read them passages from the sacred book and comment on the text with their real and universal erudition.

The venerated ones arrived punctually at the first stroke of midnight, clad in white, with a yellow ribbon in their hair. Some of them, very old, had a majestic and serene beauty; the youngest had long somber eyelids, which they often lowered over their excessively bright eyes, full of a mystical or voluptuous fever.

The yogis prostrated themselves, raising their hands above their heads while murmuring the name of the creator forty times in succession without drawing breath.

"Aum!"

The oldest of the Brahmins then went up into a sort of pulpit open to the sky, the pink granite foot of which represented a giant lingam extended toward the stars. Next to that singular cathedra, an oval basin from which a spring poured served as a drinking-trough for the monkeys and sacred cows. The bas-reliefs on the walls unfurled an erotic and fabulous ornamentation in which animal couples mingled with human couples for monstrous embraces.

In India, no one is shocked by those licentious images, which maidens and children contemplate with an ingenuous eye.

The Brahmin preacher was carrying the book of the *Oupnek'hat*, which is the ancestor of all grimoires and the most curious monument of the antiquities of goetia. It is divided into five sections full of darkness, but fulgurant lightning flashes sometimes traverse it, recalling the gospel of Saint John, as in these phrases:

The angel of creative fire is the word of God.

The word of God has produced the earth, the vegetables that emerge from it, and the warmth that ripens them.

The old Brahmin searched the ritual magic of the Indian enchanters and read the following:

"*To become god it is necessary to hold one's breath for as long as one can, and then send one's breath mentally through the heavens and attach oneself to the universal ether. It is necessary to render oneself blind, deaf and as motionless as a stone for hours, while thinking of nothing but the Creator, who is in all animals and protects the ant as well as the elephant. The supreme voice will make itself heard in ten ways: It will be similar to the song of a bird, the clash of cymbals, the murmur of a large seashell, the song of the vina, the noise of the tal, the sigh of the bacabou flute, the moaning of the pakaoudj, the sound of the trumpet and, finally, the roaring of a cloud.*"

"Ddha! Ddha! Ddha!" said the yogis putting their foreheads in the dust.

"*At each of these sounds,*" the Brahmin went on, "*the contemplator passes through different states, until the tenth, when he becomes a god.* Do you want to be similar to the divinity?"

"We want that."

"Go, then, to astonish the world by means of your fasting and tortures. In any case, if the Faith is profound in you, the most frightful tortures will procure you an inexpressible joy."

"Aum is great!"

"Nothing must retain you, neither water nor fire."

"Aum is good!"

"You must brave death ten times a day."

"Aum is powerful."

"And will you suffer the ordeals of hanging, of dislocation and crushing at the festivals of the goddess Kali?"

"We will suffer them."

"Will you die if necessary?"

"We will die."

"The martyrdom of one man rejoices the divinity for a thousand years, and that of three men for three thousand years."

The Brahmin who had spoken descended from the sacred lingam, and threw a pinch of ash on the head of each of the prostrate yogis. Then he asked Nassudamy who the woman was that he had brought, for he was not unaware of anything that happened in the temple.

"She is one of ours," the young man replied, "and her zeal will serve us. We will make a pilgrimage along the banks of the Mother Ganges; we will travel piously along the sacred shore of the river of all belief; we will go without fatigue from her source to her mouth, and we will fix, on a reed-bed of floating cadavers, the little green lamp that will guide them toward the abode of liberty and glory. Shiva, who has for a head and shoulders the rocks of the Himalayas, will sustain us as he has sustained all those who have served him. Has he not supported even the weight of the river 'falling from his head like a pearl necklace whose string is broken'? We will fill vials of amber and amethyst with the divine water, which we will carry with us in golden baskets garnished with peacock plumes."

"The road is rude!"

"We will repose in the lands where the trees intertwine their branches like lovers wearied by caresses, were the flowers, swooning like violated virgins, change under the kisses of the sun into ardent gums, aromatics and poisons . . ."

"A languor will grip you."

"No, for after the delights of the dvipas[1] we will climb the Merou, the golden mountain where the gods reside."

"You will respire the soran, which will make you die."

"The Palomen will assist us."

"Then there will be the grichma, which will lead you to the varcha. The coppery vapors will expend into 'towers' and 'elephants' and the turbulence of the maussim with engulf you."

---

1 The author inserts a note defining the *dvipas* as "verdant isles," and subsequently adds notes defining *soran* as aconite, *Palomen* as Brahmins, the *grichma* as the "season of sweats" and the *varcha* as the "season of rains."

"We will shelter under the deodar and the banyan fig tree, which can cover an entire people at prayer. We will be strong, for we will have faith."

"You will be strengthened by the faith, but you will be weakened by amour."

"What do you know about it?"

"You will forget that you have made a vow of chastity, and that woman's embrace will enfeeble our astral virility."

"I love her in spirit and will respect her body. I want to consecrate her to Kali, and if the gods permit it, she will assist in the festival of the goddess, seated on the chariot."

"Can she dance?"

"No, but she will sing during the suttees; her voice is as sweet as the cooing of a dove."

"Go and fetch her to me."

XII
In Pearls, Roses and Blood

Viamalah was asleep on her bed of jasmine, and the devadasi, their hair scattered, damp with sweat and perfumes, were lying at the feet of the idol. They were naked under the mutilated flowers, with traces of pricks and bites on their breasts.

One of them had tried to juggle with daggers, and bore a profound wound on the shoulder, from which blood was escaping drop by drop, sliding under the armpit and forming a little pool on the ground, which was still expanding. A bottle of wine had spilled and the river of gold soon went to join the red rivulet, between the bodies of the sleepers.

Schahabalu was clutching a leopard-skin against her, which partly concealed her, the muzzle of the animal caressing her delicate breast. She was smiling at a pleasant dream, her lips half-closed; her long eyelashes, as soft as down feathers, cast a shadow over her cheeks, and her long hair, thrown backwards violently as if in the unexpectedness of a fall, spread out in a straight line.

Thus recumbent, abandoned and undressed, it was easier to distinguish their race.

The women of Avantika had developed forms, the bosom rounded, the lap flourishing in a triangle, and only depilated themselves rarely. They were supple and ardent.

The women of Maharashtra, perfectly beautiful, taught the young noblewomen of Benares, for two hours a day, the theory of the sixty-four varieties of sensualities, according to the Kama. They were paid very dearly and wore more precious stones than the others, with a yoni-lingam of sardonyx in the middle of the forehead.

The women of the center, between the Ganges and the Jumna, had slim waists and mauve-tinted nipples. They braided jasmine branches around their legs all the way to the sacred flower of their brown beauty, and seemed rather reserved in their embraces.

The women of Pataliputra had strong lips and eyes clouded as if in ecstasy. They were said to be indefatigable, and the Brahmins chose them for preference over the others.

The women of Punjab, with narrow, almost boyish hips, fleecy hair covered in red powder, and dainty feet ringed with opals, sought the amity of their companions, in the same way as the dancers of Malva and Andhra. The latter, with sharp eyes with aquamarine reflections, wore their hair gathered up at the top of the head by a sapphire star, and perfumed their entire bodies six times a day. They declared themselves satisfied with their lot and almost never quit the pagoda, but they were subject to nervous maladies, having frequent crises that felled them to the ground, agitated their limbs with a convulsive tremor and flecked their lips with foam. They were said then to be possessed by pitris.

The women of the Oude, Aparatika and Lat had harmonious forms, eyelids widely split over somber velvet irises, delicate legs, wide hips and charming breasts always erect. They covered themselves with vervain and sought all sorts of kisses.

As for the women of Vanavasi and the Dravidian women, they were taller than the others, wore feather head-dresses and mostly mimed the warrior episodes of ancient legends. They were believed to be insensitive and proud, in spite of their ardent beauty, their solar eyes and their undulant rumps. When they were asked the reason for their coldness, they replied: "We are scornful of men and disdainful of women. The gods visit us during our sleep."

"What gods? Incubi, then?"

"Yes, but there are also the succubi that are the goddesses of the night. Nothing can describe the sweetness of their kisses. We hardly think about men, but we evoke those voluptuous spirits."

"Hateful vampires, lemurs and larvae!"

"No, beings of joy and strength."

The women who had commerce with the pitris almost all died violently or committed suicide.

Among those devadasis, albeit so seductive and chosen with care, Viamalah was still the most accomplished. She had, above all, a penetrating and rare charm spread all the way to the nail of her little finger, an irresistible fashion of smiling, and her warm gaze enveloped people with magnetic effluvia as gently as caresses. She was also of a superior race, more refined and more valiant; an intelligence emanated from her like a perfume escaping from a corolla. Among those superb jewels, accessible to the sumptuous fantasies of the privileged, she was the unique jewel that the artist or poet seeks throughout a lifetime.

Leaning over her, Nassudamy contemplated her ardently, while pronouncing indistinct words. Then, without opening her eyes, still asleep, but obedient to his fascinating power, she got up, adjusted her veils, and followed him.

The old Brahmin was waiting, standing, serene and majestic, on the pink granite pulpit, which he covered with a flap of his white robe. Nassudamy put his hands on the young woman's shoulders and made her fold up slowly until she was kneeling before the chief.

"She's beautiful," said the others, "and could serve for our pleasures. The work of the flesh is also agreeable to the gods, and we could seek new, very rare and very difficult sensualities with this honeyed lotus, this calyx of election."

"No," said Nassudamy, authoritatively. "The pitris have revealed the future to me and Viamalah must remain a virgin for the accomplishment of the mysterious will of the divinity. I will take her through the world in order to dazzle souls."

"That's a pity," murmured a Brahmin with long, caressant, luminous eyes and sensual lips. "That's a pity! Women are beautiful fruits that the gods have put in our path to calm the thirst of amour; they have no other mission . . ."

"I think differently."

"You are going against divine intentions and giving these inferior beings an importance that might render them presumptuous and vain. It is necessary only to demand of a woman the perfection of forms and submission to the caprices of man."

"I abandon all the devadasi of the temple to you, who are no more than dolls of lust, but I am keeping this one, who is of illustrious race, and whom I have consecrated to the goddess."

"You're only a yogi!" cried the Brahmins, maddened by the beauty of Viamalah, who, with an unconscious movement while still asleep, had just unveiled the amber pink nipples of her breasts, and her back, more polished than ivory.

But the old Brahmin imposed silence on them, doubtless because his desires had not been ardent for a long time, and because, unable to possess that corolla of election, he preferred that no one else should.

"Tell them that I am right," Nassudamy begged, prostrating himself before the august pulpit.

But the venerated one opened a kabbalistic book, which he kept for embarrassing questions, and read, because he no longer had facile improvisation, and the mysteries of the sacred books responded to everything while explaining nothing.

"*The vulgar habitually mistake the shadow for the reality in everything. They scorn the light and mirror themselves in darkness. The forces of nature obey those who know how to resist them. The man disposes of the amour of others who is the master of his own. Do you want to possess yourself? Do not give yourself.*"

"I don't give myself, I take," said Nassudamy, "and my astral force is so great that I will emerge from my tomb in order to confound men. The man who sees the individual essence of beings resident in the unity, and draws his energy therefrom, marches toward omnipotence!"

The old Brahmin skipped several pages. As he was approaching his end, the idea of resurrection interested him far more than amour. He read:

"*Death is always preceded by a lethargic sleep, and is only operated by degrees; resurrection is possible, when the will has not deserted the body, and many individuals finish dying after their inhumation. A lucid energy can act on the mass of astral light and, with the collaboration of other energies that it absorbs, determine great and irresistible currents of life.*"

At that point the old man delivered himself to a few personal reflections, which the fear of dying had suddenly suggested to him, in spite of the fatigue of age, and he spoke abundantly and confusedly about many obscure questions that could be interpreted in all kind of fashions. In any case, it is observable that absurd things are the only ones that can never be combated

"My son, I give you the sacred power. It will be laudable for you, by means of a vehement emission of magnetic fluid, to slay a living being."

"That is already possible for me."

"Perhaps. In any case, your supernatural force will extend further still. You possess the astral light, the element of electricity and the thunderbolt that Shiva sometimes puts at the service of the human will. You must know, since you have commerce with the pitris, the mysterious laws of equilibrium to which the good and evil powers are subservient. But it will be necessary for you to purify your body by the proofs of artificial life and apparent death; it will be necessary for you to struggle against the vampires of the soul, the phantoms of hallucination, and to grasp the clarity that passes over us with the rapidity of lightning; it will be necessary to cut the throat of the wild dogs that bark in dreams, and measure without terror the depth of the abyss into which the slightest false step might cause you to fall . . .

"Always remember that if you are not pure of body and that if the domination of some terrestrial passion subjugates you to the fatalities of life, you will burn in your own fires."

"I'll remember that. In any case, the supreme goal is attained in two ways: the contemplatives apply knowledge, jnana, while those who practice mystic union apply themselves to works, karma. I shall imitate the latter."

"The gods have given you enough magnetic power to fascinate ferocious beasts, and, even more so, men . . ."

"I do not fear beasts or men."

"By means of the projections of your astral light, you can make the most invincible tremble. Animals only attack those they fear. Any intrepid and disarmed individual can make a tiger recoil by the magnetism of his gaze. The world is populated by wild beasts. Go and fight for the good cause!"

When he had finished, he asked Nassudamy whether he wanted the virgin to be consecrated definitively to the goddess Parvati, and on the fakir's affirmative response, he seized a bronze lingam that was reddening in the sacred fire of a stove, and touched the neophyte between the breasts.

The skin smoked and crackled; an acrid odor of burned flesh covered the perfume of incense, and Viamalah fell backwards, uttering a loud scream.

XIII
Ourvasi Sacrifices Her Hair

Meanwhile, Achilgar, who was with Ourvasi, the expert courtesan, was still thinking about Viamalah. He had seen Honeycomb and Glory of the Moon, who had told him, tearfully, about the flight of their mistress, and, being more amorously infatuated than ever, he had forgotten his grievances.

"What have I done, little man of joy," sighed Ourvasi, "for you to scorn my most ardent kisses?"

"Have I not told you that I belong to another, heart and soul? I'm not scorning anything, but I'm unhappy."

"And you want to go to the festival of the goddess?"

"I want to! This very day, in a moment."

"But you'll see her again, the woman possessed by maleficent pitris!"

"That's my dearest desire."

"And you'll quit poor Ourvasi to follow that damned woman, who will make you perish!"

"I shall perish, if it is the will of Shiva."

The courtesan was very skillful at melting the marrow and granulating the loins. Her caresses, for Achilgar, whom she was beginning to love, had an extreme recklessness. He remained extended, his nerves dolorous, and his brain seemed to him to be leaping and dissolving, stuck to the skin of the skull. She leaned over again and embraced him, but he pushed her away, stood up and tried to leave. Then she rolled at his feet, begging and weeping.

No longer knowing how to retain him, she had sacrificed her admirable hair, which she had bound into three tresses retained by cat's-eyes from Ceylon. Those trophies of amour now ornamented Achilgar's belt and proved to him the value she placed on his person.

Proud, in spite of everything, he contemplated his profile and face in Ourvasi's tall mirror, swinging the silky tails that brushed his heels. She clapped her hands, tilting her boyish head, with its strange locks, unequally cut.

"You see! You see! What greater evidence of passion could I give you?"

"You're a good girl," he said, negligently, "and you know truly astonishing caresses. But you were prettier with hair. Now let me go; the dingui is waiting by the terrace to take me to the place of the ceremony. Thank you for the royal gift you have made me. I won't forget it."

XIV
Kali, Goddess of Love and Death

The festival of the goddess Kali is the greatest solemnity in the Hindu calendar. It lasts for a fortnight, and nothing can give an idea of the enthusiasm that it excites in the fanatical crowd. When the vina and the tal made themselves heard, announcing the passing of the procession, the streets were black with people, the faithful, curiosity-seekers and foreigners whom the dobashi and the baboo—interpreters—guided to the best places, in spite of complaints and protests.

Women went by, offering the water of the Ganges in rounded bronze or earthenware vases; others were selling betel leaves; and the crows, profiting from the inattention, stole wheat, barley and rice destined for offerings from the baskets.

The crowd reeked of coconut oil and sandalwood; young women with cheeks, foreheads and noses covered with plaques and shells, or delicately tattooed, brushed past piously silent men, who were smoking hookahs while waiting for the goddess; for the religious idea dominates and effaces everything, regulating actions, tightening consciences, molding hearts, governing thoughts, surpassing interests, preoccupations and desires . . .

The sunlight fell in floods of fire over the walls, the colonnades, the cupolas and the terraces. But all the quarters of the city that were not to be traversed by the chariot of Kali were deserted. One could have traveled through the labyrinth of tangled, tortuous back-streets, past the rickety facades of pink and white houses with wooden balconies, without even encountering a monkey. The sky, glimpsed between the bastard constructions, resembled a blue festoon, running at the hazard of a puerile fantasy. Sometimes, large licentious paintings striped the walls, and one divined by their means the liberty of mores, and the expansion of a limitless prostitution, in spite of the holiness of the place.

But the courtesans were at the festival, in their garments brocaded with gems, alongside daughters of the people with animal scents, and daughters of the countryside with skin gorged on sunlight, amid the radiation of Hindu armor, with scales imbricated by sumptuous and barbaric artists.

Here come the musicians, first: the sounders of trumpets, lifting their gigantic instruments, reminiscent of bronze lotuses; the players of the macabou flute, the vina, the tal and the pakaoudj. It is a barbaric ensemble of sonorous bellowing and shrill moans. After the strident bursts of the trumpets, the deafening racket of tubas and the thunderous rolls of Hindu cymbals, the musical phrase terminates in the whine of hulottes, with small, infinitely sad, pearly notes.

Here come the maidens holding golden statuettes, miniatures of the goddess, and jasmine branches. Under the sky in fusion, all the facets of jewelry catch fire; the stones seem to be alive, like insects of light running over the bodies of the women, which they design in ardent strokes, stinging their necks, legs and arms: as crimson as braziers, as blue as alcohol flames and as green as moonbeams.

Now there is the first massive cart, with two enormous beams for axles, which carry four solid wheels. The base, of joined planks, is covered in bestial, erotic and fabulous sculptures, where embraces mingle the sexes of beasts and humans. There are priestesses loved by tigers, children taken by dragons and other more singular couplings. Over the base, trellises of scaffolding rise, forming an enormous pyramid. Silky fabrics encrusted with olivines, sardonyxes, beryls and chrysoliths descend from the summit, retained by bunches of flowers and light garlands; and at the very top, a colossal throne reigns, which contains the ashes of the god Krishna.

Krishna, the most popular incarnation of Vishnu, is adored everywhere. His fervent followers consider him to be the creator of the world, the magnificent god, eternally young and active. Women celebrate his virility and his ardor. They sing his praises in verse and prose, taking his statuettes in jade and gold to bed with them, seeing him, embracing him and giving themselves to him in their most erotic dreams. Krishna is the hero of the great poem famous throughout India under the name of Mahabharata. His standard unfurls a black dove and a bull. He is the Supreme Being, or the primordial male, upuruscha.

The idol is coiffed with a sort of tiara, with the legs together, and the hands on the knees. Stars constellate the robe of gold cloth, which falls very rigidly to either side. The god wears the jewel Samantaka, a talisman of good fortune similar to the sun.

Around that hieratical figure, perfumes burn, which rise up in acrid spirals.

Mounted on the cart, the priests excite with their cries and gesture an entire population harnessed to enormous cables, who are dragging the idol over the bodies of prostrate devotees. Limbs crack and blood flows, putting clots of somber crimson in the sand and the flowers. Chests are opened and skulls are crushed by the iron of the wheels, or carved and trepanned by spikes; intestines are ripped from bellies, still quivering, like truncated serpents. There are dislocated and broken limbs, the bones laid bare; crushed faces oozing eyes like gelatinous bubbles retained by red fibrils.

Some, with a foot, a hand or an arm torn away, drag themselves along miserably, livid, their features horribly contracted, but the watchers shove them back under the wheels until they are nothing more than bloody pulp.

Here, again, in a quiver of amulets, shells, spangles, necklaces and plaques, are brown maidens with soft and indifferent eyes of enamel. On their shoulders they are carrying statuettes with thin arms, heavy breasts and open hands applied to the belly. Children behind them are throwing flowers and whirling frenetically. They are completely naked, with black and red designs on their bodies; their faces and legs are gilded. They do not turn away from cadavers and the dying. Without pity, as without repugnance, they tread on the bodies and cast their odorous bunches at random into the blood and the mud.

Here come the cavaliers, proudly seated on their black horses, which are whinnying and prancing, and princes of all countries mounted on elephants, whose saddle-cloths and howdahs, indurated with cabuchons of peridots, amaldines and marcasites, sparkle in the sunlight. It is a singular crowd of men, beasts, monstrous divinities, penitents, executioners, the living and the dead, which announces the goddess Kali.

Here she is, on her chariot, smiling and cruel, with necklaces of vertebrae and phalanges. She is wearing a kind of cope embroidered with human teeth, and little bones forming curious arabesques against a background of crimson and gold.

Pillars enameled with polychromatic brick, lapis and sardonyx surround the chariot, linked by garlands of flowers whose petals are falling softly. The Brahmins with jaundiced, parchmented faces annealed with wrinkles, decimated by age, are marching to the right and the left, calm and majestic, their foreheads circled by cords. Others, who are younger, follow with the fakirs; and the devadasi, always in movement, swing cassolettes of perfumes, which disgorge clouds of vapor into the yellow dust.

The perverse odor of aromatics and the stormy and heavy atmosphere tense the nerves; cries rise up, demanding dances. Schahabalu and Lotus Heart detach themselves first for the lubricious steps of the "ardent corolla." Their breasts undulate, and their nipples become erect at the friction of the plaques of gemstones that strike them, while they imprint an increasingly rapid movement on their buttocks and hips. Like their companions they have veils sewn with pearls, decorated with silver, and a very low corselets meshed with sappihirines and chrysoberyls. They resemble scarabs with scintillating elytra, which stir in the sunlight.

Seated on the chariot, at the feet of Kali, Viamalah dominates them. Her face solemn, meditative, almost august, she remains motionless, like a new idol. Her breasts, her abdomen and her thighs are armored with gems, which ignite, crossing, mingling and burying a swarm of fire over her pale velvet skin.

Concentrated, her eyes fixed and dilated, she does not see the blood, the crowd, or the maidens marching indolently through the filthy detritus of crushed flesh and muscles. She is absent, lost in a mysterious dream, and swinging, at the tips of her icy fingers, a huge white orchid.

"Viamalah! Viamalah!"

That cry erupts from the crowd, and the virgin shivers. But her gaze, obscured by the smoke of henbane and datura leaves, interrogates vainly the multicolored crowd, which, undulating around the chariot, is exciting the criminal rage of the priests.

New fanatics throw their heads over the copper stoves, frenetically breathing in the odor of dried nightshade and myrrh and then, tottering and stunned, their hearts capsizing, go to plunge iron crampons into their flesh, profoundly, and, suspended from mobile poles, they describe circles and ellipses in the air, punctuated by an abundant red rain. Others gouge out their eyes and stir the bloody milk with their fingers; others strike their heads against the wheels until the brain bursts out of the skull. Almost all are horribly thin, and sometimes, foam emerges from their twisted mouths; they jerk disjointedly like puppets, leaping from side to side, crouching down, pivoting, uttering strident clamors in order to drag themselves to martyrdom, which they support, thereafter, with an absolute impassivity. Powerful fangs enter into the fleshless backs, twisting the muscles and raking the bones; the wounds hollow out, always enlarged; the tendons give way and the man, like a crimson rag, goes to be crushed upon the ground.

Those who are not subject to the torture of the poles have stamps plunged into their legs, and their bones break slowly, springing out to either side like unequal sticks. The Brahmins, animated by a murderous ardor, pull strips of flesh from beneath the chins of the patients, and make a kind of twisted necklace of them. The skin of the thighs is carved into pink ribbons, tied in velvety knots over the loins and hips, the skin of the abdomen tucked up like a sack, from which a convulsed head emerges.

Here is a young woman who has been pierced in the flesh by flower stems. She is entirely clad in blooming yellow corollas, which are pumping the warm dew from her veins. Her hands are striking golden cymbals in cadence, and she dances around the chariot, not seeming to feel any pain.

Two others open their breasts, repeatedly twisting the blades in the warm holes, and then kneel down and offer the raw wounds to Brahmins, who possess them thus, to the frantic cries of the crowd.

Other maidens follow, stripping off their veils, wanting to receive the mortal caress and begging the priests to grant their wish. So, enlaced bodies are rolling over the wounded and the dying. Gasps of amour and death are mingled.

Some present extraordinary faces in which the eyes, expelled from their orbits, are running down the cheeks like two enormous scarlet tears. With one hand they cling on to the chariot of the goddess, and with the other they open their breasts with their fingernails. Their abdomens are rippled by crazy spasms, as if reptiles were swarming under the skin, and they die slowly, gasping frightfully, because the goddess does not want anyone to finish them off.

"Viamalah! Viamalah!"

Still motionless, her pale orchid between her fingers, Viamalah seems estranged, absent, and the red carousel that is rotating over her head, causing the ardent dew of open veins to rain down along her body and her hair, is invisible for her distant gaze, misted by dreams.

The devadasi, intoxicated by the odor of blood and the acrid swirls of aromatics, twirl more rapidly, extending their loins and their rumps, bending down and raising themselves up again, squeezing the ends of their billowing scarves between their thighs was hoarse cries. Fine sweat sparkles on their brown skin, rubbed with vehement balms, and the nacre of their teeth shines between their lips, which are nervously drawn back.

"Viamalah! Viamalah!"

As if galvanized, the virgin has stood upon the chariot. The network of gemstones that armors her belly and her breast is as rutilant as the scales of a dorado. She raises her arms, bending over backwards until she sweeps the ground with the black hair of her nape, and then, slowly, like a reed tormented by a squall, straightens up again. Her entire body carried on tiptoe, she becomes a marvelous insect, a metallic dragonfly, ready to take flight above the monstrous calices of flesh and blood that are fuming at her feet. Her veils, spangled with sapphires, like sparks crackling in cold and clear water, palpitate like wings; the diamond antennae of her crown sway; she is about to take off, to flee the red, purulent, already-decomposed lake where the human larvae are crawling.

The watchers, struck with astonishment by the marvelous apparition, prostrate themselves, believing that they are seeing an ideal incarnation of Kali.

But Viamalah has bounded lightly to the ground; two arms grip her, lift her up, and carry her away, and before the Brahmins can oppose that abduction, Achilgar regains his dingui and draws away as fast as the oars can row.

XV
Viamalah's Kisses

"Finally, it's you, dear Smile!"

"Achilgar!"

"Viamalah!"

"Oh, you won't leave me again," she said. "It seems to me, now, that I'm no longer the same, and that the maleficent pitris have withdrawn from me."

"The pitris?"

"Yes, their tenebrous flight resembles that of bats, and their swarm hid the sky from me!"

"Forgive me; I'm culpable too . . ."

102

"Certainly. It was necessary to defend me, to struggle against the evil influence . . ."

"There's also something else. . ."

"What?"

Achilgar's only response was to pull Viamalah toward him and place his mouth on hers delectably. What was the point of talking about the courtesan Ourvasi? Was she not dead for the young man? Had she even existed?

"Take me," murmured Viamalah, closing her eyes and clasping him more forcefully. "I shall be delivered when I am yours. Take me!"

"Perhaps we're being followed. Do you think so, dear Sensualist?"

"Oh! You're right . . ."

"But soon . . ."

And, very gently, without her taking account of it, he detached the three tresses of hair that Ourvasi had given him, which he was still wearing in his belt, and threw them into the Ganges, in order that nothing should remain of his temporary folly.

The light and silky hair scattered in the water like black algae, drifting with the current, but the cat's-eye that the prostitute had slipped into them was suddenly animated by a vengeful flame.

Viamalah put her head on Achilgar's shoulder, and remained silent. A passivity of fatigue and exhaustion weighed her down again; it was as if a great apathetic calm took her beyond human sensations. Except for that communion of amour, she no longer expected anything, no longer hoped for anything, and was no longer touched by anything. Her being, doubled again, ceased to belong to the mysterious yogi, the master of charms and spells. She became a terrestrial creature again, a sweet and tender little girl, the submissive companion of a man, who found all her happiness in obedience, in inclining before the desire of the master like a reed in the breeze.

After a long and enervating flight over the troubled water of the river, she reentered the palace, and was received by her three maidservants, who, since her disappearance, had worn nothing in their hair but withered orchids with the venomous calices of sylvan gojis.

As on departure, she wanted to purify herself in the porphyry basin plated with enamels and paved with milky hydrophane opals, which only shine when wet; and the eight elephants' trunks circled by rubies of Sudomante poured aromatic water over her.

"Comet Flower, people are saying that you were on the chariot of the goddess?" queried Honeycomb, curiously.

"It's true."

"What did you see? Blood, blood and more blood, wasn't it? An ardent river in which you bathed your little feet?"

"I didn't see anything."

"What, you didn't see the tortures, or the red stream flowing into the distance, always elongating?"

"I didn't see anything," Viamalah repeated.

"Is that possible?"

"I was doubtless asleep, the mysterious slumber that grips me at times. And it's better thus, for I wouldn't have been able to bear such a spectacle."

"Bah! The victims don't feel the pain, and their martyrdom is agreeable to the divinities."

"Oh, why didn't you bring us back a tuberose steeped in the blood of a yogi?"

"Or a hank of the hair of a young woman scalped by a Brahmin—an odorous lock wrapped in a parrot feather?"

"Or a bracelet of faultless teeth similar to the hydrophanes in this basin?"

"Or a necklace of fingernails polished like agates?"

"Shut up!" cried Viamalah. "You revolt me with your cruel imaginations!"

"Cruel! Why? Haven't all the victims offered themselves voluntarily to the goddess? Be convinced, little Flower, that they haven't felt any distress. Those torments are nothing compared with those that the fervent adherents of the temple of Djagganath experience, who have themselves buried up to the neck and die devoured slowly by flies."

"There are also," said Glory of the Moon, "those who have themselves roasted by a small fire, very slowly, very slowly, and never cease singing the glory of the goddess, while their flesh smokes, crackles and rises up like rice-paper or light flakes of wood."

Honeycomb half-closed her ingenuous eyelids. "I shall drink the blood of tigers, like the baig shamans, in order to contemplate the divinity," she said, "and I shall go barefoot to Jajpur, the city of the sacrifice."

Glory of the Moon gently caressed Viamalah's breasts with a silk cloth imbued with the essence of sarcanthus, in order to prolong Achilgar's desires, rendering them more imperious and more vehement. She smiled as she sniffed the amorous aroma that the warm body emitted in slow or agile waves, in accordance with its gestures.

"Viamalah," she said, "tell us about the temple where you were given refuge. On that point, your memories must be more precise."

"Oh," said Honeycomb, her eyes wide, "is it true that everything we know about sensuality cannot give us an idea of what the devadasi imagine?"

"Is it true," asked Celestial Perfume, in her turn, "that the stone idol grants the wishes of more than a hundred worshipers every day?"

"I didn't see the stone idol," murmured Viamalah, wearily. "I didn't see anything, I tell you; I was asleep."

Her voice, mysterious and slow, seemed to come from very far away, from the depths of a dream. Again, the fever of the unknown dominated her; she thought about her unsatisfied ideal, the amour that impelled her toward a man, and which a sort of fatality would not permit her to satisfy. All the misery of her futile efforts flooded her heart again. She embraced her little friends, taking refuge, like a sick child, in their obliging tenderness.

"Soothe me!"

But they pushed her away, laughing.

"Achilgar's waiting for you . . . don't you want to render him happy, finally?"

"Oh, yes, I want that . . . rub me with all the aromatics that exalt the senses."

"It's necessary to put in her hair," said Honeycomb, "the powder of Tonkin musk, which makes the finch sing twelve tunes in twelve hours."

"It's necessary to pour the essence of spikenard and Bengal lavender over her arms, in order that her embraces will be irresistible."

"And lower down we'll put a precise fusion of tuberose, jasmine and almond . . ."

Viamalah abandoned herself to the expert hands of her servants, determined not to neglect anything in order to accomplish the work of the flesh, to receive and give the manna of amour.

In the exasperated stifling heat of the room, a perfume burner was smoking, which gradually intoxicated the young women, causing them to droop like lotus stems at dusk.

"You're ready now," declared Glory of the Moon. "Go, and may Kama assist you!"

XVI
The Supreme Bewitchment

Viamalah rejoined Achilgar in the garden, where he was wandering in a melancholy fashion, picking violet berries here and there, which he crushed between his fingers in order to make the golden pips spring out.

She made him sit down under a manchineel tree—for the shade of that tree, far from giving death, incites voluptuous languors.[1] The wind passed in the seething of bamboo and lantana

---

1 The machineel tree is only found in the Americas. The generic name that

bushes, the branches of which, in playing with one another, imitated the trills of reed flutes, swelling or stringing little silvery notes. Slender pink lizards ran over the stones; green parrots and bee-eaters descended continually upon the corollas to collect insects velveted with sepia and ocher, which did not even struggle, intoxicated by perfumes.

Viamalah, completely naked, her hair mingled with tuberoses, held a betel nut between her lips, which she presented to her husband as a pledge of tenderness and submission. Kneeling down before him, she recited a few strophes of the poem of Jayadeva, in order to appease the gods.

"Krishna, my soul is full of you, you whose enchanted pipe modulates chords that divinizes again the nectar of your tremulous lips. Serpents of fire dangle from your ears, and your eyes launch the fire of desire. Your hair is crowned with peacock plumes, which show their multicolored moons; your mantle is like the curtain of the azure vault, attached by the rainbow, and your mouth resembles the flower of the Bandhujiva, which swells under the kisses of virgins. Your forehead causes a stainless moonstone to scintillate, and on your breast the olivine quivers, which has the form of the macar fish on the banner of amour.

"O Krishna, my feeble mind enumerates all your graces, and although sympathetic to your injury, strives to forget and to hope! How could it be otherwise, since it cannot be detached, and has put into you all its fever of sensuality? Oh, launch its benefits upon me, as a husband launches his semen!"

Having chewed a few betel leaves, Achilgar responded with another strophe from the *Gita Govinda*, or Cowherd's Song.

"Forgive me, I shall not cause you such pain again! Only grant me a sigh, O vehement Rhada, or I shall succumb to my remorse! Do not see in me the insensible Mahesa! A garland of water-lilies

---

Linnaeus gave to it, hippomane—previously used in the present text—had previously been used in ancient Greek sources to refer to a different plant, but that was not a tree. The description implies that the tree that the author has in mind is the legendary Upas tree, *Antiaris toxicaria*, whose range includes parts of India.

ornaments my loins with its tangled clusters; the blue petals of the woodland lotus descend lower, and do not figure the somber patch of poison that Shiva swallowed! My limbs are rubbed with sandalwood powder and funereal ashes!

"O Krishna, do not bend your bow, conqueror of the world. My heart is already pierced by the arrows unleashed by Radha's eyes, black and cleft like those of the antelope. Although I have not yet enjoyed her presence; the darts of her eyes, the bows of her eyebrows, the bonds of her lips, have wounded me adorably. Armed by Ananga, the god of desire, she marches to the conquest of the universe, and I think of nothing but her embrace, of the odorous lotus of her mouth, and the pepper of her tongue, as red as the Bimba berry . . ."

The young man put a burning expression into the recitation of the Hindu poem, and, on hearing that amorous plaint, her senses became more imperiously ardent.

Having knotted his arms around Viamalah's flexible body, he covered her face with mad kisses. Then he stepped back in order to see her better. He took hold of her again, caressed her, and moved away again, with light triumphant laughter, wanting to prolong his pleasure. But as she closed her eyes already swooning, he became anxious.

"Oh! You aren't going to sleep again! I don't want you to sleep! I don't want it!"

And, his anger suddenly returning, he shook her.

"What's the matter with you?" she asked, in the voice of a little child being scolded.

"Come!"

He stood her up, took her by the hand, and dragged her through the flowery bushes at a mad run, under the mango trees, the cardamoms and the magnolias, which let their white petals fall upon them.

From time to time, he stopped, glad to see, in the quivering of her breast, that she was really alive, and, taking advantage of those abrupt halts, he made her necklaces of kisses, stringing the gems of his desire along her arms and her legs, and slid precious clusters into all the delectable coverts of her body, covering her like an idol with a network of fire, lingering in the secret nest of her young beauty . . . and she fainted again.

With one bound he came to his feet, and started to run, pulling her after him in spite of her plaints.

"Ah, there are the pitris again, the accursed incubi disputing your body with me. Let's chase them away! Look, can't you see them? They're forming a whirlwind hovering above us . . . they're rising up, hesitating, disappearing in the bamboo!"

"Mercy!"

Her heart beating in great sonorous thumps, she let herself fall in the flowers, and he recommenced collecting kisses from her like a bee collecting pollen from a great corolla, until the moment when her lips remained inert beneath his own.

He was exhausted by that game, and feared no longer being able to make her his profoundly. While his beloved's breast was heaving tumultuously, he threw himself upon her and embraced her—but Viamalah's flesh suddenly froze, her knees came together, and no effort could triumph over her cataleptic rigidity.

Then, lying on the virgin's inanimate body, the young man wept for a long time, in bewilderment and despair, kneading that insensible flesh with his fingernails, biting in rage the heavy black hair whose balms mingled with his tears.

XVII
By Incubi and Succubi

After that crisis, Achilgar resigned himself to not seeing in his wife anything but a mystical being of grace and splendor, a spiritual beauty inaccessible to human caresses.

He adored her fearfully, and found, even so, a bitter sensuality in living with her, in respiring her perfume, in putting his lips on jewels that she had just taken off and in the still-warm folds of her garments.

Once again she belonged, body and soul, to the yogi charmer whose memory haunted her. He had taken up residence within her, inciting her to strange follies, breathing culpable thoughts into her, on which she dared not linger, while regretting the ineffable joys that she had savored in dream.

If it is true that incubi and succubi are spirits intermediate between demons and humans, astral forms that obey yogis and do the work of the flesh in their stead, without deflowering virgins, Viamalah was certainly possessed.

Conscious at times, she reflected on those things, and shivered in thinking that, according to certain beliefs, the role of incubi and succubi was also attributed to Parsis evoked from the Tower of Silence, and that while she slept she had felt the breath of charnel-houses on her lips.

She knew that at a point advanced into the Indian Ocean, a hundred feet above Bombay, towers receive the cadavers of Parsis, fire-worshipers of the Zoroastrian religion whose sacred book is the *Zend Avesta*. Those towers are pierced at a single point for the introduction of bodies. Three compartments in the interior receive men, women and children—or, at least, what remains of them after the vultures' repast. The latter, always hungry, stretch out their goiterous necks and spread their somber wings above the sinister edifice, awaiting new prey.

In an hour, the cadavers are torn apart, stripped and scraped and their bones thrown into the interior shaft of the tower; but the souls of the Parsis, according to Hindu belief, undergo eternal tortures, and come back to visit the living until the day when they succeed in being reincarnated. Fire, earth and water, which are venerated by the Mazdaists, unite to chastise those criminal souls, and their bodies, abandoned to the birds of prey, seem even so to transmit funereal desires to them. To the demonic aspect of that possession is added the even more disquieting aspect of vampirism.

But Viamalah did not linger over those frightful suppositions, preferring to believe that she was under the influence of a powerful suggestion that came to her entirely from the will of Nassudamy. By means of black magic, in order to avenge himself on her or those close to her, he was imposing these ordeals upon her. Perhaps he also loved her in his manner, and was seeking to slake his strange passion without violating the vow of chastity by immediate contact with a woman.

Achilgar, seeing her pensive, asked: "What is troubling you, dear Smile?" but she dared not respond, bowing her head or, more affectionately, kissing his hands.

Her little confidantes resolved to make certain fumigations, and to wear prayers to Krishna written on the skin of dholes— wild dogs—in amulets. Glory of the Moon, who had domesticated a flying squirrel, wanted to sacrifice it to Shiva.

"What's the point?" sighed the young woman. "Keep your little flying friend; I sense that everything you attempt will be futile. Abandon me! Kill me, and let my beloved spouse be happy with someone else."

However, Celestial Perfume and Honeycomb collected datura and henbane leaves in the street, which they dried and burned in honor of the maleficent pitris. They remained prostrate for three hours and exhausted themselves in passionate objurgations. Finally, a benevolent Brahmin immolated a he-goat, after having whispered precise recommendations in its ear.

But appeasement did not come.

Viamalah studied the sacred books of the Brahmins, and learned to know the mysteries of sexual love: why that passion is only truly durable between two unequal natures, two opposite characters; why, in amour, as in all fêtes agreeable to the gods, a sacrificer and a victim are required; and why the most vehement passions are those that can never be satisfied.

Glory of the Moon sometimes read a chapter from the Baghavata Purana in a delicate voice like the cooing of a dove, and they were the favorite passages, incitements to sensuality:

Under the guidance of the Govinda commenced the amorous games celebrated with him by the enamored women, as brilliant as metallic flies.

*The round of Rasa, embellished by the presence of the gopis, was
led by Krishna, who, using his magic power and placing himself
between them, multiplied himself, holding them embraced, and each
woman believed that he penetrated her irresistibly.*

*Then a rain of jasmine fell from the sky and the couples fainted in
the flowers, while the rings of feet, amulets and the studs of precious
stones produced a confused noise.*

*New gopis demanded the kiss. They struck the ground impatiently,
snapping their waists and making their breasts leap like nacreous
shells lifted up by a squall.*

*One of them respired the sandalwood perfume from the Master's
hair and licked the sweat from his brow with the tip of her tongue*

*Another, seizing the lover's propitious hand, initiated him into
the secrets of her delicate body.*

Another already found pleasure in the friction of his knee.

*And all of them, their ears ornamented with pink campanulas
and their mouth redder than perfumed pepper, arched their bodies
with desire amid the buzz of alarmed bees . . .*

Viamalah was inflamed by these lascivious readings, and every
night was an exhausting orgy of dreams for her.

Certain chapters of the sacred books also regulate the question
of precedence between the sexes. They prove that, the natural
force of the woman being the force of inertia or resistance, she
only has to refuse herself adroitly to vanquish all difficulties and
hold the heart of a man in slavery; but that, on the contrary, she
ought to do nothing, or have any ambition, that demands a kind
of masculine audacity, nature only having given her a little of the
muscular force necessary for the struggle and a ridiculously thin
voice that cannot make itself heard in the midst of the tumult.

*The woman who aspires to the functions of the other sex must
inevitably lose the prerogatives of her own,* affirms the Baghavata
Purana, in order to curb the ambition of beauties.

Alas, all that did not tell Viamalah why a demonic incubus
was possessing her against her will.

He came every night, and she felt his presence in the tumultuous movements of her heart. At first there was something like a very soft music of the vina and macabou flute, a trickle of infantile notes, like pearls tumbling down a crystal stairway, but coming from a distant echo; then a gust of perfumed air drowned her face like the falling petals of wild flowers, and a strange sadness ran through her limbs. It seemed to her that a thin cloud of blonde smoke glided toward her; her eyes closed invincibly, while hard, cold lips drilled into hers, and an intense and profound caress penetrated her, effacing all terrestrial sensualities.

She died and was reborn twenty times in one night, and her cloudy eyes and languid poses, when she awoke, frightened Achilgar.

"What's the matter, dear Smile?"

She was troubled, bowed her head and avoided meeting his gaze. Then he drew nearer wanting to take her hands, but she pushed him away.

"Are you in pain?"

"No."

"Tell me what's disturbing you."

"I can't. Don't interrogate me, and if you have any affection for me, let me leave. I'm not worthy to live in your house, for evil spirits have entered in my wake."

"We'll expel them."

"They're more powerful than you."

"No, for love triumphs over all the forces of the world."

She huddled against his heart, weeping, and said to him: "You're right; keep me, protect me! If you knew what I experience! But you'll never know, and I'll cut out my tongue rather than confess those things!"

The day went by without notable incidents. Achilgar, indulgent and tender, tried to distract his beloved, his sick child, by means of a thousand puerile games, and the little confidantes sang or danced with the frivolous grace of their age.

Everything went well until the hour of dreams, which brought back the specter of amour, the passionate, insatiable, irresistible vampire whose caresses corroded the nerves, emptied the arteries and marrow, and pumped life from its very source. The vagabond spirit, the astral body of Nassudamy, possessed the soul and the abandoned body of Viamalah then, recklessly.

PART THREE

I
Ourvasi Returns

"What do you want?"

"Nothing but your kiss."

"No."

"Why refuse me? I'm not threatening; you can see that I'm very humble and very docile."

"I have, however, forbidden you to enter my dwelling."

"Yes, I know—but my amour has been stronger than my pride."

Ourvasi, the celebrated courtesan, the seller of pleasures, is requesting that she be given a little pleasure in her turn. She has been caught like an innocent by the cajoling voice and proud beauty of Achilgar, and she thinks incessantly about the exquisite hours of his presence.

For ten days she has been prowling around the palace, waiting for a favorable opportunity, for she thinks that her lover will be defenseless against the memory of the excessive sensualities that she lavished upon him.

"I've come because you're alone. Viamalah and her little servants have gone to the temple of Durga, who destroys enchantments and curses."

"What enchantments? What curses?"

"Oh, don't try to deny it. You have never been your wife's husband, and by loving me you wouldn't even be betraying her."

"That's possible, but I only have affection for her."

Ourvasi has knelt down and put her brown head with the long caressant eyes on the young man's knees, and her feline lips, drawn back, allow a glimpse of the flash of pointed teeth, in need of kisses or bites.

"I love you . . ."

"What does it matter to me?"

"I'm beautiful . . ."

"Others will tell you that."

"It's you that I want, because you reject me. Until now, no man has insulted me thus, but that insult, coming from you, I forgive."

"It isn't an insult."

"Yes it is, but I adore you."

She has taken Achilgar's hands, and her burning mouth devours the palms with avid kisses. The short curly tresses of her hair recall the sacrifice she made, not long ago, in order to retain him. Those caresses, however, importune the young man, whose heart, too full of another, is closed to pity.

"Oh, leave me alone." And for the second time, he murmurs, with ennui: "No."

Ourvasi tries all the subterfuges that she knows in order to bring him to desire. She wraps herself in the crimson gauze of her dupatta, causes her jewels to click and glitter, uncovers one by one the florid corners of her brown flesh, palpitates, leans back and stretches, appeals to him by languorous plaints, seizes him, grips him, caresses him and strikes him, sometimes serpentine, sometimes a tigress. Her throat sobs and utters passionate cries; she prays and blasphemes, demands and triumphs . . .

But Achilgar has got a grip on himself again, and while she remains swooned in the disorder on the cushions, he draws away from her scornfully.

"Get out!"

She remains immobile, pretending not to have heard him, and he repeats, more brutally: "Get out."

"You're expelling me?"

"I'm ordering you to go."

"What! After what I've given you?"

"What you've given me . . . ? Here, we're quits."

He has taken clasps and cameos of great value from a cup and holds them out to her with a disdainful gesture.

"Keep your presents. What I offered you can't be paid for, because I haven't only made you the gift of my body and my desire; it's also my virgin heart that I've put beneath your feet. Nothing that you possess is precious enough to compensate such a treasure. Whatever you attempt, it's still me who will have given you alms."

"So be it; I won't argue, and I admit my unworthiness."

Quivering, Ourvasi still attempted to doubt, in no hurry to leave. Then he turned his back on her.

"Achilgar," she said, "I will strike you and I will avenge myself. I will avenge myself cruelly, and all weapons will be good for me!"

She lifted the curtain that separated her from the terrace and went away, mad with rage, her eyes full of tears.

II
Benares by Night

Night was beginning to fall. The corollas, heavier now, exhaled their soul of perfume, and large nocturnal moths, reminiscent of green and pink bats, agitated their plush wings feverishly. On the threshold of the garden, Ourvasi met Viamalah, who was coming back from the temple, leaning on Glory of the Moon.

"Who are you?" asked the young woman, with surprise. "And what are you doing in my house?"

The courtesan prostrated herself and replied, with assurance: "I was looking for you."

"What do you want from me?"

"A little attention and benevolence, in exchange for good advice."

"What is that advice?"

"Don't tempt the gods."

"What do you mean?"

"Don't return to the temple to implore the divinities that are contrary to you."

"How do you know that?"

"I know the secrets of stones and plants. The signs of destiny are revealed to me, and every night I consult the stars. Your entire life is written on high."

"You could tell me the future, then?"

"Yes."

"What is it?"

"Come to my house tomorrow; I will kill a goat-kid in your honor, and you will know what you want to know."

Ourvasi gave her directions to her dwelling and took a few steps, in haste to put her plans into execution, but Viamalah retained her.

"One more word. You affirm that you are not the envoy of Nassudamy, the yogi of the temple of Durga?"

"I affirm that to you. Nassudamy is the rival of both of us, for he has commerce with the maleficent pitris and his science has turned toward evil."

"Adieu, then. I shall see you tomorrow, as you ask. Until then, I shall pray to Kama, the god of amour, with Celestial Perfume, who is in his good graces, and takes him the dying flowers from my couch every morning."

Ourvasi drew away rapidly. The cries of merchants of curcuma and pâtés of mahua had ceased. Only the sellers of sensuality were crowding the streets, their hips free under metal belts with glaucous cabochons, their eyelids burned by make-up and late nights. Like nocturnal birds they went along, hugging the walls, pursued by large monkeys whose almost-human faces were grimacing.

"It's Ourvasi," said one of them. "Ourvasi, can't you take me home with you? You have no gallant, and we can make one another confidences."

"I can do that too," cried a thin girl who made ivory amulets rattle over her flat chest. "The Palomen have revealed their voluptuous secrets to me, which I can teach you . . ."

"You're boasting; only Hanuman, the god of monkeys, can have coveted you."

The child started to laugh, showing the sharp teeth of a kitten. "Hanuman wouldn't displease me; it's said that he has no peer for initiating virgins."

There was a burst of hilarity.

"In that case, Titimini, he'll arrive too late!"

"Who can do more can do less. I'm not demanding, and I go half way along the road . . ."

"Is it the sun of amour that has consumed you, Titimini?"

"The sun and the moon! Admit it, at my age it's quite glorious, Anyway, my first lover was the stone god."

"The devadasi witnessed the sacrifice?"

"Exactly, and I showed exceptional courage. This is a commemorative fetish that Lotus Heart, the sacred dancer who assists young neophytes, gave me."

The child chose from among the amulets that covered her breast a lingam crudely carved in an Oxus ruby with dark transparencies.

"The sacred natis has done things well; we know that you've been a good pupil."

"Yes, a pupil such as is rarely seen, for I've been going back for a month, and have linked myself in amity with Schahabalu, who is scarcely older than me."

Interested, Ourvasi took the little girl by the hand. "Take me to the temple."

But Titimini frowned. "No, not this evening; I'm tired, and I'd prefer to spend the night with you."

"We'll go home afterwards when Lotus Heart has informed me about something very important to me."

"Oh, that's different," said the child. "Come on, then. We'll be allowed to enter without difficulty. Do you have any essence of Gazipur roses? I offer it to the devadasi when I go to see them."

"I don't have any essence, but my necklace of Tibetan sapphires will please them, I hope."

"Good luck!" shouted the courtesans, resuming their indolent march alongside low houses with wooden galleries, through the tortuous and somber streets, propitious for gallant encounters.

III
Titimini and Schahabalu

The temple was silent. They traversed the lateral galleries and went around the sanctuary. Above the bas-reliefs, carved in the red marble, the divinities seemed to be rising up tumultuously to prevent them from penetrating any further. Often, a single statue charged with several attributes evoked a complex being endowed with multiple powers. There were idols with four arms, and the head of a goat or a terrifying elephant. Bats entered through the windows, and the green eyes of two enormous owls shone in an abandoned niche.

They went down several steps, and took a secret passage that the Brahmins used in order to go to the devadasi when their desires were particularly ardent. Against the walls, glittering with shiny dots, an infinity of fantastic beasts stuck out their claws and opened sightless eyes. Serpents had feet, bulls had wings, gigantic fish with human faces stood up on their tails, makna elephants raised their flower-crowned trunks, wolves labored with gazelles, tigresses caressed onagers, and the heads of nagas emerged from all the corners, darting their forked tongues.

They were the strange creations of delirious brains, nightmares of opium with obscene or frightening fantasies. Paws, skulls and mutilated trunks lay everywhere, hindering the march, and the two courtesans, jostling one another in the long tunnel, arrived with difficulty at a low door. Titimini uttered a kind of prolonged mewl, and the devadasi came to open up.

"Is it for the stone god?" asked Lotus Heart, who was guarding the entrance.

"No, I have no more need of it. Don't you recognize me?" said the child, laughing.

"Titimini!"

"I've brought one of our best natis, who wants to ask you something."

Ourvasi unhooked her sapphire necklace and offered it to the sacred dancer, who kissed her between the breasts to thank her.

"Speak, what do you want?"

"It's quite simple; I want to see Nassudamy; I know that he's attached to the temple."

"Nassudamy is praying. Since the feast of the goddess Kali he doesn't want to see anyone."

"Tell him that I've come on the part of Viamalah; he won't refuse to receive me."

"All right. Wait a moment."

When Lotus Heart had disappeared, Schahabalu, who was lying in wait behind a pillar, threw herself on Titimini, arching her back and spitting like an angry cat. Then the two girls rolled around like felines, scratching and biting one another gently, everywhere that their greedy mouths could reach. The others made a circle around them, exciting them with voices and gestures.

"Courage, Titimini!"

"Well parried, Schahabalu."

"Oh, she slithers like a snake."

"She's won this time!"

Tousled and breathless, Titimini got up again and drank a full glass of sugared and spiced wine in order to recuperate.

"Shall I tell you a funny story about something that happened to me the other day."

"Yes, yes, tell!"

"Two Chinese, who wanted me, stopped me in the street and, as they seemed amiable and well off, I asked them to follow me to a sugar house in order to question them at my ease. There I had curcuma and ginger cakes washed down with a little cinnamon bark and pink lotus wine, enjoying myself the while. My baboons took liberties, thinking they were sure of triumph."

"They had a right to be."

"Then, to amuse myself a little, I got up, simpering, and made them a few small caresses, and then, gently—very gently—while they were rolling their charmed eyes, I attached their long pigtails to a side-table laden with creams, syrups and fruit jellies. They didn't suspect a thing, putting their arms around my waist, drawing me toward them and making gallant proposals. I detached myself and, striking my most lascivious poses, I mimed the best scenes from the Kama Sutra. They were exultant, stamping their feet, begging me to choose between them, for those singular men don't like sharing. Then I took the tuberose from my belt and threw it at their feet. They dropped on to all fours; the shelves with the syrups rocked, and . . . oh, I'm still laughing at it! If you'd seen them in the jam!"

<h1 style="text-align:center">IV</h1>

Incantations and Black Magic

"Ourvasi," said Lotus Heart, who had just come back, "Nassudamy is waiting for you."

The courtesan resumed the route that she had already traveled, and, guided by the devadasi, penetrated the presence of the yogi, who, lost in his practice of bhakti—prayer—did not hear her.

In a redoubt vaguely lit by a jade lamp, Nassudamy was prostrate before a statue of Shiva crowned with the seven heads of the sacred reptile, whose emerald eyes were glittering strangely. He was burning sticks of incense and coconut oil in red clay lachrymatories.

The courtesan clicked her ankle-rings to attract his attention.

"What do you want with me?" he asked, finally. "And who are you?"

"I am Ourvasi, and I want vengeance."

"A lover who has left you?"

"An enemy of mine and yours."

"I have no enemies."

"Yes—Viamalah's husband."

Nassudamy shivered, and his features took on a grim expression. However, he continued in a calm voice: "Achilgar hasn't done me any harm."

"He's an obstacle to the accomplishment of your projects."

"I have no projects."

The courtesan started to laugh. "Why pretend with me, since I tell you that I know everything, and that I'm ready to serve you. Doubtless you've already tried suggestion for the wife and bewitchment for the husband. They haven't accomplished the work of the flesh, but they love one another, and your science can do nothing against the sincerity of their tenderness. The suffering you're inflicting on Viamalah hasn't rendered you master of her sentiments, and although you govern her actions and her thoughts, her heart remains entirely the beloved's."

"The heart is nothing, the soul is everything. The soul, under my influence, escapes the body and assumes the astral appearance, under which it belongs to the superior powers."

"It's true nonetheless that terrestrial amour still looms up between that woman and you, and that she's invincibly submissive to matter. I've come to offer to liberate her."

"How?"

"By killing Achilgar."

"Vishnu doesn't want him to be killed."

"Shiva will absolve you, and it's him you serve particularly."

The young man closed his eyes, letting evil thoughts come to him, which crowded like wasps upon the honey of his tenderness.

Sure of victory, Ourvasi waited, and her fleshy lips curled back slightly in a rictus that was habitual to her.

"Think," she said, "of the joy that the entire possession of Viamalah will give you—how strong the two of you will be, and how avidly the crowd will listen to your words."

"Yes," murmured the young man. "I wanted to take her to the countries where the powerful trees intermingle their branches like lovers thirsty for caresses, overflowing with sap that changes into perfumed gums and exquisite fruits . . ."

"And also into poisons. The palomen know all the secrets of the mountains and the forests. Soran kills without leaving traces."

"What are you saying? Don't tempt me."

"There's also the datura that one smokes delightedly, and which puts one to sleep while soothing the imagination with the sweetest dreams. Give me the herbs that cause death, Nassudamy."

"No."

"Who will know? Like you, I have every interest in remaining silent."

"Oh, I have no fear of the justice of men."

"So? You know full well that the gods are for you. What does one existence more matter? Don't you sacrifice thousands of the faithful at the festivals of Kali?"

"They're voluntary victims."

"No, since they're acting under the influence of suggestion. In any case, those hecatombs only serve your cause temporarily, whereas the disappearance of Achilgar will ensure you a durable triumph."

"Viamalah would certainly be ours, and through her, we'd accomplish great things."

"You see!"

"Go away for a while; I'll interrogate the pitris, and perhaps they'll deign to manifest themselves in an astral form."

Ourvasi lifted the curtain that separated Nassudamy's cell from the secret passage, and hid herself in the shadows.

The fakir had thrown dried plants into the red clay lachrymatory, but the fire was extinct. Without relighting it, he prostrated himself, touched the ground with his forehead and murmured mysterious words.

Immediately, a very soft sound escaped from the vase, something like the rustling of reeds agitated by the breeze, and a crystalline note similar to the amorous lament of a toad became audible at regular intervals. The recipient, still isolated from the yogi, began to oscillate, drawing gradually nearer, and the vibrations became sharper and more rapid.

Nassudamy pronounced a few words in the language of the gods, Sanskrit, of which the pitris are particularly fond.

It was the 243rd sloca of the fourth book of Manu.[1]

Darmapradanam pouroucham tapasa hata kilvisam . . . Parolo kam nayaty açou basouantam Kaçartrinam.

Which means: "The man whose actions all have virtue as a goal, and whose sins have all been effaced by pious acts and sacrifices, will reach the celestial abode, radiant with light and clad in a spiritual form."

Immediately, the green stems emerged from the vase, grew, produced fresh leaves of an infinite delicacy, and blossomed in glorious flowers like a vegetal firework. An exquisite perfume of jasmine and tuberose spread through the room and came voluptuously to caress the nostrils of Ourvasi, who was still standing in the darkness.

"Master," she said, "the spirits have come."

But he did not reply; he traced a circle on the ground with a red liquid that might have been blood, and drew away as far as possible.

He seemed exhausted; drops of sweat were trickling from his forehead, and a feverish tremor was shaking his hands.

Suddenly, Ourvasi became agitated.

"I'm scared!" she cried. "Spare me! Don't attract the wrath of the shadows to me! I can see vague forms coming toward me . . ."

"If you're afraid, go away," said Nassudamy, in a changed voice. "This is the moment of mystery. Above all, don't speak again."

The flowers leaned over on their stems and their corollas withered slowly. The petals, becoming detached, flew away and

---

1 The "slocas" of the Book of Manu are cited in numerous texts by the French occulist and travel writer Louis Jacolliot, including *Voyage au pays des fakirs charmeurs* [Voyage to the Land of Fakir Snake-Charmers] (1881), from which other details in the text are also taken.

disappeared. Then a green flame rose up to a great height, so brilliant that the fakir closed his eyes.

Now, singular calices, similar to gigantic and smoky lily cotyledons, monstrous vaporous flowers with a luminous pistil and stamens, were swaying above the vase.

"Astral forms of distant souls, whom I venerate, perfect androgynes of the universal power that elaborates and renews the luminous secret of the universe, essences of the abyss, potential generator doubles, waters that fecundate the divine breath, reveal to me the arcana of the future!"

"I'm scared," sobbed Ourvasi, again.

"Woman," breathed the fakir, angrily, "may the pitris annihilate you if you trouble their sublime manifestation again!" And he continued, solemnly: "O you who know the beyond of life, what should I do? Is it necessary, to serve my holy cause before the gods to become criminal before men?"

The smoky forms swayed more actively, and confused voices rose up that Nassudamy seemed to comprehend.

"Is it necessary to kill?" he asked, again.

New sounds, alternatively muted and shrill, became audible, and then the vapors disappeared, while the yogi collapsed in ardent adoration.

After a moment, he got up again, and lifted the curtain. "You can come in again," he said to Ourvasi.

The courtesan was trembling in every limb. "Doubtless I've acted badly and the pitris are against me?"

"No, they approve, and I shall satisfy your desire."

"Oh!" she said, joyfully. "Do you have the poison?"

"Yesterday, I mixed the bitter narcotic sap of henbane and hemlock with the caustic milk of the tithymalus. I have extracts of *Aconitum lycoctonum* and mandrake."

"Give . . . give . . ."

"But this is a sovereign plant that I will not name to you."

"Is it not the datura? What does it matter, anyway? I'll offer it to Viamalah, assuring her that it destroys evil spells and bewitchments."

"But explain to her carefully that these leaves must be smoked slowly in this gourgouri enriched with peridots and chryosberyls, gems agreeable to the pitris. Achilgar will go to sleep quietly, without feeling any pain."

The fakir gave the precious pipe to Ourvasi, with a dried plant, from the ruddy leaves of which a slight perfume of bitter almond still spread.

"Thank you, Master," said the young woman, kissing the end of the scarf that wound around Nassudamy's loins. "You can count on me, until death!"

V

The Heart Pierced by Thorns

Outside, she breathed deeply, filling her lungs, wondering whether she had not had a bad dream. But the maleficent plant and the gourgouri of precious stones were there to convince her of her complete lucidity.

The shadows of the night were beginning to dissipate and almost all the prostitutes had gone home. Only the most wretched were still wandering, rattling the silver rings on their ankles in a more feverish stride.

Having returned home, Ourvasi spent the morning hiding the licentious images that ornamented the walls and setting up a kind of altar, near to which she disposed cassolettes of perfumes, as well as the heart of a kid, the blood of which she had collected. Her servant received the order only to allow in the visitor she was expecting, whatever names and qualities were given.

When the young woman finally presented herself, the courtesan was beginning to despair. She helped Viamalah take off the veil that covered her from top to toe and showed her the altar on which a statuette of the god Kama stood.

"We were waiting for you."

"You've prepared the philter?"

"Yes, you'll be satisfied, for you'll have the joy of receiving and giving other than in a dream. These are mahua flowers and rice grains, which it's necessary to dispose of in accordance with the rites; I shall offer the blood of the victim, mixed with the juices of henbane, belladonna and black poppy."

"You swear to me to defeat the evil spirits?"

"I swear it to you."

"Without danger for the one I love?"

"Without danger."

"Give it to me quickly, then."

"One moment. It's necessary, first, to accomplish the customary ceremony."

Ourvasi played her role conscientiously, not wanting to leave anything to chance in order to strike the young woman's imagination. She picked up the heart, withdrew the long thorns with which it was pierced, and, raising it above her head, started to dance around Kama, calling him the sweetest names, while red tears trickled in her hair.

"Little god of lust . . . tresses of the sun and diadem of stars . . . you who preside over everything that makes great down here, you who penetrate and retain, fecundate and vivify, deign to smile upon us!"

She put an ardent ember on the heart, which crackled, and seemed to utter an amorous plaint.

"Now, Comet Flower, the charm is broken, and you can return to your husband. Here are the enchanted leaves that you will make Achilgar smoke, and he will possess you for life. That's all."

Viamalah slipped the pipe and the maleficent plant into her bosom, and asked the courtesan what she owed her.

"Nothing," said Ourvasi, with a smile. "Should women not assist one another?"

VI

Viamalah Refuses to Tempt the Gods

"So, Comet Flower, this remedy is sovereign?"

Curiously, Glory of the Moon, Honeycomb and Celestial Perfume examined the peridot gourgouri and the russet leaves with the scent of bitter almond that Viamalah had just set before them.

"One thing is tormenting me. What reason could that woman, whom I don't know, have for being interested in me?"

"What reason could she have for doing you harm?"

"I don't know. Might she not be one of those accursed natis who protect the yogi?"

"Since you went to her house, you ought to know what you're dealing with. The natis don't leave the temple."

"And then," said Celestial Perfume, "a devadasi wouldn't dare to risk the anger of Kama."

"Perhaps Kama is against us—that god is so capricious."

The little servants shivered. "Don't accuse him! He's the sole benefactor of women."

"He's also their torturer, and doesn't deprive himself of sacrificing us to his pleasure."

"O Kama, forgive her!" sobbed Celestial Perfume, fearfully. "She accuses you, but she has no intention of offending you. Only lovesickness—your sickness—makes her speak thus. Smile upon her and all will be forgotten."

"You'll see," said Glory of the Moon. "It's necessary to try the charm this evening."

"Yes," said Honeycomb, supportively. "We'll hide behind a curtain, as on your wedding night, and lend you assistance if necessary."

Viamalah reflected, torn between her desire and baleful presentiments. Since everything had failed thus far, it was scarcely probable that this remedy would have any more success than the others. Why should that unknown woman be able to succeed where so many famous oracles and pythonesses had failed?

"What are you risking?" asked Glory of the Moon, again. "Achilgar will smoke these marvelous leaves, and won't die of it."

"On the contrary!" proclaimed Honeycomb, in a burst of laughter.

"They must have a delicious taste."

"Yes, this parcel on my tongue is making me think of the intoxicating delights of homa."

"It seems to me that desires are already igniting within me."

"I can hear a sound of kisses!"

"Don't you want to let me smoke a little leaf? Only a very small one?"

"No," said Viamalah, "not even a tip of a root. You're crazy enough without that."

"Go find Achilgar, then . . ."

"And we'll watch . . ."

But Viamalah put the mysterious plant and the gourgouri in a little ivory casket.

"Perhaps that woman was telling the truth, and only has good sentiments for me; perhaps, on the contrary, she's serving Nassudamy's cause, and her helpful intervention is only a wicked game. At any rate, I don't want to use such means to destroy the bewitchment that weighs upon me and upon Achilgar. Time will doubtless appease the anger of the gods."

"Time won't appease anything, and the pitris will possess you more and more."

"Alas," sighed Viamalah, "I sense the same strange disturbance every night; an occult presence manifests itself."

"And you're subjected to the odious kiss of vampires of amour!"

"It seems to me that my life is escaping through the secret wound in my heart; I open my arms in the void."

"And you give yourself to the daityas of the air and the raksha-sas of the dream, without profit for anyone, for the shadows don't count. Why, you're just an egotist!"

VII
The Mysterious Lovers

Viamalah's torments were further augmented. She no longer obtained any pleasure from bathing in the great porphyry basin watered by the eight elephant trunks gemmed with rubies. However, Honeycomb attached, with the same delicate care, three golden stars on her breasts and her lap, and sometimes shook powdered Tibetan sapphires into her hair, and sometimes powdered Oxus garnets, depending on the weather, for it is necessary for the beauty of women to submit to the caprices of the sky. The servants still collected the flowers from her couch in order to offer them to Kama, but they were so mutilated by the feverish dreams that the little god doubtless did not care about them. Very weary, the young woman lay down for long hours, and her lovely friends exhausted themselves searching for new amusements.

Honeycomb, clad in a dupatta florid with golden calices, played the most stimulating pieces, and Glory of the Moon, indefatigably, marked the measure on the tal and the malatan. They ventured all attitudes and all advice, without ever triumphing over the melancholy of their young mistress.

Sometimes, Achilgar witnessed these frolics, and Viamalah, who could not offer him the ardent cup of her flesh, begged him generously to take another woman.

"I'll resign myself," she said, weeping, "to being no more for you than a friend. Since the joy of belonging to you is refused to me, I don't want you to suffer any more for me. Honeycomb or Glory of the Moon would be happy and proud to replace me. Choose between them . . . unless you prefer Celestial Perfume, who cares so nicely for her little god Kama."

But Achilgar rejected consolations.

"You're not entirely mine," he replied, "and my male desire is sometimes exasperated; however, although I can't have your body,

I possess your heart, and that is a great felicity. Let us remain like this for as long as it pleases the wrath of the gods . . ."

Viamalah bore Achilgar's hand to her lips, with tenderness and gratitude. "Oh, how we'll make up for it later!"

He slid necklaces of kisses all along the adored body. He lay down on the sparkling rings of her hair. With his mouth he refreshed the feverish palms and the little feet ringed with opals. The light of the sun and the stars were like the splendor of her skin, something supernatural and adorable that only belonged to her. The polish of her fingernails contained the softness of the gems that covered her wrists and fingers, the nipples of her breasts resembled two pink seashells opening over the amber sand of her flesh.

Sometimes, they went down the Ganges in a dingui, stopping outside the city in order to adore some god lost in the bushes and long grass. Above their heads, birds of prey disputing human remains fought furious battles. On the ground there were huge vultures finishing dying, twisting their goitrous necks back and forth. Others had been dead for a long time, and nothing any longer remained of them but the debris of skeletons mingled with the ashes of pyres; others, half-eaten, seemed still to be darting phosphorescent gleams through the enlarged holes of their orbits.

Green and blue flies were circling around, as well as tiny birds like living gems, which were hopping.

Viamalah carried flowers and fruits to the idols, dragging Aschilgar a long way into paradises of verdure refreshed by some hidden spring. Behind them extended the pink plain bordered by mountains. Here and there, a coconut palm inclined on a hill of sand, and in the distance, orange rain struck by a last ray of sunlight resembled a silvery gauze scarf extended over the sky. Rumbles of thunder rolled above them, sometimes muted and sometimes vehement. In the upheaval of nature the lovers seemed to find a little relief from their own tortures; they remain silent, emotional and grave, listening to the great confused voices of nature.

Evening came, bringing a sharper ardor to the scattered perfumes. There was the incense of aromatics, the honey of herbs, the odor of the earth refreshed by the storm, the breath of plants and wilted corollas: an entire powerful bouquet that intoxicated to the point of vertigo. The verdure was drowned in the blood of the sky, soaked in an agonizing clarity. The water had nostalgic smiles, seemingly carrying the embers of some gigantic pyre.

When Viamalah and Achilgar reposed after those long walks, they had the retreat of the shady garden, where the little paths, at the slightest breath, rolled to their feet medusae of sunlight in the tresses of dwarf ferns. There were blind alleyways of verdure in which suspended lianas extended flaps of light drapery, enameled by mauve calices, from one tree to another, and through a thousand rips in the canvas, a fine dust of radiance fell.

He lay down at her feet, his forehead on her knees, or braided garlands of rare flowers that he had acquired for her. They were unfamiliar corollas, eccentric and feverish, as disquieting as excessively beautiful girls, morbidly beautiful by virtue of having blossomed. They were hairy or silky, like tentacles, as light as feathers or as curly as fleeces. A few had the hue of dead leaves and autumnal dreams of copper, blood and rust. Erect on their ambitious stems, or lost in the moss, they danced sarabands, formed crazy rounds in which all colors vibrated. Some had the ragged collarets of gamines, tapering ruffs of precious guipure, allowing a glimpse of a pale velvet, exceedingly tender heart. Others, in their white cotyledons, were reminiscent of priestesses of the sacred fire, keeping their virginal robes chastely closed. Others immodestly cast to the wind the foamy dupattas of voluptuous natis, showing their brown stamens all the way to the bottom, so open that the hand could reach into them without touching them at all. And all of them, with the voice of perfumes, sang recklessly passionate canticles that troubled the lovers of the dream, causing them to agonize with futile desire.

Then he threw his embalmed crop over her, and attempted a thousand games with the supple branches, to which she lent herself, shivering and sighing when the caresses were too direct.

Braced or indolent, she offered herself, and fainted. The vertigo of the gaze of her drowned eyes went astray in the shadow of her lashes, and her breasts flowered like lotuses, their frail gold-starred cups swelling.

When they wearied of the enervating dream that never finished, they had a meal of mangoes, bananas and rice. Sometimes, too, Glory of the Moon composed a strange salad of bamboo and curcuma with her carmined fingertips, which ran in their veins like fire.

One evening, when the young man was more feverish than usual, Viamalah summoned her little confidantes.

"Take them," she said, "I want you to be happy"—and she pushed them into Achilgar's arms.

In order not to insult them, he drank a little pink lotus wine from their fresh lips, the taste of which is so intoxicating, but he did not want to accept anything else.

VIII
The Charmer Evokes the Vampires of the Temple

Meanwhile, Nassudamy, after having spent a month in retreat, in constant communication with the pitris, believing himself to be sufficiently sustained by their occult power, resolved to reclaim Viamalah. He assigned her a rendezvous in the temple, convinced that she would not be able to escape his magnetic power. The young woman only covered half the route, however, before she was stopped by a sudden revolt.

He found her in one of the tortuous back-streets of the city, her forehead on Ourvasi's shoulder, shaken by hectic sobs.

Interested, the courtesans had formed a circle around them and were interrogating her curiously, trying to understand her trouble.

"Is it a gallant who has left you?"

"Or rather, for you're pretty, do you fear not being able to satisfy his excessively ardent desires?"

"I'll teach you the means of always triumphing. There's no enemy that a woman can't vanquish, when she knows the secrets of the struggle."

"Unless she's dealing with the stone god," interjected Titimini, swinging her frail body, semi-naked under necklaces and amulets, in a droll fashion.

"Be quiet, Titimini, you always have ludicrous thoughts in your head, and only Schahabalu, the devadasi of the temple of Durga, would be capable of competing with you on that terrain."

When the fakir appeared, the courtesans stood aside respectfully. He approached Viamalah and put a finger on her shoulder.

"Follow me," he said, softly—and without speaking, she obeyed.

He took her to the redoubt where he had meditated so much for a month before the statue of Shiva, the terrible god, the symbol of the destructive principle. According to the Puranas, Shiva "wanders the earth surrounded by a legion of demons intoxicated by carnage; he is naked, his hair sparse, and retains the ashes of funeral pyres on his body." The image represented him with three eyes and crowned with the seven naga heads.

"Prostrate yourself," said the yogi, "ask the god's pardon for having resisted him. Do you not know that it is to give him joy that men throw themselves under the wheels of his chariot, are harpooned in the ribs and oscillate at the whim of enormous iron pendulums? All succumb without a cry, in the midst of the most frightful suffering."

"I'm suffering too."

"What have you done by comparison with those martyrs?"

"I love, and I cannot be with the one I love."

"No fate is better than yours. You will not know either satiety or disgust. Love passes quickly when the senses are satisfied, and only those who remain in their desire adore eternally. Then too, why do you cherish that man? Am I not as handsome as him?"

"You are too far above me for me to be able to love you. In any case, I only give my heart once."

"Listen—I know marvelous secrets; with me you will regret nothing."

"You're cruel."

"No. I have never killed. Do you know what the Brahmins do? They respect animals, but they make oracles with the heads of children that they tear off slowly."

"That isn't possible!"

"I've witnessed those sacrifices more than once, and while the devadasi twirl madly, the sound of brass instruments covers the screams of the victims. Here, look."

In a hollow in the wall the fakir showed Viamalah the desiccated heads of children. Emerging from each mouth was a golden blade with magical characters; asphodels and vervain flourished in their orbits.

Viamalah turned away from those nightmares, horrified. Her brain was phosphorescent with astral light.

"The ground on which we're treading," said Nassudamy, then, "is made of human ashes furnished by more than twenty thousand pyres. We live here in death. These walls . . ."

"Shut up," she said. "You horrify me!"

"Why? I repeat to you that I've never killed. I've never even tasted the flesh of an animal, and I only drink water. Look again at the work of my predecessors, and compare us!"

He struck the wall with blows of a pickax; it crumbled partly, and skeletons appeared, immured in the thick walls.

"Everywhere I strike, a corpse would appear, and that brown color you see on all sides comes from spilled blood. This refuge is full of larvae that attract obscene stryges and lamias. Monstrous debauches were accomplished here. I am never alone, and temptation claws me night and day. Understand, however, that I have never succumbed."

"Then everything that is said about the terrible things that happen in the temple is true?"

"What is said is below the reality."

"Oh!"

"You've heard mention, haven't you, about the Khonds, who invoke the goddess of the earth, Tari, and immolate victims, *meriah*, to her?[1] The crowd hastens to butcher them, and in certain villages, they're burned slowly, for the red tears of their flesh fecundate the soil. Well, here, in the same way, many children are burned, whose families offer them in great pomp, their foreheads crowned with jasmine and their bodies covered in jewels. Every chief receives a finger of one of the little beings, with which he rubs the threshold of his granary, and which he then places under a stone. The ashes, the bones and the entrails are mixed with seeds in the fields."

"You've done that!"

"We've imitated the sacrifices of the temple of Djagganath. In any case, you've witnessed the festivals of the goddess Kali."

"Unconsciously, as you know full well. I was asleep, I didn't see anything."

"Pilgrims often sleep as you have slept. They're drunk on opium, have respired fuming stoves, and martyrdom only attains their anesthetized flesh."

"But those children that you burned weren't asleep?"

"No, alas. You also know, don't you, that the Khonds no longer have daughters? As soon as a daughter comes into the world they put her in an earthenware vase and bury her at a place indicated by an astrologer as haunted by evil spirits. Well, here I've seen the throats of as many as a thousand virgins cut on the altar of Shiva. The priests violate them before the lascivious dances of the devadasi, who cover their plaints with songs and

---

1 All references to the Khonds, their worship of Tari and the naming of their victims *meriah* appear to derive from *An Account of the Religion of the Khonds in Orissa* (1852) by Samuel Charles Macpherson. The account was summarized in French in *La Terre* (1872) by Elisée Reclus.

laughter. The blood flows like a red river . . . and I dare not give you other details . . ."

"Let me go! I'm stifling here!"

"Listen again, Viamalah. Although I live with the unquiet shades of victims, I repeat to you that they are favorable to me, because I have never killed. My power can magnify everything that surrounds you."

The fakir collected himself, pronounced a few words, and from everywhere, marvelous corollas sprang, a flora apotheosis of inconceivable splendor. And they were not the familiar forms of terrestrial flora but singular calices, as ardent and mobile as faces, with glaucous eyes, and tender lips open for a kiss. Stamens of light departed like rockets, radiating at great heights, sometimes seeming to emerge from a blaze of precious stones. Flowers agitated their petals like fingers, speaking to one another and caressing one another with voices softer than a canticle. There were all forms and all colors. They covered the walls, emerged from all the cracks, and rose from the ground in perfumed waves. The cold cell was a living flower-basket.

"How beautiful it is!" said Viamalah.

"You see what my amour can create! It isn't Achilgar who can offer you that magical crop."

"You're too powerful, and that's why I'm afraid."

"Do you love me?"

"No, I mustn't love you!"

That evening, he did not retain her any longer, knowing full well that she would be his completely when he wished it.

IX
Glory of the Moon's Means

Viamalah saw the charmer almost every day now. An invincible force drew her out of herself, obliged her to go to the temple, to put on the costumes of the devadasi, to submit to the enervating and dangerous suggestion that she only savored in dreams and reluctantly . . .

On returning from those ordeals, she remained dazed and weary, her eyelids swollen, her limbs fatigued.

Achilgar, however, did not suspect anything—but the little confidantes were anxious, suffering from their impotence to triumph over the evil.

"Don't you see," said Celestial Perfume, "that Viamalah is consuming herself more every day?"

"That she's frailer than a reed and more colorless than the lotuses of the sacred pool?" sighed Glory of the Moon.

"And that Achilgar does nothing!"

"In his place, I'd try something, no matter what . . . but I'd prove that I'm a man!" said Honeycomb.

"What is he doing with his desire, then?"

"He doesn't even want our consolations."

"That's very humiliating for us."

"Certainly, since Viamalah consented . . ."

"He could have initiated us into the conjugal delights that are refused to her!"

"What harm would we be doing?"

"None: we'd be ensuring the joy of the husband and calming the remorse of the wife."

"They would both have been tranquilized by us."

"And it would also have given us a little pleasure."

"On the one hand, thanks to us, terrestrial satisfactions; on the other, mystical sensualities with an inviolate wife."

Glory of the Moon shook the somber curls of her regal hair angrily, and Celestial Perfume, who was usually always laughing, put on a sulky expression in thinking about the poor wilted flowers that she offered to the little god Kama.

"It's necessary to do something," advised Honeycomb

"What?"

"By rendering the husband his . . . only reason for living."

"He's exhausted all the philters, and the oracles are disinterested in his fortune."

"There remains one means," said Glory of the Moon.

"Which one?"

"The mysterious plant that Achilgar has to smoke in the peridot gourgouri."

"It's in the ivory casket."

"Let's go and fetch it."

And while Nassudamy retained Viamalah at the temple, Glory of the Moon offered the sovereign remedy to Achilgar.

X

The Poison

In the depths of the palace, on cushions of parrot feathers and in the acrid smoke of the poisonous plant that he had just smoked, Achilgar lay, surrounded by the three confidantes. He was stirring feebly, for delirium had come with the agitations of fever. Removed from the sentiment of the present life, his troubled sight could no longer distinguish the surrounding objects. In an invincible torpor, he felt himself transported to an ardent mountain that was spitting fire, lava and blood. Sometimes, a slight tremor ran through his limbs, and his irises capsized, as if in death-throes.

Glory of the Moon, who was weeping, then brought a pinch of herbs with vehement scents to his nostrils, and a little life returned to him. But soon, his face, mortally weary and drawn, and his blue lips, revealed the progress of the poison again.

Terrified, the little servants heard his voice, which had become the sobbing voice of a child, stifled and moaning in a puerile fashion, break and die away in a sigh of anguish. He remained in a dolorous disorder, invaded by the sentiment of an irremediable physical change of his entire being; he had the sensation of an occult power that was lifting him from his couch and carrying him away toward infantile sensations.

His staring eyeballs, and his eyelids striped with brown contusions, no longer had any movement or flutter; his hands sometimes rose up in a weary gesture as if to remove a crushing weight from his chest.

"Oh, don't die!" sobbed the adolescents. "What shall we say to Viamalah, who forbade us to touch the maleficent plant?"

But the poison acted poorly.

After an hour of distress, Achilgar recovered consciousness with a great frisson of his entire body. He looked for his beloved, and asked: "Where is she?"

"She'll come—don't tell her what you've attempted."

"She doesn't know, then?"

"She certainly wouldn't have wanted it, for fear of what might happen. Oh, if we'd known . . . but you'll be cured . . . it's only a temporary malaise. How do you feel?"

Glory of the Moon, the most culpable, held the burning hands of the invalid in hers, and interrogated him with an anxious gaze.

He smiled to reassure her. "I feel better, much better . . ."

Celestial Perfume and Honeycomb were prostrate, imploring Kama:

"O god of flowers and fruits, god of butterflies and lovers, beneficent and gentle god . . . O god of joy . . . !"

Their voices trailed in a plaintive and caressant fashion, inflating or becoming lighter than a thread of spider-silk.

"God of the moon and the stars, god of moving sands and majestic mountains . . . By the hidden symbols, by the fluidic soul of the earth, by the eternal silence and the eternal harmony, by the adoration of all that surrounds you, O Master of occult forces of the world, come to our aid!"

They swayed gently, still murmuring vague incantations, and then striking their foreheads on the ground.

A cloud obscured the sky, swirling leaves entered madly through the open windows; the wind in the trees had furious sighs.

In the green-tinted daylight, amid the disorder of his cushions, Achilgar seemed increasingly languid, with hollow cheeks, a pinched nose and lips parted by hoarse breath.

No longer doubting, they curled up on the couch, uttering moans and squeals. Then a dusk descended upon them, and of all the clamors of the hurricane, the deluge and the heavens, they no longer perceived anything but the indignant plaint of their hearts.

XI
Death

Achilgar, however, was reanimated by the return of his beloved. He wanted to feel against his chest the firm roundness of her small erect breasts. Resuscitated momentarily, he paraded groping hands over her flesh; all his sufferings vanished in the passionate desire that invaded him like a final fever.

He plucked the somber flowers of her eyes, the animate corolla of her mouth, and the quivering anguish of her entire being.

The air now seemed to be full of light flakes, vagabond seeds, impalpable pollens steering toward mysterious nests of kisses. It was like a cottony flight, a warm down of turtle-doves, a glittering dust wandering in the light.

The sun descended over a blaze of topazes and rubies, apparently making its exit through a door of flame open to a sidereal furnace of unsustainable splendor. Sprays of blue light sprang from the magical conflagration, rising up in a flamboyance of hyacinth, onyx and sardonyx, while all the voices of nature swelled and burst forth, tearing apart in a formidable gasp of amour.

It was the delirious intoxication of violins sighing over the sharp chanterelle, in a fanfare of brass instruments, hectically sounding the eternal hymn of sensuality.

There was nothing astonishing in that, since the Beloved was present.

Achilgar expired on Viamalah's heart, and she did not know how that misfortune had occurred.

Green fires were lit round the couch, where the deceased, as handsome as a young god, was asleep in the ardent roses, and the mourners made the palace resound with long moans. All the relatives and friends filed past, bringing perfumes and flowers; then virgins draped in white lay down side by side and Achilgar reposed on them, warmed by the mildness of their young flesh.

Viamalah resolved, in accordance with the custom of suttee, then in its full force, to die on the liberating pyre, to join her ashes with those of the loved one, and finally to unite after death that which had been unable to mingle down here in accordance with the law of amour.

She therefore abstained from all nourishment, only chewing a little betel to sustain her. But Glory of the Moon braided her long hair every day, steeped it in essence of Ghazipur roses, and rubbed it entirely with unguents and powders, without forgetting to paint two golden stars on her breasts and to shake powdered Kurnool diamonds over her shoulders. She no longer wore any but dupattas of yellow gauze, fastened by cat's-eyes from Ceylon, for, in spite of her dolor, she had to appear faultless in order for the gift of her life to be judged more meritorious.

Impatiently, believing herself to be culpable of weakness and treason, she awaited the moment to throw herself into the arms of Agni, the god of fire, who purifies infidel hearts. She wanted to wash herself in the flames, as others wash themselves in the sacred waters of the Ganges in order to liberate themselves from their sins. Thus, her expiatory ecstasy, augmented by fasting and prayers, became a sort of mystical joy, her soul springing forth toward astral splendors.

In the Flames

Under the tents disseminated along the streets, merchants of amber and coral necklaces were selling depilatory creams, resinous balls of perfumes, cobweb veils embroidered with chimerical birds, cakes in the form of crescent moons, and syrups of flowers.

The road, paved with pink and blue cobblestones, led to the place of the pyre, the odiferous wood of which was erected in a large uncovered area. At the corners, vases full of burning aromatics stood, maintained by young women clad in glass plates and tinkling bells. Interlaced garlands of roses gave the sinister platform a festival appearance.

People came from all directions to enjoy the spectacle. Curious faces leaned over terraces between foliage hung from balustrades, and children massed in the square were striking tambourines frenetically, announcing the imminent torture in shrill voices. At the foot of the pyre, six yogis were swaying, howling incantations, while the devadasi of Durga were executing a bizarre round-dance, curling themselves up and launching forth like wild beasts, making their dark hair undulate, spinning madly, and ending up falling, breathless and bathed in sweat.

The spectators watched, awaiting the sacrifice with serenity. Young men stopped in front of shops, haggling over embroidered fabrics, caskets encrusted with nacre and ivory, cassolettes and the essences that they would offer shortly to the god of fire in honor of the illustrious victims; and little girls went through the ranks holding out their baskets filled with mangoes, banana slices and snowy pink mangousteens.

Since the death of Achilgar, Nassudamy had not quit the temple, where he was plunged in profound adorations. Warm and supple hands had caressed him in the shadows, the bodiless hands of virgins who had died in honor of Kali. Those tapering childish hands, still ornamented with precious rings and terminated by the sacred bracelet of the lingam-yoni, had traced luminous and prophetic characters in the air.

One infantile finger had written: *Through Viamalah you will know all celestial joys.*

A gilded palm, posing on the wall, had left its beneficent imprint there.

Retire with all that you possess of the most admirable to the mountain of Merou, an index finger ornamented with a marvelous ruby had written.

We will love you in the Beloved.

Thorough her you will know us.

And we will mingle our kisses with hers like roses with roses.

We will visit you by night.

It's necessary to do something for those who perished for amour.

. . . Since only amour exists!

. . . Which will flourish again in astral souls!

The characters of fire radiated in all directions, and all those hands of feverish dead girls emitted a penetrating odor of woman.

The hour of the supreme proof had come. It was apotheosis or death, the glorious reign of occult forces or the shameful fall into darkness. In order to render the pitris favorable, however, it was necessary to evoke them fervently for three days and three nights, and also to gain the protection of the Brahmins, whose collaboration was indispensable.

At any rate, the plan that the yogi had decided upon was to allow a part of the funeral ceremony to be accomplished, to set fire to the pyre, and then, when it was drowned in the swirls of smoke, which would be further thickened by the slow combustion of certain herbs, to precipitate himself into the flames, and carry Viamalah away through the midst of the Brahmins, who would close ranks around them and hide her from all gazes.

The place of the torture was not far from the temple, and the realization of the project, even without the protection of hidden powers, was not overly adventurous. The devadasi, with their frenzied dancing and cries, would occupy the attention of the spectators; and, if veritable victims were necessary, they would be found among the pilgrims, always glad to offer their lives for a holy cause.

"What do you want to do with that woman, my son?" the grand master of the temple had asked.

"I've already told you. That soul is acquired by us, and by means of it we shall accomplish miracles."

"Perhaps, if you are able to put our cause above your desire. She is young and charming; will you have the strength to vanquish yourself?"

Nassudamy had protested his devotion and had sworn to take Viamalah in his pilgrimages to the most venerated places, in order to preach the good word, and to deliver himself to mysterious practices of which he had the secret.

Sure of the support of the Brahmins, he crouched down in his cell again, murmured passionate mantras, and, by means of the internal projection of his will, gradually fell into a state of complete catalepsy.

Doubtless the pitris came to visit him and gave him the astral force to overcome all the obstacles, for he woke up full of confidence, went on foot to the pyre where he wanted to mingle the herbs of the odorous stoves with a special plant collected in a sacred forest twenty-eight miles from Benares.

But the time was approaching, and the dense crowd was giving a few signs of impatience, for the heat was humid and a suffocating dust was rising from the ground in heavy acrid clouds.

Pilgrims were presently selling prayer-wheels, amulets carved in orange cinnamon stone, moonstone or hydrophane, which only shine when wet and which are rubbed with the tip of the tongue while pronouncing vague incantations.

The great sacred monkeys of the temple had invaded the pyre and were leaping from branch to branch, inhaling the odor of the cassolettes voluptuously. A few were intoxicated by opium, like the fakirs, and they abandoned themselves to the caprices of courtesans who passed their necklaces and scarves around their necks.

When the sounds of the vina and the tal were heard, announcing the cortege, Brahmins bearing on the forehead the signs consecrated to Shiva and, around the body, the triple cordon of initiates of the priestly caste placed themselves behind the pyre, and Nassudamy, naked to the waist, with his hair attached to the top of his head by a crimson headband, stood before them.

A deployment of magnificence, perhaps even greater than those for betrothals and weddings, accompanied the last kiss of the husband and wife. The day of the sacrifice remains, in the annals of the family, the holiest and most glorious date. The young widow, in expiring on the body of the deceased, delivers him from all the pollutions of sin, assuring him eternal joys.

The lamentations of the mourners resume, punctuated by shrill tomtoms, and the sobbing notes of viols and flutes. Metal instruments ring out a relentless carillon under the percussion of hammers and sticks. Virgins appear, throwing flowers; they mingle with mourners veiled in yellow, who are walking slowly, and seem to be the disquieting apparitions of an unknown world, creatures of tenderness or malevolence.

They surround the mortuary cart, which dominates all the others. At the very edge of the platform hung with golden cloth, in the irradiation of Hindu armor, Achilgar is lying, his face uncovered. A sunburst of diamonds shines on his breast and an azure mantle sown with stars descends from his shoulders all the way to the wheels. His visage is calm; he seems to be asleep.

The Brahmins take possession of the body and lay it on the pyre, while the devadasi, in their violet simarres, fixed to their breasts and hips by precious clasps, stimulate the flaming embers by waving ostrich-feather flabella at the end of long golden reeds, with sabbatical gestures, in order to burn powders of myrrh and red sandalwood, and seeds of male incense.

The cortege accumulates in the square, but at a sufficiently great distance from the Brahmins—very numerous now—who surround the pyre with a white line. The area in front of them is free for the sacred daces and the various ceremonies that precede the sacrifice.

The eye pauses at hazard on the sumptuousness of the décor, dazzled and blinking. To begin with, there are the musicians, clad in indigo and yellow, the horses with painted legs and heavy pearl necklaces. There are the relatives and friends, mounted on elephants with saddle-cloths and howdahs encrusted with scintillating carbuncles. Grouped on platforms and carts decked with flowers is everything that Benares has of the most aristocratic and the most elegant.

There is an extraordinary crowd, a strange mixture of people, horses, elephants, armor scaled with precious stones and flamboyant embroideries: a fanfare of colors that is indescribable.

But the crowd undulates like an immense wave, and a cry goes up:

"There she is!"

On the colossal Sikh horse harnessed with silver and turquoises that she rode on her wedding day, Viamalah advances. Her favorites, Glory of the Moon, Honeycomb and Celestial Perfume are holding the edge of her long robe of blue gauze, starred with sapphires, the sparks of which patter like stardust. Two diamond lotuses retain the delicate fabric over her pale nipples, and she is covered by such a profusion of jewels that scarcely anything can be seen of her but her little dolorous mouth, her palpitating nostrils and her long hazy eyelids, which, indolently lowered, hide the strange flame of her gaze.

By her sides, in a tremor of silk, amulets, gauzes, little bells, feathers and roses, young women are carrying perfumes in curiously sculpted vases, and garlands of tuberoses and jasmines, which they will throw into the fire as the supreme homage to their beloved companion.

The spectators draw apart, and the great Sikh horse is led to the foot of the pyre by the Brahmins, who help Viamalah to descend.

XIII
The Pitris Intervene

The master of the temple exhorted the victim to the dignity of death, courage, and the joy of sacrifice.

"Through you," he said, "Achilgar will know the supreme happiness. You are proving to him that you love him enough to scorn all terrestrial wealth, and your fidelity will charm his astral soul. What would you do down here, alone? A woman ought to have only one husband, and her duty is to die for that unique amour."

He said other beautiful things, slowly and with complaisance, for it was a rare opportunity for him to make the most of himself, given the rank of the spouses and the choice audience.

Priests of lesser importance attempted to make Viamalah drink a philter and respire narcotic herbs, but she refused, feeling that she was strong enough to brave the pain.

Glory of the Moon, Honeycomb and Celestial Perfume removed her adornments in order to give them to her friends. The stars of her breasts, her diadem, her necklaces, her fastenings, her emerald clasp and her girdle of emeralds passed from hand to hand to their respective destinations. When the young woman, stripped of her gems, showed herself in the glory of her admirable nudity, only covered in blue gauze, there was a long clamor of admiration.

Without being sustained, she climbed up next to Achilgar, prostrated herself before him, and adopted lascivious attitudes designed to awaken his desires. She made her breasts and belly move in voluptuous frissons, animated her hips with a profound rocking, emphasized the dimples of her buttocks, raised her arms and swayed her entire body as if in the combat of amour.

Then, having tilted her head back until it was above a stove placed behind her, she stood up with a cry, and her incomparable hair caught fire from the ends to the roots, striping the sky like a gigantic rocket.

That was the signal for the dances. While Viamalah knelt down beside her husband, putting her lips on his, the devadasi enlaced one another in a frenzied pantomime. They made their amulets clink, mingled the erect nipples of their breasts, heightened with paint, and agitated the heavy rings of their ankles. An indefinable odor, warm and tenacious, mingled with vanilla and pepper, emanated from them, and their skin gleamed like gold under the floating gauzes. They seemed to be inebriated by opium and datura, laughing and howling, tearing off their last veils in an indecent frenzy.

"The fire! The fire!" cried the audience.

The Brahmins had, in fact, just set light to the base of the pyre, and the flames were issuing up on all sides, hiding the last kiss of Achilgar and Viamalah.

But a new cry of amazement resounded. The three little confidantes, Glory of the Moon, Honeycomb and Celestial Perfume, had leapt into the furnace with a single bound, not wanting to survive the adored master whose death they had unwittingly caused.

There was an indescribable tumult. For several minutes, nothing more could be seen. The Brahmins, however, had come together behind the pyre, and Nassudamy, carrying something in his arms, disappeared confusedly into their close-knit ranks.

XIV
The Road of Amour and Glory

Horribly burned, Viamalah suffered for long days in the depths of the temple, in the retreat of the sacred dancers. Nassudamy, constantly present, took advantage of her convalescence to initiate her into the great mysteries of the occult sciences, for he wanted, sustained by her, to travel throughout India spreading the benefits of his strange power everywhere.

"We shall go," he said, "into the lands where the trees mingle their branches like caressant arms, where the pollen of flowers is so thick that it forms an odorous cloud, where the waters flow in streams of azure and fire, where the corollas open like parasols of watered silk and velvet. And I shall astonish the world with my miracles!"

She smiled vaguely, without the strength to resist. What had happened to her was so strange that she ended up believing that it was her divine mission.

And they departed.

At first, it was an enchantment. They visited the valleys of the Himalayas, contemplated at close range the glaciers and the snows thrown like a silvery cope of magical brightness over the spine of Kanchenjunga. But no one has trodden those terrible summits of light and death, and the voyager, lost in space, an ephemeral plaything of terrestrial tempests, has before him the clearest perception of his humility.

They saw arid mountains and landscapes of unparalleled splendor. Mutely, they admired the effort of the tormented ground spitting fire, exhaling whirlwinds, rearing up in indescribable spasms. From what frightful seeds have those prodigious mountains, with nightmarish vegetation, emerged? What deluges, what thunderbolts, have violated the ingenuous calyx of the Earth in order to frame those monstrous pistils of ice or fire?

Nasudamy caused seeds to germinate in the snows solely by the imposition of his hands. In order to be agreeable to the inhabitants of a small country with which he had been satisfied, he magnetized an enemy troop, who laid down their arms without having fought, and he was adored like a god. The daily exercises of fakirs seemed child's play to him. By virtue of the prodigious gifts of Maya, he had the power to rise up from the ground and make himself invisible.

Through him, virgins knew the most dangerous sensualities without being deflowered by them. Imitating Krishna, he gave satisfaction to all the gopis who begged him for amour, by multiplying his body infinitely. Herdswomen danced the rasa around him, and then each one quit the round, and believed that she was embracing the supple body of the fakir, who possessed her for a long time, with a thousand delectable inventions, dissolving into her as a liquid mingles with water. By means of that marvelous communion, the bodies of the little lovers were adorned with the rarest gems, and when they resumed the dance, they resembled a necklace of fireflies strung out in the flowers.

All of them cherished the yogi, all of them, burning with ever renascent desires, offered him the honey of their lips, demanding the delights that he alone was able to give them. Twenty times in a single night, without wearying, he plucked the secret corollas of their flesh on the sand of the road, or led them into a caressant stream in order to make them his more gently. However many there were, each one thought that she possessed him fully. Under the glaucous water, the bodies came together in bunches or clusters, with their scintillating gems, reminiscent of the mysterious constellations of an unknown sky.

Nassudamy was the amour and the hope of virgins, for the most vivid of his caresses left them pure physically, worthy of a husband. But his greatest occult ardors went to Viamalah, the elect of his heart and his mind. As before, she sometimes felt the caress of an avid mouth on her lips, an invisible mouth, all of whose carnal sinuosities were nevertheless revealed. Two arms gripped her forcefully, and the kiss whose softness she savored penetrated more profoundly, removing all sentiment of reality. And always, on awakening, she found herself covered in flowers without a pleat of her garments having been disturbed.

Incomparably beautiful and charming, they accomplished prodigies everywhere they went, and the multitude kissed their footprints. The electric rains that inebriate the ardent forests also made astral possessions delirious with desire, and while the calices were fuming in the sunlight like living censers, they slept side by side, possessing one another recklessly in dreams.

For years they traveled through India, and knew its unique marvels, its giant mountains, its impetuous rivers, bounding from one ocean to the other, and the mystery of its inexhaustible flora. They were limited to the North by the most redoubtable chains of mountains that the interior fire has ever caused to emerge from the ground, like menacing monsters looming up toward the stars: the peaks of the Himalayas. To the East and West they stopped at the banks of the Indus and the Brahmaputra, and pushed South as far as the Indian Ocean, which is known by turns as the Sea of Oman and the Gulf of Bengal. They dazzled and charmed the ancient cradle of the world, which is also the cradle of mysterious sciences, black magic and enchantments.

Brahmanic cosmography represents the world to us in the form of a lotus corolla floating gently on the ocean. The pistil—the sacred lingam darting its desire into the azure—is the Himalaya, the giant of the globe, the mountain venerated among all. And it was in its magical valleys—the calyx or yoni—among the beauties of a nature in delirium, that Nassudamy loved women recklessly and multiplied himself infinitely for the mystery of amour.

Then he wanted to brave death herself, and had himself put in a coffin after subjecting himself to magnetic sleep. When he was disinterred a fortnight later, he had been miraculously conserved by the astral light, remaining in a complete state of lucid somnambulism. His hair exhaled a sweet perfume of vervain, his lips seemed still red and moist with kisses.

Facts so extraordinary were reported in his regard that people made pilgrimages to see him, to the great detriment of the ancient sacrifices of Djagganath, which, until then, had claimed ten thousand victims every year. The maleficent gods of the Blue Mountain no longer saw streams of blood running at their feet, and the wild dogs no longer came all the way to the temples to devour the dead and the dying.

Such a state of affairs could not endure. The high priests of Shiva and Parvati, disturbed by such competition, sent Brahmins to the place of the miracle in order to destroy the charm.

For the twelfth time, Nassudamy had himself placed in the tomb, while the gopis, drunk on desire, wept around him.

After being plunged for a week in profound mantras, having begged the pitris to assist him in that ordeal, which was to last longer than the others, he had proceeded with the necessary preparations: the maceration in the balms, the depilation, the absorption of certain philters composed of extracts of hemp, asclepiad and datura tastuosa.

On the place of the ceremony his nostrils and ears were blocked with wax, his eyelids were glued and his tongue was turned backwards.

Viamalah, draped from the nape to the heels in uniform yellow silk, watched those preparations, impassive and grave. She presented the white sheet in which her friend was to be wrapped, and wanted to sew it up herself with tight stitches. Then, as had been done in the other experiments, the supple body was placed in a wooden box, sealed and padlocked, which was lowered into a deep hole.

One by one, the faithful threw flowers, Ganges water, perfumes and stones from the Sacred Mountains over the soil. When the ditch was full, Viamalah lay down on the ground and remained thus for three days and three nights, in constant communication with the mystical lover, who was never more passionate, while the gopis danced the rasa around her.

In the preceding ordeals, the charmer had been exhumed after a few weeks. Before the pilgrims and the crowd of curiosity-seekers, the padlock had been opened, the seals broken and the coffin opened. Nassudamy, in the white sheet, seemed to be asleep; his features, imprinted with serenity, conserved their sovereign beauty. Viamalah, kneeling on the freshly removed earth, removed the wax that closed the eyelids and the nostrils, and kissed him on the lips. He opened his eyes, extended his arms and resumed living.

Everything would doubtless happen in the same way. The curious crowd awaited the resurrection, pressing around the ditch,

154

where mysterious calices of crimson and gold had flowered, spreading an indefinable and delicious aroma.

Meanwhile, the Brahmins of Djagganath watched with the other priests, but they conserved somber visages and remained in prayer for longer.

When the term of the proof arrived, Viamalah, her hands full of roses, went to the tomb. For several days she had been trying in vain to evoke the soul of the charmer. Lying on the ground, among the flowers, so rapidly blossomed, which had withered, she had awaited the habitual ecstasy for a long time. No occult kiss had come to magnify her dream. She was anxious and feverish, and she fainted when the damp shroud was eventually unwound.

As troubled as she was, the Brahmins leaned over the body. Nassudamy appeared, and there was a cry of amazement in the crowd. His eyes were wide-open, filled with an unspeakable terror; his limbs were icy; and two nagas—the serpents of Shiva—were gnawing his face.

He was buried definitively beneath a banyan fig tree, the incorruptible tree that can shade the witnesses of a sacred ceremony, and forms and entire forest by itself.

Since then, other fakirs have traveled India, but none has been as famous.

Nothing more is known about Viamalah. In the annals of the priestesses of amour, she remains the ideal lover, the creature of election who, although a virgin, knew all kisses and all embraces, by means of the mysterious science of Kama.

brahma's courtesans

PART ONE

I
A Feast in Delhi

Orpha entered the arena, clad in his golden armor.

It was a day of rejoicing in Shahjahanabad, for the son of the Rajah submissive to the Great Mogul was to measure himself against the most redoubtable wild beasts, in order to show the people their strength and their suppleness.

All around the tamascha[1] the sacred elephants were gathered, supporting important guests. Motionless women with large dark eyes circled with antimony resembled idols of ivory and gold, and the pleats of their silky garments fell around them without a frisson, so calm was the atmosphere. The crowd was still arriving, following the banks of the Jumna, whose waters were displayed metallically, seeming to join the sun in the distance in liquid radiance. The city rose up, all roseate, on the edge of the river, with holes of light over the bulbous cupolas, domes with golden belfries and pointed steeples like feathers in the rutilant helmets of temples and pagodas. Further away there were velvets of ver-dure, and mauve and gray washes of anemiated plants beneath an intense blue sky.

Assilinia, Orpha's fiancée, was holding upright the sacred lotus that she had to present to the victor, and her profound eyes were nuanced with green beneath the band of aquamarines and sardonyxes that covered her forehead.

---

1 The word *tamascha*, in this meaning (a kind of spectacle) is employed in Abraham Anquetil-Duperron's traslation of *Oupnek'ha*t, but is otherwise extremely scarce.

"You say that Ramo has never been defeated?" she asked a young woman who was agitating a flabellum of peacock feathers with a jade handle above her head.

"Ramo, the black panther from Java, is more redoubtable than the great tigers of Bengal, may the gods protect us!"

"Ah!" said Assilinia, and a brief flame starred her glaucous eyes. "I shall know whether the Master destined for me is truly courageous."

"Do you doubt it? Orpha possesses valor and beauty. You can be proud of his choice."

The young woman had an enigmatic smile; then her fleshy lips, designed in a crimson heart, immobilized, and a more intense gleam caused the golden sand of her irises to sparkle

The festival was taking place in Delhi in front of the palace of Shah Jahan,[1] a gigantic construction of red granite that seemed stained by the blood of the arena. From the height of the terraces the motionless sentinels contemplated the massive cupolas of temples, the shiny needles of tall minarets and the gray line of the ramparts knotted over the flanks of the city like a steel loincloth. In the distance rose the tombs of Rajahs and ancient fortresses with somber memories of battle and carnage.

The crowd gathered more compactly around the privileged individuals who had been able to obtain places near the combatants. The horses covered in gold and silver tapestries pawed the ground; camels laden with spectators stretched out their melancholy heads toward the platforms where cymbals of iron and bronze burst forth, where the beaters of boa-skin drums and blowers of bamboo flutes with clear stridulations were playing frantically.

The spectators were swarming from all parts, and the various Indian languages mingled like a susurrus of cicadas intoxicated by the sun. Girls with frail pale bronze bodies, tattooed on the

---

1 Shah Jahan (1592-1666) was the Mogul Emperor of much of India from 1628-1658. He founded Shajahanabad, nowadays known as Old Delhi, in 1639.

breasts and ankles with blue arabesques, were offering bananas, dried fish, freshwater mussels with turmeric, and chapattis kneaded in ghi and flour. They were laughing, showing all their sharp kittenish teeth, and the silver rings in their nostrils put pale circles over their backward-tilted faces. Carts passed by drawn by buffaloes; the most sumptuous were decorated with brocades, ornaments were ivory figurines or metallic blades bristling like the leaves of reeds.

The Djaths, the Babou and the Omraos, cultivators, merchants and noblemen, came from far away to the tamascha, the marvelous spectacle of the great contest of men and wild beasts.

The Bhai-Tchokri,[1] bayaderes with red lips and eyelids tinted with kohl appeared, half-recumbent in bhaeli, two-wheeled carts surmounted with a cone of gold cloth, drawn by pink oxen with horns florid with saligram.

Elephants, some wild and others domesticated, had amused the audience to begin with. Those pachyderms, their hides painted in vivid colors and their tusks tinted red, had advanced staggering, drunk on arak, which they had been made to take in order to excite their bellicose humor. When one of the enormous beasts fell, twenty horses caparisoned with ruby velvet and cabochons of precious stones dragged it out of the arena.

Then there were cock-fights, combats of buffaloes, wild boar and antelopes. Tigers fought one another, and the sacred monkeys from the tower of Qutub-Minar simulated a Hindu wedding without anything missing. The bride, a tall she-monkey whose hair was divided into bangs like a woman's, falling in stiff tresses under a diadem of sardonyxes and opals, simpered as

---

1 I have reproduced this term as the original text renders it; it does not appear to exist anywhere else. It seems to be compounded *ad hoc* from Bhai [friend, although usually translated as "brother"] and chokri [girl]. Many other terms used in the novel seem to be improvised or invented by the author, including "bhaeli" from this same paragraph, and "saligram," which might be a misunderstanding of shaligram, a kind of stone associated in legend with Vishnu; I have rendered most such terms as given without further comment; the author was clearly peppering her narrative with invented terms as a stylistic device.

she dragged her long gold-spangled garments through the dust. And when the fortunate husband finally received the price of his constancy, that was the signal for inextinguishable laughter in the audience.

Now it was Orpha's turn, replacing, after a stirring pass, two Himalayan Gurkhas, the vanquishers of royal tigers.

Orpha, with his rutilant armor and his dupatta embroidered with fine pearls, wound several times around his loins, advanced, proud and supple, his eyes enlarged by two streaks of kohl under the curly fleece that covered his forehead. He was of medium height, but harmonious and robust; one sensed that he was habituated to triumphs and sure of his power; a slightly disdainful smile creased his lips, and his somber eyes had cruel glimmers. He put his left hand to his heart, and then to his lips. Looking at Assilinia, and the young woman lifted the lotus flower higher.

A murmur of admiration ran through the crowd; rounded or tubular turbans, ornamented with feathers and torsades, oscillated; rings of precious stones rattled on the quivering arms of women. There were a few cries of anguish and desire, and breasts offered at the edges of balustrades like amorous cups palpitated more feverishly.

Shah Jahan, the King of Kings, the omnipotent Mogul, who had deigned to preside over the fête, directed his sharp eyes at Assilinia. He had coveted the young woman for a long time, and Orpha, who had acquired her, would become a complaisant husband compensated generously by a high rank in the army. Shah Jahan, the voluptuous monarch, jaded by all pleasures, often profited from the weakness of Rajahs, who would deliver their daughters to him for a few honors.

It is a custom in India that the Rajahs who are neighbors of the city in which the Emperor resides come in turn to mount guard before the palace and live under tents with their Rajputs to honor and protect the Mogul. Amarsin, Assilinia's father, had deserted his post in spite of the warnings of his friends. When he presented himself before Shah Jahan, one of the secretaries of state made him a few reproaches for his lack of assiduity in service, and the Rajah, who believed that he had been insulted, drew his dagger and struck the minister, whose blood spurted all the way to the Emperor's breast.

That murder was punished immediately. Amarsin fell under the thrusts of the officers assisting Shah Jahan, while the Rajputs, avenging their master, massacred the people outside.

Assilinia, Amarsin's only daughter, remained captive in his palace for a long time; then the Emperor, smitten with her ardent beauty, resolved to marry her to Orpha in order finally to triumph over her rigor, and to have her all to himself.

This fête, given in honor of the princess, was to deliver her, at the same time, to the kiss of the husband and the sovereign. But the young woman, suspicious and disdainful, disinterested in the exploits of Orpha, did not seem to notice the shining gaze of the Emperor.

Hallabab, her friend and confidante, dropped the peacock-feather flabellum that she was agitating with a weary hand.

"Do you at least love him, your handsome fiancé?" she asked, sighing.

Assilinia reflected for a moment, and then declared, with a hint of sadness: "I don't know. What does one experience when one loves a man?"

"Oh! Are you ignorant of what amour is?"

"Yes. Inform me, little Hallabab, if your heart has already quivered."

Hallabab lowered over her gold-flecked irises the fringed veil of her long eyelids and murmured in the tremulous voice of a sylvan flute: "These things are understood without explanation. Anything I could tell you would seem strange or puerile to you. A life without amour is a landscape without sunlight, one of those desolate Himalayan landscapes that the snows cover in every season."

"Those white expanses have their beauty."

"Perhaps, but under their cold shroud nothing grows, and the earth is like a dead woman lying in her tomb."

Orpha was now fighting the wild beast, a tiger with fur striped with somber velvet and elastic loins agitated by furious tremors. A few paces from the prince, ready to bring him help, sowars waited, and the flashes of axes and the frissons of swords appeared at the end of their arms when the combatant seemed to buckle and the fangs of the beast came too close to his flesh. But the young man made light of the attacks he provoked; his body, the slender and supple limbs lightly coated with balms, gathered, crawled and spun incessantly, and red droplets were already starring the thick fur of the beast, putting ruby rings on Orpha's fingers.

It required an incredible skill to escape the abrupt attacks of the monster, which twisted, bounded and reared up with mighty roars, astonished by the human cunning that its strength could not vanquish.

The smiling Emperor encouraged his favorite by extending the glaucous star of his scepter toward him; then his burning gaze sought Assilinia, enveloping her with a magnetic wave of desire. Weary of the favors of the begum, his daughter, he coveted the disdainful Rani madly, and was ready to make the greatest sacrifices in order to possess her.

Orpha rolled in the dust, got up again, and his arm, defending him like a steel spring, struck the howling beast and put coral clasps to its tawny pelt.

Small nervous hands threw flowers, and gems knotted in valuable scarves at the combatant; courtesans uncovered breasts with gilded nipples and plunged fingernails into the flesh as a sign of admiration and tenderness. Orpha was the elect of the day, the man that every man envied and that every woman desired. Perfumed couches, he knew, would be open to him after this exploit, honeyed kisses would be offered to him, and his pride would flower like the red lotus of sacred pools.

164

Another tiger was brought, which reared up to its full height and looked the young man in the face. Its body was immense, its paws and loins incredible in their muscular energy. Orpha waited for the impact; then, leaping on to his enemy's back, he plunged his dagger between the shoulders, in the midst of the frenetic applause of the assembly.

Hallabab was following the phases of the combat passionately, while Assilinia, bored, turned her gaze away, fixing it on the buzzing flight of a metallic fly in the calm air or the zigzag flight of a pink lizard along the steps.

Young women appeared in the gap of a doorway, passed before the wild beasts' cages and, drawing them from gold filigreed baskets, scattered sprigs of tulsi—sacred basil—around Orpha. The last lowered toward him banners embroidered with pearls and amethysts in his colors and those of the Rajah, his father. Those maidens, who lived in the shade of temples, had a morbid and touching beauty. Diamonds were set in their hieratic faces, and serpents of aquamarines coiled around their narrow hips, joining the inviolate clasp under the dupatta garnished with crystal beads that hung down to their knees. They threw their odoriferous petals slowly, while barbaric instruments of bronze and silver clamored a chant of amour or war.

When the prince had turned his short dagger three times in the throat of the tiger, gasping at his feet, all the triumphant fanfares burst forth at the same time.

There was then the vision of gold and pearls of the royal dancers, gliding around the red pools and dipping the tips of their toes therein, gemmed all the way to the opaline nail with cabochons of rubies and emeralds. They leaned over the mirror of blood as if to contemplate their images therein, and brushed it with the hem of their veils, which acquired borders of crimson. The odor of the murder made their nostrils quiver, and the nacre of their sharp teeth appeared beneath the lips, raised in a desire for kisses or combat.

The prince turned toward his fiancée and smiled at her passionately.

"Oh, how I would love to be in your place, Assilinia!" said Hallabab, her eyes showing their whites in admiration. "Aren't you going to give your lotus to the victor?"

"No," said Assilinia. "I'm waiting for the black panther to judge the courage of the man. These tigers are intoxicated by opium and datura; they scarcely defend their life. I aspire to more valiant combats."

Hallabab murmured: "Now the Master is looking at you; his eyes are strange, Assilinia!"

The parting of draperies revealed an ivory throne encrusted with green and red gems, and Shah Jahan, standing up, saluted the crowd by putting the splayed fingers of his left hand on his chest. The Mogul appeared distinctly. He was clad in a yellow robe, and on top of it, a sort of gold plastron was fastened to his shoulders, rutilant with a diamond sun and stars. Behind him, a long cloak constellated with sapphires and opals was displayed like a peacock's tail. His arms were so laden with gems that, although they were bare, the color of the skin could not be perceived.

The dancers uttered a sort of guttural cry and seemed to swoon, as if they had all received the marks of royal desire. Bodies thrown backwards, they projected the amber flowers of their breasts, and extended their trembling hands toward the Master.

After the frail maidens, the Hedjera appeared, eunuchs, hermaphrodites and mutilated women appointed to guard the Zenana, for Hindus practice castration on little girls as well as boys.[1] The Hedjera women are tall, strong and possess a masculine

____

1 The existence of "female eunuchs" called "Hedjera" in India was alleged in a report made to the Societé Orientale in Paris in 1843 by a Dr. G. Roberts, who reported that he had seen three of them in 1841 and that an old Brahmin had told him that they were produced by the injection of the juice of an unripe thelpeut [sic]. Roberts then went on to give a description of these strangely masculinized women, of which La Vaudère's description is an accurate synopsis. Roberts' account echoes an earlier account of "female circumcision" given by Raymond-Henri Fourcade, which also mentions hedjeras and an oblig-

voice with tones as profound as the vibrations of the chilamchi. They show themselves completely naked, with a beryl clasp at the place of their mutilated sex, and experience neither frissons nor desire when the gazes of men pose on them. Naturally depilated, they raise their plump and polished arms in cadence, and their breasts, devoid of roundness, have light nipples scarcely darker than their skin. When very young they have been subjected to the sting of long needles steeped in the unripe fruit of the bhel-phoul, and their femininity is atrophied within them as a mango is desiccated on the tree after the bite of a cobra.

Those cold priestesses are particularly in favor in the temples, where, in their turn, they mutilate children after having intoxicated them with ganja, and are delivered to the morbid curiosity of fakirs. To the sounds of sitars and dhols, they nevertheless simulated sexual intercourse on the fuming sand of the arena, and seemed to swoon in strange intoxications that the sacrificers of Kali, the red Brahmins, followed while shivering.

The Hedjeras are very influential with the Emperor. They can obtain mercy for a culpable, and four times a year, they are summoned to the palace in order to read the mysterious signs of the stars and deliver themselves to the evocations and spells of Yogis.

Assilinia often went to the temple of Kuthu'l to consult Hadj-Hidi, the old sorceress with the long-troubled eyes of bewitchment, and she knew in advance of the combat that her fiancé would be defeated.[1]

---

ingly informative old Brahmin, but in this instance the injection is said to be of the fruit of the bhel-phoul (a kind of tree), as rendered by La Vaudère. Fourcade does not, however, allege that the treatment produces the masculinizing effects described by Roberts. Everything we now know about female genital mutilation or ovarian atrophy suggests that the operation described in the novel could not possibly have the effect described.

1 There are references in some 19th-century French sources to a mosque in the region of Delhi called Kuthu'l-Islam, which is presumably where La Vaudère found the name, but she has obviously transformed its meaning.

Hadj-Hidi, while following the lascivious dance of the mutilated virgins, smiled at the princess, as if to encourage her resistance. Twice she put her curved index finger to her forehead, and
Assilinia slowly inclined her head toward the golden lotus, which
she bore to her lips.

"What are you doing?" Hallabab asked.

"I'm reassuring Hadj-Hidi, who thinks I'm devoid of strength
before the will of the gods."

"So, before even knowing the result of the combat, you're
listening to the advice of the guardians of the Zenana!"

"Why shouldn't I listen to it?"

"Be careful!"

Assilinia did not deign to respond, and her brown eyelids
lowered over the ardent ecstasy of her dream.

Orpha had disappeared, and the Omraos, in the shade of a
crimson and gold tent, were soliciting the honor of rubbing his
flesh with beneficent balms in order to give him a new vigor.
Bhai-Tchokris, sumptuously adorned with diamond-encrusted
dupattas, were bringing rare essences and offering their carmined
lips to stimulating caresses.

"With our aid," they said, "you will be invincible. Let us place
the armor of our kisses over your breasts and your loins. Under
their tight mesh you will remain sheltered from wounds, and
nothing will be able to reach you but the wrath of the gods!"

Sending away the Babou and the Omraos, Orpha made a sign
to the courtesans that were kneeling beside him.

The Hedjeras had concluded their dances; for the supreme
combat, the sowars, with their square bucklers bordered with
strips of monkey-skin, their pikes and their sears, arranged themselves in the arena.

The population of Bigaris and Djaths was still increasing
outside; heavy bhaeli crushed marauding dogs; saermi—racing

camels—with hooded heads and backs covered with large red cloths emerged from the arena with the quarrelsome tattoo, the eunuchs and the hermaphrodites. There were patches of ocher and cobalt under the solar haloes that floated everywhere, and a glittering dust swirled at times when the swell became too forceful. Little crystal bells and golden chains tinkled after the intermittent fanfares of the chilamchi.

Hallabab leaned toward Assilinia.

"It's the moment," she said. "My heart is full of trouble."

Assilinia opened her weary eyelids slightly. "In truth," she murmured, "nothing is quivering within me, and I won't even be able to experience the pride of triumph."

II
The Black Panther

It was announced, however, that the prince had requested a few more minutes of repose, and the lions were sent in, which were not destined to fight that day.

Surprised, the enormous beasts swept the ground with their tails, raising their heads as if to sniff the odor of the human prey destined for them. Shah Jahan decided that three men condemned to death, who were due to be executed the next day, would be abandoned to the beasts. There was Ouraidi the harkarat—a courier—who had stolen a Rani's bracelet; Karysas, who, intoxicated by ganja, had insulted a Babou outside the great mosque; and finally, Mimiose, who, in his speeches, had shown scant respect for the omnipotence of the Emperor.

Mimiose, the idol of the Bigaris and the enemy of the Babou and the Omraos, possessed a certain eloquence that transported the crowds. He was said to be a revolutionary, dangerous to the government, which had been seeking an opportunity to suppress him for a long time.

A shrill fanfare resounded, and the two red battens of the prisoners' cell were overturned, allowing Ouraidi and Karysas to pass through. As for Mimiose, with one bound he had taken the lead, and was already confronting the lions.

He was a young man about twenty-five years old, tall, with a proud bearing, a supple and fine body, with long dominating and caressant eyes. He planted himself in front of one of the lions, which sniffed the air, dazzled by the daylight and astonished by the tumult. Then, lowering his spear, he put himself on guard and withstood the impact of the wild beast so victoriously that the animal went past, carrying away a bloody rose whose petals were flowing over its muscular flanks.

The lion stopped, uncertain, and then fell with an increased wrath on Karysas, who extended his dagger. Another rose bled next to the first, but the beast came back and plunged its claws into Karysas' belly, who was felled, borne away and tossed into the air like one of those light balloons that serve as amusements for children. Meanwhile, the entrails spilled from the frightful wound and flowed over the sand.

As is done for the horses that serve in Spanish bullfights, a Sakri with a long needle brought the flesh together and the man, whose belly swelled, was able to stand up. After having drunk a few gulps of arak, he picked up his dagger, and, his hand trembling, awaited the impact of the monsters.

As if disdainful of that excessively facile victory, however, the lions turned toward Ouraidi, who had not budged. With a thrust of the paw, one of them knocked him down, and, covering him with its body, plunged its fangs into his throat. Ouraidi, however, succeeded in getting to his feet; he traversed the arena, staggering as if he were drunk, floods of black blood erupting impetuously from his wound and striping the sand with intermittent zigzags. He was choking, his two hands at his neck, his respiration increasingly hoarse; finally, he fell near Mimiose, who attacked the enemy courageously.

The bronze instruments sounded all at once, and four teams of horses, splendidly harnessed, entered at a gallop to take away the cadaver of the harkarat. It was attached to the end of a rope fitted with a crampon, and the team dragged away that human debris, still so full of strength and life a few moments before.

A beras came with a basket full of soil to sprinkle on the pools of blood, where green flies were already beginning to swarm.

Karysas' wound had reopened while he was fighting feebly with one of the lions; he was the target of more bites, and his right hand, severed at the wrist, was hanging from the inert arm, only retained by a few filaments. Mimiose delivered him by plunging his dagger into the throat and eye of the wild beast, which collapsed, got up, and hurled itself with a terrible bound on to the young man, whom it covered with blood.

Life is manifest in carnivorous animals long after death, so one could have believed, given the lion's convulsive and disorderly movements, that it was still alive. Soon, two other agonies followed its own. Mimiose fought so valiantly that the Ranis asked for mercy for him, Assilinia foremost among them.

"That man," she said to Hallabab, "has killed three hungry lions, while the prince only vanquished two tigers intoxicated by opium. Mimiose has strength and beauty."

"You think so? He's only a bigaris, without birth and without money."

"What does that matter to me?"

"Mimiose is not only of obscure origin, but he has gravely offended our master by conspiring against the Omraos and the nobles of the Empire."

"He was right. I hate Shah Jahan, who killed my father the Rajah."

Hallabab looked at the princess fearfully.

"How can you dare to say such things, Assilinia?"

"What would prevent me from saying them?"

"Your relatives, your friends . . . the amour you have for your fiancé."

Silent laughter creased the young woman's painted lips, and she lowered her long somber eyelids slowly.

"My fiancé!"

"Yes, yes, the one who is going to fight for you!"

"He hasn't yet triumphed over the black panther . . ."

"He will triumph . . . I certainly hope so!"

"Little Hallabab," said Assilinia, "your heart is more smitten than mine."

Hallabab lowered her head in confusion.

"Is it forbidden," she murmured, "to admire the qualities of skill and bravery of those who exhibit themselves for our pleasure? We're watching a marvelous tamascha, and we have the right to give our opinion of the valor of the combatants."

"Yes, little Hallabab. You protest your innocence with too much ardor for my clairvoyance to be mistaken. You're more than a spectator, you're revealing yourself to be an ardent admirer. But then," Assilinia concluded, yawning, "it's indifferent to me. You can love Orpha, whom I disdain . . ."

Hallabab sighed. "You don't know how fortunate you are! Oh, if I were in your place . . ."

Mimiose, alone in the arena before the huge lions that no longer dared attack him, folded his arms and awaited the decision of the Mogul.

"Mercy! Mercy!" howled the crowd, in which the voices of the women were dominant.

But Shah Jahan remained indecisive, for Mimiose's crime was one of those that the powerful rarely pardon. He made a sign, and the sowars took the condemned man away, understanding that the Emperor was reserving the sentence for the end of the games.

Then Assilinia, in spite of Hallabab's exhortations, stood up very straight, and before Mimiose had disappeared behind the red door, held out her golden lotus toward him, smiling.

There was a long cry of astonishment from the spectators, for the young woman's action was as strange as it was audacious on the day of her betrothal.

Mimiose saw the gesture and smiled, shivering with joy. As for Assilinia, grave and proud, she sat down again beside Hallabab and paraded her sparkling gaze over the audience

"What you dared to do makes me tremble, Assilinia!" murmured her naïve confidante. "Such a scandal!"

"I rendered homage to courage, nothing more."

"What will people think of you after that inconceivable action?"

"They will think that I judge everyone's qualities freely, and no one will be astonished by my decision if it is unfavorable to the prince."

"Wait and see!" begged the young woman. "Orpha will be triumphant, I'm certain of it."

"Let the gods decide his fate."

"Here he comes. Here he comes" whispered the crowd.

Under the kisses of the Bhai-Tchokri, sellers of amour, rubbing his flesh with precious balms and stimulating his nerves with massage and incomplete caresses, the prince had recovered a new ardor. He presented himself, quivering with desire, and his fiery gaze sought an encouragement in that of Assilinia, who remained impassive.

The two battens of the red door parted again, and Ramo, the black panther, the victor in so many combats, bounded to the middle of the arena.

She was a superb beast, silky, shiny and muscular. Not as tall as a tiger, she was more elongated, with an undulating crawl and unexpected cunning. Her emerald green eyes were phosphorescent, and her large bulbous forehead seemed to be wrinkled by the effort of profound thought. Before the prince had anticipated the attack, she sank her fangs into his thigh, knocked him down, threw him over her shoulder and transported him, leaping, to the other side of the arena.

Orpha had uttered a cry of distress, and the panther could easily have made it impossible for him to continue the battle if she had not hesitated before that disarmed enemy, whom she doubtless no longer found worthy of her wrath.

She stopped, and gazed at the audience.

It is by means of a plaintive cry, modulated like a tremolo of an organ that a royal tiger announces its presence. A panther purrs like a huge cat, of which it has all the movements, by turns supple, febrile or amorous. Its surges, when it deigns to be stirred, are companied by rapid, alarming growls, punctuated like a consumptive cough; then its jowls are drawn back, its whiskers rise toward its glaucous eyes, spangled with diabolical gleams, and it spits like irritated tomcats engaged in amorous disputes. With a thrust of its velvet paw with terrible claws it can break the bones of a heifer and it carries it away without apparent effort, so powerfully-developed is its muscular strength.

Mounted on elephants, hunters of wild beasts had captured Ramo in one of the jungles of fecund and divine Java, on the shore of the black river. Hot sea, torrid sun and volcanic fire, all blazing breaths, had passed through the blood of Rano to make her an admirable beast of vigor and beauty. She had known the mortal storms of the Blue Mountains and the savage lightning that human sight could not support. Torrents of electric rain had lustered her hide while intoxicating the earth delirious with sap. And beneath the fuming sky, she had fled through the somber woods—so somber that torches are necessary there in broad daylight and the plants there, detaching themselves from their stems, become carnivorous and are no longer distinguishable from animals.

Ramo had eaten those flowers of flesh, placed so low in the morbid and oily vapors of the soil, those flowers with pistils as flamboyant in the dark as the fulgurant eye of a Cyclops. And she had retained a taste for that strange fare, never touching a vanquished enemy.

Her gaze, dazzled by the bright sunlight, was still seeking the enormous hairy vampire bats that hung down from branches and the black tigers that were, according to the Malays, inhabited by the spirit of Death.

Meanwhile, the prince had regained his feet, and, his weapon raised, was preparing to strike the enemy. With one bound the panther avoided the blow, and both of them rolled on the ground, while the audience maintained a passionate silence.

When Orpha was disengaged, he was streaked by the thrusts of claws and bites, his limbs fractured and his breast profoundly labored. He had lost consciousness, and he was carried away in order to bandage his wounds, for one ought, as far as is possible, to preserve the lives of princes.

Hallabab hid her face on Assilinia's shoulder, whose parted lips were drawn back in a disdainful smile.

"Who wants to fight the panther?" demanded a mahachalchy, in accordance with custom.

And the crowd shouted: "Bring back Mimiose!"

Shah Jahan turned to Assilinia, as if to obtain her assent, and she repeated gravely: "Have Mimiose brought back."

The bigaris was brought back in the midst of a quiver of expectation. He was calm, proud and seemed as relaxed as if he were emerging from the durbar of a Rajah after a siesta.

With a curious gaze, Ramo measured that new enemy, and then, coming to rub herself against his legs, saluted him with a seductive purr, which Mimiose welcomed with a caress. The man's hand ran over the velvet backbone of the animal, which arched her back, her eyes half-closed in an attitude of submission and ecstasy.

Then Mimose lay down in the sand and, bringing his face close to the somber head of the panther, opened the jaws gently and presented his lips to the sharp fangs.

With a thrust of the tongue, Ramo kissed the Gurkha's mouth.

"Ham!" cried the crowd, in a delirious joy; and Shah Jahan, lowering his emerald scepter, ordered that the wild beast and the man should be imprisoned in a jail in the Temple of Kuthu'l, for the event smacked of magic and only the Hedjeras could exorcise the demon that inhabited the combatant's body.

III
Assilinia

The Rani was lying on a bed borne by silver swans, with fabrics florid with turquoises and sapphires at her feet, cushions embroidered with blue pearls under her loins; and her light dupatta, open over her breast and thighs, seemed to be cut out of moonlight.

Her face borrowed a mysterious gleam from all that blue and her eyes—black stars with a redoubtable glare—launched somber lightning flashes. From the floor powdered with silver to the ceiling starred with lapis lazuli, everything had the sidereal hue by which the soul finds itself reposed, drowned in infinite space.

"Hallabab," she said to the young woman, who was kissing her knees, weeping, "I shall not marry the man destined for me."

"Oh! You'll cause his misfortune and your own! At least bring him the consolation of your kind words. You know that he's wounded, and that a child could now reckon with him. Be gentle, Assilinia, give him the intoxicating ganja of illusion, and if you can't love him, let him at least savor, for a few days, the blessed honey of the pious lie."

"I have never lied, Hallabab."

"The priests of the Jumna will pardon you in favor of the intention. Orpha might die of your indifference."

The Rani started to laugh silently.

"How little you know, my liana of the savage forests! But if the gallant pleases you, I repeat to you, it is in your power to reveal all your love to him. I only want your felicity, little Hallabab!"

The girl caused her kisses to glide from Assilinia's polished knees to her ankles, ringed with beryls and opals. Her lips passed teasingly over the Rani's supple and delicate little foot, and lingered in a submissive caress.

Illuminated by high windows circled by precious stones, Assilinia's bedroom rose up in a conch, decorated with a magic of

blue mosaics, into which entwined medallions and roses imported an unexpected grace. Her bed, on a platform, was resplendent
with gems and flowers, but the group of the two young women
seemed the most beautiful ornament in that prestigious room.

In one another's arms, now united by ardent confidences,
they whispered their desire to one another, and Assilinia, in her
body of a goddess, savored all the cajoleries that Hallabab wanted
to offer her beloved. "Oh," she said, sighing, "it's thus that everything is sweetness in amour."

"More than you can believe. Our caress is incomplete. It's
better to faint under the kisses of a man."

"That's true; you've enervated me, nothing more."

"Don't you want to know the perfect joy?"

"Yes. You've revealed strange things to me; and my desire is
ardent toward the knowledge of all human felicity."

"Come, then. The palace is dark and no one is thinking of
keeping watch on us. We can go through the gardens."

"So be it, but it's Mimiose that I want to meet."

"Mimiose!"

"He alone is worthy of loving me. Adorn me for his amour!"
Assilinia got up and approached one of the high windows.

In the distance, under the mysterious light of the moon,
the stones of mausolea, citadels, temples and palaces glittered.
Nothing was as majestic as that indefinite horizon of dead things
and dying splendors. In that epoch, Delhi, which had previously been named LalKot, Jahanpanah, Rai Pithora, Siri and
Tughlakabad, was radiant with all its power at the foot of the
great tower of Qutub-Minat. Under that cylindrical truncated
cone, with steps of red sandstone and white marble, stood the
temple of Kuthu'l, where the Hedjeras with mutilated genitals
lived, and an inscription, which stood out in formidable bloody
characters made it known that the monument originated from
twenty-seven temples demolished for the triumph of the truth.

Assilinia extended her right hand in the direction of Kuthu'l.

"I want to see the sterile women," she said.

Hallabab shivered.

"They can't do anything for you, since your desire is to consecrate yourself to amour."

"They will tell me my destiny, and what I must do in order to liberate Mimiose. Shah Jahan does not refuse them anything. A word from them can obtain mercy for the Gurkha."

"Why would they be favorable to you? What can you do for them?"

"I can offer them one thing that would be agreeable to them."

"What thing?"

"The amorous life of a child: Samjab or Pekeo."

Hallabab uttered a scream and drew away from her friend in terror. "What! You want to do that? You want to sacrifice those innocents?"

"Yes, I want to offer their virginity to the gods. Hadj-Hidi will pierce them with the long needle steeped in the fruit of the bhel-phoul."

"But a little while ago you only had mild thoughts . . ."

"What do you know about it? Before anything else, I want to save Mimiose; and them, I think that Samjab, like Pekeo, would be glad to enter the temple of Kuthu'l and be similar to little flowers whose corolla has closed without producing the dolorous fruit."

Hallabab straightened herself indignantly

"Like you, they have a right to amour, and you can obtain mercy for Mimiose without recourse to such wretched means!"

"Shah Jahan will only pardon a conspirator if the priestesses of the temple lend us their aid. He's afraid of their oracles and their maleficent influence. He believes in Mohammed, but he fears Brahma!"

"What does it matter? The bigaris isn't interesting!"

"I love him!"

✳

Having thrown a long blue veil over her hair, put up and covered in flowers, and inserted two diamond lotuses in her ears, Assilinia drew her friend into the narrow and sinuous streets bordered with brick houses, where the song of prostitutes appealing to passers-by sometimes resonated like the plaintive cry of a wounded turtle-dove. Through doors that stood ajar, or were only covered by partly-drawn curtains, the beautiful young women could be seen lying on their low beds, almost naked. In the arms of the lover of an evening they did not hide themselves any more, and passers-by were able to watch their frolics and take lessons in lust.

The sixty-four caresses of Kama were taught there, and all the young men came to instruct themselves in the arms of experts in amour. They did not hide themelves because there was no shame in sacrificing to Krishna, who, as everyone has read in the sacred books, possessed and fecundated eight hundred gopis at the same time.

Standing, kneeling or lying down, the Bhai-Tchhokri displayed themselves among flowers, and their young nudity was only adorned with a clasp of precious stones or a tuft of saligram attached by a golden thread circling the loins.

Men entered and left freely, without embarrassment, shaking hands in passing, and always came again in the midst of songs and amorous plaints.

"See," said one, "how satiny my skin is! I die and am reborn ten times in one hour! My kisses are ardent and my lips are like the red fruit of the bimba!"[1]

"Come," cooed another. "Sensuality will penetrate you like a wave of kusha oil under the white gaze of Ma, the moon. Smara will introduce you to unusual frissons!"[2]

---

1 In a verse of a prayer known as the Sri Damodarastaka, derived from the *Padma Purana*, Krishna's lips are described as being "as red as the bimba fruit," and it became a very common simile in consequence; the plant in question is also known as the ivy gourd, or tindora.

2 Smara occurs in ancient Sanskrit documents as a common noun used in reference to Kama, and it became one of his epithets in some later documents.

"Oh," murmured a third, who was not yet twelve years old, "I know marvelous games! The hornet pierces the heart of the ketaki slowly, but that narrow corolla is more intoxicating than that of the blooming roses, and the butterflies whisper it in the breeze. Soon, they will be too numerous! Respire the April flower that is only a bud as yet, passer-by!"

"My mouth," affirmed a third, "is more caressant than the calyx of the vilva!"

"I burn like the champak and the musky pepper," clamored a fifth, "and once one has bitten into the delicious fruit, one can no longer tear oneself away from it!"

Then, applying their tongue to the palate, they produced the stridulation of a cicada during the season of the grishma.

"They're happy!" said Hallabab.

"Do you think so? It seems to me that nothing is crueler than the simulacrum of amour! What torture is comparable to that of these unfortunates, who give themselves to all desires, in childhood as in senility?"

"To give herself is the woman's role. Doesn't as much pity as pleasure enter into amour for us?"

IV
The Prisoner

They went, arm in arm, through the new Delhi, which bore the name Shajahanabad—which is to say, the city of Shah Jahan. It was now a marvelous city, which only the enchantments of the Mahabharata could rival. The Great Mogul, in order to attract to it the bounty of Mohammed, had not recoiled before human sacrifices, left until then to Brahmanic superstition. Conspirators had their throats cut in the foundations of the city, and as their blood was insufficient to sprinkle that terrain of election, further victims were selected by lot. They were so numerous that the favorite sultana, Allababy, took baths in that red tide for forty days, and all the women of the harem, equipped with precious vases, sprinkled the banks of the Jumna with it. In the enclosure of Shahjahanabad eleven doors were opened and, as the city was fortified by twelve towers, an entrance was left in the middle of each gate. The largest and most magnificent served as a seraglio for the Emperor's wives.

The walls along which Assilinia and her companion went, muffling the sound of their footsteps, were constructed of bricks, with long chains of green and blue stones, firmer and more polished than marble. The chords of the vina and the dhol came through the windows of apartments, and nostalgic voices rose up in the night, sometimes as pure and high-pitched as the sounds of a crystal flute, sometimes as troubled and stormy as the plaints of the chilamchi.

Monkeys were gamboling curiously over the terraces, sticking their heads under poorly-joined curtains and sketching obscene gestures in which they seemed to be imitating the gestures of a briefly glimpsed gynaeceum.

Hallabab and Assilinia arrived at the temple of Kuthu'l, then surrounded by walls forming a vast enclosure. Assilinia gave her name to the Hedjeras that came to open the door, whispering vague threats. It was there that Mimiose, the conspirator, had been imprisoned under the guard of sterile women, sorceresses and pythonesses.

Inside, the walls forms cloistered galleries sustained by Hindu, Buddhist and Jainite columns, the different dominations having mingled their styles.

Assilinia asked to speak to Hadj-Hidi, the old priestess, whom she found at prayer over a red sandstone tomb that contained the ashes of Altamah. The walls displayed bas-reliefs of animals united for procreation, and giant lingams sprang from pedestals of jade and ivory, which the Hedjeras veiled with yellow cloths. That was the part of the temple consecrated to sacrifices. The priestesses came from the opposite side to offer themselves to the lascivious gods. In the niches, the large sacred monkeys also solicited amorous offerings, and moaned incessantly, holding out their hairy hands, covered with rings like those of courtesans, toward the women. Hadj-Hidi, having interrupted her prayer, came to Assilinia and kissed her between the eyebrows.

"Have you brought me a virgin to sacrifice to the gods?" she asked, fixing her piercing gaze on Hallabab.

Hallabab recoiled, shuddering.

"No," said the Rani, "not today. I want to see the prisoner."

"You know that's forbidden . . ."

"Oh, let me speak to him, just for a moment."

"One moment, then. But the sight will trouble your heart."

"My heart belongs to him; it can no longer be troubled. Wait for me, Hallabab, and remain in prayer, to drive the spirits of the nil ghiri and the Djagganath away from us."[1]

The old Hedjeras took Assilinia by the hand and led her into a sort of cell where Mimiose was lying next to the panther. At the sight of the Rani, the young man let himself fall to his knees and put his left hand to his breast as a sign of recognition and submission.

Ramo yawned, stretched, arched her back and came to sniff the young woman's garments.

"Here, Ramo," said Mimiose, trembling. "Let your tongue be honeyed and your claw velvet for the person who has deigned to descend as far as us."

The panther made a seductive purr audible and, like a cat begging for a caress, rubbed her electric fur against the Rani's legs. Sparks sprang from the black pelt shinier than jet, and her glaucous eyes became languid in an unctuous gaze, while her paws kneaded the ground nervously and shivers ran along her arched spine.

---

1 "Nil ghirt" means "Blue Mountains"—a term whose French equivalent La Vaudère often refers to as a quasi-mystical region, and where she believes the temple of Djagganath—a variant of Jagganath—to be. (The original text has "Djagganah" here, but that is an obvious misprint.) It is not clear why either term should be particularly associated with evil spirits.

"Here, Ramo! Don't be afraid, Princess," Mimiose murmured. "The beast is tamed."

"By what spell?" asked the young woman. "What have you done to make her submissive to this degree? Was she not the terror of the combatants of the tamascha yesterday, the black panther that no one could vanquish?"

"Beasts, like humans, obey occult and bewitching laws of amour. Ramo loves me, I don't know why, and my friends are hers. I haven't done anything, however, to merit her tenderness. Ramo guards within her the mysterious soul of the dead, and doubtless I'm the son of the pitris who inhabit her brain."

"Listen," Assilinia went on. "I want to you be free and powerful; I'm going to ask the Mogul for mercy for you."

"He won't grant it to you, for I've conspired against his power. That's the greatest of all crimes."

"You have partisans?"

"Yes, the people are for me and for Aurang-Zeb, the son of Shah Jahan whom everyone venerates."

"Bah! All masters are alike! When Aurang-Zeb has conquered power, he'll crush us with the same unjust laws."

"Perhaps," said Mimiose, "but until now he has been honest and just, while Shah Jahan only devotes himself to debauchery."

Assilinia sat down beside the prisoner. Distractedly caressing the great black panther, she said: "Yes, I know. What is said about the Emperor's orgies is true, and it's even said that after having possessed all the women of the durbar he has violated his own ten-year-old daughter, the begum Saeb."[1]

"You can see that he merits death."

"Certainly, but later. I'm not defending the Mogul, who has killed my father, has vanquished the Rajahs and is neither of our blood nor our religion. He's my enemy, as he's yours. But I be-

---

1 Shah Jahan had several daughters; the eldest was Parhez Banu, who would have been in her forties by the date of the present story, and the youngest Gauhara, who would have been in her twenties. The three young children cited in the story are all fictitious.

lieve that everything happens in its time, and that it's necessary
to wait patiently for justice to triumph. You're young, you have
the future ahead of you, and if you listen to my advice, I can have
the doors of this prison opened for you."

"Who are you, then? A Rani, no doubt? I saw you in your
box draped with precious cloth, and you seemed more beautiful
than the sun."

"I'm the daughter of the Rajah Amarsin, who was massacred
in the palace, and I hate the Master who took from me the dearest thing that I had. You can therefore count on my protection."

"Thank you," said Mimose, enveloping the young woman
with a gaze of ardent adoration. "I've heard mention of you, and
I recall now that the tamascha was given in your honor to celebrate your betrothal to Orpha, the Emperor's favorite."

"Yes, but I won't marry Orpha."

"Why not?"

Assilinia felt a sharp pain traverse her heart. Mimiose's tone
displeased her, for she found indifference in it, almost disdain.
She did not understand that the young man's calm hid a secret
irritation, all the more intense because it was repressed.

"I won't marry Orpha," she said, proudly, "because I can't love
him."

Mimiose stifled a cry of joy. "You can't love him!"

"He doesn't have the honesty I admire; he allowed himself
to be vanquished by the black panther, and he's the Emperor's
protégé."

As if she had understood that they were talking about her,
Ramo turned her gold-spangled eyes toward the Rani and
yawned, showing the pink depths of her throat between two rows
of dazzling fangs,

Mimiose remained silent, as if in ecstasy, and the young
woman, embarrassed by that reserve, said in a lower voice: "One
can't love two men . . ."

The Gurkha shivered. "You're in love, then?" he asked, with
anguish.

"Yes," said Assilinia, enjoying his disturbance.

"Oh!"

For a moment longer she looked at him with a malicious gleam in her ardent eyes.

"I love someone else, Mimiose. Can't you guess the name of the man I prefer?"

Mimiose sensed a wave of hot blood rising to his throat, and he was only able to stammer: "How do you expect me to guess?"

"Since you're something of a sorcerer and you subjugate the most redoubtable of wild beasts . . ."

"Oh, don't make fun of me! I've never frequented the durbar and I don't know the names of the powerful men of the Empire."

"Think . . ."

"You can only love a man of your own rank . . . ?"

"Who knows?"

Mimiose caused the rings circling his arms to click. In spite of his shackles, he had let himself fall at Assilinia's feet.

"Princess, I implore you, tell me the name of the man you love."

She put her hands together behind the Gurkha's shoulders, drew him toward her and murmured in his ear: "It's you."

He uttered a cry, immediately stifled, and closed his eyes under Assilinia's kisses. Her mouth slid passionately over his cheek, seeking his lips.

For a moment, they forgot themselves in that profound, infinite caress, of which the bigaris had never dared to dream, and their delirium was so great that they did not hear old Hadj-Hidi, who had come to warn them about the danger of that conversation.

"Oh!" cried Mimiose. "I want to be free! You hear? Free me! I love you! I adore you! How can I live without your presence?"

Assilinia put a finger over his lips.

"Tomorrow—tomorrow you'll be free,"

"Tomorrow!"

Their lips were fastened together again in a hectic kiss; then old Hadj-Hidi, preceded by two torch-bearers, took the Rani away, more palpitant than a wounded dove.

V

The Hedjeras

"You'll intercede for him?" asked Assilinia, putting her hands together as Hadj-Hidi guided her through the narrow corridors.

"You know that I'm opposed to amour, little Rani. Your tenderness for the Gurkha can't move me, therefore."

"I'll give you turquoises from Tibet, opals from the Yemen and garnets from Bundelkhand to ornament the sanctuary of the goddess."

"That's insufficient."

"You'll also have diamonds from Panna, sapphires from Colombo and emeralds from Jaisalmer."

"I want something better still."

"What, then? Speak; I'll give you anything I possess to deliver the adored man. Would you like my blood? Would you like my heart in a golden cup?"

"I want you to bring me two little girls between eight and twelve years old, for that offering alone is agreeable to the goddess."

"So be it. I'll bring you Samjab and Pekeo, who perfume me every morning, comb my long hair and polish my nails to render them softer than agate. They're two pretty children, who are already thinking about amour."

"Their sacrifice will be all the more precious for it."

"I'll bring them tomorrow—and you'll speak for Mimiose?"

"I swear it."

Hallabab was waiting for the Rani in a vast hall, almost dark, where the Hedjeras made their devotions.

Completely naked, they were dancing around one of their own, holding one another by the hand, and the most vigorous, standing in the middle of the circle, was whipping her companion with a sort of frenetic ardor. Every day one of the mutilated priestesses was sacrificed to the pleasure of the goddess, and received two hundred strokes of the lash on her flesh. During the torture, she swayed and sang, and ended up hypnotizing herself to the point of no longer being able to discern fiction from reality. In that state, she rendered oracles that were published to the sound of a trumpet throughout the Empire. Soon, maddened by the clamors of the victim, all the Hedjeras were swaying in cadence, and their voices, rising, attained increasingly higher notes.

That went on for a long time, and then they collapsed, rolling on the ground like pythonesses possessed by spirits. In their epileptic writhing and their furious somersaults they showed off the mutilations of their genitals, the scar that united the flesh sewn up in a barbaric and profound operation.

Their flat chests and their boyish hips made them into disquieting and mysterious androgynes. The Brahmins sought them out, and it was said that Shah Jahan often forgot himself in the temple of Kuthu'l, and that he found joys there superior to those of the gynaeceum. All the leaven of aberration that a brain overexcited by neurosis can contain fermented in that one, blasé in regard to lust, on contact with the Hedjeras with the hoarse voices and the long circled and sad eyes. They shared with certain Yogis the favors of Brahmins who, mingling physical visions with spiritual ardors, thought of Shiva, who possessed dual male and female nature, as the god of good and evil omnipotent over souls troubled by reading the Sutras of the Bhakti.

In giving birth to an extrahuman ideal in the souls of Yogis and admirers of Brahma, the ancient Hindu priests had completed the perverse work of old religions, had taken sexual desires to the extent of crime, and had given rise to strange lusts. Voluptuously morbid obsessions haunted the brains of the servants of the dark god incessantly, athirst with a stubborn desire to escape the vulgarities of society, to plunge into unprecedented ecstasies, celestial or accursed crises summoning the blood of sacrifices and the murder of victims of amour. Shah Jahan, who knew all the hysterias of vice, frequented the Hedjeras and treated them with favor at his court, where the mutilated men and women excited curiosity.

Assilinia stopped on the threshold of the vast hall, overtaken by a sort of strange magnetism. And the old Hadj-Hidi laughed silently at her terrified astonishment.

"You can see that the daughters of Annanya know how to occupy their leisure?"[1]

"Oh!" said Hallabab. "They're possessed by pitris, and their intoxication is cruel!"

"What do you know?" said the old woman. "All intoxications are equivalent from the moment they give forgetfulness!"

"I don't have anything to forget! Life seems to me to be beautiful and I'm thirsty for sensuality, healthy sensuality in accordance with the laws of nature."

"That will pass."

"Everything passes, including existence. But it's necessary to collect flowers and fruits along the road that Krishna has traveled."

"Flowers give themselves to bees, and fruits harbor a worm that eats their heart. Ma, the night star, illuminates good and evil. Everything is in everything. Shiva is man and woman for the pleasure of humans."

Assilinia, who was thoughtful, finally emerged from her reverie.

"You'll save Mimiose," she said. "Remember, Hadj-Hidi, that I have your promise."

"I have yours too. You will deliver Samjab and Pekeo to me, and we will mutilate them for the goddess Durga. In exchange, I will go to find Shah Jahan and implore mercy for the Gurkha, since you love that bigaris."

---

1 Annanya means "unique" in Hindi.

188

The old woman uttered a little snigger, which was lost in
the strident clamors of the Hedjeras, whose limbs, agitated by
increasingly violent somersaults, were writhing on the ground.
All of them opened crazed eyes, the gaze of which had climbed
up behind the lid, and foam was emerging from their lips, while
they clawed their breasts with furious fingernails.

"You see," proclaimed Hadj-Hidi, "they aren't thinking of
amour such as you want it, but it's in their occult transports that
the Emperor comes to visit them, and entire nights pass without
him emerging from this redoubt. The mutilated priestesses of
Kuthu'l triumph over the most famous courtesans!"

Hallabab took Assilinia's hand

"Come," she said, "these creatures horrify me."

On the threshold, the Rani turned round. "Remember your
promise, Hadj-Hidi. Tomorrow I'll bring Samjab and Pekeo."

VI
Shah Jahan and the Begum

When Shah Jahan took possession of Delhi, the land of the
Moguls was in its full splendor. The number of provinces that the
predecessors of Shah Jahan had been able to conquer composed
one of the most famous empires in the world. From Kandahar,
which had been conquered from the Persians, all the territory
that extends to the Ganges was submissive to the power of the
Mogul. The treasures of the palace were magical, and it was said
that one entire room was filled with precious stones of large size
and inestimable value.

The Master, however, in the midst of his people, his eunuchs,
his guards and his wives, slept with one eye open, so much did he
fear the surreptitious conspiracies and revolts that he sensed rumbling around him. His sons were already making war, thinking of
nothing but invading their father's Estates and conquering them
by cunning or by violence. On the other hand, the dethroned

Rajahs, who regarded themselves as so many petty sovereigns in their districts, were agitating on the sly and sowing ideas of rebellion in the people. The diversity of beliefs was another source of disputes between the populations obedient to the Mogul. It was doubtless for that reason that Akbar and Jahangir had formed the design of composing a single religion out of all those that reigned in Hindustan. They had found that it is more difficult to usurp an empire over the minds of people and the prejudices of their childhood than to take the sovereignty of their possessions and their lives.

When the old Hedjeras came to ask for mercy for Mimiose, Shah Jahan was with his daughter, the begum Saeb, whom he honored very particularly with his favors, although she was only ten years old.

Extended at the child's feet he had placed his forehead on her knees and was playing with the heavy necklaces that adorned her puerile grace.

"Little Saeb, I love you deliciously, because you're pretty and because you're of my blood. I adore myself in you, and what greater enjoyment can one have than that of an amour that goes back to its source? I already know the taste of your kisses, and when your gaze encounters mine, they mingle as water mingles with water, sand with sand and the breeze with the breeze in songs and perfumes. Little Saeb, give me your lips, which are mine, and your body, which comes from mine!"

The begum, however, scarcely responded to the paternal transports, and did not allow herself to be swayed by the presents that made her the most envied of the Mogul's daughters. Every morning, new adornments were offered to her; she had prestigiously mounted gems for every day of the month.

Hadj-Hidi dragged herself on her knees all the way to the bronze and gold throne that supported the august couple and rubbed her forehead on the first onyx step, stammering praises to the "Master of the World," and to the "Sovereign Star" whose splendor eclipsed the sun and the stars.

"What do you want?" asked Shah Jahan, quitting the begum, who began playing with the dolls of precious stones.

Seen thus, beneath the gigantic peacock that deployed their wings above the throne, he had a certain majesty, in spite of the stigmata that a dissolute existence had engraved on his parchmented face, annealed with wrinkles and decimated by the abuse of pleasures. He picked up the cushions that had fallen at the feet of the child in an eloquent disorder, and his emerald scepter, the sculpted metal tip of which put cold glaucous gleams on the carpet.

He was clad in yellow, and diamond stars constellated his breast beneath pectorals of emeralds fringed with pearls.

Nothing equaled the magnificence of that royal hall paved with multicolored gems, with immense sheaves of gems in the corners in the form of fruits and flowers, bursting like pyrotechnic suns. The throne was made of solid gold, encrusted with sardonyxes, aquamarines and moonstones; above it was a golden awning sustained by twelve crystal columns, gripped by garlands of roses made of rubies, olivines, amaldines, cymophanes and chrysoberyls.

Perfumes were burning everywhere, emitting clouds of aphrodisiac vapors, sometimes holed by the glaucous eye of an emerald, or the ardent fire of a ruby caressed by an oblique ray of light. Then the vapors drowned the infantile face of the begum, her short black hair, each curl of which was retained by a diamond ring, her scarcely blossoming bosom in which the fragile breasts rose up in abrupt points in a desire as yet imprecise.

In the perverse odor of perfumes, in the ardent atmosphere of that hall, the begum Saeb resembled a frail idol of lust, scarcely more grown-up than the doll she was hugging to her heart, which was rolling enamel eyes in a delicately-carved face of ivory.

Through a partly-open door, the old Hedjeras could see naked women dancing, with one hand over their epilated pubis, their thighs agitated by twisting leaps, while musciennes, similarly naked, formed a circle round them, plucking the vina and striking the dhol.

"Right hand of Mohammed, Lotus of Smara, Sun of Suns," said Hadj-Hidi, in a firm voice, "I have come to ask you for mercy for Mimiose, the Gurkha who has charmed the black panther."

Shah Jahan frowned, and his face, habitually impassive, took on an expression of sly malevolence.

"Is it Princess Assilinia who has sent you?"

"No, Master. It is the pitris who are speaking to you with my voice. In rendering liberty to the Gurkha you would be agreeable to the terrible powers of water and fire."

The Emperor shrugged his shoulders.

"Your beliefs are not mine, and I deem that Mimiose is a conspirator very dangerous to me. He's handsome, he speaks well and his power even extends over wild beasts, since he has vanquished the panther that no one, until now, has been able to confront without trembling."

"Undoubtedly he's an enemy worthy of you, but he'll be able to recognize your benefits and, by freeing him, you'll win him over to your cause."

"The Gurkhas will never submit. And it's already a great deal to spare your protégé's life."

"Oh, Master, for pity's sake, don't be inflexible. Mimiose, free, will defend you."

"No," said Shah Jahan, his voice harsh and his gaze malevolent. "Why are you interested in that bigaris? If it's to please Assilinia, I declare to you that the Rani will marry Prince Orpha. That union serves my interests; I want it to be accomplished."

Hadj-Hidi, who had spoken until then in a posture of humility, drew herself up to her full height. "You say: I want; but the gods inspire me, and I declare to you that you will be broken like a reed if you oppose their designs."

Shah Jahan stod up, trembling with rage, and clapped his hands. Two eunuchs appeared immediately.

"Take this woman," he said, "throw her out of the palace and recommend the sowars who watch over my security to keep her away from my presence for sixty days."

192

Hadj-Hidi raised her fleshless arms and said, mildly: "There is no need, Master, to take such cruel measures against me; you will only see me again when you deign to summon me to your gynaeceum. The Hedjeras are too proud in the soul to afflict with their presence a man who has expelled them."

"So, bats of misfortune, you're opening your dark wings over me! Know, then, that I will expel you from the temple with your tenebrous sisters! Mohammed reproves your shameful practices and he only mutilates men!"

Hadj-Hidi did not riposte, but her shrill laughter reverberated from the steps of the throne like a chaplet of vertebrae on a funerary slab, and she went away between the two eunuchs.

"Oh, the naughty dolls," murmured the begum, throwing her doll at her father's august nose.

VII
Projects of Flight

With a stiff gait, Hadj-Hidi traversed Shah Jahan's Tribunal of Justice, a vast portico in red sandstone, open on three sides, under a triple file of columns and arches of white marble, preciously decorated, with a ceiling of solid silver.

The laughter of the dancers was still pursuing her, and she saw once again the naked courtesans attempting lubricious poses in order to reawaken Shah Jahan's senses as he emerged from the embraces of the begum. Breasts undulating, covered in fine sweat, and under the friction of heavy necklaces, always in motion, their nipples lost the gold powder with which they were coated.

In another hall, Hadj-Hidi saw the Mogul's wives, crouched in a circle around one of their number, who was consulting Hindu cards with fantastic figures of chimeras and dragons. The bracelets, belts and rings with which they were all covered were spitting sparks in the darkness, and they had triumphant dupattas sewn with pearls, and silver branches, with breastplates of ornamental gold that extended under their arms, descended over their thighs and put a reptilian rutilance, always in motion, over their saffron-tinted skin.

As the courtesans started to laugh at seeing the old woman between the two eunuchs, the card-reader remained still, her eyes fixed on the barbaric illuminations, like a somnambulist pursuing her dream.

"Wives," said the Hedjeras, "I am as scornful of you as the indecent dancers who take the strength of an old man by means of torsions of the loins, cries of lust and rut! You dissolve the omnipotent will of the Master by the stirring of your breasts and the shaking of your bellies. You only know how to stiffen flesh and harden the muscles of your lovers, who are no longer anything but spineless after those simulacra of amour. I despise you, and your sarcasms do not afflict me."

All the women stood up in order to fall upon the audacious woman who dared to raise her voice under the vaults of the gynaeceum; but the eunuchs dragged Hadj-Hidi way and left her at the bottom of the steps of the terrace that descended into the Jumna.

On the ghats, crouching on the water's edge, she found Assilinia, who, in the garments of a Bhai-tchokri, her face hidden, was waiting for her anxiously.

"Well, Hadj-Hidi?"

"All was futile."

"The Master refused?"

"Alas!"

"What does he want, then?"

"He wants you to marry Orpha, and you have doubtless divined why."

"Orpha is of noble birth. He will deliver the Empire from its enemies, and will deliver his wife to the Emperor."

"Shah Jahan covets your beauty."

"I know that. He's already weary of the begum and the submissive kisses of his wives no longer tempt him."

"Orpha is ambitious, and will stop at nothing to obtain command of the imperial troops."

Assilinia bowed her head, dejected; then her eyes flashed.

"You haven't been able to catch him, Hadj-Hidi. It was necessary to threaten the Mogul with the occult vengeance of the pitris. He believes in spells and bewitchments, and trembles before the menace of unknown gods."

"I said what it was necessary to say, but his amorous desire is stronger than his terror. You'll be extracted from your palace and delivered to the Master, Assilinia."

"I want to flee! Protect me, Hadj-Hidi! Free Mimiose in order that the two of us can go to hide our amour in some distant solitude!"

The Rani, who was rubbing clusters of saligram wrenched from her belt between her small feverish hands, looked at the old woman with anguish.

"I'd answer for the prisoner with my head," said the Hedjeras. "I've already said too much in his favor."

"I implore you! Have pity! We'll summon the Fakirs to our aid."

Hadj-Hidi hesitated. She knew that she had great power over the Omraos and the Djaths who believed in curses and spells, but the Emperor, fatigued by lust, annihilated by excessively vivid sensation too often repeated, scarcely obeyed anything any longer but his vague desires.

"I reign in the Temple of Kuthu'l, but I can do nothing over the Master of your destiny, for he wants your possession and nothing can deflect him from an amorous folly. However, I'll come to your aid—but don't forget, little one, that I'm gambling with my life and that you'll have difficulty compensating me for my pains."

"I know . . ."

"You'll depart by night in a badjera, which devoted men will enable to glide over the water silently, like an expiatory danghi laden with the mortal remains of a Brahmin and his offerings to Shiva."

"I'll leave tomorrow, because it's necessary to hasten."

"Yes, tomorrow."

"How good you are!"

The old Hedjeras has a singular smile. "I desire that everything succeeds in accordance with your wishes, Assilinia, but I repeat to you that it's necessary, in order to bring such an enterprise to a successful conclusion, that you ensure the good graces of the goddess Durga."

"I'm ready to immolate the most beautiful parts of my herds."

"That's not enough. She wants human victims, and you've promised me Samjab and Pekeo."

"Oh," sighed the young woman. "That's true, I'd forgotten that."

"Tomorrow, little one, you'll be free . . ."

"And the doors of Kuthu'l will close on the victims of amour?"

"It's necessary."

VIII
For the Sacrifice

"Virgins, put perfumes everywhere on your flesh . . . in order that the god of amour, in kissing your mouth . . . will breathe in that kiss as if in a bouquet . . . all the lotuses of your couch!

"Virgins, put on perfumes!

"To Lingam you will give yourselves . . . only once in your life . . . and by virtue of that sacred union . . . you will be his forever.

"To Lingam you will give yourselves!

"Into you, virgins, he will descend . . . his amour will fill your hearts . . . Hastini, Chitrini, Padmini . . . of you Krishna will be the conqueror . . . like flowers, he will take you.

"Into you, virgins, he will descend!

"And it will be like honey . . . a soft and voluptuous flow . . . a gentle ray fallen from the sky . . . the profound kiss of Lingam . . . who will penetrate you to the heart.

"And it will be like honey!"

The Hedjeras sang, swaying, those verses taken from the *Torch of Amour*, by the great poet Jayadeva, who boasts of having written on every subject.

Mutilated priestesses, they circled slowly around the lingam, decorated with roses and tuberoses, which received the supreme offering of little virginal victims.

The temple is in fête, as happens every time that a young girl or a child has to undergo the operation that will consecrate her forever to the goddess.

The voices of the servants of Durga cover the cries of pain and the supplications; a golden cup, held by a Yogi, receives the precious blood of the victims of torture, and nothing equals the joy of the criminal priestesses after the immolation.

Samjab and Pekeo have entered, conducted by Hallabab, who is weeping with them, and can find no consolations except for kisses. The two little virgins are naked; their bodies have been steeped in perfumes for a long time, and their hair envelops them with a silky mantle. Hallabab makes them a necklace of her arms, hugs them madly, unable to resolve to quit her cherished companions. Like them and to encourage them, she will give herself to the lingam, but she will not undergo the mutilation, being of higher birth than Samjab and Pekeo, and, in consequence, free in her person.

The songs became increasingly vehement, the vina sobbed hectically, while the dole made rapid gasps and the sitar modulated the plaints of the "wounded dove" in a minor key. Cassolettes in which aromatic herbs were burning sent forth warm and acrid gusts. The two victims were pushed over a stove from which they breathed in the morbid effluences, and they straightened up tottering, showing the whites of their eyes, already intoxicated.

Hadj-Hidi made them chew ganja, which threw them into convulsions, and then they were taken to the seat where the crime was to be consummated. Their entire bodies agitated by febrile somersaults, they were subjected to the rape of the lingam, weeping unconscious tears of pain, while that farandole of the mutilated women with flat chests, narrow hips and hoarse voices circled around them.

"Virgins, put perfumes everywhere on your flesh . . . in order that the god of amour, in kissing your mouth . . . will breathe in that kiss as if in a bouquet . . . all the lotuses of your couch!

"Virgins, put on perfumes!

"To Lingam you will give yourselves . . . only once in your life . . . and by virtue of that sacred union . . . you will be his forever.

"To Lingam you will give yourselves!"

The Hedjeras resume the verses of the Consecration, and repreat it endlessly, while Samjab and Pekeo are carried through the galleries of the temple, where unnatural creations unfurl in bas-relief, with the abductions of naked women by fantastic animals, between spangled plants terminating in phalluses and flowers with vulvate corollas, yawning over skies violently painted in ultramarine. Under the columns of the temple, the most singular couplings triumphed, fantasies of a delirious imagination of which nothing in nature can give any idea. The unsexed guardians of the goddess Durga contemplate those scenes, exasperating lust incessantly, repeated infinitely on the walls, the ceilings, the porticos, the cornices and in any place where the gaze might settle.

The noise of instruments is still stridulating in the distance when the panting children are deposited on a golden bed for the supreme mutilation.

Eyes closed and lips dry, they abandon themselves, and Hadj-Hidi prepares the long needles impregnated with bhel-phoul and arranges within the reach of her hand a few surgical instruments and bandages of delicate cloth.

The Hedjeras' eyes are shining strangely, her toothless mouth set in a cruel rictus that hollows out the wrinkles in her cheeks, and she truly seems to be some malevolent sorceress escaped from the temple of Djagganath on the Blue Mountain.

She offers to Durga the *mahaprasad*, the sacred nourishment of the goddess. She tests with her fingers the points of the instruments of torture, and, bending over the bodies of the victims, she parts their frail knees, which two Hedjeras maintain vigorously.

But all the instrumentalists have arranged themselves around the golden bed with the bloodstained cushions, and the dances resume, rhythmed by cries of agony.

"To Lingam you will give yourselves . . . only once in your life . . . and by virtue of that sacred union . . . you will be his forever.

"To Lingam you will give yourselves!"

IX
The Badjera

While the mutilated courtesans of the temple of Kuthu'l embrace one another frenetically and roll, enlaced, at the feet of Samjab and Pekeo, who have lost consciousness again, Assilinia has rejoined the prisoner.

Pressing against him like a wheedling cat, she tells him that the hour of liberty has sounded and that he can take her wherever seems good to him.

"I've come to liberate you, Mimiose; let's flee together. You'll keep me like a little private possession and we'll hide in your homeland. Your brethren, the Gurkhas, won't denounce us. Do you want to?"

He looked at her, anxious, not daring to believe in so much good fortune.

"We'll be followed, we'll be recaptured, and the worst punishments will fall upon us!"

"No, I tell you. No danger threatens us. Are we not protected by Hadj-Hidi, who will give us her badjera and her oarsmen? Come, come—I love you!"

Ramo, the black panther, rubbed her supple spine against the Rani's legs, and her eyes shone like amorous torches. By that glaucous gleam the young couple embraced, drawing from their first caresses the courage necessary for their escape.

Assilinia's warm body abandoned itself, and the Gurkha could not weary of drinking from the cup of her lips, forgetting, in that new fever, all the perils outside.

"My adored! My adored! How have you been able to think of me and descend as far as my tenderness?"

"I love you!"

"But I'm nothing but a poor bigaris!"

"I love you!"

"Won't you blush at having given me so much joy?"

"I love you!"

And to everything that he said in his humility as an obscure and fervent lover, she responded with the divine phrase that absolved them both: "I love you! I love you! I love you!"

Then he lay her down on the quivering fleece of Ramo, the complicit panther, and, kneeling before those two bodies of nervous and lascivious beauty, he plunged into the nirvana of caresses.

A burst of laughter extracted them from their ecstasy.

"The badjera is in front of the ghats. The time has come."

Hadj-Hidi, opening the door of the cell wide, showed them, at the end of the dark corridor, the large patch of azure and gold of a sky speckled with stars.

"You have your entire life to cherish one another," she said. "Go, and may Durga be propitious to you!"

They got up, sighing, and, leaning on one another, they emerged from the bleak redoubt, while Ramo, bounding ahead of them, uttered a profound growl.

Mimiose installed the Rani in the bottom of the boat, close beside him, for it seemed to him that that flesh was already his, and he would have liked to caress it incessantly, to penetrate it with irresistible effluvia, to intoxicate himself on its sweetness and its perfume.

They glided softly over the Jumna, which runs from the north to the south of Delhi. To the north, the banks of the river and its islets constituted a dense jungle, to the south there was a vast plain whose soil was strewn with the debris of ancient cities, where the Rajahs still constructed citadels, temples and palaces. With the Moguls, other cults had replaced the religions of amour and death, the savage beliefs of the Brahmin worshipers of Shiva.

Nothing equaled, by the tremulous light of the stars, the gripping eloquence of that indefinite horizon of dying things, proclaiming the eternal struggle of man against man, in spite of all the religions of goodness and forgiveness.

"Ah!" said Assilinia, under her lover's kisses. "You'll avenge me! You'll avenge my father! It's necessary not to depart, to neglect our cause, which is the holiest of all!"

"Yes, yes, let's stay!"

Immediately, however, she changed her mind, fearing the danger to her beloved of capture, torture and death. The Emperor, alas, was pitiless toward conspirators and rebels.

The oarsmen impelled the light boat smoothly, and the entire past of Delhi passed before the somber gaze of the lovers, for Indraprastha—the Delhi of the Arya, more than two thousand years before Shah Jahan—had already known a frightful series of calamities. The metropolis of Hindustan is perhaps, throughout the entire world, the city that has drunk the most blood and has seen the most tears flow.

Delhi has always been attacked, taken and retaken by the invaders and all the heroes of India. Many religions have flourished there, giving rise to new battles perhaps more furious than those of the conquerors. Under Shah Jahan, Brahmanism still persisted, maintained by the Rajahs and the Omraos. The people always went toward their ancient gods, in spite of their vices and their cruelties; sacrifices still stained the slabs of temples with crimson before Shiva and Durga, and the victims themselves implored the favor of "Consecration" in agonizing tortures.

The badjera fled more rapidly, for the glimmers of dawn were already dressing the crouching domes of the mosques and the slender colonnettes of the minarets with a glaze of lacquer and ocher.

Nothing was comparable to the glory of that sunrise over that décor of enchantment, and Assilinia closed her eyes, as if dazzled by so much tragic splendor. The enlaced young couple dared not raise their voices. Pressed against one another, they whispered their traveling plans in fearful voices.

"We'll go toward the Himalaya," said Mimiose. "You'll be safe among my own people; but the journey is difficult. Will you have the strength to follow me?"

"Oh, yes," she sighed. "Isn't it there that the purest blood of the Rajahs is found? Let's go toward your people, who are honest and brave, toward the majesty of the mountains of ice and fire."

"Alas, little Rani, are you forgetting that Delhi is an incomparable abode, where, under the arches of every palace, the Persian distich can be read:

> *If there is a radiant paradise in this world*
> *Stop, traveler, it is here, it is here.*

"My paradise is next to you!"

She extended her mouth to him, where he drank the wine of forgetfulness without ever ending his thirst. He would have intoxicated himself insatiably at that divine cup if the young woman had not pushed him away gently.

"We're not yet safe, Mimiose. Moderate your transports. If the Emperor learns of my flight, he'll have me pursued by his harkarat, and the sowars will lock us in some bleak cell, Can't you hear the sound of his marching troops?"

"I can't hear anything."

"I assure you that spears are glinting in the distance between the branches. Shah Jahan knows of our escape!"

"No, little flower of amour, those spears of flame are only the sun's rays caressing silvery bagicha leaves!"

"That's true. Oh, how frightened I was!"

"You can be tranquil; the Emperor is asleep in his begum's arms."

He laughed; but she went on, gravely: "You're mistaken, Mimose; the Emperor no longer desires the begum Saeb. That perverse feast has been of short duration, like all his whims, and the fragile loveliness of the child no longer retains him."

"After her he'll do violence to his other two daughters, the begums Roxanara and Merniza."

"Perhaps . . . but it's me that he covets today. Then too, there's Orpha, who will only be powerful by marrying me and whose ambition is watching me."

"Orpha isn't healed of Ramo's wounds."

"I've seen him wandering around the temple of Kuthu'l."

Mimiose clenched his fists; then, clutching the young woman against him, he said: "Let him come, then, to take you from my arms!"

Ramo, showing her terrible fangs, uttered a long roar, and Assilinia had to apply the muzzle of the beast to her breast in order to stifle her denunciatory growling. Then the panther extinguished the dual flash of her pupils and ran her pink tongue with erect papillae over the Rani's velvet breasts.

"Yes, Ramo, my little darling," Assilinia continued, shivering under that caress. "We'll go to slake our thirst in the sacred lakes and we'll kiss the idol with twelve heads and twelve sexes, which reposes under the golden deota of the distant mountains. We'll dance with the ebony gods who are paraded in the villages, covered with flowers and finery."

The Rani fell silent for a moment, abandoning her little hands to the warm caress of the panther.

Now that they were traveling together, they were no longer in a hurry, simultaneously enjoying their intimacy and the vague danger that was still hovering over them.

The Rani saw once again the narrow cell where Mimiose had lived under the protection of Ramo, and the voluptuous beast made her slightly anxious, like a rival that one cannot drive away, and to whose sly affection one is subjected.

It seemed to her that she could hear once again the chilamchi, which the musicienes were striking harder with sticks of pitel, while the dance of the Hedjeras around Samjab and Pekeo was exasperated.

With a constriction in the heart she recalled the plaints of the little victims, delivered to the Lingam; then she perceived the course of the mutilated women through the long corridors following Hadj-Hidi, who had completed her premeditated crime coldly, in the midst of the most culpable intoxications.

Samjab and Pekeo, the little girls with the ingenuous gazes, were delivered henceforth to the goddess, and, as they were gracious and pretty, the Brahmins would use them as well as the eunuchs and the yogis.

"In order to liberate you, Mimiose, I have sacrificed the dearest possessions I had. Will you forget that?"

"Never, my adored."

"And when I'm yours, you'll have the same gratitude and respect for me?"

"You can't doubt it!"

"Oh, I doubt everything. My childhood was so unhappy! Those closest to me were killed; I'm alone in this world! But let's not think about the dolorous past, let's talk about you, my love."

She remained silent momentarily, and then she asked the Gurkha: "is it true that in your homeland, all the men of a family only possess one wife, and that they take advantage of her in turn without jealousy?"[1]

_____

1 The French physician François Bernier (1620-1688) spent many years in India, mostly as the personal physician to two of Shah Jahan's sons, Dara Shokh and Aurangzeb. He published an account of those experiences that was translated into English as *Travels in the Mogul Empire, A.D. 1656-1668*

"Yes," said Mimiose. "Among us we have substituted polyandry for polygamy. Never, in a family, no matter how numerous the brothers are, do they take more than one wife, with whom they live in perfect intelligence."

"Those are the mores of the Aryans, such as they are described in the *Mahabharata*."

She smiled, amused by that idea of a harem of men, in which the wife only had to choose a new lover every day.

"I'll keep you for myself alone," affirmed Mimiose.

"Certainly," she said, "I shall only be yours, since it's you that I love and whom I've taken freely. But it's no less true that that conception of sensuality is far more logical than the one admitted among us. Cannot one woman satisfy several men, my love?"

"One man, on the other hand, can fecundate several women, and nature only wants renewal, creation, incessant creation, to reproduce herself in her glory eternally."

X

Sensuality

They traveled for a part of the day. Toward evening, when luminous flies swarmed in the profound azure like clouds of golden dust, Assilinia, who had gone to sleep on the Gurkha's shoulder, opened astonished eyes.

---

and an essay on *Nouvelle division de la terre part les différentes espèces ou races qui l'habitent* [A New Division of the Earth in Accordance with the Different Species or Races that Inhabit It] (1684), an important but mostly specious proto-anthropological work that laid the foundations of much later racial theory. His passing assertion that polyandrous societies existed in the remote valleys of "Kachemire" was based on a second-hand account of dubious authenticity, but it started a hare running that became one of the most persistent myths of pseudoanthropology, with many later travelers producing equally dubious accounts, mostly related to Tibet. Although isolated instances of polyandry undoubtedly occurred, there is no evidence of any society or tribe ever having institutionalized the practice, and none of the allegations refer to Gurkhas. La Vaudère, however, found the notion sufficiently intriguing to use it as the basis of *Le Harem de Syta*, tr. in the present series as "Syta's Harem."

The solitude was profound. Only the splash of paddles troubled the tranquility of the water, sleepy between the pink lotuses of its banks. Strange metallic spiders were slipping through the foliage, and immense horned moths stained with ocher and cinnabar were chasing one another, and sometimes coupling in the air, combining the rhythmic beat of their furry wings.[1] A fecundating dust fell from the branches and the breath of eternal desire passed over everything.

"We're going, my friend, to the source of the Ganges, which is marked by three peaks clad in lianas and roses."

"Yes, those three mountains were consecrated, like gigantic altars, to Tudra, a divinity of Vedic times, whom we worship today under the name of Shiva. Himalayan maidens will offer you silver bowls from which to drink, and you'll be the queen of that land of fervor and amour."

The badjera had come alongside the bank and Mimiose, taking Rani in his arms, deposited her on a bed of dry leaves in a bamboo hut that a djath had consented to lend them for a few hours. The poor man, smiling at their happy tenderness, brought chapattis kneaded in ghi and ghour, palm wine and mahua flowers cooked in honey.

After having done honor to that light meal, the lovers sat down under a manchineel, for the shade of that tree, far from giving death, incites voluptuous languors. The wind passed through the clumps of reeds, and a herdsman's flute strung together its crystalline notes in the distance, which charmed the green parrots and great bee-eaters.

Assilinia took a betel leaf and fruit between her lips, which she presented to her lover. Applying his mouth to the flowery mouth, he savored the juice of the fruits of amour for a long time. By that communion she offered herself to him, gave herself without reserve, and very quickly, under the swirling flight of the

---

1 La Vaudère's frequent references to large "horned moths" with this color scheme are almost certainly to the Atlas moth, *Attacus atlas*, the furry antennae of which could easily be mistaken for horns at a naïve glance.

golden flies, he collected the corollas of the path and the odorous herbs of streams in order to make a nuptial couch.

In the djath's narrow hut, he dressed the altar of the caress, which was soon a glorious throne, and when there was no longer a parcel of soil in the humble shelter that as not covered in petals, he came back to the beloved, pressed against her, his mouth close to her erect breasts, and commenced his voluptuous song in the fashion of the Gurhkas, warriors and seducers.

"Kama, Smara, Annanya, the god of love whispers in the sighs of the wind and the waters. His voice, softer than a cry of the hulote, swells into a tempest and makes the waves rise!

"Kama, in the waves, mysterious Smara in the profound forests, on the earth and in the skies, exalt all day long in poems of amour.

"To your radiant body I attach my lips, quivering with fever, which will be able to cover you, like a golden mesh, with kisses, kisses and more kisses; from your dainty foot to your red mouth, in order that your heart stirs, slowly they will rise.

"Then in the secret nest of caresses, the fiery nest of desires, the god Kama for your pleasure, and the god Smara for your intoxication, will huddle very gently, and remain there for more than an hour, like the penetrating vilva."

Mimiose spelled out those stanzas from the *Gita Govinda* ardently, and the soothing poem of Jayadeva made the young woman shiver divinely.

"Take me, come into me, remain in me," she murmured, holding the Gurkha against her erect breasts. "Don't you understand that I've loved you for a long time, always, and that nothing is worth as much to me as the savor of your kisses?"

But he was still adoring her, not daring to accomplish the work of the flesh, for he respected her with a fervor equal to his desire. She was the Rani, the Omnipotent, the radiant Virgin, the daughter of the Rajah, whom he ought to celebrate in his soul and in his heart like a parcel of the golden mountain where the gods reside.

However, like all the adepts of the ancient Brahmanic cults, he had the science of sensuality, and, by means of a thousand delicate games, he maddened the senses of his beloved.

"Your happiness is mine," he said. "Above all, I want you to be happy, for the initiation will make you suffer."

"Oh, let your breath penetrate me! I want to suffer!"

Between them, Ramo purred like an amorous she-cat, passing her large pink tongue between her sharp fangs, and electric waves ran over her black fur, making the Rani shiver more delightfully. The lascivious beast sometimes stretched herself, offering her warm back to the lovers like a velvet pillow, and sometimes got up with a bound, with a kind of hoarse mewl though which all the cruel enervations of the jungle passed.

"I'm jealous of Ramo!" Assilinia wept, then. "She's always between us; she loves you as I do!"

"Ramo is only a very affectionate panther, my little queen, who has kept me company in my prison."

"She has done more for you, in sparing you in the games of the Tamascha, than I have done in opening the doors of your prison!"

Mimiose laughed, placing his hand on the beast's prominent forehead.

"Since we both adore you, Rani, of what are you complaining? Truly, all three of us are young, strong and beautiful! Who would dare to attack us?"

"Shut up!"

"I don't fear Shah Jahan, or anyone in the world, since I have your love!"

"Shh! It's necessary not to tempt the gods!"

For a long time they lulled themselves to the splash of the waves, under the protective manchineel, to the plaintive calling of turtle-doves, mingled with the mewls of the ardent and submissive panther.

Suddenly, however, the beast stood up, beat her flanks with her long tail, furrowed her jowls, and a double spark sprang from her emerald eyes.

"Ramo is troubled; some danger is threatening us," said Assilinia.

Without replying, Mimiose took the young woman in his arms, laid her down on the bed of flowers that he had prepared, and possessed her madly.

XI
The Alert

In the morning, when they were finally drowsy, after so many caresses, kisses and agonies of amour, followed by triumphant resurrections, they were woken up by Ramo's muted growling.

The panther was not roaring, seemingly understanding that her cries would betray the fugitives' presence, but, with all her fur bristling, her claws extended and her flanks agitated by profound waves, she was preparing to launch herself outside.

The djath, who was on watch outside the hut, soon came in, his face distraught with fear.

"A troop of sowars passed by yesterday, not far from here. Now they're coming back, doubtless guided by the river-dwellers who saw the badjera gliding along the river. You're no longer safe here; it's necessary to leave as quickly as possible."

"Leave!" sighed Mimiose, clutching the supple body of his beloved against his heart. "I won't have the strength."

Assilinia, her arms around her lover's neck, seemed exhausted by voluptuous fever.

"Let's stay," she said. "What's the point of fleeing and seeking other adventures? What greater happiness could we savor? Have we not known the plenitude of terrestrial felicities?"

But the djath became impatient. "If they find you here, it's death for me. Have pity on the humble bigaris who offered you his shelter for that night of amour."

"He's right," said the Rani. "We don't have the right to drag that poor man into our doom. Where are the oarsmen?"

But Mimiose shook his head. "The river isn't safe; it's necessary to flee through the forest."

"Flee without elephants and without horses? We won't have the courage to drag ourselves that far, and we'll soon be discovered."

"Perhaps the sowars will pass by without stopping, as they did yesterday."

"Oh," said the djath, "if they've come back, it's because they've picked up your trail."

"In fact," said Assilinia, shivering, "it's tomorrow that Orpha was to present me to the Emperor for the official wedding. He'll be searching for me furiously. What are we going to do? We no longer have time to flee!"

The heavy footfalls of a troop of elephants were drawing ever closer. Ramo, who was being held back by Mimiose, was making furious bounds and uttering hoarse sighs of rage.

"Are your enemies of the Brahmin religion?" asked the djath, rapidly.

"Orpha is the son of a Rajah; he believes in the old gods."

"Follow me, then, crawling through the reeds. I'll take you to the yogi charmer who lives in the jungle and has commerce with pitris in the midst of wild beasts. His protection is omnipotent."

✳

The lovers had quit the bed of roses and lotuses on which they had given themselves to one another recklessly during that unforgettable night, and the young woman, having hastily picked up her jewels and garments, allowed herself to be drawn away by Mimiose.

The ground, bristling with dry grass, crackled underfoot; they dragged themselves along on their knees, advancing prudently but surely, as far as a path frayed through the woods. The djath, who knew all the turnings and folds of the terrain, preceded them, parting the branches in their passage.

They heard the heavy troop of sowars massing behind them. Soon, an enormous rocket sprang forth above the trees, followed by other even brighter rockets, and then a veritable wall of flames hid the horizon from them, and they understood that their enemies had set fire to the bamboo hut, which was consumed with an incredible rapidity. The wind, although light, gave birth to others blooms of flame in the reeds, and the conflagration spread, opening mortal flowers with luminous petals everywhere.

"They've set fire to my home!" sobbed the djath. "I'll never recover what I've lost!"

But Assilinia, detaching her necklaces, gave them to the old man.

"This will compensate you. With these opals and sapphires you can buy a finer house, and I won't abandon you."

Monstrous girandoles of flames were now bursting forth behind them, and a menacing flock of crows and vultures soared over their heads, whose clamors stifled the other cries of the forest.

They were obliged to run in order not to be overtaken by the fire, but a broad watercourse isolated them from the danger. They gained the other shore, with difficulty, Mimiose carrying his beloved on his shoulders.

Not far from there the jungle commenced. The long florid branches of the trees were entangled in the air. The musa trees, the pandanus trees, the mangoes, the nictanies and the nagatellies, curtained with lianas, suspended strange crimson corollas everywhere, like open mouths avid for kisses. Delicate stems, like garlands of spun glass, rose along the trunks, displaying prestigious sprays, enlacing fleshy calices from which black bees emerged, intoxicated by nectar. Insects with glittering corselets were running in all directions, forming mosaics of gems. Birds with golden wings were pursuing moths with silver wings often larger than themselves; giant dragonflies were spreading diamantine wings, searching the crimson sandalwoods, nopals and dragon-trees, while blue wasps striped with ocher surrounded bushes that produced nard and cardamom.

There, everything was quietude and smiles.

Assilinia would have liked to repose beneath those embalmed arches and porticos of verdure, of a dream-like splendor and delicacy, but the djath would not permit it.

"Let's go further," he said. "Here, excessively lovely nature won't protect us; let's go into the heart of the forest; there, death struggles with life incessantly. The jungle is populated by monsters, enemies of man, which feast on flesh and blood."

"Ramo is with us."

"Ramo would be impotent against the serpents the color of aquamarine that hide under the foliage, and the tigers with yellow flanks striped with velvet, which lurk in the reeds. Only the charmer can triumph over the ambushes of the pitris with the bodies of reptiles and predators."

"Oh," said Assilinia, "nature would be imperiled by her own fecundity if she didn't harbor in her bosom that legion of devourers who engulf everything that falls, everything that falters and no longer has the strength to fight. Have not humans also said: Woe betide the weak! Woe betide those who have no claws to rend their prey, and whom pity arrests in the necessary work of destruction!"

"Can't you smell the insipid odor of musk?" Mimiose interrogated.

"In fact," said the Rani, "I feel nauseated."

"We're walking over the age-old dust of cadavers. This gray sand that sticks to our feet is composed of thousands of bones that the wild beasts have left. Under the impenetrable and burning shelter of jungles, life and death are eternally confounded. In the same way, purulence and diseases flourish in the human domain: the tetanus of covetousness, the hot fever of lust and the gangrene of crime! In the clearings, in the glaucous filtration of branches where the celestial rays penetrate, there's a rutilant swarming of enameled scarabs, plushy moths ocellated like peacocks' tails, with sardonyxes and rubies. At night, the stars seem to quit the skies to abandon themselves to implausible farandoles! The entire

Milky Way quivers in the light of golden flies, and traces before dazzled eyes the grimoires of fire and eternal mystery.

"In low places, an obscure population of filthy and viscous creatures splashes: water snakes, caimans, and monstrous salamanders with bodies pustulated with ocher and chrome. Here, one can almost see the plants growing, so irresistible is the surge of the sap. These vegetations, hectic with desire, come together, grip one another and embrace one another like lovers, and the inextricable fornication of jungles can stop an army on the march. One tree becomes a forest if its branches hang down to the ground. On the fiery contact with the ground it is animated, an infinite ardor penetrates it, and soon, under the unleashing of its productive spasms, it gives birth to new shoots, which grow infinitely."

"I'm breathing fire!" said Assilinia. "Oh, dear love, put your arm round my waist, hold me against you in order to defend me against the violation of cruel nature!"

He pressed her against his bosom more forcefully, and refreshed himself momentarily on the nectar of her lips, intoxicated by the sensuality of creatures and things.

Around them, leaves were detached from the trees and ran toward other trees. One might have thought that they were carried by the wind, if the wind had been blowing in those labyrinths of verdure.

"They're animate vegetations that nourish themselves on dew and pollen," said Mimiose, who knew all the secrets of the forest. "They've exhausted the calices that they're quitting and going to suspend themselves from other pistils, from which they will drink the fecundating sap. They're hermaphrodites, and self-sufficient. But those corollas that are opening beside you, Assilinia, those disquieting flowers that seem to be corroded by leprosy and reaching like the crooked hands of corpses, are vegetal ghouls, carnivorous plants that secrete a digestive liquid and grow fat on larvae and insects. They're equipped with curved spines that fold over and form a grille over the scarab they imprison. These droseras, these metallic green nepenthes,[1] absorb everything that lives above them."

The Rani parted the murderous corollas, some of which, tinted with verdigris and dotted with livid patches, gave off a charnel house odor.

Everywhere, scaling the trees, there was a tide of fantastic, hybrid vegetation unfurling like the waves of a dream ocean. Foliage submerged flowers in the form of gelatinous medusae, cephalopods, mollusks and madrepores—and from all those vegetal mouths a murmur seemed to emerge comparable to that of waves.

The air became rarefied, the vault became darker, and suddenly, into the ferns, a light crept like a fiery serpent. It was produced by rhizomorphs that cast a singular glow as they respired.

The young woman shivered against her friend's heart.

"I'm afraid," she said. "Everything here kills or is immolated. Enjoyment and pain are invincibly united. Amour and Death march side by side. The very stones seem to be moving and struggling against us."

She was stifling increasingly in that atmosphere of plants, where the horrible odor of musk coming from tiger-cats, vultures and cobras half-eaten by predators reigned everywhere.

Ramo, her belly brushing the ground, slid between the tall ferns, disappearing in the inextricable tangle, then suddenly showing herself on the high branch of a coconut palm, her whiskers splayed and her ears flattened, in a pose of suspicion and expectation. If any animal with delicate flesh wandered within her reach, she gathered herself, and then pounced on her prey with lightning rapidity; her somber fur glistened like jade, and carnivores sniffing her from afar, did not show themselves—for the black panther of Java is feared even by the royal tiger.

---

1 The author appears to be confusing two different genera of carnivorous plants, *Drosera* (sundews) and *Nepenthes* (pitcher plants). Her "animate vegetations" are imaginary, but similar organisms are described in Ludovic de Beauvoir's *Voyage autour de monde* (1867; tr. as *A Voyage round the world*), which La Vaudère used as a source in several of her exotic novels.

"I'm very tired," the young woman murmured. "Can't we rest for a moment? Look, my feet are bleeding and my knees are bruised . . ."

"A little more courage," said the djath.

The feverish orchids were swaying more gently and emitting putrid miasmas, drinking and spreading death insatiably, in a debauchery of sap and color.

The Rani, at the end of her strength, closed her eyes, and a faint sigh escaped her dry lips.

"Carry her," ordered the bigaris. "A few more steps and we'll be there. The charmer's retreat is here."

XII
The Yogi

Behind a thicket of plants bristling like daggers and spearheads, a glaucous sheaf of weapons above which floated, like barbaric banners, venomous flower-heads in blinding colors, a small sandy mound rose. In the middle, partly buried and covered in a sort of varnish of dirt, was a pale, emaciated, sexless individual who opened strange bright yellow and cold eyes beneath black eyelids. His mouth, with flat, clapped lips, was furrowed beneath a nose with a desiccated ridge, as pinched as that of a corpse. Extraordinarily thin arms, the arms of a skeleton, were folded over his breast. In the hollow of the clavicles, birds had built their nest.

"This is Krumilianik, the yogi charmer," said the djath, prostrating himself. "He has been here for twenty years, and the animals nourish him. He alone can save you from the others and yourselves, for he is similar to Shiva, the invincible god of Evil and Good. He will show you the way to the temple of sacrifice, where you can make a few offerings that are agreeable to the god, but he doesn't want anything for himself. Interrogate him."

Mimiose put his hand to his forehead and his breast, and then prostrated himself, as the djath had done.

"We have come to you," he said, humbly. "Can you help us?"

Without moving—for he was condemned to immobility and his atrophied limbs had acquired the hardness of wood—Krumilianik fixed his troubling yellow gaze on the lovers, and spoke in a clarion voice, strange in that desiccated body.

"I will guide you toward the god, for I see that you are of the good religion and that, like me, you hate the Moguls. Since the grim exterminator who called himself Timur Lenk traveled India at the head of ninety thousand men and devastated the banks of the Ganges, we have been in desolation! Conflagration, pillage and relentless extermination signaled the taking of our most beautiful domains. While Timur killed women and children and delivered himself to the filthiest of orgies, his lieutenants ravaged the kingdom of Lahore. Everywhere they had passed, there was the horror of ruins and cemeteries. Those hordes, laden with booty, dragging long files of prisoners in their wake, came to lay siege to Delhi, and before launching the assault, Timur had his three hundred thousand prisoners quartered, burned, impaled and murdered. In the holy city, the soldiers, more ferocious than the tigers of the jungle, rushed upon the inhabitants, marked for slaughter like beef and cattle. Women were disemboweled, children raped, hung up on walls in bloody clusters and then thrown to the vultures. No one knows the exact number of that monster's victims, but it's certain that he caused the deaths of more than two million people. However, the work commenced by Timur the lame had to be finished by Babur the tiger."

Krumilianak trumpeted his indignation in a louder voice, and the chicks that were showing their beaks in the nest of his clavicles trembled at those unexpected clamors.

"Babur," the yogi continued, "attacked Hindustan, which he wanted to reduce to his empire, and he reigned over Agra, choosing for a residence the venerated palace of our ancient monarchs. Akbar, the successor of Humayun, continued the perverse work;

he pillaged the treasures of the Rajahs, and his elephants were so covered in gems that they were no longer animals but walking mountains of millions. Our religion languished and the old gods were expelled from their temples. You, who are young and brave, revolt! It is necessary to fight for the good cause; it is necessary to liberate our beautiful land from the yoke of the invaders!"

"Ah!" said Mimiose. "I know full well that I was wrong to flee."

"Return to the Himalayas," said the yogi. "Bring the Gurkhas, your brothers, and fight for our deliverance."

Assilinia was sobbing quietly, not daring to intervene.

"Venerated father," she murmured, finally. "Mimiose loves me, and we're going toward happiness."

Krumilianak laughed scornfully, uncovering his dirty gums, profoundly eroded.

"Go away," he said. "The pitris have spoken through my voice. Go, Mimiose! Steep yourself again in the sacred source of the Ganges; go to find the fatherland of the first Hindus, which was also the fatherland of the gods, as its name, Brahma Vitra, tells you. There you will feel your heart bound with hatred; you will know fecund indignations and the desire for sublime murder will equip your arm. It is in the beautiful land of Ayodhya that the races of the Sun and the Moon were born, from which the privileged families emerged that Brahma had designated to reign over the world, as the Puranas affirm.

"After Rama, who invaded the Deccan and conquered the pearl of the Oriental seas that is called Ceylon, the great epic of the Ramayana unfurled. Sixty princes of his race succeeded Rama, and all were glorious. Our Brahmanic religion is the mother of the world, and all the people drew upon its holy information. As well as the Chinese, the Persians have obtained everything from the Hindus. Modeled on the *Baghavat Gita* of Krishna, the *Zend Avesta* of Zoroaster was written in the Sanskrit dialect. The book of the Hebrews, the *Sepher*, the *Genesis* of Moses, was inspired almost completely by the Dharma Shastra, the code of Brahamanic morality.

"Save for Christ, who was isolated, like Mohammed and Buddha, the Christian religion has also taken our god of three persons. Odin, the master of the Scandinavians, borrowed their best axioms of legislation from the Hindus in order to compose his Havamal. Hermes Trismegistus, whom the Egyptians venerated under the name of Thoth, wrote the famous emerald tablet found in the valley of Hebron under the sepulcher of the same Thoth, whose head was bronze, as Jupiter's beard was gold!

"The foundation of all the religions is similar, O poor human imagination! The various parties of the *Bundahishn* of Zoroaster, the *Chun-Tzu* of Confucius, the *Paemander* and the *Asclepius* of Thoth, the Sepher of Moses, the Havamal of Odin, the Theogony of Orpheus, and finally, all the best pages of the Koran of Mohammed, go back collectively to the Vedas and Puranas of the Hindus!

"Our Brahmanic religion alone is great, and alone is true, since all the false prophets of the world have been unable to liberate themselves from its sublime teachings, and have only embroidered puerile arabesques over the prestigious canvas of crimson and gold that has been conserved throughout the ages.

"O my son, you must submit to the sacred traditions, you must recall incessantly the glorious history of your homeland, until the moment when it was conquered by the Mohammedans. Lift up your forehead, my son, and march against the enemies of the good and the beautiful. The gods have designated you to accomplish great things! But it is necessary not to lose your energy in the arms of a woman."

Assilinia trembled. "You're condemning me? What have I done?" She was weeping.

"You are the gouge avid for its prey, the demon of lust whose kisses soften and deprave!"

The Rani fixed her proud gaze on the yogi's. "I am the one who loves and who puts over the disconcerting realities of life the prestigious veil of tenderness and illusions!"

"That is only temporary, and you abridge, by means of your perverse kisses, the days that are parsimoniously counted for each of us."

"What does it matter if I leave the memory of a few hours of felicity? Is not everything lies down here, except amour?"

"You're blaspheming!"

"Yes, I'm blaspheming, and I fear nothing but the indifference of my lover. If the gods are truly powerful, let them avenge themselves on me!"

The yellow eyes of the yogi had a gleam of rage, and for the first time, his desiccated breast, where the frightful cemetery of the ribs was displayed, rose. A cavernous sigh emerged from his dirty lips and he said, in a hoarse voice: "The Gurkha is free to follow his folly. Only let him know that it will lead him to the cruelest tortures, to shame and to death."

Mimiose, who had remained pensive and silent, drew the young woman against him.

"What do suffering and punishment matter," he murmured, "if your kisses are sweeter than honey?"

"No," said Assilinia, "it's necessary to go away from me if you truly believe my influence to be harmful. I don't want to be an obstacle to your glory."

"Glory is nothing without amour, my beloved. So long as I can press you to my heart, my joy will be complete. All that I need in order to live is the soft light of your eyes and the ardent dew of your mouth!"

Hiccups of sinister laughter burst from the hideous sepulcher where the half-buried yogi was mocking Amour and Death.

Then Mimiose lifted the Rani in his robust arms and set forth into the jungle, under the protection of the wild beasts, less cruel than humans.

PART TWO

I
Sacrifice to Ganga

The abode of the snow—such is the signification of the Hindu name of the Himalaya—is also the abode of the gods. The mountain groups in the azure its light peaks and opaline towers. By nights, ice spirits emerging from a moonbeam seem to be suspended from the golden mane of the stars, and rise toward the stars in the mad rides of white Valkyries.

In reality those prestigious mountains rise to more than fifteen thousand feet above sea level, and a few peaks, standing out from the principal chains, surpass that by a further ten or twelve thousand feet.

The Himalaya, a prodigious manifestation of terrestrial forces, summarizes India, as India summarizes the world.

From the womb of the giant mountains, good and evil, life and death, beauty and horror burst forth. Everything that the human brain can conceive is manifest by the laws of nature alone, without humans even having dared to measure themselves against it.

Although the summits of the mountains shine with an eternal whiteness, the torrents and the streams that are precipitated at their base form a marshy plain in which all the poisonous germs of malaria are born, which form frightful nuclei of corruption.

The creeping bushes with spongy roots, extending their ever-thirsty branches into the fetid water, are swarming with larvae and striped by snakes with livid hues, whose touch alone is mortal.

The north of Bengal, however, in the region where the Ganges and the Jumna obtain their source, is truly an abode of delights.

It was there that Mimiose and his lover, extenuated by fever and amour, came to put themselves under the protection of the daughter of Shiva, the divinity that escaped from the undulating hair of the perverse god and took the name of the river.

Mythology has dressed her in a tiger skin and seated her on an elephant, but in the temple consecrated to her glory she was upright, her knees parted, her arms stiffened above her head, and around her narrow loins gleamed the gems of a heavy golden loincloth whose emerald clasp hid her inviolate sex. Real hair descended from her narrow and prominent brow, falling to her thighs. Her glaucous enamel eyes gleamed against the burnt earth backcloth of her skin, and a ring of enormous diamonds traversing her left nostril covered her puerile mouth. She was frail and disquieting, with her grace of a warrior doll that rejoiced in blood.

For her, the victims were never numerous enough, nor the tortures complicated enough, and her equivocal smile demanded inventions of strange cruelty.

Around her childishly voluptuous prettiness floated a charnel house odor that seemed to delight her thin nostrils; blood reddened her bare feet amid the sapphires and the opals with which they were constellated, but flowers were equally agreeable to her.

The temple only received daylight through the doorway turned to the rising sun, and was only illuminated by a few jade lamps suspended from the vault around the idol, which stood on a granite altar covered with a thick layer of grease and coagulated blood. Perfume burners awaited the balms that only the Brahmins had the right to pour into them.

The temple was composed of several enclosures flanked with round towers and tambours. The niches, separated by partitions, contained the attributes of the goddess, and bas-reliefs ran over the walls everywhere, representing monstrous couplings of animals and humans. In the corners, the double image of the lingam and the yoni were offered to the adoration of pilgrims.

The lovers penetrated to the vicinity of the altar and prostrated themselves before the fakirs who had come to celebrate the three great rivers: the Ganges, the Jumna and the Godavari, of which the religion of Brahma made the divine triad that reigns in Prayaga and is venerated under the name of Tribeni.

Assilinia, meanwhile, asked the goddess to conserve her lover for her, and Mimiose, anxious, recalled involuntarily the words of the yogi, perhaps thinking of fighting for the good cause and avenging his brothers.

A Brahmin burned branches of sage in golden cassolettes, and the audience offered chapattis kneaded from wheat flour. The goddess had tufts of saligram placed on her arms and thighs, and her forehead was crowned with pink lotuses.

In accordance with the rites of worship, piously accomplished, to the slow chant of the mantras, accompanied by a chilamchi struck by a pitel stick that a fakir rolled between his fingers, the Brahmin who was officiating had a goat brought forth, whispered precious recommendations into its ear, and cut its throat at the foot of the altar.

The members of the audience came in turn to dip their hands in the blood that was seething on the granite steps, and the richest offered other animals that were immolated in the same fashion. The sickening odor of warm blood, mingled with the old abattoir reeks of the dimly lit temple, in which only the gems and the glaucous enamel eyes of the goddess were gleaming, was suffocating Assilinia. A sort of morbid languor penetrated her, and she pressed herself against Mimiose, wanting both his protection and his caresses.

Other couples were uniting themselves nearby, intoxicated by the emanations of the virile incense and kusha grass burned in the bronze lingam. Blinded by the dense smoke, they were seeking one another and embracing furiously, at the hazard of encounters, and their sighs mingled with the gasps of the dying beasts.

When there were no more victims to sacrifice, the Brahmins opened the warm cadavers and extracted the hearts, which they placed in silver vases for the evening meal. Meanwhile, the blood, following the inclined slope of the ground, ran outside, and the people who had not been able to penetrate into the temple rushed upon the red river, each of them wanting a few drops with which to purify himself.

A cry rose up, covering the sighs and the gasps:

"Here come the Natis, daughters of joy . . ."

The prostitutes, half-naked, were indeed arriving in a noisy troop, and their bodies, rubbed with balms with sharp effluences, provoked desire. They were holding hands and singing, to a monotonous rhythm, the glory and wisdom of Ganga.

They were obliged, with their eyes closed, to accept the lover who took them, and to accomplish all his wishes meekly. Three times during the grishma, the season of mild ardors, the Natis gave themelves to passers-by for the greater joy of Kama, the god of lust. Not far away, they lived in a temple where the laws of amour were taught, and the scholars who came to take advantage of their lessons were numerous. Everyone respected them, for the religion of Brahma counsels before everything the caress, and every act of amour is agreeable to the gods.

II
The School of Intoxications

After the sacrifice to Ganga, Assilinia went with the Natis to the temple where they practiced the sixty-four manners of Kama and prepared young women for the conquest of men. Before the celebration of a marriage, the bride was placed—as among the Hedjeras before the immolation—on the sacred image, the lingam, in order that she might be rendered fecund by the divine principle. The Brahmins succeeded the god, and the grateful victims expressed their gratitude by means of presents deposited on the altar: phalluses of precious stones equal in number to the number of officiants at the sacrifice.

The greater the number was, the more glory the initiate obtained, and it was also a great honor for her husband. The sakti, or rose mass, in honor of Shiva was also celebrated there.

Assilinia walked among the Natis, who sustained her gently, while Mimiose lingered nonchalantly, watching the pilgrims prostrated along the banks of the Ganges, who were collecting the holy water, and the yogis covered in ash, with their loins circled by cords and their unkempt hair, who, with their hands clenched on their hips, were marching rhythmically, repeating the sacred name of the divinity until their strength was exhausted.

Little girls ornamented with barbaric jewelry, their long gazelle-like eyes further prolonged by streaks of kohl, their frail hips draped in blue gauze dupattas, were offering fetishes, yoni-lingams in gold and silver, perfumed candles and dolls crudely carved in the image of the goddess.

Mimiose, his head heavy, sat down on the ghats that descended into the river. He smiled from a distance at his beloved, who was to rejoin him after the customary ablutions in the sacred water. He wanted, in his turn, to make a sacrifice to the god in order to receive the felicity of amour, shared and durable. Ramo, beside him, was purring softly, glad to have him all to herself, desirous of reconquering him.

In the Hindu religion everything is done to provoke carnal desires, from the most tender age. The bas-reliefs of temples and the sacred carts on which idols are carried in public celebrations are laden with paintings and sculptures that defy any description. Nothing can give an idea of the license of the images that decorated the hall in which the courtesans exercised and taught their lascivious science.

The temple designed a rectangle eighteen meters long and twelve wide. Under the peristyle, a yoni-lingam two meters high, erected on a jade stage, announced the object of the worship, and, almost at every step, cones, symbols of the generative organs, rose up, crowned with lotuses and roses. All around were ranks of numerous goddesses in the poses appropriate to the sacrifice, like the gopis around the god Krishna.

The walls were painted with erotic and singular subjects, animals in rut seeking one another and satisfying one another, phalluses perched on pedestals to which virgins were offering themselves, naked women pursued by monkeys, servants of Shiva solicited by Brahmins.

There, nothing penetrated of external agitations, neither the rumor of marching pilgrims nor the gasps of victims sacrificed in honor of the enchantress of the Ganges with the long black hair.

Young women who were preparing for "initiation" were gliding quietly, with balms, linen and cups full of sacred water for the ablutions. As soon as the entrance, vehement perfumes seized the nostrils; large beds sustained by adoring chimeras stood in the corners. On the onyx floor, carpets with designs of fantastic beasts supported cushions, tiger- and panther-skins; stars of silvery silk, falling from the vault, made discreet niches for couples who desired isolation.

The eldest of the Natis, who might have been twenty years old, had Assilinia sit down next to her and interrogated her gently about her life, her projects and her ambitions.

"The sole mission of a woman," she said, "is to be beautiful and to be able to charm. Do not depart from the mysterious designs of Kama if you want to enjoy a durable happiness on earth. Ornament yourself and make yourself cherished."

"I love and am loved," the Rani replied. "I have run away with my lover and I have come to the sources of the Ganges in order to purify myself."

"Why is your lover not beside you? Fear losing him!"

"What are you saying? Is he in danger? I only quit him a moment ago; he has promised to rejoin me." Assilinia had risen to her feet, prey to a great agitation. "Let me leave! I was wrong to go with you!"

But the Natis brought her back gently.

"Don't worry. Whatever happens must happen, and nothing you attempt in the future can change your destiny. But doubtless you have conversed with your friend about things other than amour?"

"I've talked to him about the god of the Fatherland, and he is going to avenge my father, the Rajah Amarsin, who was killed on the order of Shah Jahan."

"Poor child!" said the Natis, compassionately. "It is better to study the *Prem sagar* and the games of Krishna with the gopis than to seek to resist the one who is named the King of Kings. A woman avenges herself by means of the desires she inspires, not by anything she does, and it is very foolish to envy a man his illusory power. If you had been more versed in the incomparable science you would have subjugated Shah Jahan by caresses. He must desire you, for you are beautiful."

"He wanted to have me marry Prince Orpha, who is one of his sons, in order to possess me more freely."

"You see . . . and why didn't you obey the Emperor's order?"

"Because I am of a race that never yields, and that man is my cruelest enemy. Have you forgotten his crime, then?"

"I've forgotten nothing, little Rani, but by virtue of voluptuous dementia, by virtue of erudite hysterias that empty the marrows, disrupting the brain, tautening the nerves in erotic spasms, which go all the way to death, you would avenge yourself surely and without danger."

And the Natis, with her sulfurous eyes, her spoliatory and charming mouth, really was the succubus of amour, the invincible demon of monstrous sensualities.

"Woman reigns over the senses," she went on, "and her power subjugates the world. Make use, child, of the weapons that Shiva has given you; they are the best."

"Oh," said Assilinia, "I can't deceive Mimiose."

"Why? He'll only love you more afterwards. What one has lost doubles its value. The most virtuous are the most deceived! Would you like a specimen of our knowledge? Our lascivious priestesses will mime before you the sixty-four acts of sensuality according to the *Kama Sutra*, the Dharma and the Artha.

226

Afterwards, we shall celebrate the sakti with the Brahmins who are not taking part in the sacrifice of Ganga. To arrive at the number of sixty-four, which is consecrated by the Vedas, that which relates to the intercourse of the sexes, or Kama Shastra, is divided into eight parts, and in each part, eight principal subdivisions are made. The woman who is familiar with the sixty-four means of pleasure indicated by Babhravya is the mistress of the world."

"Alas," said Assilinia, "I thought that it was sufficient to love!"

"Loving is nothing. It is necessary to make oneself loved."

The Natis made a sign to her companions—sixty-three in number—who listened to her religiously. They got up, put their left hand to their forehead and their breast, and then the games commenced. Each one taught one of the manners of the Kama Shastra; alone or with an associate, she mimed graciously the act of amour, ornamenting herself with roses, sometimes played the vina or the dhol, bent down, got up again, danced to the accompaniment of the vibrant strings, and lingered in savant caresses that caused the Rani's heart to leap.

Each one had in her hair, regally unwound, a flower with a special perfume, irresistibly aphrodisiac, which symbolized the manner of the Kama Shastra that she had adopted.

"For myself," said Madja-Bod, a slim Natis with long gold-flecked eyes, "my supple and firm breasts resemble the fruits of the vilva; they are softer than the rounded leaves of nympheas that brush you under water. Do you not want to see them stand up in the battle of amour?"

"As for me," said Ranaaah, a ten-year-old girl with slender limbs and a waist narrower than the stem of a mango tree, "my tresses are so long that I walk over them as on black serpents, and their contact is more electric than the fur of felines. I make a thousand caresses with them."

And the child, twisting the gleaming skeins, made rings of them for each of her fingers.

"My arms are as slender as the Siricha tree, and the corolla of my armpit exhales more perfumes than the calyx of the ketaki.

Bees plunge into it voluptuously and follow me as if I were an errant flower."

"Ah," murmured Keraloum, a Natis with discolored hair sown with mauve powder, "my skin is as tender to the touch as the trunk of a young elephant, and my thighs resemble the polished trunk of a latanier. Little gray lizards know it well!"

But Campissino showed her delicate feet. "Are they not as pretty as the seashells of distant beaches, where medusae of beryls and opals flourish?"

"My knees are like lotus buds when I bend my legs in the water, and blue dragonflies come to settle on them."

"My lips are redder than the fruits of the bimba. They melt on the tongue like a praline and their honey appeases all burns. They have the taste of a freshly picked amra, they retain like the corolla of the kesar; they would madden the god of amour himself, and Smara has never been able to resist them. See my vermilion lips!"

And Aninya showed off an ardent mouth, with fleshy, shiny, adorably modeled lips, very small in repose, but with a thousand voluptuous creases that must have taken the measure of a kiss.

"The nest of my desires is silkier and softer than a daboia viper nestling in the moss. The kokila charmer knows the route to it. It has modulated its light songs there, like the trills of a crystal flute. And when it takes off, it is never to perch very far away. Little Rani, would you like to know the nest of sensuality?"

Assilinia learned from each one of them one of the secrets of the Kama-Shastra, and she opened her eyes wide at the enumeration of so many ingenious talents.

"And you," she asked the Natis who had held her against her, tenderly embracing her during that lesson in amour.

"Personally, little Rani, I'm reserving myself for the sakti, the rose mass that we're going to celebrate in a little while."

She got up, and the young women, after having poured essences of champak over her shoulders, enveloped her in gauze spangled with gold and silver.

III
The Rose Mass

The Natis led Assilinia into a large hall with a ceiling in a cupola charged with mosaics, which only received daylight through a round opening at the summit. At the back, colonnettes of crystal circled with gold and rubies supported an altar on which the god Shiva stood, in his dual male and female nature, black on one side and white on the other. They all prostrated themselves before him, and then embraced the symbol of eternal fecundity.

Brahma, Vishnu, Shiva,
Shiva, Vishnu, Brahma!

"O god of fire! O god of intoxication! We prostrate ourselves before you! God of infernal caresses! More beautiful than Surya and Soma! We submit ourselves to your laws! Your mouth is honey and flame, for the kisses of Ganika! And all of us guard in our souls the fecund god, the god Shiva!"

Brahma, Vishnu, Shiva,
Shiva, Vishnu, Brahma!

They swayed, sweeping the ground with their long hair, breathing in the perfume of aromatics that was slowly intoxicating them.

Then one of the Natis resumed the sacred song, while the Brahmins, clad in white, arranged themselves around the image of the god.

"Shiva, mighty god, see our ardor! We are burning like the vilva! Destructive god, creative god, penetrate us like the Amra! Shiva is sufficient for our pleasures, lover and mistress by turns. Men know his desires, women know his caresses!"

But the priestesses of amour have taken on a tragic expression. They sigh, weep, and pursue one another, howling, and the sacred poem concludes, to the heart-rending sounds of the chilamchi:

"Shiva, surrounded by demons, wanders near funeral pyres, his three eyes with the profound gaze resemble fire in the darkness. Shiva wants joy and death! Shiva demands tortures! Everything that crushes, everything that bites! Everything that kills gives him delight!"

They labor their breasts with their sharpened fingernails, rolling and moaning, offering to immolate themselves to the wrath of the god. But the officiating Brahmin calms them with a gesture. He requests the wine of forgetfulness, and young women adorned with yellow veils, their head covered with a kind of turriculated miter, pour them the aphrodisiac liquor speckled with gold, sown with precious stones, which will intoxicate them to the point of voluptuous dementia.

At the great festival of the goddess Kali, every year, a Natis must satisfy the strangest caprices of the Brahmins and die under their embraces. Her body, having been delivered to the flames, remains exposed for three days to the adoration of her companions, and that sacrifice is particularly agreeable to the gods.

Assilinia put her lips to the precious cup where the wine of folly was foaming, and immediately, her temples hammered, a flood of blood burned her face, and she desired the caresses of Mimiose.

The Natis, who had not quit her until then, headed for the altar, throwing back their veils, which undulated behind them

230

like golden reptiles. The officiating Brahmin circled the androgynous idol three times, reciting passionate mantras; then, lifting the woman in his powerful arms, he laid her down on the table strewn with flowers and consummated the carnal act . . .

✳

It is in those gatherings that affiliates, gorged on strongly spiced meats and vehement liquors, adore the sakti in the form of a woman. She is placed in front of Shiva, and a Brahmin possesses her at the whim of his caprice. The ceremony is terminated by the general coupling of everyone, each couple representing Shiva and his sakti and identifying with his divinity.

The Natis had resumed the chorus of the couplet of possession.

"Shiva, mighty god, see our ardor! We are burning like the vilva! Destructive god, creative god, penetrate us like the Amra! Shiva is sufficient for our pleasures, lover and mistress by turns. Men know his desires, women know his caresses!"

Brahma, Vishnu, Shiva,
Shiva, Vishnu, Brahma!

IV
The Invasion

The Natis had scarcely abandoned themselves to the Brahmins' kisses when a profound rumor coming from outside covered their whispers and sighs. The doors of the temple burst into splinters and a troop of sowars, led by Orpha, irrupted into the hall of sacrifice.

The men, armed with spears and daggers, fell upon the defenseless couples, stunned by sensuality, and separated them, with sniggers and insults.

Shah Jahan's soldiers dragged the Natis by the hair and attached them to the foot of the idol with the Brahmins. Then, having taken possession of golden vases studded with rubies, precious cups and the Natis' inestimable jewels, they set fire to the temple.

✵

Assilinia had lost consciousness; when she came to, a great flame was drowning the horizon, golden rockets were striping the azure of the sky, and the crackling of the first overwhelmed all other sounds. An immense crowd, on the banks of the river, was contemplating the devastating scourge without seeking to fight it. Shiva had wanted it, Shiva was the master.

The Rani found herself lying on an elephant next to Orpha, whose somber gaze was fixed upon her.

"What do you want?" she asked, shivering.

"To take you to the Master."

"Why? I'm free. It's Mimiose that I love."

"Mimiose has fled. That Gurkha is unworthy of you . . ."

"He has fled!"

Assilinia's breast rose up gently. Since her lover was free, she could still hope for his deliverance. Doubtless he would attempt the impossible to recover her.

After a moment's silence, braving the grim stare that weighed upon her, she demanded, proudly: "What do you want to make of me?"

"My wife."

"Your wife! But you have no love for me; it's ambition that drives you."

"What if it is? I don't have to account to you for my thoughts or my actions."

She laughed scornfully. "In fact, I believe you to be incapable of that frankness. It would show you in too vile a light."

"You have offended me cruelly and I would have the right to punish you. At least recognize that my intentions are generous."

"Generous?" she said, ironically. "No, Orpha, I know you too well. You want to satisfy a caprice of the Mogul, who is weary of kisses that are too facile. Even the infantile graces of his daughter Saeb no longer seduce him. But I am of the abhorred blood, the invincible blood of the rajahs, and my possession would be doubly flattering for the tyrant."

She had not attempted to hide her nudity and her disdainful gaze followed the quiver of desire on the prince's face.

"You're beautiful," he said. "Be mine."

"You will only have me by force."

Furtively, she advanced her hand toward the weapon glinting in Orpha's belt, but he understood her thought and, detaching the dagger damascened with gold and studded with rubies, he threw it on to the road.

"Killing me would be too easy, when you had put me to sleep under your kisses!"

A Thug picked up the weapon. He made use of it to kill a young herdsman who was passing with his goats, blowing into a bamboo flute. The animals were also slaughtered and taken away for the evening meal.

Assilinia, drunk with horror, shut her eyes. Orpha, hesitating between desire and hatred, gazed into the distance at the last radiance of the conflagration.

Blue-tinted smoke furrowed the sky like the fantastic mane of the dragon Aracas riding the clouds. The fiery monster was paling, retracting its tongue and its claws. Stopped by the Ganges in its murderous work, it seemed to be taking flight toward the clouds.

Orpha and Shah Jahan's sowars might not have been strong enough to penetrate into the temple of the priestesses of Shiva in spite of the resistance of the penitents and Brahmins, but he had joined forces with the terrible sect of the Thugs, the mysterious association of fanatics who had made homicide a fundamental doctrine. The crime, in any place, was the sole dogma of the Thugs. Devoted to the worship of the goddess Kali, they murdered, night and day, in order to please her, the Omraos and Bigaris they encountered on their route.

The warm effluences of human blood rejoiced that sinister idol, and no incense seemed sweeter to her. All esthetic and sensual recompenses were to be devolved in the other life to those who had accomplished the bloody labor conscientiously, so the Thugs died with much joy as they killed.

As he passed by, Orpha allowed the bloody wave to flow in the fields and the towns; his sly soul made itself crueler in that game; ancient instincts of ferocity awoke in him, while his face learned to cover itself with the mask of hypocrisy.

The Thugs, originally from the realm of Oude and the Deccan, were divided into cut-throats and gravediggers, but when executions were too numerous they abandoned the dead, leaving the vultures the care of finishing the lugubrious work.

Shah Jahan, subsequently, did not recognize the services rendered by the redoubtable sect, and although a hundred enemy cadavers were exhumed a few months later beneath the carpet of his own tent, he had the murderers killed.

Delivered to the law, and once in prison, the Thugs showed a calm and obedience that contrasted singularly with their murderous instincts. They awaited in profound quietude the death that they had often given. It was devoid of terror and shame for them. Mildly they recounted their crimes, their refinements of cruelty and their perverse imaginations. Did Kali not love rape and assassination? Did her feet not tread in the mud of entrails, and did her hands not caress the exsanguinated heads of torture-victims?

The Thugs only asked, as a sole mercy, that they be hanged, in memory of the cord that they had used for preference in their morbid work. To be hanged was to be strangled between heaven and earth!

V
The Camp

Dusk was filling the hollows of the valleys, the approaching night was blurring the blue-tinted silhouettes of the bamboos and the mangroves, but the river retained glaucous reflections in which the moon danced like a medusa of flame.

The huge somber bodies of elephants were agitating on the bank. There was a mobile sea of rumps and heads swaying under heavy bronze ornaments. The hours went by slowly in the camp that had taken a bath in blood.

The Thugs were amusing themselves with male orgies in the shelter of the tents, while the cries of the dying faded away outside and the river carried the last cadavers toward eternal oblivion.

Exhausted by fatigue, Assilinia was lying under Orpha's tent, and, in a horrible dream, the image of Shah Jahan loomed up before her. The jewels on his breast and his long crimson robe, constellated with sardonyxes and beryls, hypnotized her thought. She saw nothing but that deployment of splendors, that brilliance of precious stones, surmounted by a face hollowed out by lust and ennui.

The Emperor tipped her over on the cushions, applied his spoliatory lips to hers and crushed her in a furious embrace. Then the vision disappeared . . . Orpha, in his turn, possessed her insatiably, and she fended off the terrible specters with her feverish hands, imploring and begging for mercy.

Then the décor changed again.

She found herself in a palace of confused and grandiose style; women dressed her in sumptuous and chimerical fabrics the colors of the moon and the sun, mitered her with a tower of diamonds and poured her the wine of rajahs sown with precious stones.

In her left hand she had the lingam, master of the world. She was holding the Hindu symbol of life and strength between her woman's fingers, and the words of the Natis returned to her memory: "Your sex is omnipotent, by it alone you will triumph over man. Don't seek to reign differently."

The Rani knew what awaited her. Orpha would take her to the Master, delivering her secretly to the gynaeceum, and she told herself that she might be able to take advantage of the imperial folly to reign in her turn, to render to the rajahs their confiscated wealth and dictate her laws of justice and peace. Certainly, that would be a fine role, but Shah Jahan would soon weary of her kisses; he was too blasé in body and in soul to attach himself to a lover for long, whatever she did. And then, she loved Mimiose . . .

With a sigh, she lay back on the cushions, and again phantoms haunted her suffering thoughts. Her eyes, open in the darkness, saw palaces emerging from the ground, borne by light iridescent columns, with vaults in mosaics cemented with gold. Arabesques in lazuli and partitioned enamel ran along the cupolas with rainbow gleams.

Shah Jahan was kneeling over her, laughing; a horrible laughter that uncovered his yellow gumless teeth. He was extracting her brain through her nasal fossas with curved needles, and that explained the frightful pain that was drilling into her skull. The nightmare was accentuated; she made vain efforts to escape her torturer, but all her exerted will power could not succeed in shifting her little finger.

Perfumes were burning around her, disgorging clouds of vapor that were perforated by the cabochons of the imperial robe, like the phosphorescent eyes of felines. She could have screamed, but her screams would not have been heard outside the sealed room where the monstrous whim of the Mogul had now imprisoned her. He had stood up, with new laughter, and was making a profound incision in her left side, by means of which he was possessing her, in red floods . . .

And the widened eyes of the Rani saw the somber, green-tinted face of her torturer. His skeletal arms were linked to his shoulder like tentacles; a frisson of fever agitated him from his spine to his heels, and his teeth were chattering. The frightful gaze of the man penetrated her to the marrow. Then, suddenly, he pushed her away, and, falling backwards, started howling mortally.

Woken up, Assilinia finally breathed more freely. Everything was calm under the tent. A torch stuck on the tip of a spear illuminated the silhouette of Orpha, whose back was turned to her.

Painfully, she got up, and came to kneel before the prince.

"I beg you," she said, "let me go. Just now, I spoke to you harshly, but now I'm imploring. Other women are as beautiful, and even more beautiful, than me. Choose a spouse among them and return to the Master."

"It's you that I want!" said Orpha violently. "You've offended me! I'll be able to reduce you!"

"What's the point? If I rejected you, it's because I don't love you. Nothing has changed in my heart and nothing will ever change there. In those conditions, we couldn't be happy."

Orpha laughed silently. "When you're mine, I'll bend you to my whims."

"Better to kill me immediately, since I'm in your power. You're the stronger."

"Undoubtedly, but your life is precious to me at the moment, because I want to offer you first to the Mogul, who covets your beauty."

A frisson of disgust passed over the Rani's face. "Oh, that's true," she said. "You're as ambitious as you are cruel."

She took a few steps, and perceived that a golden chain was wrapped around her ankles, and that it would be impossible to flee. Then she let herself fall at her enemy's feet again and, hiding her face in the hollow of a cushion, wept abundantly.

Outside, the elephants were pawing the ground, making their bronze ornaments rattle

The Thugs, crouching around a fateful stove, were reciting mysterious mantras.

A little further away, Shah Jahan's sowars were asleep in the long grass. They formed confused masses, punctuated by the flash of axes and golden swords. A few, drinking arak and smoking ganja, were conversing noisily. They had butchered the goats, and had gorged themselves on meat and wine. Many were regretting not having brought the Natis, who would have occupied the hours of their halt. The murder of those women had been futile; it would have been better to keep them for durable pleasures. Where would they find other slaves of lust now? The temples scattered along their route were only served by Brahmins, and the Bhumij, the sons of the soil, guarded their daughters.

But one soldier started laughing and pointed at a young man crouching near Orpha's tent, who was trying to see what was happening inside.

"That one isn't serpent-born like us. Look at his hips and his breast."

"That's true," said the others. "His waist is slim, his breasts protruding, in spite of the bandages that are compressing them."

"It's necessary to summon him."

"To force him to undress."

"We'll soon see whether he's a woman."

One of the sowars went to fetch the boy with the soft face and slender hands, and ordered him to undress, but he refused to do so, fearfully.

"Undress? Why? I only obey my chiefs, and you're soldiers like me."

"We're your chiefs, since we're men. Prove to us that you're our equal!"

There was coarse laughter, and, as the child remained silent, his eyes moist, one of the sowars tore away his leather garments, and uncovered the proud maidenly breasts and the harmoniously rounded loins.

She uttered a cry and fell to her knees.

The man who had undressed her threw himself upon her; the others protested, demanding their share of the booty, and she was seized by the neck, by the upper body, by the legs, lifted up in clawed hands in a cluster of shoulders and chests, the bronze

238

ornaments of which wounded her. Daggers entered into flesh; the more determined, maddened by the ganja and opium they had chewed, had taken possession of pikes and clubs, with which they staved in skulls from which soft brains sputtered in floods of blood.

Orpha, disquieted by the tumult, lifted the cloth that veiled the entrance to his tent.

His gaze plunged into the obscurity toward the confused mass of combatants, who, at the sight of him, had suddenly calmed down.

"What's happening?" he demanded. "Why this tumult?"

A soldier threw the young woman, who had lost consciousness, at his feet.

"It's a woman who has penetrated into the camp."

VI
The Amour of Hallabab

Orpha took the inert body of the imprudent woman into his tent, and Assilinia, who had raised her burning brow with difficulty, uttered a cry: "Hallabab!"

"You know this woman?"

"She's my friend," the Rani replied, emotionally. "How was she able to penetrate all the way here?"

But she smiled vaguely. She told herself that only Hallabab's secret amour had driven her to this folly. The young woman loved Orpha and had doubtless been unable to resolve to quit him. Then she rejected that thought, and preferred to believe that her friend had only listened to her devotion for her.

In reality, Hallabab had obeyed her two affections, which, in the present case, had combined to dictate her conduct. The tenderness that she had for the prince and the fears inspired in her by this expedition against the Rani had persuaded her to mingle with Shah Jahan's sowars. In her warrior disguise, she had departed, with no suspicion of the rude assaults to which her compassionate soul and her virginal body would be subjected.

With a piece of cloth, Assilinia wiped her friend's face and pushed back the hair sticky with blood and dust.

"Look," she said to Orpha.

He examined the young woman with disdain.

"Well? I see a woman that my soldiers were wrong to mistreat, since she's your friend."

"This young woman is of a birth almost equal to mine."

"What does that matter to me?"

"She's poor, but I can endow her with the better part of my wealth."

Orpha frowned. "You're free to make that stupid gesture."

"Hallabab is beautiful," the Rani went on, "as beautiful as me."

"That's a matter of appreciation."

"And," Assilinia emphasized, "she loves you."

"She loves me?"

"Madly."

The prince made a careless gesture. "I can't do anything about that."

"Marry her, return to Shah Jahan's court and do your duty as a devoted soldier of the imperial cause. I'll follow my route, which isn't yours, for I can't serve the same master as you."

Orpha reflected for a moment.

"No," he said, "I can't accept what you're proposing to me. The Emperor's will is formal."

"Ah!" sighed the Rani, discouraged, "Everything is futile! What have I done to the gods that they should crush me thus?"

Hallabab came round. Her first glance was for her beloved, but then she smiled at her friend and threw herself into her arms.

"I thought I might never see you again. Save me, Assilinia! Protect me!"

"You're no longer in any danger. Orpha will watch over you."

Hallabab addressed a gaze of infinite gratitude to the prince, who had turned away in annoyance.

Coquettish in spite of everything, she covered herself with the pleats of a silver veil that was trailing amid the leopard- and tiger-skins. She huddled against the Rani, already forgetful of the outrages to which she had been subjected, only curious, in her infantile soul, to know about the amorous life of her friend and the marvels of the temple of Shiva.

At the account of the murder of the Natis near the idol with the double sex, she shivered.

"That's a presage of misfortune for us," she sighed. "The inflexible god will avenge himself for the profanation of his altar. Why that unnecessary sacrifice?"

"The Thugs are with us," said Assilinia, "and everywhere they go the red river flows. We have only left cadavers in our passage, and if we dug in the soil below this tent, dead men would show themselves. The earth is swollen by victims; under the fermentation of all those bodies, still full of youth and sap, she sometimes seems to draw breath, and her breast heaves. A little while ago I had horrible visions, and it seems to me that my reason is abandoning me."

Hallabab wept. "Oh, why did you go? It's your flight that has caused all our misfortunes!"

"And Hadj-Hidi?" asked the Rani. "Has she pricked the virginal loins of Samjab and Pekeo with her long needles?"

"Samjab and Pekeo are the most beautiful Hedjeras in the temple of Kuthu'l, and the Brahmins know it. Since their entry to the sanctuary, the ceremonies of the Lingam have succeeded one another, but the profane are not admitted to them."

"And the begum Saeb?"

"The begum has broken her last white doll, which was made of a single opal, and thrown the debris at the head of her father, whose caresses importuned her. Shah Jahan has thought about his other two daughters, the begums Roxanara and Meridza, but they're still too young. The permissible joys of the gynaeceum no longer have any charm for the Emperor."

"And he's waiting for me to satisfy his perverse fantasies?" The Rani's black eyebrows drew together like angry serpents. "I'll kill him," she said, "and the country will be free."

Hallabab and Assilinia ended up going to sleep in one another's arms under the suspicious eyes of Orpha, who had posted thirty sowars around his tent in order to prevent any attempt at escape.

Soon, nothing more could be heard in the camp but the sinister flight of vultures and the slow chant of the mantras that the cut-throat Thugs were continuing around their fateful stoves.

VII
The Perversities of Shah Jahan

Shah Jahan was waiting impatiently for the return of the pretty Rani, whom he desired recklessly.

The clever and wily monarch had been put on the throne by a strange artifice. At the succession of his predecessor, when the special envoy had demanded the usual tribute from him, engaging him to recognize the sovereignty of his nephew Bulaki,[1] Shah Jahan had collapsed, vomiting blood in abundance. He had been picked up and laid on a bed, where he had spat out his last red mouthfuls. Now, that blood was only sheep's blood, with which he had filled his mouth in order to simulate a devastating attack.

Bulaki had judged him doomed, and was not astonished by the announcement of his death, proclaimed by trumpet blasts. A funeral had been prepared with all the magnificence due to the first prince of the Mogul blood. The empty coffin, drawn by forty horses harnessed with gold and precious tones, was followed by

---

1 Bulaki is better known as Dawar or Dawar Baksh, who was briefly proclaimed Mogul Emperor before being killed by Shah Jahan, along with several other possible claimants. The anecdote related here is fictitious.

an imposing guard chosen among the officers of the imperial mi-
litia. Shah Jahan, dressing in mourning, followed his own funeral
gravely, recruiting, at intervals, squadrons of rajputs, who seemed
simply to be adding to the magnificence of the funeral pomp.

Bulaki, not supposing that the slightest revolt was to be feared
from a dead man, had decided to attend his uncle's funeral without an escort. Some distance from Delhi, however, the rajputs
had taken him prisoner and Shah Jahan was proclaimed Emperor
thereafter. The sacred courtesans, the Bhai-Tchokri, emerged
from beneath the funeral ropes and began to dance to the sound
of chilamchis, flutes and tambourines. The hearse was converted
into a triumphal chariot, and the new monarch came back on his
coffin, adorned with flowers.

Such had been the beginning of his reign, the early years of
which went by in relative calm. Once he was master of Hindustan,
the Mogul had the strength and the skill to maintain himself in
his conquest. A confederation of rajahs that had been formed in
order to expel him, was soon annihilated by him; all partial insur-
rections were repressed, and he remained, at least for some years,
in spite of his faults, the uncontested sovereign of a great empire.

The inhabitants of Hindustan belonged to various races, but
the foundation of the population, the indigenes, the most ancient
masters of the land, were the Hindus. Religions were even more
numerous than races. Some read the Koran, others remained
faithful to the old doctrines of Zoroaster; they worshiped fire and
sought the word of life in the *Zend Avesta*. But the poor-blooded
Hindus followed Brahmanism, and continued to worship their
cruel and voluptuous gods.

The Hindus were the very foundation of the nation; the floods
of invasions passed over them and curbed them like reeds, but
they got up again more alive and stronger. Conquerors elevate
themselves and destroy themselves by the excess of their ambition. They only shine briefly in order to be more thoroughly
annihilated in the very bosom of the vanquished. Conqueror
pass like scourges necessary to renew humanity. Nature has not
assigned them any other role.

Shah Jahan was waiting for Assilinia.

In order to receive her, he had prepared a chamber of great magnificence. Illuminated by the mauve and yellow windows of a cupola that coiffed its height, the room was resplendent, on its walls and its columns, with magical mosaics in which complicated jigsaws framed lascivious subjects of men and women united. On a platform, a low bed with cushions of peacock- and parrot-feathers was sustained by crouching jade tigers. Violet curtains spangled with gold and silver ornaments hung down behind the bed, which juxtaposed mirrors reproduced infinitely to the sides. Ivory stools upholstered with delicately embroidered yellow and mauve silks completed the furniture of the room, among the skins of wild beasts and the heavy rugs distributed everywhere.

A harkarat had announced the arrival of the Rani with the prince, and the Emperor, his heart quivering beneath his pectorals of precious stones, prepared to receive the woman he was already calling by the most tender names.

Shah Jahan had only had seven children from all his wives, for the Moguls had no scruple in interrupting, by culpable artifices, the fecundity of their spouses, and he counted on enabling Assilinia to profit from the privileges with which he honored the begums Saeb, Roxanara and Meridza.

The prince, as the price of his complaisance, once his marriage had been celebrated, would be promoted to the rank of general in chief of the imperial troops. The grateful Orpha had accepted all the conditions of that precious favor.

"The Rani!"

Omraos standing near the entrance door have shoved Assilinia, who has come to fall at the Master's feet.

The young woman is no longer the humble companion of Mimiose. Bhai-Tchokri have dressed her in a khelat of golden cloth, gemmed like a firmament with a profusion of stats, and a diamond-studded belt makes a circle of flames around her slender waist. Her hair, dotted with champak flowers, has been steeped in the most precious essences, and her little feet are so covered in rings that they resemble fireflies straying over the crimson of the carpets.

"I salute you, Assilinia, for you are the most beautiful among the beautiful!"

The Rani enveloped the monarch with her somber gaze and remained silent. What could she have said? Shah Jahan had killed Rajah Amarin, her father, and she hated him with all the force of her soul. She had only one desire, which was to escape the palace as soon as she was able to do so.

"Assilinia," the Emperor went on, "I have had you come in order to affiance you to Orpha, who is worthy of your rank, and who loves you. I intend that your marriage should be celebrated with great pomp, and that the Omraos witness that solemnity."

The young woman remained motionless, her face grim. Her wide-open eyes had an expression of disdainful pride. But Shah Jahan preferred that air of revolt to the habitual submission of his slaves of lust. His desires became more vehemently ardent; the resistance he anticipated redoubled for him the prize of the conquest.

"Assilinia," he said, again, "you will have to serve you as many maidservants as you please, and no adornment will be refused to you. The Bhai-Tchokri will occupy your leisure with their songs and their dances, and you will learn from them the rules of amour of Vatsyayana. Your Acharyas, or ancient authors, qualify voluptuous talents as 'dear to women.' I therefore want you to find some charm in the information that will serve you."

The Rani did not confess that the Natis had already completed her education, and that she knew as much as the most celebrated courtesans. She bowed as Shah Jahan passed by, who gave her the tip of his emerald scepter to kiss as he withdrew, and she stayed there with her arms folded over her breast while the footsteps of the courtiers drew away over the sonorous paving stones.

VIII
Projects of Vengeance

"Hallabab! Hallabab! I'm dying of sadness!"

Beside her little friend, who had been obligingly returned to her, the Rani sighed and lamented.

"Where is the beloved, the spouse I have chosen, the elect of my mind and my heart? Doubtless I shall never see him again. If he were alive, he would already have made his presence known to me. They've killed him, you see!"

Gently, Hallabab pressed Assilinia's burning forehead against her breast and tried to distract her with a thousand caresses.

"Mimiose will come back, be sure of it. If he were dead you would have been informed by an occult advice of the pitris. His astral body would have rejoined you in a dream. Cannot those who love one another communicate beyond the grave? And do not invincible bonds attach them to one another? If Mimiose had succumbed under the blows of his enemies, you would see him every night and you would feel his icy kisses posing on your lips."

"May you be speaking the truth! For I have not seen the beloved in my dreams, and I have only shivered with the desire for vengeance!"

"Princess, you will avenge yourself, but promise me to pardon Orpha, who is only obeying the Mogul's order."

"I'll pardon him on one condition . . ."

"What?"

"That you'll go to Hadj-Hidi to ask her for the herb of death."

"For whom?"

"For the Emperor!" whispered the young woman, so quietly that Hallabab divined it rather than heard it.

"What! You want . . ."

"I want to administer justice myself."

"But the Hedjeras will never consent!"

"Yes, she will, because her wealth has been confiscated, and the Mogul wants to expel her from the temple of Kuthu'l."

"How do you know that?"

"From the Bhai-Tchokri, who are very glad of the disfavor of the sterile priestesses. Shah Jahan has promised to give them Kuthu'l for the teaching of their voluptuous science."

Hallabab reflected momentarily.

"So be it," she said. "I'll go to find the old Hedjeras and ask her for the herb of death for you."

The Rani smiled cruelly. "Don't almost all the Mogul Emperors perish by poison? In their families, the mysterious plants are known that cause death without leaving traces. It will be assumed that Shah Jahan has been suppressed by his son Aurang-Zeb, who has been seeking to seize power for a year."

"Aurang-Zeb is in Golconda."

"Can he not make his friends act?"

Hallabab shook her head.

"This is a dangerous game, little Rani. I'll do as you wish but I tremble for you. Remember that you'll have no one to help you if you fail; remember that the Emperor, who is on his guard, will easily perceive your design."

"No," said Assilinia, "he desires me too madly to be perspicacious. I know that after our union, Orpha will bring me to this palace, where he will abandon me to his Master's whims. The Emperor cannot do anything to an unmarrried woman of my caste; he can do everything to a married woman as soon as her husband consents. I shall therefore be alone with that old man, who will beg for my caresses, for he is not strong enough to demand them, and I shall only give the impression of yielding momentarily in order better to attain my goal."

Hallabab put her lips on Assilinia's eyelids, caused her caress to descend along her friend's cheeks as far as the corner of her mouth, and murmured in a longer kiss: "I'll ask for the herb of death, but I'll also ask for the herb of amour, in order that Orpha will finally deign to perceive my tenderness."

The Rani repaid the child kiss for kiss.

"Oh," she said, "I desire that you make yourself beloved, but I fear that Orpha has nothing in his heart but the stone of ambition. If he has affection for anyone in the world, it's for himself."

"That can change, with the aid of the pitris, and the old Hedjeras knows all bewitchments. In your turn, swear something to me!"

"What?" asked the Rani surprised.

"Swear to me to reject Orpha's caresses when he is your husband."

"Oh, gladly."

"All caresses . . . even the most minimal . . ."

"I won't let him kiss the tip of my little finger."

"How good you are, Assilinia!"

And the amorous woman nestled in her friend's arms like a wheedling cat, asking her to hug her more tightly and to show her how to embrace adoring lovers . . . And the kisses that rained down on her did not satisfy her; she wanted others, and yet others, in order not to be ignorant of anything of the delectable abandonment of happy nights . . .

But Assilinia, out of arguments, went to sleep on her heart, and each of them dreamed of the beloved man, without ceasing to embrace one another . . .

IX

The Hedjeras' Means

"Hadj-Hidi, I have something to ask of you."

The old woman, who had fallen asleep in the middle of her mantras, against a bronze lingam, raised her head and looked at Hallabab fearfully.

"I was dreaming that Shah Jahan's sowars were expelling me from the temple . . . It's only you! What do you want with me, child?"

"What I have to say to you is grave. Let's go, if you will, into the Hall of the Consecration or that of the Ablation, in order that no one can disturb us."

The old Hedjeras' eyes gleamed. "Is it a virginal flower that you want to offer me? Samjab died only yesterday!"

"Samjab is dead!" sighed Hallabab. "What sad news!"

"The operation was carried out too late. The girl knew amour."

"And Pekeo?"

"Pekeo is more robust in complexion and less keen in sensibility; she'll survive, I think."

"Samjab and Pekeo! My best and dearest companions!" sobbed Hallabab. "What need did you have to offer them to the gods?"

"It was to gain for them the indulgence of Durga, who rejoices in sacrifices. Don't mourn them, their role is more enviable than yours. But it's not to make me reproaches that you've come, I suppose?"

Hadj-Hidi led the child through the long galleries of erotic sculptures into one of the halls of the sacrifice, which the Hedjeras had ornamented for an imminent ceremony.

"Speak now; no one is listening to us."

The cassolettes spread acrid fumes around the brown-striped altar, the stone of which seemed eroded by blood, and thick garlands of saligram and tuberoses completed the poisoning of the air.

Hallabab understood the mystical frenzies of the mutilated priestesses in that morbid atmosphere, and the clappers of bells were already hammering her temples. She stated rapidly the purpose of her coming.

"I desire the herb that gives death."

Hadj-Hidi started. "I don't know what you mean. We're servants of Durga, not poisoners. It's not at the moment that they want to expel us from the temple that I can expose myself to public anger. It's already being claimed that it's the Fakirs and the Brahmins who have cast a spell on the crops and have caused a famine!"

"They won't say it any more, if you listen to me."

"Why?"

"Because I want to propose that you reconquer your power by liberating the country."

"I don't understand."

"It's necessary to kill the Moguls who are desolating India."

Hadj-Hidi started to laugh. "But they're more numerous than the pebbles of the shore! After Shah Jahan we'll have the sultans Dara Shikoh, Shah Shuja or Aurang-Zeb, perhaps even Murad Baksh. The Moguls are invincible, they're reborn from their ashes!"

"You only have one enemy," said Hallabab, "and that's Shah Jahan, who bears a grudge against you for protecting the Rani."

"And it's Shah Jahan that you want to suppress?"

"Yes."

"I understand. He's found Assilinia?"

"Exactly. He's destined her for his pleasures and is only waiting for Orpha's consent to make her his favorite in the gynaeceum. A splendid wedding is in preparation, and as soon as the ceremony is over, the Rani will belong to the Master."

Hadj-Hidi reflected for a moment.

"The means you've imagined with Assilinia is dangerous; I know a better one."

"What?"

"The excess of caresses!"

"What are you saying?"

"I'm saying that the Rani could, if she desires, kill her aged lover more surely and without danger."

"She'll never consent to play that odious role!"

"You think so?"

"I'm certain of it. She'll lend herself to murder, but not the abomination of which you're speaking."

"Oh! That's unfortunate."

The old Hedjeras remained thoughtful; then her sharp gaze posed on the young woman with an indefinable expression of irony and cunning.

"Another might replace her."

"Another?"

"Yes—you, for example."

"Me?" Hallabab had straightened up, trembling all over. "Me?" she repeated. "But I'm a virgin. I've never read the Dharma, the Artha or the *Kama Sutra*."

"I'll teach you."

And Hadj-Hidi spoke for a long time to the young woman, who, confused and troubled, dared not look her in the face.

"Have you understood, Hallabab?"

"Certainly," said the child, weeping, "but what you're asking of me is frightful. I love Orpha, and thought that I would belong to him some day."

"Orpha disdains you."

"My faithful love would doubtless have touched him. Where would he find more tenderness and devotion?"

"They are virtues about which men care little. They hardly ever yield to anything but the maddening of the senses. If you obey me, I'll tell you what it's necessary to attempt in order to vanquish him in his turn."

"Oh! You'd do that for me?"

"Yes child, I'll give you a certain lotion that will render you more beautiful in Orpha's eyes than Ma, the moon, or Rati, voluptuousness."

"And the prince would love me?"

"As much as he can love."

Hallabab got up, joyful. "I'll do as you advise, Hadj-Hidi. I'll be as wily and lascivious as the most famous Ganika!"

"You've understood completely? Assilinia, first, until the charm operates, and you afterwards, for the invincible and mortal caress. This is the talisman that will blur the Master's reason and give you, in his erotic vision, the appearance of the Rani."

Hadj-Hidi kissed the young woman, and gave her a mysterious perfume contained in an opal flask.

X
The Dance of Desire

On her return to the palace, Hallabab found her friend in tears.

"They've recaptured and imprisoned Mimiose!" she said.

"How do you know?"

"If he were free he would already have reassured me and got a message to me!"

"That's not certain. He must be on his guard, and he wouldn't risk compromising a possible escape by his imprudence. Have no fear, Assilinia, your lover is alert and will be able to recover you . . . only the moment hasn't yet come."

"Do you have the poison?"

Hallabab knelt down next to her friend and, in a whisper, repeated old Hadj-Hidi's instructions to her.

"Caresses?" said the Rani, surprised. "Yes, perhaps. And you consent, child?"

"It's necessary, since it's to save us all. While I'm with the Master you can envelop yourself in somber garments and leave the palace."

Assilinia shivered

"What will become of me, alone in the city? Oh, if only Mimiose were with me!"

"Have confidence. Your lover can't be far away."

The two friends were interrupted by the Bhai-Tchokri, who came to find Assilinia in order to instruct her in their lascivious dances and adorn her in accordance with the tastes of the Mogul, who only liked certain colors and certain jewels.

252

Buzzing like furious bees they traversed the Divan, a tribunal of the Sultan's justice, a vast portico in red sandstone open on three sides and composed of a triple row of arches in the Arab style. The two colonnettes were in onyx of different hues. The throne, encrusted with rare gems, stood at the back, dominating the floor of the portico by several feet.

One of the Bhai-Tchokri, as a joke, had Assilinia climb up on it, and put a lotus stem in her hand by way of a scepter.

"Sacred Ganika of the Master's pleasure, we salute you!"

"Dispensatrix of the Artha and the Kama, we venerate you."

"Priestess of infinite joys and radiant dreams, we annihilate ourselves before you."

Then, still laughing, they drew her under another portico, sown with arabesques in gold and silver, and made her climb up on to the dancing stage, sheltered by two immense peacocks whose fanned-out tails where scintillating with fulgurant gleams. On the solid gold steps decorated with jewelry, fabric of the moon and the sun were thrown, along with cushions indurated with gems, and monstrous tiger skins. A crimson awning sustained by square columns plated with enamels was spread over the entire width of the platform, which could support two hundred people.

"Little Rani," said one of the Bhai-Tchokri, "We're going to teach you the steps of the Rati, which you'll dance on the evening of your wedding in order to stimulate the Master's desires. Watch carefully."

She threw back her veils, and caused her necklaces and plaques to leap over her breasts in illusory movements; serpents the color of ripe lemons seemed to be running over her skin. Then, the shocks descended her rounded flanks to her agile and expert thighs. Her entire body quivered with expectation and covetousness. She offered herself by means of a corrupt twist of her supple loins, uttered the cry of desire and rut that breaks the energy of a man and melts the will of the strongest. She became the symbolic deity of invincible Lust, the immoral Succubus of omnipotent

Hysteria, who stiffens the flesh and hardens the muscles. She remained motionless for a moment, her arms open and her loins extended, and then bounded, with a burst of laughter.

"Your turn, Assinilina!"

They dressed her in dupattas of yellow gauze embroidered with amaldines and uvarovites, put kohl on her eyelids, perfumed her ears, nostrils and lips, and threw a profusion of fulgurant gems over her breast, her arms and her ankles. In which the rubies of the Oxus, the diamonds of Sambalpur and the pearls of Ceylon were triumphant.

"Your turn, little Rani! Show the Master that you know all the secrets of amour, and that you're worthy of sharing his couch! Here you are, dressed in chimerical and sumptuous fabrics, with the Lingam, master of the world, in your hand, the symbol of omnipotence and omnibenevolence. Come on, dance in your turn. Why don't you want to?"

Mute, Assilinia did not seem to see anything or hear anything. She had taken the phallic plaything that the courtesan had given her mechanically, and was rolling it between her feverish fingers. Concentrating, her eyes fixed, like a somnambulist, she watched the amusements of the prostitutes, full of delirious charms and active and mad depravities.

Then they brought her down from the platform and, putting her in their midst, they forced her to follow the phases of the mime, insensible and visionary.

The Bhai-Tchokri, drunk on cries and movement, accelerated their lubricious dance. Their breasts undulated and rose up under the friction of the plaques and cameos; a fine sweat glistened on their skin among the diamonds; the rings, necklaces and clasps spat sparks, and the Rani, in their midst, with her dupatta patterned with red tones and her golden breastplate, let herself go to the enraged rhythm of the luscious round.

Suddenly, however, she uttered a cry.

It had seemed to her that she saw Shah Jahan on the stage, presiding over the games, impassive, his legs together and his hands

254

on his knees. She gazed, terrified, at his brown face, decimated by age and passions, his flaccid cheeks, annealed with wrinkles, his little eyes, blinking with evil lust, and his slack lips parted by a cruel smile.

"Let me go," she said. "I don't want to learn the dance of the Rati."

"Why are you refusing to know the amorous science?"

"I'm suffering, can't you feet that my hands are burning? Can't you see that I can hardly stand, and that a breath would knock me down?"

"In fact," said one of the dancers, "she's all a-tremble."

Assilinia felt a profound distress. Her numb lips stirred without articulating any sound, tears rose to her eyes, and she let herself fall, fainting, into the arms of the courtesans.

XI
The Lover Rediscovered

While the Rani was carried away, inert, in order to give her the care that her condition required, Hallabab left the palace furtively, went past the Mosque of Pearls and ventured into the back streets of Shajahanabad, the Delhi of those days. She went to the Mosque of Jama Masjid, which is one of the largest in India and possesses, along with relics of Mohammed, a copy of the Koran written in the Cufic characters of the time of Ali. The monument is erected on an eminence that permits the gaze to embrace all the quarters of the city.

With the aid of the muezzin, whom she bribed with a few offerings, Hallabab made the ascension of one of the two minarets, and looked around. Her anticipations were not deceived. On the ghats that plunged into the Jumna, a man was sitting, his eyes raised toward the palace.

He seemed exhausted, and profound sighs were raising his chest. Lying beside him, a black panther was resting her head on his knee, seemingly begging for a caress.

"Mimiose and Ramo!" said the young woman, joyfully. "I knew that the lover would find the lodgings of his beauty again."

She descended in haste and ran to find the young man, without worrying about the growls of the beast, which rose to her feet grimly.

"Peace, Ramo," said the Gurkha.

"Don't you recognize me?" asked the child.

He enveloped her with his somber gaze and seemed to hesitate for a moment. "You're the Rani's friend?"

"I'm Hallabab, and I have good news to give you."

"Speak quickly, then. I'm dying of anxiety!"

"Assilinia is nearby. She has not forgotten you and still loves you."

"Is she in any danger?"

"Not for the moment."

"Can I see her? I beg you, take me to her."

But Hallabab shook her head. "Impossible. The Rani is a prisoner, and it's necessary that no one suspects your presence here, for you'd be doomed."

"What can I do?"

"Wait patiently. Assilinia will be returned to you."

Mimiose sighed. "Are you telling the truth? Those who are guarding her are omnipotent. I know that she left with Orpha after the burning of the temple of Shiva, and that Orpha wants to make her his wife."

"He's marrying her, but he's destined her for another . . ."

"For the Emperor!" The Gurkha uttered a roar of rage, and dug his fingernails into his breast. "The prince is adopting an infamous métier," he said, scornfully.

"Certainly, but he'll be paid well for his complaisance, and many others at the court have set examples of submission to the Master's whims. The Emperor has always had all the women he has coveted."

The young man revolted again. "I don't want this crime to be accomplished."

"It won't be accomplished, I swear to you."

"What occult influence do you count on invoking against imperial omnipotence?"

Hallabab scrutinized the shadow of the ghats with her piercing gaze. Apart from a few danghis and a few badjeras that were gliding smoothly over the river, everything around them was silent and deserted. Then the young man leaned toward the Gurkha's ear and talked to him for a long time in a whisper.

She told him about the advice of Hadj-Hidi, and how she counted on devoting herself to the Rani's cause.

"I'll remain with Shah Jahan in order that he'll be torpid in the mortal caress, and Assilinia, in disguise, will traverse the palace in order to come to join you. Wait here with Ramo, and pray to the gods to assist us!"

"I'll obey you," said Mimiose, "and I'll make sacrifices to Shiva to implore him to come to your aid."

"For my part, I'll offer Durga a nazir of twenty golden candles engraved with mantras and honey chapattis."

Hallabab and the Gurkha prostrated themselves and addressed their passionate supplication to the divinities of the air, the waters, wind and fire:

> *"Indra, god of the etheric spaces, never hide the stars of night from us!*
>> *Enlighten us!*
> *"Varuna, god of the tranquil waves, may the river have the smoothness of oil for us!*
>> *Direct us!*
> *"Pavana, god of the wind, guide our frail badjera toward the port!*
>> *Protect us!*
> *"Agni, god of fire, maintain in our souls the hearth of eternal amour!*
>> *Inflame us!"*

And Ramo concluded the prayer with a profound growl that must have made Yama, the god of the infernal regions, shudder.

PART THREE

I
Forced Union

The great noise of a howling crowd, a gallop of men and women, running toward the temple of Kuthu'l in order to see the cortege of Assilinia and Orpha go past, undulating slowly in the square swarming with people, and heading toward the Mogul's palace. On the terraces, heads protrude, curiously, and young women throw flowers, calling out the names of the happy couple. Children, mute with admiration, hold out their little hands in order to receive the small coins and sweets that the guests distribute to them.

The blare of trumpets, and the hoarse sound of dhols and tamburas, is pierced by the cries of beasts: the roaring of lions, tigers and leopards, which young boys were holding on leashes, two by two. Carriages pass by in a dazzle of flesh and gold, escorted by saermi camels with red pompoms, heras bearing palanquins and harkarats clamoring the news of joy and amour.

Here come the goddesses of Fecundity and Sensuality, perched on the shoulders of superbly blossoming women, their hips broad and harmonious, their breasts erect in the pride of desire; here come the terrible idols with the heads of goats, dogs and bulls, Lingam-Yonis surrounded by roses preceding the god Lingam, a colossal statue with a phallus three feet long, carried on a triumphal chariot drawn by forty young women from the temple of Shiva. The bas-reliefs of the chariot unfurl an unusual variety of unnatural creations incensed by perpetually agitated cassolettes, which spectators, worships of the sacred principle, come to kiss.

In tall jars, rare wines are fuming; on jade trays, honey chapattis and pyramids of fruits for the ever-famished gods are displayed.

Hundreds of fakirs, almost naked, their hair floating and their eyes crazed, sang hymns to the Principle of Life, the Lingam, the symbol of ancient beliefs that still triumphed over new religions and always will triumph, since nature has only one will, amour, and only one end, death.

Soldiers in scarlet langoutis ribbed with iron and bronze, crossing their spears, surrounded the priests of Brahma and Durga, whose long yellow robes were trailing in the dust. They were singing more loudly than the fakirs, and some, raising their bare arms and displaying their shaven armpits, were playing the vina or shaking tamburas covered in snakeskin. Others were whirling like dervishes, making their robes billow; and there were yogis too, leading sacred cows with curved horns covered with leaves of gold and wrapped in flowers.

Bellowings and trumpetings mingled with the roars of the wild beasts and the precipitate chords of the barbaric music. Behind the fat cows, ornamented with necklaces and roses, like idols, came the swinging gray trunks of elephants with saddle-cloths and howdahs decorated with roses of gems carved with a thousand facets, brilliant cabochons that seemed like fragments of the sun. And the enormous beasts were so numerous that the rest of the cortege disappeared behind the painted towers, gilded and draped with glittering silks, that they carried on their backs. A few of those brilliant kiosks, preciously carved, surpassed the summits of the surrounding buildings, launching their spires ornamented with pennants high into the azure.

The goddess Parvati came next, drawn by twelve naked young women linked to one another by chains of roses. Perfumed candles were burning on the cart and doves, attached by invisible threads, were fluttering incessantly, forming a dome of quivering wings over the idol.

Here come the eunuchs, sabers in hand, sacred Hermaphrodites showing desiccated breasts over a green silk langouti spangled with silver; here come the Hedjeras, gliding smoothly and slowly, one arm extended, the other folded level with the face, holding a white lotus. They wear a sash from the right shoulder to the left hip attached by rows of pearls, and a sort of tiara covers their foreheads over their short-cropped hair. They have calm, sad faces, and their song rises, hoarse and powerful.

The Bhai-Tchokri, educators of amour, dance backwards, throwing shredded tuberoses on to the chariot on which Assilinia is standing, motionless, more elaborately adorned than the omnipotent statue of eternal Fecundity.

The meditative face of the Rani is adorned with a circle of diamonds placed on her hair, divided in the fashion of virgins of Benares, and on her dupatta sewn with pearls, embroidered and re-embroidered with sapphires and opals, a kind of golden breastplate grips her waist, its inflamed mesh overlapping, spitting sparks at every movement. Gems run over her arms, her shoulders and her ankles like fulgurant scarabs. She attracts and retains the gazes, for no other is as beautiful.

The Bhai-Tchokri, smiling, dance around the bridal chariot; they are only clad in lucid minerals, which an enamel clasp between the breasts and a tight belt around the top of the thighs, fastened in the middle beneath clappers of peridots and chrysoberyls that undulate and clink with a crystalline sound. Their bellies are rounded, wound around with gold, stamped at the groin with mauve verses, and they are quivering in their most lascivious dances. Some have vinas, tals and macabou flutes, which accompany their high-pitched voices, contrasting with the deep and seemingly ragged songs of the Hedjeras with mutilated sex-organs.

But Assilinia has shuddered. Mimiose is standing in the front rank of the spectators, contemplating her with an ardent gaze, His two fingers are splayed at the level of his forehead, and she inclines her head slightly. She has understood that her beloved will be under the ghats at the second hour of the night, and she responds to the agreed signal with a great frisson that shakes her from the nape of her neck to her heels.

Orpha, who is following on an elephant, decorated by such a profusion of gems that it resembles a marching sun, has seen nothing. At least, his features remain impassive; his eyes have not ceased to contemplate a Bhai-Tchokri who is dancing backwards in front of his elephant. That is Yaminah, the prince's favorite, an undulating Natis whose fiery eyes burn more brightly than the fruit of the asteracantha, and who knows all the games of amour.

Yaminah, by means of erudite hysterias, has been able to re-awaken the somnolent desires of the prince, and he loves her as much as he can love. She knows the aphrodisiacs that stimulate dormant covetousness; she uses all the apadravyas that the Kama Shastra teaches, and no one has yet resisted her.

The Bhai-Tchokri surround the favorite, encouraging her with torsions of the hips and rumps. Will she not replace Assilinia, shut away with the Emperor, during this wedding night? Is it not necessary for her to be at the height of her mission?

And Yaminah continues the lubricious dance, which the spectators applaud from the height of the terraces. Her breasts undulate and lift their rose pistils like plants thirsty for sunlight. Her bracelets, her belts and her plaques throw off brighter gleams under the shaking of her belly and the quivering of her thighs. A long pendant, from which a cascade of pearls streams, beats the inside of her thighs. She really is the great venereal corolla that reawakens the lethargic senses of a man, the living flower rolled in balms, smoked in incense and in myrrh.

While the Rani, intoxicated by her rediscovered amour, was smiling at Mimiose, Orpha, his eyelids partly closed, was gazing at Yaminah, who was promising him a joyful night far from the nuptial couch.

He told himself that one woman is worth as much as another, but that the most learned is even better. However, his gaze, beneath the grille of the eyelashes, sometimes drifted toward the legitimate spouse, and an ironic smile creased his lips.

II
The Bridal Toilette

On returning to the palace, after the rajahs' meal, washed down with lotus wine, speckled with gold and precious stones, Assilinia, at a sign from the husband, has quit the banqueting hall furtively. Sending away her surprised women, she has only accepted the cares of Hallabab to prepare her for the voluptuous sacrifice.

Accompanied by her friend, she has gone to the sumptuous retreat adjacent to her chamber, where a silver basin equipped with ascending and horizontal jets of water is set out for the concerns of her beauty. At the sides of the basin, twelve heads of dragons and chimeras with ruby tongues and aquamarine eyes deliver honey water, the milk of almonds and roses, and essences of takeoka, jasmine and tuberose.

Assilinia, naked before an immense mirror that stands at the back of the room, examines her charming body, blossoming like a tea-rose under the first rays of the dawn. Her face is meditative, solemn, and almost august; she is not thinking about the extravagant charms revealed by that inspection, nor the active depravities that seem to be demanded of her. She is telling herself that it is necessary to be beautiful in order to vanquish, similar to the symbolic deity of indestructible Lust, to the monstrous, indifferent Beast that kills for the sake of killing, because such is her mission, and she does not know any other. She is that fateful power, the supreme force that triumphs unconsciously by good as by evil, by the splendor of divine amour or the magnetic abjections of debauchery,

Her eyelids became heavy with tears, and Hallabab, on her knees before her, proceeded with the intimate concerns of her beauty. Then she put a kiss on her breasts and sought, among the pots and flasks, for those containing ointments, pastes, and lotions that might be useful. She counted on making her friend a chimerical Rani, and making herself up in her image, in order that the resemblance might be perfect and the Emperor would not be able to distinguish one from the other.

She spread rouge on her cheeks, made use of pastes of serkis, emulsions of lilies of Kashmir and musk, Chinese inks, Japanese gold, and, by means of small ivory nacre and silver instruments, strigils, stamps and crepons, metamorphosed Assilinia into a princess of sensuality.

"My turn," she said. "It's necessary that I am identical to you."

The Rani, consulting the tall mirror that sent back her image, then rendered to Hallabab the cares she had received, rose-tinting the corners of her eyes, her nostrils, her ears, her lips and her breasts, blurring the eyelids, designing the mouth in a crimson heart, arranging the hair in light curls over the temples.

Two similar scarves, sumptuous and diaphanous, veiled their rounded loins, a diadem in the form of a tower, streaming with pearls over the temples, ornamented their heads, and similar flowers fell from their shoulders in perfumed clusters all the way to the knees.

Thus ornamented, they resembled one another like two sisters, and, taking one another by the hand, they looked at one another, smiling, in the mirror.

"You're beautiful, Assilinia!"

"You're beautiful, Hallabab!"

And, like a coquette embracing her reflection, the Rani put her lips to the lips of her little friend, insufflating her with her desire for vengeance.

"You saw him during the procession, then?"

"Yes, he'll be waiting for me this evening at the agreed place."

"Courage, Assilinia! Everything will succeed to the will of our desires."

But the young woman sighed.

"Orpha quit me with a nasty look. Do you think he suspects something?"

"What can he suspect? We haven't confided our secret to anyone."

"Yes, that dear spouse believes me to be in the Master's arms at this moment. He is saying prayers for me to intoxicate the perverse monarch with my most expert caresses, and he has no other ambition than that of seeing me share the imperial couch for as long as possible. Does not his future depend on my complaisance?"

"Perhaps you're calumniating him. He's obeying an order, nothing more."

"At any rate, I'm not without dread. What if he saw Mimiose?"

"He scarcely knows him, and Yaminah's dances were absorbing his attention, you told me. Oh, that thought gives me chagrin! But the Hedjeras has affirmed to me that he will love me one day . . . Do you think he will love me?"

Assilinia nodded her head.

"I hope so, since that amour grips your heart so much . . ."

But a discreet rap on the partition warned the friends that they were awaited, and two eunuchs lifted the curtain that veiled the entrance to the room.

"Have you forgotten anything?" Assilinia whispered in Hallabab's ear.

"No, nothing. I have the mysterious powder that the Hedjeras has given me. Courage!"

III

The Emperor's Kisses

In Assilinia's chamber everything was ready to receive the august visitor. The young woman threw herself on the couch strewn with jasmine and roses, while Hallabab slipped behind a curtain.

Around the bed, on golden tripods, perfumes were burning, disgorging clouds of vapors; everywhere, flowers with yellow and white corollas emerged from precious vases, ran in garlands round the columns and the vault, covered the floor, and fell upon panels of fine mosaics and indented ledges filigreed with gold. Through the oval opening in the ceiling, the moonlight danced, frolicsome and blue-tinted, over all the flowers, which seemed to be ornamenting a funeral couch.

Assilinia contemplated the red calyx of the passion within her, which, in spite of everything, opened victoriously, and she drew from that amour the strength for the struggle and the will to triumph.

The eunuchs had disappeared immediately, and the uneven tread of the Mogul resonated on the paving stones in the distance.

"Here he comes," breathed Hallabab. "When you judge that the moment has come, lift the curtain and I'll take your place. Do you have the wine of forgetfulness?"

"It's on the ivory stool. Think about the caresses that engender eternal sleep!"

"I'm thinking about them, and my heart is beating as if to burst from my breast. Can't you hear it?"

"No, I can only hear Shah Jahan marching toward death."

The curtains were parted violently, and the Emperor appeared, in his golden khelat streaming with gems.

His icy face had nothing alive but the eyes, which were as phosphorescent as those of a cat, and were coveting the elongated body of the Rani passionately.

He advanced toward the couch, presenting the tip of his emerald scepter to the young woman's lips for the kiss of submission. She got up, put her hands to her forehead and prostrated herself before the Master.

In the perverse odor of perfumes, in the suffocating atmosphere of the room, the stimulated senses of the monarch acquired further ardor. He took Assilinia's wrist and drew her toward him. Complaisant, she let him do it, docile to the lessons of the Natis and the Bhai-Tchokri, which advised beginning with the most entire obedience to the caprices of the man whom one wants to vanquish.

She therefore threw off the scarf that covered her breasts and drew away slightly from the pink candles that were burning near the bed, as if in a movement of modesty.

With the crooked hand of a miser, he palpated that treasure of youth and amour, deliriously detailing all its perfections.

He recognized the arms softer than the stems of mango trees in flower, the breasts as delicate and as firm as the fruits of the vilva, whose buds tickled his palms. He took pleasure in seeing them erect with emotion, as hard as the overturned golden cups in the temple of Kuthu'l. He compared her arched pelvis to the agile curve of a daboia viper rearing up against the breast of a charmer. He dispersed roses on her pubis, which was as pure and marvelously rounded as a lotus emerging from the Ganges in the shadow of sacred herbs, and on the thighs softer and more harmonious than the polished branches of young banana trees.

Assilinia lent herself to those games, her eyelids closed, her thoughts distant, remembering other caresses and trying to superimpose illusion over her present lover.

Her lips parted in the expectation of amour like bimba berries, and her teeth, whiter than the jasmine of Araby, gleamed in the half-light of the candles.

The Emperor lingered over the flavorsome preface of the erotic poem, knowing that he would not reread the same chapters twice, and that he ought not to squander the hours of joy that Mohammed gives us.

When his feverish lips strayed too far, the Rani pushed him away gently, but he returned obstinately, determined in his will to know everything.

Finally, feeling excessively enervated, she got up, declaring that she knew the thirty-two musical modes of Radha, and that she was going to sing, accompanying herself on the vina.

But the Emperor pulled her toward him again.

"You can sing later, when we're both weary, and I'll go to sleep to the profound tones of Krishna's lover. Enable me to know the amorous science. You little servants of Brahma must know all the secrets of amour of which our women are ignorant. You're more complicated and more perverse, being only raised for the pleasure of gods and men!"

"Yes," said Assilinia, "our religion is a religion of sensuality, and the Ganika are venerated by all. We go abroad with our faces uncovered in order that nothing of our beauty is lost, and our body serves as an altar to Kama."

"Adorned and perfumed you wait, smiling, and ever-ready to celebrate the sweet sacrifice in honor of Smara with all those who pray to him?"

"Once it was thus. In the provinces of Bombay and Bengal the devotees of Krishna, in imitation of the games of Krishna with the gopis, exalted in common to the point of frenetic paroxysms, enlacing all night long, but now, only the Natis serve the pleasure of all."

"Be for me a Natis is ardent to the point of dementia! Do you know all the kisses?"

"Certainly," said the Rani. "The courtesans have instructed me in the art of charming men. I know the kisses that soothe, those that inflame, those that madden and those that kill."

"I only want to know the first two. Make me, little Rani, the kisses that console and intoxicate. It is necessary to observe the rules of the Shastra while passion is moderate, but the wheel of Kama has turned for us and you will inspire yourself with your own desires."

Assilinia feigned a great disturbance.

"I dare not unveil myself thus before the Master, and I shiver with alarmed modesty."

"What, for a few kisses?"

"Your Majesty impresses me. You are so powerful and I am so obscure by comparison."

"You're the daughter of a Rajah . . ."

At the memory of her father, killed by Shah Jahan, a blush of anger rose to the young woman's face. The kind of languishment that the Emperor's caresses had brought about in her dissipated rapidly. She turned her gaze toward the golden cup that contained the wine of forgetfulness, and showed it to the Master,

"Drink," she said, "and I will drink after you in order to penetrate myself with your amour."

"So be it. Let us drink in order that our embraces are durable and profound."

He drank half the contents of the cup and presented it to the Rani, who made a semblance of wetting her lips therein.

"Drink again," she said. "After you, the wine is better. See, I have already effaced the trace of your mouth."

The Emperor emptied the cup a second time, and his troubled eyes closed.

"Come," he murmured, "come close to me."

Assilinia lifted the curtain, and Hallabab slid into the Master's arms, quivering.

While the young woman commenced the mortal work by means of the terrible caresses that Hadj-Hidi had taught her, recommending her soul to Durga and Shiva, her friend, enveloped in somber garments, slipped out of the room furtively.

The eunuchs were asleep outside the door, and the women, extended on low divans, did not pay any attention to the Rani, whom they mistook for one of their own in an amorous torment. Did they not know that the new favorite was with Shah Jahan? The idea of a flight would have seemed insensate to them, when so many others would have been proud of the imperial conquest.

Only Orpha, who had not wanted Yaminah's habitual caresses, was on watch near the voluptuous chamber, where Hallabab was accomplishing the sinister task among the lotuses and the roses . . .

IV
The Banks of the Jumna

At the light rustle of the Rani's feet, the prince emerged from his hiding place, summoned the sowars, and followed the fugitive at a distance, knowing that he could overtake her when he wished, for she was not habituated to marching, and the long garments that enveloped her, wrapping around her legs, prevented her from advancing as rapidly as she would have wished.

The young woman heard the imperceptible noises in the darkness increasing until they became a formidable clamor. She thought that she was risking her life in fleeing again, and, in spite of the assurance of Hallabab, confident in the advice of the Hedjeras, she doubted the efficacy of the subtle caresses. The Emperor might wake up, and launch the redoubtable Thugs on her trail, who would strangle her along with her lover this time.

She emerged from the palace still warmed by kisses, troubled and feverish, sensing the persistent, intolerable movement of the arteries that were beating with a redoubtable pulse in her temples. She went forth in the night, with a jerky tread, sometimes turning her head to assure herself that she was not being followed. Had Shah Jahan not groaned? Had she not perceived a shrill sound like the string of a musical instrument breaking?

Involuntarily, she stopped momentarily, listened, darted anguished glances into corners where it seemed to her that she could hear sighs, to see menacing forms agitating. The cry of a vulture that was flapping its heavy wings resonated in her taut and dry eardrums like a rumble of thunder, shaking her enfeebled brain further.

She had traversed the audience hall, the hall of the ministers and the hall of the peacocks, where the Bhai-Tchokri had taught her the voluptuous dance that was to awaken the senses of the monarch for a night of amour. Now she traversed the interior courtyard, and the emanations of the Jumna, which ran at the feet of the ghats, struck her sense of smell and intoxicated her like the morbid perfumes that cause malaria. She tottered, sometimes leaning against the pedestal of an idol taken from the ancient temples and placed there ironically to serve as a perch for the marvelous parrots whose plumage was as bright as bagicha flowers.

The Rani had never experienced a similar disturbance, but never, however, had she desired so ardently to avenge herself and reconquer her liberty. A rustle behind her made her turn round with a lurch of the heart so violent that she nearly cried out, and she saw the bushes moving and growing larger. She began to experience strange hallucinations: enlacements of men and women were affirmed all around her, the garden entered into rut, and the quivering bodies were so numerous that she did not know where to place her feet in order not to disturb that lascivious ecstasy.

She raised her head; the stars were seeking one another in a vertiginous race, melting into one another, and the moon, swooning, was straddled by an unknown star that had the form of Hanuman, god of monkeys, crowned with the seven naga heads!

She was so cold that her teeth were chattering, and she imagined that she was plunged in an ocean of ice. However, she made an effort, emerged from the garden, letting herself slip along the terraces, as Hallabab had recommended. Dholes started barking on the banks of the river, and she mistook their howls for the roar of the waves and the din of a tempest. Her blood was seething in her veins, and yet her entrails were as icy as if death had already paralyzed them.

A soft mewl informed her that Ramo was nearby; unconsciously, she headed toward the ghats where Mimiose had been waiting for more than two hours, lying on a step. She hastened without advancing; it seemed to her that her body was separated into two, and that her feet were no longer connected to her legs. Nevertheless, she went down the damp steps that led to the Jumna, and two arms suddenly knotted around her shoulders.

"Assilinia!"

"Mimiose!"

"I thought that I would never see you again! Oh, how I've suffered!"

"My beloved! My lover! If you knew what I've done . . ."

"What have you done, my love?"

"The Emperor . . ."

But she stopped. A shadow, growing at the height of the ghats, appeared to reach the sky. She raised an arm.

"Don't you see anything?"

He sounded the darkness with his piercing gaze.

"No, nothing."

Ramo purred tenderly, like a cajoling cat, and leaned her ardent head against the young woman's flank, begging for a caress.

"Oh, I see enemies everywhere! All these events have driven me mad!"

"Rest for a moment on my heart; then we'll flee through the low quarters of the city, for the river isn't safe. That's where they'll look for us first."

But Assilinia wanted to leave immediately, and Mimiose, passing an arm round her waist, drew her toward the smoky back-streets where prostitutes, sitting behind clay lamps, were appealing to passers-by in a nostalgic voice.

The Rani was having difficulty walking. The heavy necklaces that she was wearing were crushing her; she imagined that the cabochons of gems were entering into her flesh, and that her shoulders were denuded to the bone.

"What is your plan?" she asked. "Do you have horses to reach open country?"

"No, that means is dangerous. I've reflected for a long time; the best thing, I think, is to hide here until tomorrow; then we'll see how things stand. By acting otherwise we'd attract attention, and it's in cities that one can hide most easily. In any case, you're too weak to support the fatigues of a long journey."

"I'll do whatever you wish."

"I have many projects, my love. You'll know them later."

Naked women standing between placards were offering their beds and their kisses for a minimal salary, while the frolics of couples could be glimpsed behind half-closed doors. Girls with red lips and eyelids tinted with kohl appeared on the arm of a mahajan or a subedar whom a perverse whim had brought there. But many preferred the plump and curly-haired catamites whose commerce was conducted in another quarter. Men were running through the streets, touching one another in the open air baths along the river, but the spectacle did not revolt Assilinia, habituated to the free amours of the religions of sensuality.

Mimiose was seeking a house that he knew to be hospitable, which would be ceded to him for a price paid in advance. He advanced with precaution, still supporting Assilinia, whose dark clothing did not attract any attention.

The cascading notes of scithos and macabou flutes escaped from light constructions, often ornamented with flowers and festoons of gilded paper. The laughter of women crackled more shrilly than the sound of the instruments, and in luminous doorways rumps and breasts agitated, gleaming as if rubbed with gold. Young women with slender limbs, laden with plaques and necklaces, lay down on low beds, and an entanglement began immediately: female bodies embracing one another amid flowers and perfumes for the greater joy of audiences whom those games incited to new pleasures. Men embraced the polished flesh of the servants of Smara, who emerged from every corner, replacing one anther on the low divans, to the sounds of chilamchis and frenetically-shaken dhols.

In the streets inhabited by Muslims, the houses remained closed. Sometimes, on the doorsteps, eunuchs coiffed in yellow miters showed themselves, interrogating one another in infantile voices, exchanging provisions of betel and areca nuts.

V

The House in the Flowers

Assilinia and Mimiose were still walking, hiding alongside walls.

"Haven't we arrived yet?" the young woman interrogated, who felt herself fainting more and more on her beloved's shoulder.

"Soon, my love, we'll find the refuge. I've chosen one as far as possible from the palace, and no one will discover us in this remote quarter."

To encourage her, he pressed her against him, and kissed her lips for a long time, passionately. Then, in spite of her lassitude, a more vibrant blood seethed in her veins, an impression of divine hope, gratitude and unknown poetry drove away regrets and fears. A new soul was disengaged from itself and spiritualized her sensations, as if another humanity had taken possession of her person.

She hesitated over telling Mimiose everything. She put off her painful confession until later.

A keener wind rose, sweeping the moon, which reddened under the scintillation of the stars. Groups of pedestrians jostled them; rapprochements of the sexes were still being accomplished in the high-ceilinged rooms open to seekers of forgetfulness. In the depths of holes of brutal light naked dancers of both sexes were moving; indecencies blossomed at every step before idols charged with roses and tulsi, wooden lingams stood in the corners. And again, bodies embraced, mingled as if at random, amid the warm perfumes and the empty cups.

The Rani was not paying any attention, half-fainted in that orgy of flesh, displayed everywhere, which stirred her organism and caused her to clasp herself more tightly to her lover's breast.

They had arrived at a low building, painted pink, so burdened by climbing plants that it resembled an embalmed bagicha adjacent to a more sumptuous dwelling.

"This is it," said Mimiose. "How do you like the nest?"

She extended her lips to him silently, and they went into a room ornamented with a few lascivious paintings, where everything had been prepared to receive them. A low bed was displayed in a corner, mats covered the golden sand padding the ground, and two horn lamps cast mysterious gleams over everything.

"O dear Delight!" she sighed, throwing herself into Mimiose's arms.

He laughed and wept, unable to find enough kisses to prove his happiness in having her with him after so much sadness and misery. When they were weary of caresses given and received, and their thirst for amour had been slaked, he wanted to know how she had quit the palace and put the jealous surveillance of the Mogul to sleep. She told him about the ruse employed by Hallabab, and spoke, shivering, about the criminal act advised by the Hedjeras.[1]

"Tomorrow, no doubt, we'll hear about the death of Shah Jahan, killed by the very excess of his perverse passions."

"Tomorrow . . ."

Mimiose's brows were furrowed.

"Are you not satisfied?" she asked, anxiously.

After a silence, he exposed his projects.

"I would have preferred to vanquish the tyrant by means of other weapons. Murad Baksh, the son of Shah Jahan, is advancing toward Delhi with Aurang-Zeb, his brother, in order to take possession of power. By joining the army I would have fought honestly and surely, for the two brothers have considerable forces at their disposal and the Emperor has no suspicion, being unable to believe in the treason of his sons. The pass of Manddo, surrounded by forests and mountains, has already been accomplished without difficulty, thanks to my advice, and here, there is no thought of anything but fortifying the capital, while leaving the posts that might prevent the army's approach free."

---

1 The author seems to have forgotten that Hallabab has already told Mimiose about her plan.

"How has Murad Baksh, who has an honest heart, been able to approve of Aurang-Zeb's designs?"

"His father's death had been announced to him, and his ambition stifled his remorse. Hazard has determined that the death in question is veritable. The enemy will triumph without a battle."

"It's necessary not to regret that, my friend, since we shall not be separated again, and we will savor in peace the happiness that is our due."

Meanwhile, Orpha had followed the fugitive couple and discovered the love-nest hidden among the flowers. The thin walls of the lodgings allowed the lovers' words to be overheard, and the prince, after having listened to the dangerous conversation that informed him of Hallabab's crime and Aurang-Zeb's projects, drew away rapidly in the direction of the palace, recommending his sowars to mount good guard.

Daylight appeared, and the merchants, profiting from the coolness, set up their displays along the narrow streets where the houses of sensuality had opened a little while before. Some suspended from nails khelats that were still fresh; dupattas woven in gold, the color of banana, saffron, tulsi or maida; langoutis fringed with pearl, decorated with little crystal bells or light embroideries in silken thread. Shops offered barbaric jewelry in copper and silver, inlaid with coral and turquoise, ivory amulets, yoni-lingms and precious weapons. Others, reeking with bizarre mists, presented sachets containing dried salamander, aconite, scarabs pickled in vinegar for headaches, torpid cobras in nets, mandrake and cantharides, which transport women with smoky eyelids to desires always extended toward amour or murder.

But he quit the quarter of prostitution for the sumptuousness of squares, displaying red temples and the erections of palaces of marble and gold. He ran, without seeing anything around him, uniquely possessed by the thought that he might perhaps save the Emperor, and that the service in question would assure him the highest destiny.

Shoving the guards, eunuchs and women out of the way, he headed for Assilinia's chamber, parted the crimson curtains that veiled the entrance, and remained motionless, his gaze directed toward the couch on which Shah Jahan lay . . .

VI
Hallabab's Murder

The Emperor was lying on the bed strewn with flowers, in the attitude of a man asleep, and one might have been deceived by that if he had not been bathed in blood. His breast had been pierced by a dagger-thrust, and the murderous weapon was still in the wound. On the far side of the room, kneeling in the shadows, Hallabab was weeping copiously.

Orpha had already ordered the eunuchs to bring the palace physicians. Half asleep, they arrived, and hastened to Shah Jahan, palpated him, turned him over, and observed that he was emerging from a profound faint, but that he was still breathing. Cares, already belated but hasty, were lavished upon him with so much success that they succeeded in reawakening the sentiment of life in him.

The prince, reassured, at least for the moment, regarding the Emperor's fate, had taken possession of Hallabab, who continued to sob quietly, without seeking to flee.

"Why did you want to kill the Master?" he demanded, when the young woman was able to speak.

She had recognized the man she loved with all her strength, and who, without knowing it, had put the weapon in her hand—for perhaps she would not have accepted the odious role that she had taken on if the hope of breaking the marriage of Assilinia and the prince had not sustained her.

She fell to her knees, and raised her hands in anguish, seeking to seize the prince's langouti, but he pushed her away.

"Forgive me," she sighed. "I love you!"

He sniggered disdainfully. "You love me? And you believed that you would prove that fine amour to me by accomplishing the greatest of all crimes!"

"I was jealous of the Rani whom you had just married! I favored her escape in order to get closer to you."

"And you've stabbed the Emperor?"

She shivered from head to toe and wept more forcefully. That was not the way that she had promised to make Shah Jahan perish. The old Hedjeras has informed her of a better means, but all her virginal modesties had awoken at the same time, and in the disgust of the act that she was about to accomplish, she had drawn the weapon that the Mogul carried in his belt and she had struck him, in a paroxysm of revolt and hatred.

"Forgive me," she repeated. "If you only knew what tenderness I have for you!"

She clung to his knees, bearing her lips passionately to the hem of his garments.

Furiously, he took a few steps back. And as she dragged herself toward him, he pushed her away with his foot, summoned two eunuchs, and ordered them to lock her in one of the palace dungeons, until the Emperor had decided her fate.

✳

A few days passed in the alternations of dread and hope that awakened public sympathy for the aged monarch, who was weakened by so much excess.

As soon as he judged that the Master was in a condition to listen to him and understand him, Orpha made him party to the secret that he had discovered in the little house in the low quarter where Assilinia and Mimiose had taken refuge.

"Your two sons Murad Baksh and Aurang-Zeb are preparing to attack you in your own empire in order to snatch power from you; it's time to take the measures necessary for resistance," he concluded, after a detailed account of what had happened.

As the ambitious man had hoped, the Emperor was grateful for the service rendered.

"Henceforth, I have only one son, and that son is you," he said to him, when the physicians had assured him of a prompt recovery. "My children want to expel me from my own domain. I am withdrawing my affection and my esteem from them in order to gratify you with them. Go, Orpha, go and fight for the good cause. I give you command of my army, and I have confidence in your worth. If Mohammed is sensible to my prayers, he will bring down their father's malediction on the rebels!"

Putting his hands to his forehead and then to his breast in a sign of submission and gratitude, the prince assured Shah Jahan of his profound devotion, and declared that he would be able to render himself worthy of the noble mission that had been confided to him.

VII
Night of Amour

Meanwhile, Assilinia and Mimiose, huddled together in the little house in the low quarter, after the fatigue of their first intoxications, told one another the story of their struggles and their misery. But that conversation was frequently interrupted by further kisses, more tender and more profound.

"Oh, how sweet it is, my Mimiose," the amorous woman murmured, "when the sound of bells expires in the towers of Kuthu'l, to share with you the long-solitary couch in which I appealed to you so ardently!"

"You are mine, my adored, and the evil spirits of water that separated your lover's slumber from your voluptuous slumber will no longer loom up between us. But you're falling asleep, Lotus of Flame, and here you are, devoid of strength, against my heart, like a flower on the river bank that a tempest has battered. Repose, then, on my bosom, and let me feel the warmth of your flesh penetrate me ineffably to madden my senses! The moths of dream will descend, buzzing, while I watch your beautiful eyes close. Their plushy wings will strike your forehead, more polished than the shield of Smara, and the translucent dust of their flight will mingle with the blue vapor of perfumes.

"The goddesses of the night are kissing their ivory scithos, interrogating the sonorous strings, which respond to the beating of their hearts, still ablaze, and then pause on a chord of bewildered tenderness, which prolongs their divine spasm.

"After the annihilation of pleasure, they gaze at one another, lean toward one another, consult one another, still embracing, confounding their gleaming hair, and heir red lips come together in the ecstasy of a new fantasy, for desire is born of desire, and the spirits of the air make love as bees collect pollen. Let me—for I have wept for you or a long time—let me forget the tears that are still burning my eyelids, in the phantasmagoria of these charming dreams! You can sense that the phantoms of amour are brushing us with their hasty, mobile, inconstant flight, which rises like a wave borne by the incoming tide, and descends likewise, rolling in its fugitive curl all the colors of the scarf of Durga, when the sea, at the end of a tempest, comes to break, expiring at the ultimate point of its immense circle, against the prow of a vessel . . ."

Thus spoke Mimiose, while rocking his lover, and it was like a serene melody, accompanied by the purring of Ramo, huddled against the couch like a chilly cat. The panther closed her emerald eyes, stretched out her powerful paws, the amorous velvet of which hid the claws, and she too seemed a beast of dream and sensuality.

"Have you seen," the Gurkha went on, "along the walls of Shahjahanabad, when they are struck by the vermilion dawn that regenerates the world, a long line of somber men with bruised eyelids and teeth grinding with rage and hunger, with red and stupid gazes? Some are crouching like brutes, others remain standing, leaning against pillars, half-buckling under the weight of their extenuated body? Have you seen them, mouths slightly open to inhale one more the air embalmed by the bagicha? Thus I was before the palace in which I knew you were captive, and I would have given my blood for one of your smiles!"

Assilinia only replied with kisses to her lover's ardent words. However, at one moment she sat up, shivering.

"Don't you hear something?"

Ramo, all her fur bristling, had roared dully.

"I can't hear anything," declared Mimiose, after a few moments of silence

"It seemed to me that men were whispering around the house. Might we not have been followed?"

"Followed? By whom? Everyone in the palace was asleep when you quit the Mogul?"

"At least, I don't think I attracted the attention of the guards and eunuchs—but we have a more redoubtable enemy."

"Orpha?"

"Orpha, my husband now, who might have been watching for me in the shadows."

They both remained silent for a few moments, trying to catch the noises outside. But Assilinia started laughing at her fears herself.

"I'm crazy to frighten myself thus! Take me against your heart again, dear lover, and put a betel nut between our lips in order for me to take it, mouth against mouth. Since we cannot marry in accordance with the sacred laws, a Purohita will disengage me from my criminal union and will make the Homan, the sacrifice of fire, in order that our union will be eternal. Afterwards, we shall be one another's for life, and will no longer have anything to fear from malevolent pitris."

Mimiose hugged the charming body of his mistress more tightly against his bosom.

"Oh," he said, "I'm beside you and I'll defend you to the death. No one will dare to take you from my arms!"

"I'm afraid of the darkness! Is it not because of me that Shah Jahan is dead?"

"You have avenged yourself and you have accomplished a divine mission. Let your lips press my lips, my beloved, and let the nectar of your mouth descend in me like a flood of honey."

"Reanimate those lamps, which are paling," she said. "Demons, as you know, fear the odorous vapors of candle-wax and oil."

He got up in order to obey, but Ramo barred his passage. The panther's green eyes flashed briefly, and her jowls were drawn back over her sharp fangs.

"Peace," he said, passing his caressant hand over the beast's head.

She did not calm down, growling more loudly, while rapid waves passed over her somber fur. In spite of Assilinia's tears, Mimiose went to look outside. Everything seemed calm. Only the sounds of songs and kisses troubled the silence of the night.

The young man sprinkled a few flowers in a cup of milk perfumed with saligram, and stoked up the fire of the perfume-burners. The flames curved around the circular edge of the stove, leaned over and drew closer together, brushing it with their golden lips. Soon, the milk was hot, and the lover offered it to his mistress, drinking thereafter where she had drunk, in order to know her amorous thoughts.

The intoxications of the night had numbed the Rani's senses. Involuntarily, she saw the phantoms of her imagination pursuing one another in the obscure corners, and dancing in the smoke of the odorous candles. She heard strange rumors; she distinguished voices, alternately grave and menacing, insulting or ironic. And, as in a supreme refuge, she nestled against the tumultuous breast of her friend, wanting further caresses in order to forget even the memory of her fears.

VIII
The Living Wall

"We're betrayed!"

"What are you saying?"

"The dwelling is surrounded!"

By the first gleams of daylight, Mimiose had seen the spears of the soldiers around the house of amour and the men lying in front of the threshold, forbidding entry.

Assilinia got up, shivering, throwing over her shoulders the mingled tresses that covered her face.

"We must flee!"

"Flee? But how?"

"Has the house no other issue?"

"No, we're occupying the only room in the building. If I were alone, I wouldn't fear anything, but for you, dear Lover, the slightest danger seems redoubtable to me."

"I'll be brave, my love, as brave as you!"

"Come, then . . ."

He slid an arm around her waist and armed himself with his dagger in order to hold the enemy at bay.

At the first step he attempted outside the house, a sowar precipitated toward him.

"You cannot pass," he said, "by order of the Emperor!"

Mimiose started to laugh.

"Your Emperor must be dead by now."

"Dead!"

All the soldiers had risen to their feet, consternated. However, they crossed their spears in front of the lovers, and the one who had spoken and seemed to be their leader ordered them to go back inside.

"No," said Mimiose, "we're leaving in spite of you."

"In spite of us? You're alone with that woman, who can't defend herself. Don't attempt the impossible, and await the Master's orders with resignation."

"I want to pass," cried the young man, raising his dagger against the soldier. Twenty weapons were immediately directed at him, but the panther, as rapid as lightning, bounded into the group with a mighty roar, and her powerful fangs sank into the throat of the leader.

Abandoning the palpitating body, which was convulsing in the last efforts of the death-throes, Ramo, her back arched, braced herself to pounce on a new prey. And at every moment her long supple body collected itself for a more forceful attack. Every man attained was a dead man.

282

With an infinite skill, she leapt to the left and the right, avoiding the most unexpected thrusts. It was evident that her back was tensing and relaxing with an indefatigable ardor. Shreds of flesh were hanging from her claws; her muzzle was red: also red were her royal pelt, the earth, the walls, and the enlaced lovers, who advanced gradually through that rain of blood toward deliverance.

Finally, the route was clear; with a great cry of joy, Mimiose and the Rani, pressed against one another, stepped over the convulsed bodies of the last combatants, and disappeared into the indecisive gleams of the dawn.

IX
Forward Ho!

Orpha, invested with the supreme command of the imperial army, marched to meet the rebel sons and intercept them on the banks of the river Ugen. As it was the season of the Grishma, the water was low and easy to ford. Aurang-Zeb, who was leading the advance guard of the enemy troops, presented himself first, and, while the rest of his army waited, he limited himself at first to preventing Orpha's troops from reaching the other bank. The regiment of the two brothers arranged themselves outside their retrenchments, but they did not rush forward to attack, fearing that they might get bogged down in the mud. The heavy cavalry and the formidable reserve of elephants could not be deployed there, which gave the advantage to the light imperial troops.

In the camp of the two brothers there was no longer the fine ardor of the day before, the irresistible force that had impelled the two brothers when they imagined that they would find the field clear and would be able to fall upon a defenseless prey. Shah Jahan's army fought doggedly, but, in accordance with the Emperor's recommendation, it did not strike the first blows, waiting for the enemy to deliver themselves.

In the evening, however, everything changed. Orpha, running out of patience, led new regiments into battle. He multiplied himself, racing to the assault at the head of his squadrons, and not recoiling from the range of the enemy sabers.

Aurang-Zeb's army was primarily composed of cavalry, for the Moguls were still better cavaliers than the Persians. Covered in complicated armor, they were mounted on gigantic and heavy horses. The princes and the chiefs were fortified in towers placed on the backs of elephants. Once launched into the plains of Hindustan, nothing could resist their formidable impact. Orpha's army, by contrast, formed of cavalry squadrons with horses lightened of ancient armor, and infantrymen who could handle muskets, bows and spear with equal ease, was as ready to attack as it was to retreat, disrupting the calculations of Aurang-Zeb and Murad Baksh.

Although the river was already laden with cadavers, the soldiers precipitated themselves to the assault, howling. They collided with the armored breasts of horses, and fell, decimated by arrows, under the iron of spears, but returned to the charge even so. In the rising tide of that human flood, the crimson and gold standards of the rebel bothers began to buckle.

Through the jungles, the plains and the streams the human waves poured, incessantly increased by discontented djaths and bigaris. They announced that Shah Jahan, at the head of a new army, was coming to crush his sons. The battle was interrupted, and Aurang-Zeb asked for a negotiation; but Orpha refused to hear him, and launched his troops to attack the retrenchments.

The prince, at the head of ten thousand men, reserved himself to support them at the decisive moment. All the barbaric instruments burst forth at the same time, melting into an immense sonority in which the howls of the vanquished, and the agonized cries of the wounded and dying, were annulled.

✺

Orpha was now returning, triumphant. He was, however, marching through the midst of revolt, carnage and fire. Cadavers and pyres marked his route; the Thugs had passed that way and blood was spurting under the hooves of the horses. In the outlying districts of Delhi, bands of men drunk on arak were going from house to house dragging out Hindu women by the hair, raping them, murdering them and stealing their jewels. Heads were swaying on the ends of pikes, as well as the bodies of little children, transpierced and still palpitating, their eyes widened by terror. The gilded idols and lingams set up at the corner of every street disappeared under mud and filth. The air was hazy with burned things, in the vertigo of beasts of burden expelled from their shelters, which were galloping at random, frenetically. The crowd was crowned at every moment by a standard, a pole topped by a severed hand, a heart splattered with black blood, or formless red things, which floated, letting warm droplets fall on to faces contacted in fury.

The same cry always resounded: "Death to the idolaters! Death to the Shivaists!"

There was a push, a sword glinted and a bloody head, its eyes put out, was hoisted on a pike and brandished, like a glorious wreck. Laughing soldiers sometimes plunged a flaming torch into the mouth of a torture victim, shouting that he was about to taste his last pipe of opium and that its smoke would be agreeable to Brahma.

Men in chains, their noses, hands and ears cut off, were wandering lamentably, weeping and begging for mercy; women were displaying their mutilated breasts, disemboweled girls were trampled by the crowd.

In the distance, barbaric weapons bristled, punctuated by swords, amid the sparkle of armor and breastplates, and the resounding rumble of cavalry reentering the palace.

In the squares the Bhai-Tchokri were dancing for the pleasure of the victors, showing their gilded nudity beneath gleaming gems. Sometimes, they uttered a screech and slipped in the blood, but the soldiers picked them up again, exciting them with voices and gestures, mingling with their dance and dragging them in a mad race through the luxurious streets, where the pillage was less active.

The sacred monkeys from the mosque of Qutub Minar gamboled with them, rejoicing in the murder. They ran after the mutilated heads, black with mud, which the soldiers amused themselves with by rolling at their feet. And always the crowd swelled, rushing to the massacre.

The most peaceful stopped before the shops that punctuated the quarters like the alveoli of a beehive. The merchants were forced to remain behind their displays, in order to distribute their fabrics and their jewels, with which the drunken soldiers adorned themselves. On the steps of the Hindu temples, the Brahmins showed themselves in their white robes, folding their arms and defying the murderers of women and children. The Muslims accused them of celebrating by night in the shadow of idols, after having created a void around their prodigious vices. Many were killed on the steps already reddened by murder, and hung up by the midriff under the vaults, where they swung like great white birds.

Human forms shoved one another on to the ghats, and the sound of a splash announced the fall of a body at every moment. The dead and the dying were hurled pell-mell into the Jumna, which broadened under the pressure of the cadavers. Soft floating masses flowed under the moon, whose silver light illuminated the summits of temples, the tips of columns and obelisks, arches, cupolas and slender minarets, the gold of which was flamboyant, puncturing the sky. Channels disgorged black liquid with a drunken gurgle.

And still the groups passed by, carrying bodies that plunged into the river, under the splashing water, and then reappeared further away, open-mouthed, sniggering at the stars.

Meanwhile, Aurang-Zeb and Murad Baksh had withdrawn, leaving, along with the prisoners, five hundred horses and two hundred elephants. Shah Jahan refused to pursue them, in spite of the advice of his ministers, who foresaw that the monarch would soon succumb, vanquished by the ambition of his sons, equally avid to reign.

After three days of pillage and murder, the city gradually resumed its customary occupations, in spite of the mourning and the ruins.

The captives, thrown into frightful prisons, awaited death. And among them, Hallabab, resigned, prepared herself for the torture, knowing that her crime was one of those expiated cruelly. From behind the bars of her cell she saw the eunuchs, mitered in yellow, chasing slaves with great strokes of the whip, sowars aligning their armor, splashed with blood, and sometimes, with the points of their spears, pricking the vanquished, huddled like beasts in the depths of their cages. Trumpet-blasts passed in the distance, announcing parades, the emergence of corteges protecting Shah Jahan, who was showing himself to his people.

X

Embraces for Embraces

"Master, it is appropriate to inflict on that woman a punishment equal to the crime."

Shah Jahan, a gleam in his yellow eyes, was interrogating Orpha.

"You say that she wants to kill me by means of an excess of caresses."

"Yes, it's the Hedjeras who counseled her to commit that frightful murder."

"But what interest did she have in my death?"

"She loved me and she was jealous of the Rani."

"So she took her place beside me?"

"Yes, in order to permit Assilinia to flee with her lover."

"Do you know what has become of them?"

"No, Master, but we'll find them. No torture will be cruel enough for them."

The Emperor reflected momentarily. "I know what torture it's appropriate to inflict on your wife. We'll commence with Hallabab, her friend, in order to experiment with the idea that I've just had, and we'll see how many embraces a human creature can support in one day."

"What, you want . . . ?"

"I want all the soldiers in the Imperial Guard to profit from her virginal body, which you'll attach between the seven lingams of the temple of Kuthu'l. And if she resists those savage attacks, we'll summon the troops from the city, until death puts an end to that monstrous debauchery."

Laughing, Orpha approved the Mogul's project.

"Ah! Her small breasts with rigid tips, her smooth torso, as fine and pure as a golden lotus, her noble face with the large eyes dappled with light and shadow, her mouth thinner than a musky pepper! Do you think our men would refuse such a feast?"

"No," said the prince. "And even dead, with her smile of atrocious sensuality, she won't have any shortage of lovers."

The victorious regiments filed in front of the palace, bearing green standards with golden stripes, or crimson with splashes of blood.

Shah Jahan showed himself on the terrace beneath the famous motto of the Mogul capital: *If there is a heaven on earth, here it is! here it is!*

In the distance, under the red rays of the sun, loomed the mosques, the temples, the tombs and the fortifications of all epochs of the Hindu art of ancient Delhi, overturned by the Moguls. Then there was the palace of Firozabad, containing the pillar of Asoka, the ruins of Indurpont, the tomb of Humayun, the mosques and the colonnades of Qutub. On a sort of eminence, the tower of Victory, elevated in the thirteenth century, dominated those edifices. A sheaf of columns, divided into five stages by circular galleries, seemed to absorb the light more particularly, and large sheets of crimson and silver glass scintillated like lighthouses.

But Shah Jahan directed his gaze toward the Mosque of Jama Masjid, the largest in India, which he had constructed for his personal worship, and which crowned a rock covered with jade and ivory, curiously sculpted, like a surplice of rigid lace.

A portal of pink marble, with copper ornaments, was visible from the terrace, between polychromatic colonnades of porphyry. Three Gothic arches surmounted by a metal dome and four minarets gave access to the imperial pagoda.

"It would have been a pity," said the Mogul, extending his hand toward the sumptuousness of his city, to lose all that! I have raised Shahjahanabad from its ruins; I have made it the pearl of India and the admirable capital of my empire. No one can contest such benefits. And, certainly, I have not shed as much blood as my predecessors. Indra Prastha, the Delhi of the Arya, knew all the evils of war many centuries ago. It paid for its title of the metropolis of Hindustan in a particularly horrible fashion. Personally, I have only fought to defend myself, and, this time, again, I have only taken up arms against my ingrate sons. Have I merited so much hatred, then?"

Orpha put his hand to his heart, too troubled by the Master's words to try to respond to them. There are silences more eloquent than the greatest eulogies.

The sun was still flamboyant over the city of the ancient rajahs. In the distance, yellow and pink stripes marked the extreme limit where the sky and the earth seemed to unite behind the debris of tombs and dismantled fortresses.

But Shah Jahan, with a sigh, redirected his gaze, suddenly saddened, toward the delicate mosques with rutilant domes, which showed themselves closer to him between the tamarinds and Indian lilacs with fragile clusters of fruit. There, the white marble and the incrustations of precious gems brightened the sky; the obelisks of pink sandstone, the columns dotted with agates, cornelians, lapis lazuli and conglomerates of Jaisalmer shone like an immense firework in the melancholy of the distant décor.

"You see," the Emperor went on, "after the long and terrible battles, after the fratricidal struggles that dishonor humanity, one experiences a need to make a halt in the gardens of amour, and to respire perfumes sweeter than those of battlefields. If I have loved women a great deal, I have scarcely done any harm to my subjects, and, without the ingratitude of my sons, my reign would have been a peaceful one."

The old Emperor sighed again, as if he had divined that defeat was imminent and that he was enjoying his marvelous city for the last time, ornamented, like Mohammed's wife, with all the jewels of the earth.

XI
In the Blood and the Roses

The temple of Kuthu'l presented a marvelous interior of incense, light and flowers. The reflection of lamps escaped through the windows in multicolored jets, and metal trumpets sounded hectically, summoning the soldiers of Delhi to the murder of amour.

The Hindu people listened anxiously to the sounds swayed by the wind in waves, sometimes grave and slow, sometimes light and brief. Young women bore the fetishes and the amulets of the goddess to their lips, for, since Orpha's victory, tortures had succeeded one another in the vicinity of the palace, which the vultures haunted with their somber flight.

No one was aware of Hallabab's criminal attempt of the Emperor's person, but they knew that a young woman, in expiation of her sins, was condemned to perish in mysterious tortures between the seven lingams of the temple of the Hedjeras.

The mutilated priestesses went into the hall of the Immolation, each with a silver lotus embroidered on the shoulder, her head mitered with glaucous gems, with long veils falling vertically over their frail bosoms.

The din of chilamchis struck by nervous fingers mingled with their sacred songs. Their hoarse voices had profound rips, similar to the plaint of waves breaking on rocks; they revealed the tempests of the soul and the senses, the despair of eternal impotence.

The guards of Shah Jahan, the regiments of the Moon and the Sun presented themselves before the temple, already drunk on arak. The eunuchs had distributed ganja and opium to them, and they were marching slowly, their brains invaded by strange desires.

To their right the Jumna was radiant, with its flat katarras, its badjeras, its houlaks and its danghis, on which somber shadows weighed, pink and grey shadows of languorously falling veils. On the far shore, the ruins of ancient cities were profiled, their bleak silhouettes in the azure. Via the swarming streets, other troops arrived, whose weapons and standards passed over heads like migratory birds en route toward the light.

In the midst of the Hedjeras, in the florid hall of the temple, nervously, Hallabab squeezed the hand of Pekeo, her former companion, now the mutilated servant of Durga.

Hadj-Hidi, the aged and sinister priestess, whose breath ran over her sweat-soaked hair, placed the lingam, master of the world, between her breasts, and ordered her to submit to the will of the Master, since the gods had not wanted to intervene to save her from the torture.

"Oh," said the young woman, "you know full well that I tried to follow your advice, but, alone with Shah Jahan, I felt the furious revolt of my thought within me at the act that I was about to commit, and I struck at hazard, in a kind of delirium, no longer knowing what I was doing."

"You were wrong," murmured the old woman. "My vengeance was sure and devoid of danger for you."

"Perhaps. But I would not, however, have made Orpha love me. What is the good of living without amour?"

"Oh, amour comes when one wants it. For that, too, it was necessary to rely on my experience."

The child sighed, and a pale smile parted her lips.

"At least will the others, those I saved, be happy?"

"It's necessary not to seek to know the secret of the gods."

"I would die more tranquil with the assurance of the happiness that I had created . . ."

Hadj-Hidi was about to respond, but the door of the temple opened, giving passage to the first soldier, surrounded by eunuchs in crimson robes.

With a terrible scream, Hallabab veiled her eyes . . .

XII
Calvary

However, the flight of Aurang-Zeb had only been a feint. With new forces he was returning toward Delhi. Shah Jahan, indignant about the knavery of his sons, had proposed in his council of ministers to direct the decisive campaign himself, supposing that Murad Baksh and Aurang-Zeb would not dare to fight against him.

Undoubtedly, the Emperor would have given proof of his wisdom in employing that expedient, for Murad Baksh, whose heart was good, was not obstinate in his revolt. The friends of Aurang-Zeb in the council deflected Shah Jahan from that resolution, by representing to him that the dignity and authority of the sovereign would be compromised thereby, and that, in addition, his health did not permit him to expose himself to the hazards of such a perilous campaign.

One minister devoted to the rebel son spoke to him very eloquently in those terms; it is even claimed that the large eyes of his wife and the tears of the begum Saeb had a great deal to do with the Mogul's decision.

Orpha was, therefore, invested with the supreme command of the army, as he had already been once before. Very glorious after his first victory, he hoped, after having vanquished the rebels, to conquer Persia and enter into Turkey. By means of adroit rumors spread among his troops, he animated the courage of all of them. Two thousand elephants, charged with their towers, and five hundred horses equipped for battle, followed the convoy.

To see those warrior waves spreading out in the environs of Agra, one might have supposed that the prince would only have to show himself to be victorious, but a certain leaven of hatred was fermenting against that improvised chief, whose sudden favor rendered him suspect. The grandees of the Empire thought of avenging themselves for the dishonor that Shah Jahan had thrown upon them by seducing their wives, several of whom had not quit his harem.

Orpha, full of self-confidence, emerged from the fortress of Agra in sumptuous apparel. The camp, designed on the plan of a city, had its streets, its bazaars and its courtesans. Cohorts were paraded in the glare of the sun, with their musicians, whose long curved trumpets launched splendid fanfares that punctuated the muffled sounds of snakeskin dhols. In the distance, there was a violent movement of horses harnessed with gems, elephants with long tusks sculpted with gold, with howdahs in tiger- or crocodile-skin, soldiers sharpening their weapons or trying on coats of mail imbricated with iron. Chiefs were wearing tight-fitting armor of tortoiseshell, bronze or silver and passing by on their nervous horses, whose nostrils were fuming. Camels stood up, swaying their bony heads, obedient to an order from their conductors. There were distant roars of chained lions, the mewling of leopards and the yelping of monkeys.

Close to Orpha's tent, the richness of the camp was incomparable. Young boys, naked or clad in parted robes, were plucking scithos and vinas and singing in shrill voices. A few were spinning, arms extended, in flights of bright cloth and clinking jewelry.

Next to the curly-haired catamites with delicate bodies there were the fanatics of Mohammed, the mystical adepts who went into frenzied convulsions to the sound of barbaric instruments. The rhythm always accelerating, the excitation and dizziness of the dancers led to a commencement of physical insensibility.

Taking one another by the arm they threw their heads backwards and forwards, as if they wanted to hurl a ball into the audience. Gradually, their eyes only showed the whites and foam emerged from their lips. After a thunder of instruments unleashed in unison, the music ceased to an abrupt halt, which produced the effect of a rip. Their eyes crazed, their fingernails digging into their breasts, the fanatics resembled furious wild beasts. They bit and swallowed pebbles, snakes and scorpions that they introduced into their mouths, falling down and uttering frenetic clamors.

The brief chords of tamburas with taut skins resonated everywhere, with the light rills of bamboo flutes extracted by feverish lips. In the blue-tinted shadow of the streets the Bhai-Tchokri combed their hair, steeped in balms, depilated themselves or spread mauve and brown powders over their bruised eyelids.

Orpha's tent was crimson embroidered with gold, starred with topazes and opals. Tapestries closed it, covered with chimerically precious designs. In the half-light of the interior, where horn lamps burned slowly amid cassolettes and flowers, the prince was lying, holding against him the svelte brown body of Yaminah, very proud of that amorous glory. Behind the enlaced couple, intoxicated by perfumes, kisses and caresses, two eunuchs were agitating flabella made of hanging curved lotus leaves.

"So," asked the young woman, after having surrounded her lover's neck with her silky hair, as if to prove that she held him enchained by the bond of caresses, "you've never been Assilinia's husband?"

"You know that."

"She fled, on the evening of your marriage, with that Mimiose, who has gone over to the enemy?"

"So it appears . . ."

"It's said that the Gurkha is now a counselor of Aurang-Zeb, who has confided the command of a part of his army to him."

Orpha made no reply, but a frisson passed through his limbs.

"It's also said," the Bhai-Tchokri continued, "that Mimiose has sworn your death, and that he's as brave as a lion. Are you at least sure of your men? There are a great many malcontents in the imperial camp. In your place, I'd be watchful . . ."

The prince frowned.

"I don't fear anyone, that adventurer less than anyone. He wouldn't dare measure himself against me!"

"Has he not already vanquished you on the day of the Tamascha, when you fought the tigers for the beautiful eyes of the Rani?"

Orpha pushed his mistress away. "Think before you speak," he said. "No one can vanquish me. I withdrew from the arena, disdaining to measure myself against a Gurkha, a bigaris that I want to ignore, who isn't worthy to carry my palanquin!"

Yaminah pressed herself against her lover seductively, wanting to make him forget the audacity of her speech. She offered him the honey of her lips, and gave him evidence that she was burning with the most ardent desire for him. And while they rolled among the cushions, the impassive eunuchs continued to make the great reed flabella flutter above their ecstasy, with a regular movement . . .

But there was a stir in the camp and officers came to warn Orpha that the enemy was approaching. A skirmish has already taken place the day before. In the trampled fields, the cadavers of men and horses lay here and there. A road of death extended its red ribbon between the two armies.

Extracting himself from Yaminah's arms, the prince assembled his regiments, which pushed forward in disorder, in haste to vanquish and not doubting their triumph. The prince was ignorant of military science, but he had confidence in his star, which had already protected him.

A pond bordered the route, cannonballs slid into it without reaching Aurang-Zeb's troops, disposed in squares on the other side. The cavaliers launched themselves into the water then, uttering their war cry, hoping to put the enemy to flight, as they had the first time. But Aurang-Zeb drew his men back, contriving a sort of hemicycle, into which he thought that the prince would not hesitate to advance with his troops.

In fact, Orpha allowed himself to be drawn into the trap, and when the enemy infantry parted like a curtain, unmasking the gaping maws of cannons and sharpshooters lying in the long grass, he did not have time to retreat. The reckless individual felt a cold sweat slide between his shoulders; his troubled gaze stared into the distance; no idea germinated in his numbed brain, still anesthetized by the courtesan's vehement embraces.

The cannons thundered, and in the spirals of thickening smoke, at times, the sowars could be seen galloping for the other side of the pond, the golden flashes of their armor punctuating the black clouds.

The elephants charged, but they got stuck in the marshes, and their enormous masses, immobilized, like the debris of some volcanic eruption, cut off the retreat of the fugitives. Peppered with gunfire at short range, struck by thrusts of spears and daggers, crushed beneath the hooves of horses, the soldiers of the imperial army did not have the time either to reassemble or to defend themselves. Some of them, under the cover of the smoke, tried to slip between the cadavers; others, throwing away their weapons, bounded at random in a folly of terror.

New regiments were arriving incessantly from the enemy camp; Orpha had to vanquish or die. His men were crowded together, stifling one another, fighting one another, falling into the pond, where the bodies were so tightly grouped that the water was overflowing.

The carnage lasted for hours; then night fell over the gasps of the dying and the imprecations of the vanquished.

Meanwhile, Mimiose, mounted on a horse as black as the night, had driven straight toward Orpha, and summoned him to surrender. The trembling young man realized that he was dealing with an adversary of uncommon robustness and dexterity, but he responded that he would not abandon the imperial cause for anything in the world.

Under the furious assault of the enemy, his saber trembled in his hand; he half-slid from his mount, and tried to hold on to its mane, but the wounded animal fell beneath him, and it was only after minutes of effort that he succeeded in disengaging himself. He palpated himself, took a few steps, and observed that his men had fled and that he was alone with the Gurkha. Mimose, who had stepped down to the ground, waited with his arms folded for the prince to be in a condition to defend himself. When he saw that he was not wounded, he presented his dagger to him and engaged him to continue the contest.

Orpha, his gaze troubled, interrogated the area in the hope that some help might arrive from his own men; thick smoke drowned the pool, where the submerged elephants were still struggling.

"To me!" he cried. "For the land and for the Emperor! To me!"

Then the Gurkha launched himself upon him and they wrestled madly, rolling on the ground, animated by the same murderous fury.

Orpha's bones cracked under the furious pressure, blood flowed between the mesh of his gem-embroidered khelat.

His face sweaty and his features convulsed, Mimiose finally got up, withdrawing his blade, red from the point to the hilt, from Orpha's breast.

Clamors fused behind the victor. The shadows of tall cavaliers in scale armor ranged themselves round the group. In the direction of the army of Aurang-Zeb, in the silvery enlargement of the moonlight splitting the clouds, there was now a dazzling gleam of rutilant armor, swords, spears and pikes, raised toward the stars in a flutter of banners with enamel plaques, and Hindu flags with embroidery imbricated with fantastic jewelry.

"Are you wounded?" Aurang-Zeb asked, his horse prancing in blood.

"No, but I've killed Orpha. Look!" And he pointed at the cadaver, whose khelat as gleaming under the lunar light.

"Someone cut off his head," ordered the prince, "and fix it on the longest of your pikes. It will guide our march to victory. But are we not triumphant already?"

In fact, the imperial army was in full rout. The soldiers, undermined and softened by a long peace, had buckled at the first impact of the enemy. Covered with powerful armor, Aurang-Zeb's cavalry, with their heavy horses, advanced like angry waves, breaking all obstacles. Behind them came the elephants, whose towers, striping the sky, seemed intent on scaling the stars.

Orpha's head, brandished before the troops, guided them toward Delhi. The towns in their route were put to fire and blood; conflagration, pillage and a merciless extermination of all those who did not want to submit signaled the passage of the rebel army.

While Murad Baksh and Aurang-Zeb accomplished these exploits, lieutenants worthy of them ravaged the kingdom of Lahore. Everywhere they passed there was desert. Assendy, Toglukpur, Panissat and Luni, flourishing cities, were changed into heaps of ruins. All those hordes, charged with booty and dragging long files of prisoners reduced to servitude in their wake, came to lay siege to Delhi. Before launching the attack, however, the rebel son murdered more than a hundred thousand captives.

It was thus that he prepared to conquer the city of all sensuality and all magnificence . . .

XIII
The Last Kiss

Shah Jahan, devastated, had taken refuge in the palace of women. The dusk enshrouded the gardens in violet vapors, and lights were shining in the windows of closed houses where people were talking about the massacres of the day and the day before. Voices lamenting the dead rose up in lugubrious waves from all directions, for the cruel orders of the old emperor had succeeded the vengeance of the sons, and again blood was flowing in the poor quarters, while the Jumna was carrying decomposing cadavers, poisoning its banks.

The gurgling of the river resembled the hiccupping of drunk-ards, and all the green-tinted faces turned toward the sky launched mute imprecations toward the stars.

Mimiose had rejoined his beloved, who had been confided to Ramo, the panther watching over the woman. After the confidences of the return, the tender words and the embraces, they headed toward Kuth'l, where they thought they might find Hallabab. Natis on the threshold of their flowery house had told them that, in expiation of an unknown crime, the young woman had been subjected to the rape of drunken soldiers in the great hall of immolations, between the seven lingams of the temple.

"She sacrificed herself for me!" Assilinia wept. "But perhaps she isn't lost and we might save her?"

Hadj-Hidi, the old priestess, shook her head lugubriously on seeing them.

"Come," she said. "Hallabab is in the midst of the Hedjeras at prayer, and you can embrace her one last time."

They followed the old woman into the long galleries with the monstrous bas-reliefs.

The torture-victim was lying under roses at the very place where she had suffered the criminal caresses until death. Her body, purified and steeped in balms, was displayed in its svelte harmony, and she seemed to be asleep, so calm and mild was her face.

The Rani scattered a few tuberoses over her, and put a sprig of the sacred basil named tulsi on her breast.

"Brahma! Brahma! Receive her in your bosom!" she moaned, kissing her hectically on the cold lips that had once lavished such tender intoxications upon her.

"To the palace," said Mimiose. "The hour of punishment has sounded. Aurang-Zeb ought to be with his father by now."

✳

Streets opened in front of the lovers, which pools of blood rendered slippery. Long crimson ribbons indicated the flight of the wounded, at hazard, straight ahead. The waters of the public drinking fountains was red, and also red were the porticos of the temples under which the Brahmins were exhorting the crowds with cries of anger and supplications. Houses displayed mysterious holes, in the depths of which the victorious soldiers were knocking down the prostitutes, who allowed themselves to be taken while laughing, knowing full well that the daughters of amour had nothing to fear.

A swarming life was blooming in a daylight dense with equivocal perfumes, the stink of murder or feasting. The indifferent sum illuminated scenes of murder and scenes of joy simultaneously.

In their luxurious dwelling, the Bhai-Tchokri opened the curtains of their beds with columns of gold and jade and sat up, semi-naked, as the warriors passed, their breasts bruised and their lips dry, wearied by their feverish night. They stretched their limbs, yawning, blinking their somber eyelids, still tinted with kohl.

Assilinia and Mimiose arrived at the palace, where soldiers were waiting, surrounding the sowars who were carrying the disheveled head of Orpha on the end of a pike.

Rajahs mounted on elephants with enamel-plated howdahs were following Brahmins whose white robes, secured at the waist by cords, were trailing in the dust. They had come to impose their conditions on Shah Jahan, not knowing yet in which direction to turn their preferences.

Aurang-Zeb had gone in some time before to speak to his father, to summon him to desist in his favor and accept exile. The response of the old Emperor, who was known to have taken refuge among his women, was awaited anxiously.

A great noise rose from the terraces where the eunuchs were being murdered. Their blood was flowing along the walls, and the soldiers, with a thousand gibes, were amusing themselves pricking them with their spears and pulling them outside the marble balustrades. Sometimes a eunuch clad in a yellow miter crashed to the ground at the feet of the horses.

XIV
The End of a Reign

A bronze door opened suddenly, exposing a long corridor into which Mimiose drew Assilinia. The panther bounded in front of them, holding the guards in respect.

They traversed the immense halls, similar to the interior of mosques, with columns surrounded by golden and silver flags with sumptuous irradiations. The ceilings, divided by beams with curious gold inlays, had galleries at the edges, and the rooms were separated from one another by porticoes with incrustations of jade and ivory.

Here are the hall of ministers, the hall of the throne, with its platform of solid gold protected by stone peacocks with deployed tails, the hall of the tamascha, with its onyx basins and its jets of perfumed water. Everywhere, there are beds of damask, draperies sparkling with hyacinths and sardonyxes, vases on pedestals of translucent minerals encrusted with cat's-eyes from Ceylon, cymophanes and sapphirines with complicated scintillations. On the floor-tiles, there are mosaics exalting the barbaric triumphs of Mogul emperors, in the midst of monstrous magical plants shining crazily. On the ceiling, in chimerical paintings, there are skies imbricated with fulgurant gems, suspending clusters of peridots, olivines, amaldines and uvarovites from a flamboyant azure.

But a surprise awaited the lovers in the gynaeceum. Shah Jahan, holding the begum Saeb against his heart, was talking to Aurang-Zeb, who was standing in front of him, while the Bhai-Tchokri, to the sound of dhols, vinas and tamburas, were gliding smoothly, smiling at the young prince.

"Lord," said Aurang-Zeb, "your recent malady and weakness render you incapable of reigning. End your days in retreat, enclosed with your beloved women in the delightful gardens of Agra, where the proudest mortals would like to live. We do not envy you the light of day, which shines for monarchs as for big-aris, but cede to your children a place that you dishonor by your weakness and your senile follies . . ."

The last words were too much. A great cry rose up in the harem, and the women, drawing the daggers that were shining in their belts, launched themselves toward the imprudent.

But Shah Jahan extended his hand to protect his son.

"Listen," he said. "If I am unfortunate enough to be de-throned by rebel children, be courageous enough, my son, to defend Delhi against all the attacks of my enemies. I cede power to you, and I hope that you will render yourself worthy of my confidence. I am, indeed, only good any longer for the seduc-tions and the tenderness of the gynaeceum, the faithful caresses that I shall savor in my citadel of Agra."

Meanwhile, in the gardens, the soldiers had put to death the guards, the slaves and the last eunuchs. They entered the apartments of the women, whom they seized with eager arms and threw down on the cushions. A few, using their weapons, defended themselves, screaming. There was yet more blood and kisses, gasps of amour and death, while Aurang-Zeb, surrounded by his officers, took the old Emperor away.

The ranks opened before them. They reached the grand terrace of the palace, where the prince showed himself to the people, saluted by unanimous clamors. All arms were raised and thousands of mouths uttered the same cries:

"Hail Aurang-Zeb, Master of the World! Aurang-Zeb, the King of Kings!"

Aurang-Zeb was the best and the most humane of despots since Prayadesi. He died as a warrior king in his camp, after having won brilliant victories. His favorite and his adviser was always Mimiose, whom Assilinia's kisses sustained in life in the midst of the attacks and the conspiracies of the envious.

A son, as handsome as the gilded crow of the Himalayas at sunrise, was born to the tenderness of the Gurkha and the Rani. For some years he played between the caressant paws of the panther, whose emerald eyes had infinite amorous gleams for him. The beast watched over the games of the fragile and thin infant, whom they loved to confide to her. Then she rendered to Brahma's heaven her soul of a wild beast, which many humans might have envied her.